The World in

Reverse

Latrivia S. Nelson

The World in Reverse

RiverHouse Publishing, LLC
1509 Madison Avenue
Memphis, TN 38104

Copyright © 2013 by Latrivia S. Nelson

ISBN: **978-0-9839819-5-4**

All **RiverHouse, LLC** Titles, Imprints and Distributed Lines are available at special quantity discounts for bulk purchases for sales promotions, premiums, fund-raising and educational or institutional use.

www.riverhousepublishingllc.com

www.latrivianelson.info

This book is dedicated to my dear friend of many years, Walter Gunn, for all of your expertise, even during important save-the-world work. Thank you for being there *always*.

Acknowledgments

This book would not have been possible without the support of Karen Moss, my editor and my friend. Thanks so much for taking time to not only work through my ideas but also make this process fun. I am so grateful for our friendship and your dedication.

I would like to thank my beautiful family for all of their support during this book including my daughter, Tierra, and my son, Jordan.

A special thank you goes to my mom, Linda, aunts, Sheronda and Sandra and grandmother, Ella, for always encouraging me to write as a little girl.

Prologue

The fiery heat of an angry, record-breaking summer had finally subsided for a few hours under the thick clouds that covered the night's sky. A welcoming storm poured down on the city of Memphis in fat, heavy raindrops mixed with gusty winds. People scurried to get out of the weather and retire to their homes after a long day at work; however, Nicola Agosto had gotten used to the climate over his years in the Bluff City and was enjoying the muggy, rainy evening with a late-night run.

Pushing past the burn on his lungs, he checked his watch and kicked himself into full gear for the last leg of his ten-mile jog. It was part of his weekly regimen to drive his body to its breaking point, though he had long passed the need to be in tip-top shape on the force since he had climbed in rank.

Vanity was what pushed him now. He refused to get fat and old, refused to get slow and passive. Edge was necessity in this job. In fact, he needed to be a serrated edge. The job was demanding. Life even more so. This kept him ready.

Cars with their lights on and their windshield wipers violently wiping away the storm passed him as he hiked up Peabody Avenue, passing the back entrance of the West Precinct. Under the radar in jogging pants and a gray hoodie, he appeared nonthreatening as he ran by a few guys doing a drug transaction under an oak tree near an old, bricked apartment complex. They didn't know that he was packing a Glock tonight and more than capable of busting them on site.

Don't worry, he said to himself, *there is always later.*

Glancing over to make their faces quickly, he continued on with his ear buds in his ears and his mind clearing.

It had been a long disappointing day. He had been forced to close an investigation on a local counterfeiting ring that had traceable firearms linked to a known Russian mob boss, but he was informed by his superiors that one of his arch rivals, Anatoly Medlov, was officially *hands off* from now until kingdom come.

Motherfuckers!

There was no telling who the Medlov Crime Family had paid off to get that shit done - ongoing amnesty wasn't cheap. He had been after the Medlov family for years now, and not once had he ever gotten close enough to really do any damage. Sometimes, he wondered why he even bothered with this profession. For every perp he locked up, there were ten more that got away.

Still, he did it. He guessed that he was a glutton for pain or maybe it was because he cared about the families that he helped, the communities that were able to sleep just a little better at night. But mostly, he cared about his sons' futures. He didn't want them to grow up in a cesspool where no one gave a damn about anything that really mattered. *Some things had to matter.*

Truth had to matter. Honesty had to matter. Honor had to matter. Family had to fucking matter.

He grunted as he got to Cooper Avenue and turned south headed towards the center of the Mid-town party district. Cars lined the streets by the many pubs and restaurants. He ran harder past the drunk, young couples and groups of wild partygoers headed in and out of their destinations. He ran past the people walking their dogs and the homeless looking for shelter. As the sidewalk cleared, and the rain began to pour harder, he ran even harder. His strides became more powerful and suddenly, he was like a shadow in the night, only visible as he passed under the streetlights. Arms rigid, legs powerful, he moved with purpose and then interrupting his groove, his phone began to buzz in the pocket of his jacket.

Pulling out his iPhone, he abruptly stopped and stood under a large oak tree for cover. "Yeah," he answered, wiping the rainwater from his face.

"Agosto, it's Deputy Director Warren."

Nicola tried to catch his breath. "How can I help you?" he asked winded, looking around as the cars passed him quickly on the road and splashed water against the sidewalk.

Was he in the middle of a flash flood? It was raining cats and dogs out here. But his mind had wondered off so far until he had not even realized it until that very moment.

"I know that this is short notice, but Director Amway wants a meeting with you tonight at his office." Warren waited for his response.

"Sure. What time?" Nicola asked.

"What are you doing right now?"

"Running in the rain apparently, sir." Nicola looked down at his body now soaked and felt the chill of night air start to cause goose bumps to form. If he didn't get out of his clothes, he'd have the flu soon enough.

"Well dry off and get here. Is thirty minutes okay?" Warren asked.

"I'll hump back to my house, change clothes and head up there," Nicola said, sensing that whatever he was being called for in the middle of the night was more than serious.

"Great. See you in thirty."

The phone went dead, and Nicola turned back the way that he had come, moving faster than before.

***

Thirty-two minutes after his phone call, Nicola stood in front of newly appointed director of the Memphis Police department in jeans and a gray t-shirt, hair slick to his head and gun on his hip. His badge rested against his chest, gleaming in the dim light. He scanned the room quietly, covering his mouth as he coughed.

All the players were at this *unofficial meeting*, which meant it had to be major. But why was he here? He knew that it wasn't because he was in trouble. He had been in trouble enough to know that he would have been hauled to internal affairs for that, during office hours, not on a Saturday night.

Amway was a damn good cop who had been tapped by the mayor for the position of director because of his hard stance on crime and his love for his community. An African-American man in his early forties, Amway had come up the ranks with Agosto through the years, but had managed, *where Agosto had not*, to stay out of trouble and still stay in the public eye. He had cracked some pretty tough cases, saved a lot of lives and accumulated a hell of a lot of jail time for criminals who deserved nothing less.

"Have a seat, man," Amway said, sitting back in his chair with his left arm perched on the armrest. His index finger rested under his chin as he furrowed his thick brow in thought.

"What brings me here?" Nicola asked, looking around the room.

Amway looked over at his subordinates.

Warren jumped into the conversation quickly. "Are you familiar with the Baby Boys murders?" He walked over and slapped a confidential file in front of Nicola on Amway's desk.

"Who hasn't?" Nicola said, opening it to find pictures of the dead children he had read about in the news and heard about on the job.

"Detective Luke Johnson is currently on the case, but we need to bring you in," Amway interjected.

"Why me?" Nicola stared at Amway for an explanation.

Amway sat up and knitted his large fingers together. His gold wedding band gleamed against the light. "We need to close this. We need to find the man *or men* responsible for this and let people sleep again."

"Men?" Nicola's interest peaked. There had never been anything leaked about their being more than one killer.

"*Unofficially*, we think there is a sort of organized crime group behind this," Warren said, waving his finger. "But that's off-the-record info. We need you to confirm it."

"And you know organized crime better than any-one," Amway said sincerely.

"And we know that you know the players in Memphis," Warren said, sitting on the end of the desk.

Nicola brushed off the compliment. "Is Johnson okay with me coming aboard?"

"That is not Johnson's call," Deputy Chief of Investigative Services Magnelli said, sucking his teeth.

Nicola looked over in the corner and spied the older, Italian man in the corner, staring out of the window. The two knew each other well, considering he used to be his boss back in the day.

Agosto's current boss spoke up. "You've seen the news. We're drowning in bad PR. We're adding you to this case to make the people of Memphis feel better. Everyone was impressed with how you handled the Caesar case and a hundred since then. Folks know you and like you *for the most part.* Do this and stay in the good graces of those who matter," Deputy Director of Special Operations Stan Hilliard said, standing up. He walked over to the coffee pot and poured him a cup of hot, stale coffee.

"You're not really leaving me in a position to say no," Nicola said, closing the file. He had seen enough for the moment.

The men laughed collectively.

"That's the whole point," Amway said, smiling. "How long have we known each other?"

"A long time, man," Nicola said, clenching his jaw. "But this is one of those cases that could make or break you. And if I'm going to work it, I need all resources available to me and no closed doors."

"Look around you. Everyone on our command staff is here tonight and with whom? You. We mean business. Solve this for us and you can write your own check in the department," Amway said, making sure that his team heard him. "*No* closed doors."

"You're guaranteed to go back to Lieutenant after this," Nicola's boss promised. "That little incident a few months ago can and will go away."

"You can just erase it from my file?" Nicola asked.

Amway put up his finger to cut them off. "Why don't you guys talk about that offline? I don't want to be party to anything that is not *by the book*. What I want to know in this meeting is, are you with us?"

Nicola looked around the room again and chuckled. "Do I really have a choice?"

There was a tilt of his head as the technicality of it all was laid on the table. "You always have a choice," Amway said, eyes saying otherwise. "But I'd like for you to choose this, choose us. Hell, Magnelli is retiring soon. You might find yourself in his job. And the mayor is on my ass…bad. He had a press conference on Friday morning where the reporters spent most of their time busting my balls. I need a comeback. And the people of Memphis need to sleep better."

Nicola nodded. "Fine. I'll take the case."

"Great, we will let Johnson know to fully cooperate," Amway said, standing up. He offered his hand. "Welcome aboard."

Nicola shook his head hesitantly. "Thanks, *I think*."

***

The rain poured down from the heavens on the Three Wise Men, *as they had aptly dubbed themselves*, while they sat under large black golf umbrellas alone on the bleachers at Southwind High School's football field trying to strategize behind one of the men's most recent screw ups.

Looking around to ensure that no one saw them, they huddled together and spoke in whispers like Romans plotting to kill Caesar.

Sitting on the far end of the small huddle, the youngest of the group, was a cop of reasonable means and power. He heaved a great sigh and gritted his stained, crooked teeth together. "Who is going to clean this mess up?" He asked, hoping that they understood that it could not be him. Delving into the cover-ups of their on-going relationship had boundaries in order to protect himself and his affiliations, plus he knew all too well the thoroughness of the homicide investigative unit and crime scene detectives.

The man responsible for the mess rested his head in his large, manicured hands in quiet desperation. "How was I supposed to know that the damn drug was going to kill them?" His arrogance perfumed the tense situation with more petulance.

The fatter man on the other end of the huddle spit snuff on the bleachers and cursed. "Shit, I don't know. Maybe the first two fucking kids might have been a clue that Molly is too damned potent for their small bodies. I mean, have you ever tried it or do you just force feed it to your victims?" He kept the rest of his thoughts to himself. He wanted to call the man a thousand names, speak to his deep-rooted prejudice of the man's race and slap him down the bleachers. But he kept his cool only because their relationship promised to yield too much financial gain to look away from.

"It works sometimes," the arrogant man said, index finger pointed up in the air. "It has worked before. And no, I've never tried it. I don't need to. I'm not the one who needs to be relaxed for the encounter."

The cop cringed. *Encounter?* It was rape and then murder.

"Look, we aren't a part of your *constituency,* so please stop trying to feed us that politician mumbo jumbo. We're here because you can't keep your shit under control. And when I say shit, I'm referring to fucking all these young boys and doping them up to the point where they have heart attacks and seizures and shit. Now, you're not going to get elected mayor; super cop over there is not going to be tapped for deputy director of shit by you after the election, and I'm not going to close this deal with the East Coast guys on these fucking drugs that I have sunk *everything* into if you get us caught." The fat man's face reddened with heat even in the chilled rains. "And I promise you if that happens, I'll kill you myself."

Waving his hand, almost dismissively, the man in the middle of the bunch calmed the situation. "I've seen the error of my ways. There will be no more children until after the election. I just need you to get rid of this last pair of bodies. They're still at the playground…"

The cop winced again at the conversation. The bed-fellows he had acquired made him sick to his stomach. Still, these were the men with the power and his only means to his desired end.

"This is the last fucking time," the fat man said, voice raised and finger pointed directly at the middleman. "I'm not cleaning up one more of these messes. My guys are all twisted in the head after. I damn near have to put them down like dogs after they have to do that shit."

"It will be the last time," the middleman said with finality. "You have my word."

"The word of a pedophile really don't mean shit to me right now," the fat man said, standing up to leave.

"There is one other thing," the cop said, trying desperately to get back on task.

The fat man could tell that this wasn't going to be good news. Sitting back down, he propped his foot up on the bleacher stand in front of him. "What is it now?"

"I just received word that Sgt. Nicola Agosto was assigned to the Baby Boys case, as of today actually. The powers that be are meeting with him now."

"You've got to be kidding me," the fat man grumbled. "I can't think of a worse cop to put on this case. He's going to find us out. I know the cocksucker. He's like a damn case of genital warts that won't go away."

The middleman did cringe at that statement. Turning to the fat man calmly, he raised his hands. "What am I here for, if not to help in that regard? I can formulate a plan to get him kicked off the case as quickly as he was put on it. I do have the ear of the people."

"You're going to need more than an ear with that asshole on the case. We gotta get rid of him. I've put too much into this shit to see it all go up in smoke," the fat man snarled, eyes blazing.

"He's right," the cop said. "Everyone knows that if anyone can solve this case and put all the pieces together, it's Agosto."

"I said that I would take care of it, and I will. All I need is his file, which I will acquire, and I'll need your guys to put surveillance in his house. In order for this to work, I'll have to ensure that we know what he knows," the middleman said even calmer now that he was back in a position of control.

"Don't go acting like you're doing me a big fucking favor. These damn kids are your fault. All I wanted to do was sell some drugs and get filthy rich. Now, I'm waist deep in dead bodies." The fat man stood up again. "Is there anything else to report? Did someone kill an entire elementary school or happen to piss off the CIA since the last time that we met?"

"Like I said, *if you help me*, then I'll make this go away," the middleman reiterated.

"With all that fancy education to that Ivy League school and all the fucking trouble you've caused with that *specialty sex* of yours, you'd better fix it," the fat man said, walking down the steps to the bodyguards waiting on him. "Or I'm going to fix you."

1

The oldest set of the Agosto twins' birthday party had to be brought inside due to the lightning, thunder, and heavy rains beating against the house like water against a ship. The soggy, golf course-like knoll of their impeccable lawn was flooded, unfit for young children.

It was a complete disaster.

The forecast had originally anticipated only a twenty percent chance of rain with a slight overcast. It would have been a perfect day to play outside. The night before Nicola had stayed up setting up the yard's birthday signs, a huge inflatable bounce house, and tons of benches and chairs - all for nothing.

The rain had started at ten that morning and continued all day.

Nicola stood looking out of the patio door at his masterpiece going to shit with a crooked grin on his face. *That was life.* At least, that was his life.

His kids, of course, blamed him. "Why, daddy?" they had asked. He couldn't give them a reason. "God wanted it to rain, so it rained," he had said before he began carting things inside. Kids didn't question God. So, it was easier to incorporate Him in everything.

By mid-afternoon, over thirty children ran through the old Victorian home screaming and playing, four of which belonged to the Agosto's. However, despite the unforeseen weather, Nicola refused to let his boys' birthday be ruined. He pushed the large leather couches to the backs of the walls, moved all of Ivy's china out of the way and turned on the 60 inch television in the entertainment room to play SpongeBob on loop. The other parents chipped in as the normally impervious dining room was turned into a picnic table complete with red and white checkered tablecloths.

Nicola emerged from the kitchen clutching a 52-piece Spiderman cake in his hands, while Ivy followed carefully behind him, coaching him with every nerve-racking step.

"Don't drop it Nicky," she begged, hands ever so lightly touching the small of his back.

"Baby, I got this," Nicola answered, barely missing a little girl in pigtails, who came whirling by with a squirt gun.

"No honey, you can't have those in the house," Ivy said, turning from Nicola to chase the little girl down the corridor.

Setting the cake in the middle of the table, Nicola stepped back and raised his brow. "It's big, huh?" he said to his friend and colleague Moss, standing across the room drinking a beer and talking to his wife.

"That cake is pure sugar, man. You're going to have these kids hyper as shit. I'm leaving Malika here with you tonight. Hell, you can babysit her," Moss said, walking over to the table to take a closer look at the red, blue and white cake. "They definitely supersized it."

"No shit," Nicola said, a little surprised himself. "I just wanted to make sure that I had enough. You know the boys like Spiderman." He crossed his hands over his chest and ran his tongue around his bottom gum line.

"What's wrong?" Moss asked curiously.

"I'm bummed about the rain," Nicola answered.

Moss couldn't help but laugh. "This is supposed to be the twins' party, not yours."

Nicola didn't agree. "Hey, baby. Did you give *little man* his medicine? I hear him coughing again," he called into the next room.

Ivy stuck her head into the entryway with raised brows. "No, I thought that you did."

"Well, you better get it out," Nicola said just as both sets of his twin boys came running in the room soaking wet.

"What in the world?" Nicola shrieked.

"Daddy, we got the slip and slide out and put in the back yard. Can we use it?" Adamo asked, wiping the rainwater off his flushed face.

"No. You're not even supposed to be outside. It's raining cats and dogs out there," Nicola said, grabbing a napkin to wipe the floor. He bent down and quickly cleaned it up.

"It's not raining *cats and dogs*, daddy," Madison said with a frown. "It's raining *rain*."

"I don't mean it literally, Maddy," Nicola said, standing back up.

Just then two more people came through the front door, dodging the heavy rain with a large Nike umbrella. The grandparents. Ivy's parents to be exact. Lugging bags of gifts, Sadie and Madison walked into the dining room and looked around.

"Some kind of birthday, huh?" Madison asked, shaking Nicola's hand. "How are you, son?"

"Pretty good, sir," Nicola said with a smile. He leaned over and kissed Sadie on the cheek. "Hey, Ma."

"Hey, baby," she said, setting down her purse on the dining room chair. "Well, worse things could happen on a birthday," she said, picking up on the disappointment. Ivy had told her how long Nicola had spent yesterday putting everything together. She was sure that he was bummed.

"Like what?" Ivy asked, hugging her mother.

"Like…a tornado," Sadie laughed. "The point is that we're all here." She winked at her daughter. "Trina and Emerald sent a gift from Seattle and they send their love, of course."

"Yeah, I know. Emerald landed some huge development deal. So he and Trina said that they would try to come down later in the summer when things cooled down," Ivy said, hating that her only brother and her best friend couldn't make it.

"That is one huge cake," Madison said, leaning over the table. "Happy birthday, indeed."

"Grandma! Grandpa!" the kids screamed, rounding the corner. They burst into the room with arms wide and eyes wider. Both sets of the twins now in dry clothes hugged their grandparents all at once, nearly knocking them down and making them damp.

"Look at my wonderful boys," Sadie said, kissing their cheeks.

"When are you guys gonna give me a girl?" Madison asked, looking over at Nicola.

"That's what I keep asking," Ivy said with a giggle. "I feel outnumbered here."

Nicola looked down at his son, Madison, named for his grandfather, and grinned. "Are you ready to open your gifts?" he asked, rubbing through his mass of curly hair.

"Yes," they said in unison.

"Okay, go and get all of your friends rounded up. You think that you can do that for me?" Nicola asked.

"On our way," Adam said, bolting out of the room. "Come on, Maddy!"

A little slow to react, Madison turned around and followed after his brother, determined to catch up.

Putting one of the boxes that had fallen off the table back on top of the large pile, he heard his work cell phone ring loud in his pocket. It wouldn't have been more unwanted if it had been a mistress calling.

Ivy suddenly froze, back rigid and a small vein protruding out of her neck. She stared at him as he pulled out his work Blackberry.

"I'm sure it's nothing," Nicola said to her as he turned his back. "Yeah," he answered. He listened on and then his shoulders dropped in defeat. "When?" He listened again. Looking up at the wall, he sighed and shook his head. "I'm on my way." Hanging up, he turned around to face Ivy. "Baby…"

Ivy's finger pointed like she wanted to hit Nicola. "Don't *baby* me, Nicky. This is their birthday for God's sake. They have been looking forward to this party for months." Tears started to form in her eyes. "Can't someone else…"

"It's *my* case," Nicola interrupted, voice strained. Walking over to her, he rubbed through her long tendrils and tried to get her to calm down. "And I wouldn't go if I didn't have to, but someone else's twins were just found in a dumpster." He tried to say it low just in case there were children around.

Ivy's disposition suddenly changed. *Children?*

Moss's chimed in. "Need me to ride with, man?" he asked, stepping away from his wife.

Nicola ran a hand through his tousled black locks and gritted his teeth. He could feel the tension from all the women permeating the room. "No, man. Thanks. If you could, just keep an eye out here for me. I'll be back as soon as I can."

"You aren't even going to wait to sing happy birthday?" Ivy whined, voice pitched high.

"We...we have to make it quick," Nicola said, disappointed in himself for having to leave. He looked at his watch impatiently.

Quickly, Ivy ran out of the room, calling the kids together as fast as she could. He could hear the desperation in her voice, the need to cry but the will to keep it buried down with the rest of the crap that he had put her through.

"She'll be okay, man. You gotta do what you gotta do," Moss reassured in a low voice. He nodded at Nicola, trying to make him feel better.

Nicola barely blinked. "Try to explain that to the kids."

2

The rain had not let up a bit by the time that Nicola arrived at the scene of the crime. It was only about ten minutes away - a little over five miles-from his house - at Overton Park, a well-known place for families to take their children, dog walkers to take their animals and couples to come for romantic picnics. Only today, there was nothing harmonious about the setting.

Pulling up in his black Escalade, he turned off his truck and watched from the window as the hordes of policeman ran through the raging storm to a garbage dump in the back of the park pushed up against an old fence, adjacent to the Memphis Zoo.

His headlights shined on the green, banged up dumpster about ten feet away. Rust had eroded the sides of the container away and large cockroaches crawled out of the bottom and fell into the pool of dirty water below it.

Several trash bags had been pulled out and set side-by-side on the concrete - marked in orange as EVIDENCE. And based upon the uniformed officers who were not used to the smell of decaying bodies, the putrid odor of rotting carcasses was overwhelming even in the open air.

An uncanny nervousness swept over Nicola, making his stomach clench tight as he watched. Sure he had seen plenty of bodies over his career, but there was something very disturbing about seeing a child that had been mutilated, raped and murdered.

Every time that he was forced to view one, the image burned indelibly into the back of his mind and haunted him for weeks. He could see it in his sleep, when he daydreamed, when he blinked. This was the hardest part of the job.

Stepping out in the rain, boots landing in a puddle of mud and grime, he pulled his badge from under his damp t-shirt clinging to his muscular frame and let it hang like a dog tag on his chest. The gleaming gold of the badge against black leather caught the reflection of the streetlight and gleamed in the gloomy setting.

The cold rain beat against his body as he stalked over past the onlookers and ducked under the yellow police tape, crossing into the restricted scene of the crime.

"What's up, Agosto," homicide detective Luke Johnson said with a handkerchief over his mouth, looking up from the top of the dumpster.

Detective Luke Johnson was an ethnic enigma. Fair-colored, deep-set brown eyes, arched black brows, bald head, muscular body and deep voiced, he was a mirror image of Vin Diesel in build and appearance, and he had never once told anyone if he was black, white or *other*. As far as anyone knew, he was just Johnson, and Agosto figured he liked it that way.

"Nothing is up, man," Nicola said walking over.

"I heard about the demotion," Johnson added with a smirk. "What? You didn't like being a lieutenant?"

"It wasn't that. I didn't like punks pissing on my female cops. So I made an example out of a couple of them. Who knew that they had good lawyers?"

Johnson raised his brow. "You're lucky that all you got was a demotion. Shit, from what I heard about the ass beating you gave those guys, you should have gotten shit canned."

"I'll remember to count my lucky fucking stars from now on," Agosto said, tired of telling the same story over and over. It had been months since that incident had happened. It should have been old news by now.

Johnson could see Agosto's irritation and chose to move on. "So what good thing did this call ruin for you? Because I was in between a beautiful brunette's thighs. Damn shame to just get up and leave her."

Nicola chuckled. "I was at my kids' birthday party when I got the call. My wife is pissed," he said, stepping up on wooden crates to look over into the garbage can. His eyes narrowed on the two twin boys discolored and duct taped with their hands behind their back. "Shit," Nicola cursed disgusted. Fighting the urge to gag at the sight of the maggots crawling out of one of the boy's ears, he jumped off the crate back into a large puddle of rainwater and took a deep breath.

"Not a pretty picture," Johnson said, stepping down beside Agosto with a little more grace.

"Do we know who the vics are yet?" Nicola asked, spitting.

"Yeah. A couple reported their kids missing about a week ago. Hunter and Hayden Naples, age 7. They were abducted while riding their bikes down Peabody. They live off Avalon and belong to a Dr. and Mrs.

Naples." He handed Nicola a small container of Noxzema to put under his nose to kill the smell.

Nicola slipped a little under his nose. "I live on Peabody."

"No shit?" Johnson said surprised. It was a pricey neighborhood, far too expensive for a cop's salary.

"No shit," Nicola answered, shaking his head. He was thinking about the proximity of the crime to his house. *Much too close for comfort.*

"So let me get this straight. The chief wants you on this why?" Johnson asked, pulling off his latex gloves as the crime scene investigator finished taking his pictures for the case. "You're a gangland cop last time I checked."

"Organized Crime," Nicola corrected, trying to focus. He looked over at the dumpster again. "The speculation about this being a serial killer is off in every way. The MO changes every time with every kid. It's not indicative of a serial killer. It's not indicative of one person. Right now, I'm in the middle of pulling all the pieces together. But I truly believe that this is part of a large organized crime thing and so does the brass."

"But why wouldn't they sell them instead of killing them here, if it's OC?" Johnson asked intrigued by Agosto's theory.

Nicola huffed. "That's what I'm trying to figure out."

"And not to poke holes in your notion, but why would they shit where they eat? The two kids that went missing before these two were from Memphis and were found in Memphis. Normally, if it's organized trafficking, they cart the kids off to some other city *or country for that matter*." Johnson moved out of the way as the coroner prepared to move the bodies out of the trash.

Nicola stopped talking out of respect for the boys as he watched the men pull the small bodies to the ground. A petite hand fell over, discolored and cut. Johnson made the sign of the cross and mumbled something under his voice. Nicola cursed again.

Finally, he managed to pull his attention away from the kids. Turning his head from the van, Nicola looked at Johnson. "We're making national news with this. Every day the outcry from the community gets a lot louder. I don't plan to step on homicide's shoes, but what if I'm right? Wouldn't it be worth it to work together and stop this instead of letting more kids end up like dead? We're at four now?"

Johnson threw up his hands. "Hey, I'm not arguing or complaining. I've pulled one fucking out of an abandoned car trunk and another out of a hole in the ground and all in the last month. If you know some way to make it stop, I'll give you a fucking medal, not a hard time. I just don't see why some group would do this here and risk getting caught. A serial killer I can understand…the other just doesn't make sense. If you come up with something, you let me know. Plus, I got the word from Amway just like you. I'm not stepping on his fucking feet."

"I plan to figure this out," Nicola said, wiping more water off his face. "And I plan on putting the bastards responsible for this under the jail."

Johnson looked down at Nicola and bit his lip. "I was thinking more about putting them under the fuck-ing dirt, *but that's me*. Hey, you need an umbrella or something? You're getting soaked out here, and you can't be much help to me with pneumonia," Johnson said, snapping his fingers at one of the uniform officers standing close by. "Give the lieutenant...my bad, give the *sergeant* a fucking umbrella," he shouted.

Nicola ignored the slick joke. "Have the parents been notified?" he asked, walking over to look at the boys' faces before the coroner zipped up the little black bags. He wanted to remember their faces, remember their torture for the days to come when he'd be forced to work his ass off and risk pissing his wife off further. It would keep things in perspective.

Johnson passed Nicola an umbrella. "We're getting in touch with them now."

"Mind if I'm in on it?" Nicola asked, tilting his head as he looked at the boys' faded eyes. He felt a sorrow that words could not describe for the children. They had to be his sons' ages. *Such a waste.*

Johnson felt his lunch coming up as he looked at the kids. Popping a cigarette into his mouth, he stood holding his umbrella over his head and puffing on a Kool. After a long drag, he exhaled. "No. I don't mind at all. I could use the support. These kinds of personal notifications fuck me up," he said, looking at the black bags as they were loaded into the back of the coroner's truck. "No matter what kind of day you were having before this, you can't tell me that this doesn't put things into perspective."

Nicola didn't respond. He was too far away now, thinking about his own sons and what he would do if something like this ever happened to them.

A uniformed officer walked over to Johnson and passed him a folded up piece of paper. "Here is the address, phone number and names of the parents," the woman said, eyes red from tears.

Johnson took the paper and stuck it inside of his pants pockets. "Thanks. First time seeing a dead body?" he asked the young woman.

She nodded quickly. "First time seeing *dead kids*," she reiterated, looking over at the coroner's van. "I hope to never see another."

"We're in Memphis, the leading city for infant mortality. You may want to get into another profession if you don't want to see another dead kid." Just then Johnson realized how cold he sounded and instantly hated himself for it. Patting the woman on the back, he tried to give her a smile. "Why don't you go and do something that will make you feel better. Get with Officer Masterson over there and secure the area. We don't want those fucking reporters to get too close to the crime scene."

Still shaking her head, she walked away obediently.

Nicola watched the woman as she went to the police line and began to chorale the onlookers. "You got someone in the crowd in plain clothes?" he asked, scanning the large group of spectators.

"Two. They are both looking for someone who might be *revisiting* the crime scene one last time," Johnson said, pulling out his keys. "You ready to go and visit some very unfortunate parents?"

"No," Nicola answered, rolling his eyes. "But we have to."

"What a fucking Saturday, eh?" Johnson said, wiping his eyes. "You want to follow me over in your truck? I know you don't like cigarette smoke, and after this I plan on chaining like a motherfucker for a few days."

"Yeah, I'll drive," Nicola said, scratching his neck. "This shit has to end, man."

"Sooner than later," Johnson said, as he watched the coroner's truck pull off.

***

The rain seemed to come down harder as Nicola pulled into the driveway of Dr. and Mrs. Naples. He put his truck in park right behind Johnson's unmarked squad car and gazed out of the window grimly.

The house had been newly built, and reminded him of the bricked homes on Chicago's east side with a quaint little swing and pots of flowers on the closed-in porch. There was a University of Tennessee orange flag waving in the wind and two Volvo station wagons in the curved drive.

Everything about the place screamed normal, middle-class family. It would be a shame to have to shatter their dreams today with the news that nothing would ever be the same for them again.

Johnson was the first to jump out of his car. Throwing down his cigarette on the well-kept lawn, he looked back at Nicola and motioned for him to join him. Nicola did so quickly, stepping back out into the miserable weather.

"You do the honors," Nicola said, as they hiked up the sidewalk to the front door.

"That's what I brought you for," Johnson said, pulling his badge from under his shirt. "I'm horrible at this shit."

"Aren't you supposed to be the homicide detective?" Nicola asked.

"I don't do the kid thing well," Johnson mumbled. He looked over at Nicola and frowned. "But then again, who does?"

Nicola shrugged.

"Well let's see who they warm up to first. Whoever they like gets the job," Johnson said with a huff. "Agreed?"

"Yeah, yeah. Sure thing," Nicola said, sucking his teeth.

The knock on the wooden door was hard and foreboding. Standing side-by-side, the two men waited as a petite white woman in a ponytail came peering out of the door. Her eyes had dark, black circles under them, and her face was white as a sheet.

Nicola knew that she had been worrying herself to death, just like Ivy would have.

"Yes," she said, voice quivering.

"Mrs. Naples," Johnson said, void of emotion. "I'm with the Memphis Police Department. Do you mind if we come in?" He held his badge up where she could see it.

She looked at the badge and then back up at Johnson. "Did you find them?" she asked, opening the door a little wider.

"It's best if we talk inside," Nicola chimed in. He looked over at Johnson and stepped forward.

Moving out of the way hesitantly, she allowed them inside of the house.

Nicola looked around at all the tables covered in MISSING flyers with pictures of their sons on them and walls that were papered in maps and post-it notes. Evidently, they had teams of people helping them search.

No matter how trained a cop was in doing this, there was no way to describe being the messenger of such horrid news.

Dr. Naples entered out of the kitchen quickly looking as tired as his wife. As soon as he made eye contact with Nicola, his shoulders sank. He went to his wife and put his hands around her. "Officers," he said gloomily.

"Why don't we all have a seat," Johnson offered as he motioned towards the sofas in the living room.

"I prefer to stand," Mrs. Naples said, tears flowing.

Johnson reached into his coat pocket and pulled out a Ziploc bag with a photo inside. "I'm very sorry, but I need to make a positive ID." He couldn't wait a second longer. This was killing him. He just wanted it over already.

Nicola looked over at him with a what-the-hell glare in his face.

Mrs. Naples nearly fainted. Her husband caught her in his arms, but could not push back the grieving moans that pushed up from his aching diaphragm. "Oh Lord, no," he said, tearing up.

Nicola took the photo and walked over to Dr. Naples. Moving around the woman, he lowered the picture where only the doctor could see.

Sobs escaped his tired eyes. "That's them. Those are our boys," Dr. Naples said, pulling off his glasses. He grab and held his wife tight. They both cried in the middle of the floor, nearly collapsed on top of each other.

Both Johnson and Nicola were forced to just stand there and watch. Suddenly a small dog came running past their feet. He stopped in the living room and looked back like he could sense the anguish.

Nicola looked at Johnson and raised his brow as if to insinuate that he should get on with the news.

Johnson cleared his throat and shifted his weight on his left side. "We found them about an hour ago in a dumpster in Overton Park." He gritted his teeth. "I'm so sorry. I promise you that the Memphis Police Department is doing everything in their power to find the person responsible for this."

"My children make four babies dead," Mrs. Naples sobbed, visibly trembling. "What are you going to do to stop this instead of just picking up after this bastard?"

Johnson wished that he had the words to comfort her, but he knew that she was right. All the leads had gone nowhere, and it did feel like he was just the cleanup guy. Looking over at Nicola, he shook his head, begging him to help him explain this.

"I have twin boys the same age," Nicola said, out of character and definitely unprofessionally. "Your kids were abducted only a few steps from my door. Even if they hadn't been, this case would still be a priority, but I want you to know that we will find the person or persons responsible for this, and we will bring them to justice. Your children will not be forgotten."

Nicola's words seemed to calm her just a little, though not much. She wiped her eyes and nodded. Letting go of her husband, she went to the sofa table and picked up a silver frame of the boys recently taken at a family event and gave it to Nicola. "That picture barely looks like my boys. I want you to take this so you can remember that they were once *living, breathing* children. Find who is responsible for this, please."

"I swear it," Nicola promised, taking the framed photo.

Johnson's eye twitched. Swearing was a no-no, but he wouldn't tell Nicola that now. The look on Nicola's face was as rife with anger as Johnson ever seen a man. Now was not the time to trifle with protocol.

"Thank you," Mrs. Naples said, touching his hand as she began to cry again.

Nicola nodded and looked over at Dr. Naples. "We'll need you to come down to 201 Poplar for follow up, but for now, I would seek grief counseling for yourself and your wife. This process is not going to be easy. If you have family, now would be the time to lean on them, and if you have a faith, I would call on your parishioners for spiritual support."

Dr. Naples's voice would barely carry. "We do. We will." He looked down at the floor, broken and numb.

Mrs. Naples found her way to the sofa, where she sat holding a pillow in front of her chest, rocking and crying.

Nicola stood in the middle of the floor watching her in a total state of sympathy. His feet were locked, unable to move; he simply took it all in…the sounds of mourning, the pain, the weariness. He looked around the house, a place once filled with love and felt the emptiness as it seeped in like a foul odor. This family had been robbed of life's most precious gift, and the only consolation that he could give them was that they were "working it." It was hardly enough.

"Agosto," Johnson said, pulling Nicola out of his daze. "Yo, man. We gotta go," he whispered.

Nicola nodded and turned away from the woman. Looking at Dr. Naples, he passed him a card. "If you need anything..."

The doctor took the card and nodded.

Drained and depressed, Nicola and Johnson made their exit back out into the rain. As soon as the door closed behind them, Johnson spoke up. "You swear it? Really?" he asked as they stood on the top step of the porch.

Nicola turned and looked at him with a stone face. "I don't break a promise, Johnson. I haven't in many years."

"Look, dude. You can't make this personal. Every man I've ever known who took this shit home with them ended up without a home," Johnson warned.

"Babies are being slaughtered, *if you haven't noticed*. In my opinion, that makes it okay to make a fucking exception on what you take home," Nicola said, stalking back to his car.

"Look, I know that this must get to you, but..."

Nicola cut him off. "I'll see you at the precinct."

On that note, Johnson threw his hands up and left the guy alone, because in his mind, it was never okay to take work home - no matter what. Everyone who he ever came into contact with in this line of work was a victim or a perp; everyone deserved the same amount of attention, and he couldn't move them all in with him. So, his motto in life was *you lose some, you win some*. This situation - no matter how grotesque - was no different. But Nicola acted as if someone had lit a fire under his ass. More power to him. As long as he solved the case and made him look good, why did he care if the guy was over zealous?

3

A little after midnight, Nicola pulled back up to his home, exhausted and a little nervous. He had missed the boys' entire birthday party and left Ivy alone with a house full of guests and wild children on the day that she needed him most. Words couldn't express how sorry he was about the entire situation. What was worst was that he had not told her yet that he was taking the Baby Boys case.

Normally, they discussed their career moves with each other first. Every promotion she had taken, every big client she had gone after, she had discussed with him preemptively. In the same manner, he had discussed his caseloads with her, remained transparent about his course of action regarding this ascension and dissension in the department and never kept her out of his work life. It was how they stayed grounded, and how they stayed together. Both of their jobs were demanding. Both of their lives were full; so juggling was something that they did to help each other.

Only in order to juggle, both parties had to be aware that there were balls in the air, and Nicola knew that he was about to hit Ivy in the head with one of the biggest dropped balls of yet.

In between running around like a chicken with his head cut off that day, he had managed to text her quite a few times, but each time the tone of her texts became more and more frustrated. As a peace offering, he had promised to be home to tuck the kids in by ten, but that got blown out of the water when the medical examiner had called him and Johnson back down to her office.

Getting out of his SUV, he slammed the door shut, hit the alarm and threw his jacket over his shoulder. Crickets chirped loudly out in the lawn, drawing his attention back out into the street. It had finally stopped raining and now the muggy fog was back, thick enough to cut through and stick to the skin. Low visibility made him nervous. He sloshed through the puddles in the driveway up to the front door and stuck his key into the lock. As he turned the knob, he felt the door pull away from him.

In gray jogging pants and a purple college alumni shirt, Ivy opened the door for him and stepped to the side.

"Come on in," she said, eyebrow cocked.

Now, I need permission to come into my own house? He thought to himself. He must have been in deeper shit than he first thought.

The house was spotless and quiet. There were no signs that a mob of people had been there only hours before. He looked around and felt even worse. So she had worked her ass off all day with the kids and then worked all night to clean up after them. *Great. Just wonderful.*

Nicola stepped passed her meekly and threw his jacket on the black iron coat rack in the corner. "I'm sorry, baby," he said, waiting for her to blow up on him like he deserved. His heart thudded in his chest cavity awaiting World War III.

Ivy crossed her arms over her chest and looked down at the wooden floor. Her fuzzy pink socks played with a spot that she had missed with the Swiffer. Her voice was low. "So, what's this about?" she asked, running her tongue over her bottom teeth. "Are you cheating on us again?" Her voice was weary, like she had spent hours waiting to ask, thinking about it, mulling over the right way to broach the subject.

Nicola's heart skipped a beat. "No, I'm not cheating on you guys *again*," he said, walking up to her. He lifted her chin and made her look at him. "I'm not," he said sincerely.

She looked at his wall of a chest protruding out and the 3-D muscles pushing up against the soft cotton fabric and huffed. How could she stay mad at a man who looked so good? "Your job is a pretty hard mistress to compete with, Nicky," she said, biting her bottom lip. "And every time you get too involved with her, we suffer." Sometimes, Ivy wished that she only had to contend with another woman like most wives, but not here. Nicky was known for spending inappropriate amounts of time chasing perps. The Memphis Police Department and all of her trappings was his mistress, tempting and lustful, promising glory and distinction that no woman could. He was ensnared in a career-based love affair that she hated almost as much as she hated the idea of what could happen to him as a result of it.

Nicola eyed her pouty mouth and realized what he hadn't done today. Rubbing her back with the flat palm of his hand, he let out his gigantic secret. "I took a big case, Ivy, but I can handle it."

"Nicky…" she said, shaking her head. She tried to pull away but Nicola's strategically placed hand held her there, unable to bolt on him without hearing him out first.

"The Baby Boys case," he explained further, narrowing his eyes. "And I know that we normally talk about these things…"

Determined not to just stand there and be forced to digest his bullshit, Ivy wiggled out of his embrace. She knew that he would not grip her, hold her too tight. Turning on her heels, she headed out of the foyer toward the kitchen. "I can't believe you! You *are* cheating." She threw her hands up in disgust.

Nicola followed a few feet behind her. His large boots echoed throughout the house. "Baby," he said, calling after her. "Baby, wait."

"Nicky, why would you do that? Why would you except the biggest case in Memphis since the Lester Street murders?" she asked, going to the refrigerator. Her long fingers grasped the stainless steel handle and with unnecessary force, she yanked it open. The condiments on the top shelf jingled together against the pressure.

"Why?" Nicola shrugged. "I didn't have a choice. This case is a big deal to Memphis and to Memphis families. We're losing kids left and right and…"

"No…uh-uh, don't pitch me," she said, whipping around to face him. The door to the refrigerator hit her on the hip. "I'm a publicist, okay. I know all about the sell."

"I'm not *pitching* you," Nicola said, voice high. *He was.* "I'm telling you that *this time* I honestly did not have a choice. Director Amway called me into his office three nights ago and practically begged me to head this case." He thought the news might soften things for him, explaining that his orders had come straight from the top.

He was sorely mistaken.

"Three nights ago?" She could literally feel a blood vessel about to pop in her head. "You've been holding on to this for 72 *whole* hours?"

Never had Nicola heard 3 days sound so long. He stuttered. "When I first found out you were in the middle of the CD release party for that guy, remember? Then the kids' birthday party preparation." He sighed. "I was looking for the right time to tell you."

"Do you mean when they mentioned your name on the television as the lead on the case or when you're standing in front of reporters answering questions with the Director of the Memphis Police Department?" she asked, turning back around. She pulled a wrapped up plate out of the refrigerator and walked it over to the microwave.

"The news conference isn't until the day after to-morrow." He might as well let it all hang out now.

She huffed, hating that she was always right.

"You know that I was going to tell you," Nicola said, scratching his brow. He watched her carefully as she moved around at the counter. "I was just looking for the right time."

"And did you find it?" she asked snidely. "This *right time,* I mean?"

"No, I didn't," Nicola said, sitting down at the kitchen table.

"Nicky, this case is huge. It's nationwide already. The pressure surrounding it will be stupendous. Then there is the issue of what if the case doesn't get solved. They'll persecute you. Parents everywhere will blame you for not saving their children. You don't want to live with that."

"I'll solve it. I always do," he snapped.

"And if you don't? This is a PR nightmare for the city. They are not going to handle this without rolling some heads. Citizens are demanding blood. The mayor has had over four press conferences or town hall meetings about this already. Families aren't letting their children go out to play."

"I know that!" His voice boomed like a drum from his diaphragm.

Ivy was unmoved. "And you're willing to offer your head and your career?"

"I'll solve it. If it's the last thing I do…I'm going to solve this damn case," he promised.

"The last thing you do?" She sounded exasperated. "Do you realize how morbid that sounds?"

"Well, I'll tell you one thing. I know how morbid this case is. Children are dead. They have been brutally murdered and there is no end in sight unless someone stops it. No one is safe-not even our own kids."

Ivy felt an urgent possession over him now. "Then don't take this case, so you can be there for them…for our children."

"I've already taken this case. I thought I made that clear." He held on tightly to the end of the table, gripping it until he thought that it would break.

"Then tell them that you don't want it," she growled.

"Why would I do that?"

"Because I…" She looked around the room and ran a nervous hand through her hair. "Because I don't want you to take it."

"That's not a good enough reason for the MPD."

Her voice cracked. "Fuck the MPD, Nicola. I'm trying to watch out for my family here. This case is disaster."

"That's why I was brought in. Evidently, they have more faith in me than you do."

"I have to live with you well after this case!" she screamed. "You got demoted after a man pissed on one of your female officers. What will you do when you actually get your hands on the person responsible for these murders? You'll end up behind bars."

"I can stay professional."

Ivy gave him a look that let him know that she knew that he was lying.

"What is really bothering you, Ivy? You've never been like this about a case before? You know I'll watch my back. What is the problem? Why now is my job such an issue?"

Ivy paused. She looked at him like she wanted to say something. Her eyes were panicked, her breathing heavy.

"What, baby? Spill it," Nicola begged. His voice was more understanding now. Although he was the one being attacked, he freely opened himself to anything that might help things.

Ivy got control of her breathing and sucked in a breath and the words that were on the tip of her tongue. "It's just not a good time," she said, voice nearly at a whisper.

"I love you. I'm doing this for all of us," Nicola said sincerely. "I need you to believe that, and I need you to support me."

Arguing with his wife was completely exhausting - worse than chasing perps. He was never right with her, and she was *never* wrong with him. It had been like that since before they married, and it would probably be that way until the day that he dropped dead.

Only the sound of the microwave heating the food filled the room, but Nicola could hear his wife silent screams.

He kept his eyes on the table but he could feel her glaring at him, burning through his body with her intense *you-fucked-up* stare. She was waiting on him to say something, defend himself, so that she could swoop down like the mighty angel of the Lord and smite him. But he wouldn't fall for it tonight. He kept quiet.

When the microwave beeped, Ivy turned from him and took the plate out with brown pot holders by the stove. Setting the dish in front of him on the table carefully as not to splash any food near his face or body, she stepped back. "Eat your dinner," she ordered in a low voice.

Nicola tried to hide his grin. She couldn't have been too mad at him. She had managed to fix a home cooked meal for him and his favorite at that. It was the kids' birthday. They were full of cake and pizza. "Thanks, baby," he said, getting ready to get up and grab a beer and some eating utensils.

"I'll get it," Ivy said, walking over to the drawer. She pulled out a fork and knife and grabbed a Bud Light from the refrigerator. Setting it down in front of him, she sighed. "I hate being mad at you, Nicky, but you deserve it…always trying to be sneaky and it just blows up in your face."

"I hate you being mad at me," Nicola said, grabbing her hand. Looking at her wedding ring, he pulled her to him and made her sit on his knee.

She did so reluctantly, hating herself for giving in.

Rubbing his head against her bosom, he sighed. "Umm, I just want to melt into you and go to bed right here."

Ivy knew where he was headed. "No sir. You're not getting off that easy. You left me here with a house full of heathens, *four of which belong to you*. You hid from me the fact that you were on the biggest case in Memphis, and you broke your promise to be here to tuck the kids in. Making love is not an option for you tonight." She stood up and put her hands on her hips.

Nicola liked when Ivy got all fired up. He watched her now, completely oblivious to how turned on he was, and licked his lips. Picking up his fork, he stabbed his Manicotti. "You don't have to be so cruel. What is that they say? Don't turn away your husband."

"Don't *turn* this on me," she said, pursing her lips together.

He bit into the food and lowered his voice. "Food is good, but I'm sure that you taste better." He cut his brown eyes at her and winked.

Ivy rolled her eyes in return. "Whatever," she said, unable to hide her blush. "Goodnight, Nicky. I'm tired. I'm going to bed and getting some rest before I have to be up for church in the morning."

She turned to walk away but Nicola grabbed her arm again. This time he lifted her and put her on the table right beside his plate.

"Boy, what are you doing?" she asked, laughing. "Let me go!" She felt his cold hand slip down her leg and into her jogging pants. Closing her eyes, she tried to curse him. "I said no making love," she whispered, wanting him to take her right then.

"Who says we have to make love?" He leaned into her and sucked on her neck with a nimble hot tongue. "We can do other things…" He adjusted his fingers down into the warmness of her panties and let out a groan.

She found his mouth and kissed him slowly. "Like what?" she whispered, tugging on his bottom lip as she held the sides of his face in her hands.

Nicola grabbed the waist band of her pants and pulled them down to her ankles. "Fuck, screw, pump, smash, twirk…"

"You have such a dirty mouth." Ivy laughed as she watched him pull off his shirt. His impatience with his own clothes let her know that this was going to be quick. He kicked one boot under the kitchen table and the other across the room into the stove. When he got to his jeans, he yanked them down along with his underwear.

"We can do whatever you like," he sang part of the rapper T.I.'s song, returning to her naked.

She giggled and looked down at her name tattooed on his chest across his heart. How could she stay mad at him while looking at something like that? He was her teddy bear, her biggest baby. "You should have told me, Nicky," she admonished one last time in a much quieter voice.

"I know, baby. I'm sorry. Forgive me, okay?" He lifted her chin and kissed her lips softly. His tongue slowly licked at her mouth. "Don't be mad at me. I can't take it. You're all I've got in this world besides the four *heathens* upstairs."

"You'll say anything to get what you want," she said in a whisper as she felt his hand running over her skin.

"Let's make up, right here, right now," he begged.

"Right here? Right now? Having sex on the table isn't sanitary," she reminded him as he pushed his body up against hers and melted into her. "The kids have to eat here in the morning for goodness sake."

Nicola grunted, turned on by her body and desire to reconcile. "Okay, I'll bleach the damn thing after," he said, pulling her legs to the end of the table.

"After what?" she asked, closing her eyes. She could feel the warmness of his throbbing penis pushing between her steaming thighs and suddenly she couldn't think of anything else. Swallowing hard, she wrapped her arms around his neck.

Nicola bit his lip and watched her face. "After this," he said, pushing inside of her.

4

At the crack of dawn on Sunday morning with the crickets still chirping and glistening dew on the ground, Nicola crept out of the front door of his house before the alarm could go off and wake Ivy for church. Quickly loading into his truck with a cup of premium roast coffee and a microwave egg and sausage sandwich, he pulled off into the quiet streets of Midtown listening to talk radio and getting his mind right for the long day ahead.

He truly hated to leave his family again this morning considering he had been gone all day the day before, but the medical examiner had come across a very important piece of information last night - too important to ignore or push off until Monday.

To follow up, Nicola and Johnson were going to visit one of The Five Families today. The Five Families were the top crime syndicates headquartered directly out of Memphis and moving illegal products nationally and/or internationally.

Even though Memphis was a smaller metro, it had two very distinct characteristics that made it a prime spot for smuggling: the river and the largest international cargo airport in the world. On any given day, to get things in or out of the country, all it took was a dirty customs agent, a starving delivery man with a contracted truck, a cargo hold and an 18-wheeler and any major dealer could be in business.

There were many crime syndicates in Memphis that kept the Organized Crime Task Force very busy, but most of the major crime was streamlined through five distinct organizations. These organizations knew about any of the real money in gambling, guns trafficking, prostitution, auto and identity theft, illicit and prescription drugs, burglary and murder-for-hire.

The Fly Boys were the most notorious of all five organizations, known for selling prescription drugs, illicit drugs and even over-the-counter drugs that would be flagged if purchased in bulk at stores. Started by one drop-out med student and one reject Air Force Pilot, the two men had grown the business considerably in the last five years, but oddly enough they had chosen to stay in Memphis.

Through his investigations, Nicola had been able to find out the truth behind the reason that the duo wouldn't jump ship. Twist, the former pilot had a child with his ex-wife in Memphis. He worried that if he left, he might alter the relationship that he had with his son or even worst, risk putting he and his mother in danger without his protection.

Cane, the other half of the dynamic duo, was happy in his long-time home on the farm that he and Twist stayed on right outside of town. Cane was a good old boy who started out wanting to run his father's pharmacy but ended up running a multi-million dollar drug business instead.

Nicola had busted the Fly Boys on a few occasions, but never had enough evidence to keep them. Usually, he did just enough damage to make them change their

operations mildly. He never kidded himself with
thoughts of grandeur when it came to the five families.
They had too much money behind them individually
and collectively. But he did hope that one day, someone
would mess up on a grand enough scale that they would
bury themselves.

Today, however, he wasn't going to shake up The
Fly Boys or spend time interrogating them. He was
going to ask them, practically beg them for a favor.
Normally, even thinking about such a thing would be
above Nicola, but considering there were children
involved, he would use all resources available to him.

But first, he had to make a stop downtown off of
Main Street to pick up Johnson from his condo. Evidently, the guy wasn't a morning person, so Nicola
offered to pick him up instead of waiting for him to
show at Republic Coffee shop, his favorite meet-up
place on the West side of the city.

Johnson claimed he was a night owl from years of
being on delta shift before transferring to homicide.
Prior to serving on the police department, he had been a
0311 infantryman at the Marine Corps stationed at
Camp Lejeune in North Carolina. And before
that…well, Johnson's story is a mystery. He never
speaks of family, friends or life before the Corps. And
being the type of guy that Nicola was, he didn't ask.

Nicola didn't like to rock the boat.

While the Memphis Police Department was over
2,500 men and women strong, almost everyone knew
each other directly or indirectly. If a cop had a reputation, good or bad, everyone knew about it. Stories
circulated among the watering holes about the amazing
and most often bizarre situations that a cop could find

themselves in on any given day. Johnson was one cop who had a serious reputation on the force. Dubbed a ladies' man, charged with being excessive with force at times, tough in the interrogation room, fast on his feet and feared by the OG's, Johnson had worked hard for his badge. While on uniform patrol, he had managed to turn in more arrest tickets then anyone on his shift at the West Precinct. His continual harassment of drug dealers and gang members made him prime for the Organized Crime Unit, but he had already bid for a spot in homicide, which is where he had landed. Since then, he had solved more cases than he had left unsolved and helped put a few major criminals in jail through forensic evidence and pushing witnesses to actually testify.

Nicola liked Johnson from what he could tell of the man. He reminded him a great deal of himself prior to marrying Ivy. When Johnson wasn't on the job, he was always chasing girls, for instance, something that Nicola had received a citywide reputation for over the years. And even after he was married, he had to often worry about running into one of his old flames out in public with his family. They would often try to slip him their numbers or offer to meet up later, but he would always decline.

That part of his life was over now. Thank God.

He had become a new man, found a new reason to live and changed his old ways, but he didn't fault the guys who lived his old life. That was just part of growing into a man. In fact, he lived vicariously through their stories without the side effects of crazy women showing up at his house unannounced or endless paternity tests and close calls. In the six years of marriage to Ivy, he had never had one affair. True there had been close calls. Women still found a man with a badge and gun attractive no matter how many children he had or how married he was, but he had managed to stay on the straight and narrow. At times, he had found it trying, but the one thing he knew was that he loved his wife and he would do anything to keep her.

Plus Ivy was a good woman. She was a hard work-er. She had a great job that she loved. She was a great mother to his children and an even better wife to him. He couldn't ask for more, except longer vacation time and more hours to sleep on any given night. But his life was his own and he took immense pride in it. People always complimented him on how beautiful his family was and how lucky he was, and unlike some who only looked that way from the outside, his family and his life really was good.

***

Pulling up to the Riverbend Condos off Riverside Drive not far from his old place before marrying Ivy, he parked his truck and meandered up to Johnson's place with his coffee still in hand. He had never been to Johnson's place before, but he liked the look of it. It screamed bachelor pad with bricked, zero lot, three-story condos overlooking the river. Smart sports cars and SUV's lined the quiet street as early morning runners and dog walkers went about their daily rou-tines. Birds chirped up in the strategically placed trees near the street lights and the sound of cars in the distance on the nearby freeway made for urban tranquil-ity.

Hitting the doorbell, Nicola took a sip of his luke-warm coffee and waited patiently at the front door. He squinted at the sunrise coming up over the horizon, slipped on his shades and ran a hand through his black curls. Leaning against the black rail of the staircase, he looked at his watch. Impatiently, he rang the doorbell again.

Minutes later, Johnson came to the door and opened it slightly. He peered out with red eyes at Nicola, who tapped his watch.

"What the fuck, man," Nicola said, pushing his way in.

"Sorry. I didn't realize the time," Johnson growled as he stepped back. He was in a pair of black briefs and bare-chested with only his dog tags hanging from his neck. Tattoos colored his deep olive-tanned skin over the thick, concrete muscle.

"Well, get dressed so that we can head out to Eads," Nicola said, looking around.

Johnson had a thing for Scarface. Everywhere he looked there were large, black and white photos hung up of the movie and other random memorabilia on the coffee table. The guy was a real movie enthusiast.

"Where's your kitchen?" Nicola asked, walking through the living room.

"Back there," Johnson said, scratching his chest. He looked over at the stairwell as a woman in a man's dress shirt came walking down. Cracking a smile at the young brunette, he pointed at Nicola.

"Agosto this is…." he waited for her to answer.

"Sam," she answered with a frown.

"Samantha," Johnson said, raising a brow. "She's a friend."

"Nice to meet you, friend," Nicola said, walking toward the kitchen. "We've got ten minutes," he called out to Johnson.

"Whatever you say, boss," Johnson said, saluting Nicola sarcastically. He turned on his heels. "Baby, let's go up and get dressed. I gotta get out of here in a minute. You heard the man."

"Why don't I just stay here and wait on you?" she asked as he walked up to her and kissed her lips. Holding on to the banister, he planted himself in front of her to prevent her from coming down stairs and getting comfortable.

"Hmm," he growled as he ran a hand down her exposed thigh. "Not a good idea, baby. I don't know what time I'll get back and my mom is supposed to stop by later and clean-up. Trust me, you don't want to be here when she gets here."

"I'd love to meet your mother," she said with a smile.

Johnson sucked his teeth as he prepared to exhale a lie. With a faux-distant look in his eyes, he fibbed. "She's overbearing, overprotective and she runs all my girlfriends away. I'd rather introduce you myself later," he said, turning her around by her voluptuous hips. "Now up the stairs with you."

"Girlfriend?" Sam repeated. "But you just called me your friend."

"Yeah, my *girlfriend*. Do you think I just bring random girls home?" Johnson asked, trying to keep a straight face. "Now come on. You heard the man. I've got ten minutes. Don't make me look bad in front of my boss."

Nicola shook his head at the conversation. *Textbook player*. The next thing he would be doing is telling the girl that he'd only been with a few girls and had never felt this way before. Wow, he didn't realize guys were still using the old green as grass routine. He went into the kitchen and popped his coffee into another cup to warm it.

Just as the microwave sounded, Nicola's phone beeped. He pulled it out of his pocket and checked it. It was Ivy.

What are you doing? She asked.

Sorry to leave so early, baby. I've got a lead. Once I'm done, I'll be home, he typed.

It's Sunday, Nicky. He could actually hear her tone in his head.

I know. I'll be home soon. I promise.

We're going to church without you. More tone.

Say a prayer for me. I love you guys.

There was a pause before Ivy responded.

I love you, too. She responded back with a smiley face. *But you have dinner duty tonight at seven. So unless hell freezes over you had better be here.*

Nothing will stop me, Nicola typed back. *Have a good day.*

He smiled and put his cell phone back in his pocket. Just one more example of why he loved his life more. There were no names to remember, no quick escapes. She'll be there when he got home, waiting for him just like every night for the last six years.

Exactly ten minutes later, Johnson had seen Sam off in her red Mini-Cooper and had loaded into Nicola's truck. Sliding into his seat and slipping on his shades, he groaned. "Shit, I've got a fucking hangover."

Nicola started the truck and smirked. "So, you're a lightweight, huh?"

"No, I'm a fucking alcoholic," Johnson said, reaching into the pocket of his hoodie to pull out a flask. "Want some?"

Nicola nodded no.

"Fine." Johnson took a sip of the strong drink and slipped it back inside. Letting out a growl, he blew out a breath, making his lips flap. "Okay, so we're headed to Eads to see the Fly Boys, right?"

Nicola turned onto the expressway and adjusted his rearview mirror. "Yep. The medical examiner said that each of the children had one thing in common. They all had the Molly in their system." He looked over at Johnson. "And you know who produces that pill."

"The fucking Fly Boys," Johnson said, raising a brow. "Yeah, I get that part. I got that last night. What I don't get is why we are just going to knock on the front door and ask Twist and Cane, *of all people*, to help us out. Call me crazy, but I've never known drug dealers to be helpful in a police investigation."

"Well, I'm not so sure that Cane will be helpful. He doesn't have any children and by all accounts of the word is a fucking redneck, but Twist might just help us out."

"Why?"

"Call it a hunch," Nicola said with a shrug.

"How about I just call it a fucking mistake," Johnson said, resting back in his chair. "Wake me when we get there."

5

At the large imposing gates of a sprawling horse farm on a few miles into Eads, TN, Nicola pulled up and looked into the camera focused on the driver's side of his vehicle. Taking off his shades, he flashed his badge and stuck his head out of the window.

"I'm here to talk to Twist. I need a favor," Nicola screamed at the camera. He knew there was no need to give a name. Twist knew him well and would either see him or would not.

Nicola's voice rattled Johnson awake. He sat up in the seat and yawned.

A female voice came over the buzzer after a few moments. "Wait there. Someone will be out," she said in a dry, flat tone.

Nicola sat back in his seat and looked at Johnson. "Are you up, sleeping beauty?"

"Yep, just in time to get my ass shot off," Johnson answered, checking his weapon.

"We're going in for a discussion, not to clean house," Nicola reminded.

"Hey, you have a right to trust who you want to trust. Me. I don't trust anyone."

Nicola turned up his lip at a thought, but kept quiet.

A few minutes later, a white golf cart pulled up to the gate as it opened with two women in pink polo shirts and khaki shorts. They greeted Nicola and

Johnson with bright smiles, although Nicola was sure that they were anything but cordial if ordered.

The driver of the golf cart, a taller blonde with sparking blue eyes and a funny twisted mouth, walked over to Nicola's side of the truck and looked inside. The closer that she got, the more worn that she looked. He could see the worry lines in her face that she tried to hide by an overuse of makeup. Instantly, the thought of a Monet, beautiful from a far, but a mess up close.

"Morning, sir," she said, eyeing Nicola then Johnson.

"Good morning," Nicola said, tapping his fingers on the car door. "So, is Twist going to see us or not?" He chose to skip the theatrics.

"What is this about?" she asked, eyes intense.

Nicola smacked his lips and huffed. "Like I said, I need a favor," he said, refusing to elaborate, especially to someone's hired hand.

Sensing Nicola's aggravation, the woman turned away from Nicola and spoke into her earpiece. After a few seconds and a few replies from the other end of the transmission, she turned back around and walked back up to Nicola's truck. "Follow me," she said shortly.

Nicola gave her a condescending salute. "Yes, ma'am," he said, winking at Johnson. "This bitch..." Nicola said under his breath before he could catch himself. He hated want-to-be bad guys. She was all of 135 lbs. Unless she was more lethal than him with that weapon, she could never be a threat to him at 258 lbs. of mature muscle. And the mere suggestion by her attitude that she thought she was a bad ass, only pissed him off.

"Are those his bodyguards?" Johnson asked amused by the interaction between Nicola and the woman.

"Yeah, didn't you see the gun under the back of her shirt?"

"Yeah, but I was more impressed with the double D's in the front," Johnson laughed.

"While you're watching her tits, she's going to try to attempt to blow your ass off," Nicola joked.

"I'm always up for a good *blowing*," Johnson said with a chuckle.

Following the golf cart into the gate, they drove slowly down the gravel driveway to the main house where they parked in front of the circular drive, and then followed the women inside.

"Nice place," Johnson said, looking around the marble entryway. His voice echoed throughout the elaborate but hollow hallways.

"You haven't been out here before?" Nicola asked. He had quite a few times.

"No. You?"

"Couple times," Nicola answered, but did not elaborate.

"Sometimes, it makes me wonder…" Johnson said under his breath.

"Wonder what?" Nicola asked.

"Why we choose to stay on the right side of the law, when all the damn money is obviously on the wrong side."

Nicola chuckled. "But the health benefits suck." He avoided telling Johnson that he was born into wealth. It might unbalance the already shaky relationship.

Johnson smirked. "Life expectancy is about 30 in the drug world, so you're living on borrowed time in their world."

"I'm not even 40 yet," Nicola frowned. "Do I look it?"

"No. Of course not," Johnson lied.

The two women stopped and turned around. The same woman who had done all the talking before spoke again. "Twist and Cane will be right out. They've asked that you all make yourself comfortable in the living room." She pointed at the sofa. "Can I get you something to drink while you wait?" Her demeanor had changed since the gate. Evidently, she had found out who Nicola Agosto was.

"No," Nicola answered, walking to the sofa. He avoided the thank you, part of his manners. Fuck her. There was no way he was going to be polite to criminals unless they were giving him something he *really* wanted. He sat down and rested back, checking his cell phone.

"A coke will be fine," Johnson answered the woman, raising his brow suggestively, "for now. I'll let you know what else comes to mind."

She gave a lingering smile at Johnson and turned around, disappearing into the house.

Johnson turned to Nicola and smacked his lips. "I'd hit it," he said in a matter-of-fact tone.

"I'm sure that you would," Nicola said, rolling his eyes. "She's a criminal, you know."

"I don't do criminal background checks on my booty calls, dude. I'm not around long enough for it to matter," he said, sitting down.

"Didn't anyone ever tell you that if you lay down with dogs, you'll get up with fleas?"

Johnson paused and raised his brow. "Yeah. That's why I never lay down without a little protection. OFF seems to do the trick."

Nicola gave up. The boy was hopeless.

The duo wasn't made to wait long. Within in minutes, a dapper man in perfectly pressed khaki pants and an apple greet polo rounded the corner with a bright smile on his face. He was slender and tall, blonde with bright brown eyes and clean shave.

"Twist," Nicola said, nodding his head. "Good to see you."

"Shit, I don't know yet, man." He walked up to Nicola as Nicola stood and shook his hand. "Every time I see your ass, I end up in the clink."

"Not today, man," Nicola said with a grin.

Twist looked over at Johnson still sitting and tilted his head curiously. "Johnson?" He looked back over at Nicola. "Did someone die?"

"Yeah," Nicola said, rubbing the back of his neck. "That's what I'm here to talk to you about."

Twist smacked on his Double mint gum, blowing and popping a bumble simultaneously and shook his head. He was processing something in the back of his mind but refused to speak on it. "Yeah, alright. Why don't you guys come on back? The boys and I are playing Madden. We can talk in there. It's only room I know for sure in this house that isn't bugged."

"Madden. You got the new one?" Johnson asked, standing up.

"Come on, man," Twist said in a deep southern drawl. "This is Twist you're talking to. I've got the one that hasn't come out yet."

Nicola shook his head. The young guys, no matter their profession, were always in the same shit. Girls and games. He stayed away from both - one out of necessity, the other out of sheer dislike. He had grown up in a time where boys went outside and played football, swam and surfed on their downtime. They didn't sit around together playing video games and watching porn. But that was a discussion for another day. For now, he would simply grin and bear it.

All three men walked casually through the elaborate halls of the mansion to a media room in the back of the house that opened up to the pool area. Five men with guns in their holsters sat strategically around the room watching while three others monitored the women out swimming in the pool and working on their tan.

It looked like Twist and Cane were having a private party.

Johnson took a seat on the couch beside Cane, who moved over a little and tapped his friend to pass him another controller.

"What's up, Johnson," Cane said, picking up his beer. "What the fuck brings you out here?" He passed Johnson a controller and raised his beer.

Cane was a heavy-set, tall man with an awkward body, who had only put on the extra pounds since his new found success in the drug industry. A country boy who still wore John Deere hats, Ole Miss T-shirts and dipped religiously, no one would ever have imagined that the man was a scientific genius and one of the biggest drug dealers in the southeastern hemisphere. He had jolly locks of auburn hair on his large head that matched his jolly cheeks and deep set green eyes that were only brought out by the red freckles that dusted his face. But as innocent as he looked, he was that much more treacherous. Cane had been a hunter since he was nine and loved a good weapon. Good with a shotgun, he often disciplined his men with buckshot and the various tools that he kept in his barn.

Johnson was all too familiar with Cane. He had hauled him in on several occasions regarding dead drug dealers, but he could never make anything stick. Cane always had an alibi and always had a lawyer. So after a few idle threats, Johnson would be forced to cut him loose. Still, their relationship had not made them sour on each other.

Both men respected that it was all business.

"I'm just here with Agosto," Johnson said, looking back at his partner who was talking in the corner to Twist. He'd let Nicola ask for the favors of these guys. He had no intention of doing so. What he could not take by force, he didn't want.

"Want a drink?" Twist asked Nicola as they walked over to the stocked bar alone.

One of the bodyguards who was sitting on a barstool towards the end of the bar quickly got up and moved when he saw Nicola's pensive stare lock on him. Everyone knew Agosto. Mean as a rattlesnake and hard as nails. No one wanted to get in his crosshairs accidentally.

Nicola turned his attention back to Twist after the man had moved out of his sight. "You're lady guard out there already asked me. I'm good," Nicola said, looking back at Johnson. "But I think Johnson wanted a coke."

"Make it a beer," Johnson answered quickly, letting Twist know that he was still in ear shot and could monitor both situations while playing the video game.

"Sure thing," Twist said, opening the refrigerator. He pulled out a beer and passed it to one of his bodyguards. "Take this over to Johnson."

"With the cap still on," Nicola added.

Twist took his hand off the cap of the beer and smiled. "Don't trust me?"

Nicola grinned. "You're a dealer. I think you know the answer to that."

"Scared I'm going to slip you a Mickey?" Twist chuckled.

"Well, you are a pill dealer."

"I don't know what you're talking about," Twist said, winking his eye at Nicola.

The bodyguard quickly took Johnson a beer, with the cap still on, and then took a seat by the door.

Nicola sat down at the bar and heaved. "I need a favor, Twist."

"Not what I expected," Twist said with gleaming eyes. "But okay. I'll bite. How can I help you?"

Nicola moved in closer to the bar, fists balled up tight. He lowered his voice and looked Twist in the eyes. "You've heard about the Baby Boys Case?"

Twist leaned in very dramatically. "Who hasn't?"

"Well, we got the tox report back and the one thing all these kids had in common was that they had Molly in their system." Nicola sat back up and loosened his fists.

Twist stood back up and looked around the room. Running his tongue around the ridge of his mouth, he thought intently on something else before he spoke. "So what does that have to do with us?" he finally asked.

"*Aww*, shit, Twist. What do you think? Now, we both have kids. You and me. Would you want what happened to those kids to happen to yours? Because I sure as hell couldn't sleep at night thinking that I had something...anything to do with his. Someone is using your *signature* synthetic drug to rape, torture and kill elementary school kids," Nicola said with a growl in his voice. "Now, I know that you're a son-of-a bitch, but I don't think you'd have anything to do with this." He only prayed that the man had a little conscience left, otherwise, he might as well be pissing in the wind.

Nicola could look in Twist eyes and tell that he didn't know anything about it, but the trick was getting him to help him despite their obvious conflict.

"Let's say that it was *my* Molly that helped kill all those kids - and I'm definitely not saying that it was...," Twist said in an even lower voice. "What the fuck do you want me to do about it?"

"I could come in here with a warrant, throwing folks around on pure accusation - and it'd be bad for business. Even some dealers might distance themselves from you on just principle-or you could help me by finding out which one of your guys is selling to a guy that fits the profile I'm looking for."

"So you do have a description on this guy?" Twist asked. That was news.

"No," Nicola huffed in frustration. "The FBI lent us one of their profilers. We have an idea based upon the kills of what the guy at least executing some of the kids must behave like, maybe even look like."

"I've seen that on one of those cop shows. A profil-
er. Yeah. Okay. Then what?" Twist asked intrigued. He
had never spoken with a cop about an investigation that
didn't concern him directly. It was refreshing in a way
to not be the target of an investigation.

"All I want is your dealer to point me in the right
direction so that I can stop this guy, these guys..."
Nicola didn't think that he was asking a lot considering.

"So now there is more than one?" Now he was confused.

"That's why I'm here. I think it's all connected to a
ring, but I can't be sure until I get one successful lead."
Nicola let Twist fill in the blanks.

"And you won't go after my guy?"

"I purposefully did not leak the contents of the children's tox reports to the media so that I could come to
you. You're the only one in the fucking region selling
Molly. You won't let anyone else into the market. All
roads lead to you. So, I figure, you should be the one to
help." Nicola's eyes became greedy. He had explained
too much. He wanted answers now.

"In exchange for what?" Twist continued. "Shit,
I've got my own problem at the moment. I've got Rick
Amherst trying to take over my entire operation. "There
was an urgency in his voice that didn't quite fit the
normally cool Twist.

"A get out of jail free card," Nicola said with cool-
ness in his brown eyes.

Twist turned his lips up. "My lawyers cost me $750
an hour. I've got a *get-out-of-jail-free* card on any day."
He popped another bubble with his gum at the tip of his
tongue and looked at Nicola to sweeten the deal.

"I've got an inside tip on a shipment coming in, Twist. It's good Intel. Now, you know that I never turn my back....ever, but I will this time. Even though I've got a hard on for this case with regarding you, I'll not only let the shipment come in but I'll turn my back on the pickup crew and the drop off. Now, I know you get shipments in weekly and I've recently learned where about 70 percent come in. I know that you can't afford to change everything right now. I know you can't afford to re-staff and you sure as hell can't afford to change your MO. So, work with me and I'll work with you. Trust me when I say, my Intel is good and I would have enough to lock you up on it, but at the moment these kids are more important than your drugs."

Twist sucked in a dramatic breath and put his hands on his cheeks. "What to do? What to do? First you come in here with a favor and then it turns more into a rape," he said, taking a crystal tumbler stacked up on the side of the bar and turning it over. He poured himself a hefty helping of Gentleman's Jack and knocked it back. Slamming the glass on the bar, he smacked his lips. "Damn, that hit the spot. I gotta tell you, Agosto, you have the worst timing in the world."

"It's my collar, Twist. You give me something. I give you something. We both win." Nicola waited.

"I want Amherst's head on a plate. He's talking to my suppliers, fucking with my money flow. Can you do something about that?"

"You're really asking me to lean heavy on another drug dealer for you? Come on, man. You know I don't do that shit. Hell, this is not my style. Coming to you is like...making a deal with a devil."

"Better the devil you know," Twist said in a huff.

"This really isn't a good time."

"When is it a good time? At least you won't have me on your back. You can do what you do…for the moment," Nicola said with warning. "This offer is only good for as long as I'm in this house. When I leave, I come back with an army."

Twist wiggled his fingers like he had just figured Nicola out. "What if I do help you find this guy and then you just bust me next week?"

"I'll give you a month head start to change shit around after I bust this guy before I even look your way."

"Two months," Twist negotiated.

"A month and a half, and that's a lot for me. You know it." And Nicola wasn't lying. It was more than he had ever offered in his life.

Twist scratched his chin. Nicola Agosto was a good ally to have - the best. He never bent for anyone, which meant that he wanted the kid killer bad. "Alright. I'll help you find this fucker. I'll get my guys together, find out who has been selling to your *mystery boy* and then get back to you. But you fucking owe me. And I won't let you forget it."

"You have my word. Now, I need it quick," Nicola urged.

"I know. I see the news every damn day," Twist said. "When are you going to get me the profile so that I can tell them what we're looking for?"

Pulling out a red metallic jump drive, Nicola slid it over to Twist. "I don't have time to waste. Kids are dying. Everything you need is on there."

Twist took the jump drive and slid it down into his pocket. "Give me until tomorrow afternoon *at most*. I'll have something for you."

"Thank you," Nicola said, pushing the words out. For that kind of favor, he could be polite.

6

The Agosto house was alive by nightfall when Nicola pulled up after a long day from home. He and Johnson had followed up on a few more leads regarding the case, took some statements, took more photos and studied everything that they had in the war room to try to come up with more clues. The day had been exhausting, and essentially they knew that they were depending on a drug dealer to point them to the killer, which meant it had also been emasculating for Nicola.

All the lights throughout the entire three-story bricked, colonial were on, including the porch lights and floodlights that illuminated the large mansion from the street. For some reason, Nicola immediately thought of his utility bill and how his children were hitting him in the pocket every time they flipped a light on - especially since they never turned a light off.

The family dog, Meko, barked in the backyard as an ambulance passed a few streets over, and wind rustled through the shuddered windows as it brought with it dark clouds that covered the full moon.

It was a peaceful night. No kids were found dead today and no horrible media stories had broken about the investigation. God was giving him a break.

He walked inside gratefully, inhaling all the wonderful scents that made his house smell like a home - cinnamon, spice, baked goodies and happiness. Every day, he waited to walk through his door and smell that exact fragrance. Every day, he could not wait to see his family. Every single day, they did not disappoint. They were always there for him, always ready to receive him with open arms. He needed it tonight.

Kicking his boots off at the front door, he threw his jacket up on the hook behind the door and walked quietly down the corridor, listening to the multiple high soprano giggles come from the TV room.

The kids were lined up on the sofa watching television and eating popcorn in the dimly lit room, completely oblivious to their surroundings, while Ivy sat at the large wooden desk in the corner nook reading an email on her laptop and eating nachos out of a bowl. She had on her headphones to drown out the sound of children, something Nicola could never do in the house while he was babysitting. He was too paranoid.

Stealthily, he leaned against the door and watched them as they went about their business - safe from everything that was outside of these walls. His oldest boy slapped his twin brother in the head and called him a booger right before the youngest of his sons told everyone to smell his feet. They were all *boy* - gross and untrained.

He cherished all four of his sons - every single one of their many idiosyncrasies.

He found their chatter to be soothing and their problems to be a break from the *real* world. All four of his children adored him, praising him constantly and always looking to him for answers. It made him feel needed in a different way than people needed him on his job. His children needed him to help them survive,

to grow and become catalysts of change in their community - world shakers.

And his Ivy…

Words were not enough to express how much he
loved his wife. Each and every year they fell deeper and
deeper in love, despite the arguments, the sofa deploy-
ments, the rolling eyes and snide remarks. That was just
a part of marriage, ask any old person. But his wife was
his shelter and his foundation. She kept him grounded.

Her voice cracked across the room like lightning.
"Turn that TV down. I can hear it above these dang
earphones!" Ivy screamed, pulling an ear bud from her
ear.

"It's Madison's fault!" Adam screamed.

"No, it's not!" Madison argued, slapping his brother
in the ear. "It's your fault."

"Enough hitting! If one of you hit each other ONE
MORE TIME, then I'm going to start paddling people's
asses!" Her voice was harsher now, full mommy-mode.

Nicola snickered to himself at Ivy's feeble attempt.
She tried to be so tough. It only made her softer.

She caught a glimpse of her husband's large shadow
in the corner and stood up. "Nicky?" Suddenly, her
voice was a mix of excitement and surprise.

"Yeah, baby," Nicola said, stepping inside the door.
He winked at her. "*Paddling asses*?" He laughed.
"Since when do you paddle anything?"

"Daddy!" the kids sang, turning around on the back
of the sofa to look at him. All four sets of eyes burned
through him, looking for treats.

"Did you bring us anything?" Madison asked.

"Forgot. I'll fix you a treat with dinner," Nicola
said, slapping his pockets.

"What are you doing over there?" Ivy asked, walking over to him.

"Just checking you guys out," he said, pulling her to him. He noticed that she was glowing - her skin was radiating like the sun was right under the surface.

She hugged him tight. "You made it."

"I told you I'd be here to cook dinner," he said, nuzzling his nose into her hair. "I try to never break a promise."

"*Try* is the operative word," she said, looking up at him as she held on to his waist and weaving her fingers around his gun. "Now that you're here, I'm going upstairs and run a hot bath."

"Can I get in?" he growled into her ear.

"Nope. Mommy needs some *me* time," she said, stepping away. "Kids. He's all yours." Patting him on the back, she disappeared down the hall.

***

Two hours later, two sets of little kids ran up and down the front staircase chasing each other and screaming, while *SpongeBob* played in the den.

Madison and Adam, the oldest twin boys, led the gang, followed by Michael and David, the three-year old twin boys, who worked hard to keep up with their older siblings.

Pleased with the racket, Nicola cooked a large pot of spaghetti in the kitchen as he watched the news, and Ivy counted socks in the adjoining TV room, coupling them together every time that she found a match.

"FYI. This is not how I want to spend my anniversary," she said sarcastically as she heard one of the kids scream again. "So, despite this case, you had better be planning something great. You have a little over six weeks to reserve hotels and first-class tickets, buy me an awesome piece of jewelry…you know a diamond-*esque* anniversary gift and…"

"Wait. How do you know that I haven't already done that?" he asked with a serious face.

Ivy turned her lips up in a smirk. "Because I've been married to you for six years."

"And?" Nicola said with a frown. "Every year I do something amazing."

She said his name slowly, over enunciating every syllable. "Ni-co-la…you know I love you, but your anniversary gifts always suck."

"Baby!" Nicola said appalled. "How can you…" He shook his head as if he could not process her words. "The massage thing that I bought you with the prongs to work your deep tissue…"

"A dildo," she said throwing down a pair of socks into one of the kids' baskets. She rolled her eyes at him.

"That was *not* a dildo. I bought that thing at the mall by one of those massage chair things. And what about the Dead Sea bath salt big basket bullshit I bought you that one year…" he argued.

Ivy cut him off. "That shit broke me out. I had to go to a dermatologist, Nicky, remember? It changed my complexion forever."

Nicola snapped his fingers and pointed at her. "The diamond tennis bracelet."

"You got me pregnant right after that."

"*But* you liked the tennis bracelet, right?"

Ivy shook her head. "Plan something nice, Nicky. I'm not playing. I deserve it."

"What? This is great," he said, adding sage to his special sauce. He tasted the spoon and smiled, revealing deep dimples in his well-tanned face. "We're all going to sit down like a family and have dinner and..." He looked down at the red sauce as it splattered on his apron. Rubbing his finger against the stain, he slipped his finger in his mouth. "Finger-licking good." He smiled at Ivy.

His boyish charms still made her heart skip a beat, but over time, she had learned to hide it.

"You know you still like what I do with my fingers, girl," he joked. "And my tongue for that matter. The other night I almost lost consciousness in that leg-lock, death grip you put me."

"I don't know what you are talking about," she chuckled.

"Oh, you don't know what I'm talking about. I damned near saw stars when you let go of me. You practically smashed my entire head."

Ivy laughed this time, recalling the encounter.

She looked up from her pile of laundry and gave a cool smile. "You're in a lot better mood now, huh? Since you have come clean about your investigation. The few days before that you were edgy." She observed as she placed a large bundle of folded clothes in a clean hamper to haul upstairs later.

Nicola raised his brow while he dumped more oregano in his sauce. "I'm always in a better mood when I'm with you guys," he said, stirring the food. He looked at her for a moment with a half-smile, his large, brown eyes sparkled with phony calm, but Ivy could see his pain. She stood up from her chores and walked over to the counter. Leaning against it, she reached her hand out and touched her husband's face.

"Want to talk about it?" she asked. Her voice was low and soothing, as normal.

"What? Talk about what?" He took his eyes off her and focused on the spaghetti.

There was a slight hint of frustration in her voice when she realized that he was going to try to avoid any resemblance of a discussion about his work. "Talk about today?" she continued. "About yesterday? About any of it? This can't be easy. I've been giving it a lot of thought and it's the only way you're going to survive this case."

He stopped stirring his food and looked up. His long eyelashes flapped like wings. "No, baby, I don't want to talk about it." His face was like stone now. Shutting down immediately, he turned his back to her again, putting up his invisible yet fully recognizable wall.

But Ivy continued, only in a softer voice to convince him into sharing. "Well, you need to talk to someone. It's not healthy. You're going to..."

"Going to what?" he interrupted. He turned back to her with narrowed eyes. He thought that she was going to say fail - going to say what he feared the most. He watched her mouth as the words formed on her lips.

"Explode." She lowered her voice and looked around to make sure that the children didn't hear her. She lifted her eyes and nodded. "You're going to *explode*, Nicola, if you don't talk to someone." She bit her lip.

Nicola turned off the stove, the knob clicking with his rough handling of it, and pulled off his apron. Setting it on the table, he walked over to her and pulled her into his arms. "Listen to me. I don't bring my work home. That's the one thing that I've learned *not* to do -

especially after that shit that happened out in West Wood."

Ivy shook her head emphatically. "Some things are easy to separate, Nicky. When it was drugs, guns, prostitutes, you could separate it. But it's children now...like the four you have in there," she motioned towards the loud noise coming from the stairs. "There is no separation, and you and I both know that. You're a father first, no different than the rest of the fathers out there. You're not thinking like a cop...I know you."

"Even if I did want to talk to someone, if I spoke to the shrink at the station this early in the case, they may pull me off the case completely," he said, rubbing her arms. "I'm too close to just get yanked, Ivy. I'm *so* close. I've got a viable lead just dangling. I've damned near offered my soul to get it." His voice pleaded for her understanding and his eyes were intense with the passion that she'd seen on a hundred other cases.

It was confirmed. Nicola was all in.

She took his face in her hands, cupping his chin in her palms. His big brown eyes gazed at her, seeking approval.

After a moment of staring at him, pondering to her-self, she nodded. "Then talk to my shrink."

"There you go with that shit again," he shook his head. That wasn't the response he was looking for. He quickly changed the conversation, knowing that it was easy to get her off track. "And why do you need a shrink? You have everything a woman could ask for."

"I do," she agreed with a certain amount of sarcasm in her voice. "I have a wonderful husband, who enjoys playing cowboy in the most crime infested city in the country. I have a job that at times drives me crazy, especially since I'm so close to making partner. I have four kids. Four. And I've just turned thirty."

Nicola waited. His intuition told him that there was something else that she wasn't saying - something to add to that already long list. But for some reason, she had stopped there.

"Okay, maybe you do need a shrink," he said as they both laughed, "but...baby, I can't go to your man-hating, man-eating, psycho babbling, women's lib..."

Ivy interrupted him. "She's great. I tell you what. I'll make you an appointment myself. You can talk to her and get some of this off your chest before you explode and do something crazy." Her warm smile reassured him.

Nicola pulled her closer. "Something crazy?" He ran his hands down her back and grabbed her buttocks. Biting his lip, he picked her up off the ground and forced her to wrap her legs around him. "Something crazy like...take you on the floor right here?" He slapped her backside and growled. It was amazing how quickly she could turn him on. "You know how horny I get when you wear that Steeler's t-shirt with no bra on under it. His deft fingers grazed over her pebbled nipples as he bit his lip.

She laughed and tried to keep him from pulling up her shirt. "Nicky! You better not! The kids...*what about the kids*?" She laughed infectiously. "I keep telling you that you can't do that kind of stuff in front of the little babies!"

He pinned Ivy against the wall and held her in his arms. Burying his head on her chest, he inhaled her perfume and sighed. "Shit. I forgot about *all* those damned kids." He rubbed his hands against her jeans and felt an erection growing.

"Look at what you're doing to me," he said, trying to make her feel guilty.

"Oh, you poor baby." She ran her hands through his curly locks and kissed him quickly. The feeling was mutual but would have to be hampered for now. "Kids! Come down! Dinner's ready!" she screamed in his ear.

"Ouch, my ear," he said, deafened by her long-range, outdoor mommy voice.

Sliding down from his embrace, she patted him on the back and giggled. "We'll pick this conversation up later, chief."

"That's right," he said watching her walk away. "Put daddy's shit on the back burner."

"Daddy's stuff is always X-rated, "she said, turning back to look at him. She flashed her bedroom eyes.

"And that's fair, how?" he asked, pushing down on his crotch to adjust his growing manhood.

She laughed.

Nicola rolled his eyes. "Yeah, keep laughing. I'll pull you into the broom closet and get you pregnant," he shouted after her. "It'll take me like four minutes, five tops." Throwing up his hands at her, he went back to his spaghetti.

Ivy bit her lip and paused. She watched him while he worked on his food. Her voice was lower now. "You've already gotten me pregnant," she said, walking back into the kitchen. The kids ran past her to the dinner table.

Nicola turned his head. "Come again". His eyes bucked.

Ivy pushed the smaller boys up to the table and looked over at him. "I was looking for the right time to tell you."

Her smile told him that she was happy with herself.

Nicola couldn't blink. He stared at her in disbelief. PREGNANT.

Walking over to the cabinet in the corner where their medicines were housed, she pulled out a small gift box and brought it over to him. "You weren't the only one keeping a secret. I wanted to wait until our anniversary to tell you but with everything going on, I felt it best just to put it out there."

Nicola opened the box to find an EPT test. His long fingers grasped the white handle of the test as he stared. It was positive. He swallowed hard and looked down at his wife. "How long…how far along are you?" He was truly lost for words.

"Seven weeks," she said with a small smile. Leaning into him, she smirked. "This is the part where you jump for joy or *commit suicide*."

"Commit suicide? Why?" Nicola reached down and picked her up in her arms. Swinging her around, he screamed out. "That's why you've been so crazy! You're knocked up again! Damn, I hope it's a girl."

Ivy laughed and then caught herself. "Wait. What do you mean *I've been acting crazy*?"

Nicola set her down and kissed her forehead. "I mean rabid ass, strait-jacket crazy." He kissed her again.

"I want a girl, too," she said quickly. "And this is our last one. I want my tubes tied." She pointed at him like this was all his fault.

"Why?" Nicola asked sarcastically.

"Because my vagina can't take one more of your Agosto seeds," she laughed. "And I think we have enough now. We won't be able to fit them all at the table soon."

Nicola looked over at his sons. "A table full of Agosto's," he joked. "Damn, baby. I'm so happy. I mean..." he was lost for words. "This is amazing. You know, we said we wanted a big family when we got married and now look. We're at number five in six years."

"It's cult like," Ivy said under her breath.

"Who knows already? I know that you told someone. You can't hold water. Man...we have to celebrate," he said, rubbing through her hair affectionately.

"I figured that you should be the first to know," she said, walking over to the children. "I haven't told anyone yet."

"Not even Trina?" Nicola asked of her best friend and sister-in-law.

"No one," Ivy said, shaking her head. "Not a soul. And I talked to Trina just today. She called and we spent about an hour on the phone talking about the kids, Emerald and Brooks."

He really wished that his dead friend was here to celebrate with them, but he quickly pushed the painful thought out of his head. "I'm breaking out a bottle of the good shit, and after dinner I'm going to give you a *big girl* massage with that thing I bought you for your anniversary and then we're going to...."

"Daddy, you cursed," Adam said with a frown.

Nicola winked at his son. "What did I say?" he asked sarcastically.

"You said *shit*," Michael answered as clear as a bell while he dug in his nose.

"Michael Agosto!" Ivy admonished, narrowing her eyes on her son. "You do not use that language in this house. I don't care what your father says."

"Aww, let the boy say *shit*. It should be his favorite word from the look of his underwear. He uses his boxers like tissue paper," Nicola said, going back to the stove to fix their plates.

"You are not helping," Ivy said, trying to repress a laugh.

Just then the doorbell rang. The echo of it clanged through the house like the sound of broken glass.

Ivy turned around and looked towards the doorway.

"I'll get it," Nicola said, putting down the plate.

"Who could that be at this hour?" she asked, looking at her watch. It was nearly nine.

"Don't know. That's why I'll get it," Nicola said, walking out of the kitchen.

As Nicola peered out of the front door peep, he cursed. "Fuck," he said, opening the door.

Johnson smiled. "Hello to you, too, beautiful. Can I come inside?" He leaned against the door opening.

Nicola stepped back and opened the door wider. "Sure." Closing the door behind them, he pulled his department cell phone from his pants pocket and frowned. "I didn't get a call. Is there another body?" His chest constricted.

"You could say that," Johnson said, looking around the large house. "Damn, is your wife rich or something?"

"No, we both work for a living," Nicola said, trying to get his attention. "So why are you here and how did you find me?"

"I got your info from Cory at the office," Johnson said, shaking his head. He looked back at Nicola. "Somebody somewhere has to be rich in order for you to afford this, man. We don't get paid nearly enough to…"

"Johnson, please just fucking concentrate," Nicola said, snapping his fingers. "Why are you here, man? Is this a social visit? You having problems?"

"Homicide just found Twist's body inside of a car, blown to shit downtown. I wanted to get down there to check it out before it was completely processed."

"Twist is dead," Nicola repeated, rolling his eyes. He let out a sigh. "Fuck!" Wiping his face, he grabbed his boots from the corner and sat down on the bench to put them on. "This is not coming at a good time. I'm supposed to be cooking dinner for my babies; my wife…"

Ivy came around the corner, looking curiously at the man who stood in her doorway. She wiped her fingers on the kitchen towel clutched in her hand and spied Nicola putting on his shoes.

"Baby, what's going on?" she asked. "Where are you going?" Her frown was unmistakable.

Nicola stood up and walked over to her. "Baby, I'm sorry. I gotta go."

"You just got home," she growled. "And what about the news I just gave you?"

He held her slender shoulders in his hands. "I know. It's fucked up. I know, but I promise not to be too long.

I've gotta go. I think I just lost my only lead in this case."

Ivy rolled her eyes.

Johnson looked over at them with shock and awe in his eyes. Agosto had a black wife...a fine black wife. Who would have ever thought it? He always pegged him as being married to a small, blonde woman - a Becky, an Amy, a Cathy but not a sister.

Ivy looked over at Johnson for an explanation of who he was and why he was in her house.

"Detective Johnson, ma'am," he said, sticking out his hand. "Nice to meet you."

"Ivy Agosto, Nicola's wife," Ivy said, seeing the surprise in his eyes. She was used to it after six years of marriage to a white man in the city where Dr. King was assassinated. Some things just never went over well.

"Sorry, baby," Nicola said, motioning to Johnson. "This is my new partner." He had to stop himself from rolling his eyes.

"Nice to meet you," Ivy said, trailing her intense gaze back to Nicola. "Don't be all night, Nicky. You and I have unfinished business." Her voice was flat now, knowing that she could demand all she wanted, but more than likely it wouldn't happen.

"I won't." Nicola kissed her on her forehead. "I promise." He blinked as he said it. How could he tell her anything but that even though he knew it might not be true? He would try his best. That was the truth.

"Nice to meet you, Mrs..." Johnson paused.

"You're his war partner. You can just call me Ivy," she said with a half-smile. "Watch his back out there okay?"

"Yes, ma'am," Johnson said, saluting her.

7

Nicola followed Johnson's unmarked squad car in his truck with the lights flashing as they barreled through the city streets to downtown Memphis off of Madison Avenue directly across from the Madison Hotel, where a parking garage had been quartered off by the police.

Onlookers from the hotel, the law school directly across the main thoroughfare and the gym gathered around speculating and pointing, while anxious news crews tried to get a glimpse of the action for a live shot.

Pulling up out front of the crime scene, Johnson and Nicola quickly jumped out, waved their badges and went under the tape.

"What time did they find him?" Nicola asked as they walked past detectives standing around talking.

"I got the call fifteen minutes before I came to your place. So, not too long before that," Johnson answered, nodding towards a detective he knew. "Where's the body?" he asked the guy.

"Second floor," the detective said, pointing up. "Can't miss it."

On the second floor of the garage in the nearly vacant lot, flashing lights from crime scene cameras danced around the concrete structure as a woman in a black top and jeans took more pictures.

Nicola and Johnson walked up to the Range Rover, covered with bullet holes and broken glass and stopped.

"Why do these motherfuckers always drive Land Rovers?" Johnson asked quizzically.

"They are normally good urban warfare vehicles. They can maneuver in just about any terrain," Nicola answered.

"So can a Hummer," Johnson said, taking his eyes off the dead man to look at the woman as she bent over to take photos of the blood dripping from the interior of the truck to the ground.

"Well, he got fucked off regardless, didn't he?" Nicola said, rolling his eyes.

"You think," Johnson said, tilting his head and looking inside of the window at the dead body. "Looks like buck shot," he said, looking at Nicola.

"12-gauge pump more than likely," Nicola said, putting his hand on his hip. He exhaled a sigh. "Cane's favorite. The bastard was right under our nose."

"So you believe he killed him over our case?"

"I don't believe in coincidences," Nicola said with a frown."

"Hey, don't fuck with my crime scene, gentlemen," Detective Aubrey Graham said, walking up to the men. Graham was a mid-forties, black heavy-set woman with dark skin, black glasses, a thing against wearing make-up and a mean streak. Barely five feet tall, she had a reputation for being a hard ass on the streets but everyone loved her on the force. She nodded at Johnson and then stuck her hand out to shake Agosto's hand. "So, do you think that this guy had something to do with the Baby Boy murders? Cuz I was told you guys weren't working shit else until you solved it."

"He may have had some useful information that could have helped us," Agosto said, careful not to give too much away. "Why'd you call Johnson on this?"

Johnson looked over at Nicola and scratched the back of his neck. *Where was the trust?*

Detective Graham smiled at Johnson. "He asked me to give him a call on any murders until he cracked the case." She turned looking at Twist. "So you think he had something to do with it?" She asked again, just in case Nicola didn't hear her the first time.

"No," Nicola answered finally. "I just think that he could have helped."

"Any possible idea of who might have killed him?" she asked, yawning. "I scratch your back. You scratch mine."

Nicola rested his hands on the back of his head and yawned also. "Cane. His partner. He's got a rap sheet a mile long. You might want to start by dusting the truck for his prints. I'm sure you'll find them, and I'm sure that he'll say that they lived together and shared the damned thing."

"When you say partner?" she looked over at Nicola suggestively.

"I mean *business* partner," Nicola said, shaking his head.

"Hey, it's a new world. You have to be very specific these days," she said with a chuckle.

Nicola stepped closer to the scene. "Did you find anything in his truck? Any data devices or anything?" He looked back at her.

"Not yet, but I'll let you know once we haul it in to check it out," Graham said, seeing that one of her detectives needed her elsewhere. "I'll get back with you boys later."

Nicola moved closer to the truck and looked inside without contaminating the scene.

Twist's eyes were still open. His dead gaze was set on the wall across from him. Evidently, someone had stepped in front of the car and gotten his attention. But the shot that had ended his life, came from the driver side window. Blood splatter indicated it and the large hole on the side of his head and body. His right hand was still clenching the gun but the poor bastard never got a shot off.

While Nicola was looking inside, Johnson gave Graham the skinny on The Fly Boys and their operations before they gracefully bowed out.

"You want to go down to the coroner's office with the body?" Johnson asked.

"Nah," Nicola said, looking at his watch. *Damn it was getting late.* "Just tell Amy to call me if she finds anything that might be useful."

"Will do," Johnson said, fishing his keys out of his pocket. "So…you wanna tell me how you got to be rich?"

"I'm not rich," Nicola said in a matter-of-fact tone.

"Well, how'd you get the house?" Johnson probed.

Nicola spun around aggravated at Johnson and the hour.

Johnson put up his hands defensively. "Hey, I'm a detective. You can't expect me not to be naturally curious. If you're on the take, then just…"

Nicola wouldn't even let him finish that statement. "My family has money. I have money. My wife makes a good life for herself, over six digits. We're blessed.

Now end of discussion about my finances. I haven't been on the take, and I'm not ever going to be on the fucking take. I'd rather die first." He raised his brow. "Anything else, detective. You wanna know if I'm a boxers or brief kind of guy?"

"Yeah as a matter of fact, I do have one more question. Does your wife have a sister…with money?" Johnson asked with a smile.

"Get the fuck out of here," Nicola said, shaking his head. "No, she doesn't, but she does have a very beautiful brother if you're in to that sort of thing."

Johnson laughed. "Yeah, well, I'm sure that you've heard this a thousand times before, but you have a beautiful house, a beautiful wife and a seemingly beautiful life. That's hard to come by this day and age. I know dudes on the force who have been married like four times by forty."

"I'm not fucking forty," Nicola protested.

"You're missing the point."

"Look, don't think I don't know that I've got it made at home. Okay, I had to basically jump through a fire-blazing hoop with gasoline on my balls to get my wife," Nicola said, pointing at Johnson as he made his point. "That's why I try my best to protect my family. I've got two sets of twin boys who think the world of me. I'm there fucking Superman. That's why my home life has to be completely separate from my work. I don't like to mix 'em. So, showing up at the house is a no-no unless it's a social call. Call me on my cell. Let me come to you. I don't like to get the wife worried, and trust me. She is a worry wart. She'll be texting me all damn day."

"I'll remember that in the future," Johnson huffed. He quickly shifted gears again. "Well, I never thought you'd be married to a black woman," Johnson said out of the blue. "That shit blew my mind. When she came walking around the corner in your house, I was like…damn! You just don't seem like the type."

"And what's *the type*?" Agosto asked defensively. He had been told the same thing a hundred times and it always rubbed him the wrong way.

Johnson shrugged again, turning up his lips as he did. "I don't know…open minded."

Agosto laughed. "Yeah, well since you're into getting personal, just what the fuck are you?"

Johnson wiped his mouth off and looked up in the air. "What do I look like?"

"You look like fucking…Vin Diesel," Agosto joked. "A broke-ass, wanna be, cock strong Vin Diesel stunt double."

"Fuck you. I'm not broke. But you hit the nail on the head. Italian and Black all the way baby. Which means my dick is twice as long as yours. And considering the pedigree, don't be surprised if your kids don't end up looking like me when they grow up, a bunch of Vin Diesel look-a-likes. "

"*Shiiittt.* My kids will never be that ugly," Agosto said. He let out a sigh. Without intention his mind had drifted back to Ivy and her news. He was going to be a father…*again*. The idea excited him and overwhelmed him, but the timing was way off. Plus, he knew that she was at home stewing over him having to leave again and disrupt their night. He wasn't sure how he was going to make things up to her, but he knew that he was going to somehow.

"I know how this sounds before I even say it, so I'm just going to go on and put the disclaimer out there that this case means as much to me as it does to you," Nicola said, turning towards Johnson.

"I think it means more to you based up on that scene at the Naples house."

"Ivy's pregnant. She just broke the news to me tonight and we didn't even have a full conversation before you rang the doorbell. I really need to get back to her before long. You know how women are. Me leaving can't be the lasting memory in her head about my final kid."

"Final?"

"So she says."

"Hell, with four already, I don't blame her. But yeah, okay. Let's get a move on. Congrats by the way. You're a daddy again. I'll have to buy you a drink sometime. You still can get out, right? You're not on one of those off-hour lockdowns where you can't leave the house unless it's work related."

Nicola shook his head. "No. Ivy's normally really cool about anything I want to do. It's just the situation. A drink sounds cool."

Johnson nodded. "So where are we going? Back to Twist's place?"

"For what? You really think Cane's gonna tell us anything now? Fuck that. I doubt they'll have surveillance tapes of the murder. They would have been smart not to leave any evidence over here. This was set-up, planned. Plus, all we have is a theory about the buckshot. We can't just show up there at his place now. The best thing we can do is track his phone, see if we can get a number and try to find out if anyone will come forward."

"You don't really think that the Molly dealer is going to come forward now, do you? That would be suicide and for what? He doesn't get anything out of it. His boss is dead, just in case you haven't noticed," Johnson said pointing back at Twist. "Best thing is to kick this dude's door in and drag him downtown."

"Without a warrant?" Nicola laughed. "I've dealt with Cane, okay. He called his lawyer before he capped this dude. Not a judge in the city will give us a warrant based upon the evidence we have and not a lawyer in the city wouldn't take the case if we fucked this up."

"Well, we are running out of options. We have to do something. Okay. My idea is obviously out. So what now?" Johnson asked, scratching the five o'clock shadow staring to form on his face. "We've got no video here, but there must be surveillance somewhere in the area that we can use to narrow down who was in this place during the time of the murder."

"Let's go across to the Madison Hotel. I know the manager there. He's cool people. Maybe he'll let us view the camera footage from that vantage point and get an idea of who came in and out of here right before and right after the murder without a fucking subpoena."

"Good idea," Johnson said, winking at Nicola. "You might just be useful yet."

***

Nicola and Johnson only had a small window to snoop unofficially. It wouldn't be long before Graham and her homicide detectives actually assigned to the case made their way across the street for the same reason. In preparation, Nicola had asked the manager to keep their inquiry confidential. The manager had agreed reluctantly, but owed Nicola a favor from a few years back.

Quickly, they ran through the tape and found that four cars had come through in the last hour. Twist's Rover was the second car in, followed by two additional vehicles.

"The Mercedes Benz that came in before Twist had a man and woman inside. They came across the street to the hotel," Johnson said, logging the information down in his notebook.

"Yeah, they're not who we're here for," Nicola said, sucking at his teeth. "The two cars that came in after Twist... they both had tinted windows. A Dodge Ram and a Ford Mustang. Ten minutes apart. Can we zoom in on a tag?"

The security manager zoomed in on the back of the car. "We lose a little clarity on the Ram, but it's a Tennessee tag."

Johnson wrote down the number. "I'll have it called in."

"And the Mustang?" Nicola asked, leaning closer to the monitor.

The manager ran the tape forward and then stopped as the Mustang pulled into the garage. "It's an Arkansas tag."

Johnson wrote down that tag number as well.

"Now fast forward to when they are coming out," Nicola said, anxiously. He prayed that he had a good shot of Cane's face.

He had no such luck.

Both cars barreled out quickly into the streets, a clear picture unattainable because of the light missing in the front of the building and dark tint. But they could tell that the Dodge Ram had two occupants, both white males. One was heavy set, the other smaller framed. The mustang was being driven by a black woman. From what they could tell, she was alone.

"We need to find out who these people are, where they are and what they were doing there," Nicola said more to himself than Johnson.

"On it. I'll get it run tonight. Now let's get out of here before Graham shows up. She's going to have our asses if she catches us in here," Johnson said, standing up.

Nicola stood up also, taking one last look at the screen. "Thanks so much, Richwell," he said, shaking the older white man's hand.

"No problem. Any time," Richwell said, reaching over to shake Johnson's hand as well. "You gentlemen have a safe night."

***

By the time that Nicola got home, everyone in his house was asleep. Inching through the hallways in the dark, he checked the doors and windows downstairs, then rearmed the alarm. Walking slowly up the staircase, he held on to the alabaster banister praying for enough strength to get out of his clothes and into the shower without passing out.

At the top of the stairs, he went down the left wing of the house to check on his sons. The first bedroom down the hall belonged to his elder boys. He opened the door to find them in their twin beds asleep. The room was a complete mess. Toy soldiers were strategically placed around the room for battle tomorrow. The television had been turned on after Ivy had put them to sleep and turned down low to be undetected. Clothes were thrown in the corner and a huge ball of Play Dough sat top one of the boy's study tables drying up.

Nicola went in and kissed each boy on the head, turned off the television and carefully tiptoed out of the room, trying not to fall over anything.

When he got to his younger sons' room, the mess was basically the same. Ivy normally got on to them and made them clean up before bed, but he knew that tonight she was exhausted. He nuzzled in to David's curly black hair and kissed his forehead, tasting spaghetti sauce on his lips. That was his boy...messy as hell. The funny thing is that he probably made it through a whole bath without removing that speck of sauce.

Michael in the twin bed beside his brother and was hugged up tight to his brown teddy bear, sleeping without a care in the world. Nicola bent to kiss his forehead, then turned off the lamp beside him. Before he walked out of the room, he looked back at his boys and felt a deep since of pride. Nothing mattered more than them. These children and the woman in the next room was his reason for living. That's why he felt so strongly for the parents of all the victims. He knew that he could not stand in their shoes. He could not have been as strong as many of them had been.

Courage had many faces. The women and men of the children were all courageous, but they needed someone on their side, someone who wouldn't tire out, give up or punk out. And he had been tapped by the powers that be to be that man.

Coming out of the room, he looked down the hallway at his office at the end of the hall and debated whether or not he should go in and check a few emails and do some work, but his body reminded him that in order to do anything for anyone else, he'd first have to take care of him. So he opted to head down to the right wing, where his wife was surely asleep and probably would not feel him when he finally slipped into bed.

The door to the bedroom was open, which was nothing new for Ivy. When Nicola wasn't home, she always kept the door open to hear the children. She was nearly as paranoid as he was but not about burglars and other criminals, but about fire, falls and mishaps.

He walked slowly to his side of the bed and noticed that she had pulled back the covers for him and set his pajamas on top of his pillow. Again, even when she didn't have to - shouldn't really- she made life easy on him in ways that only she could.

You're too good for me, he thought to himself as he watched her sleep. Her hand was up near her face and the other was cupped under the pillow. Her black inky mane splashed across the white pillowcase, so inviting that he wanted to rub through it now, even in his exhaustion.

She slept quietly in the dark with only the glow of the moon shining through the blinds to light up the room. Her brilliant brown skin, blemish free, make up free and absolutely beautiful. To him, she was his symbol of peace. He stood there for a moment, drinking her in before he picked up his pajamas and went into the bathroom to change.

Closing the door, before he turned on the light, he slowly released the knob and set his clothes on the chair by the wall. As he was about to pull off his shirt, his cell phone rang, booming through the silence like a thunder bolt.

"Shit," he said, fumbling for his phone. "Hello."

"It's Amy down at the morgue," a woman said in a nasally tone. "Strangest thing. We found a jump drive inside of your vic."

Nicola leaned against the sink and looked at himself in the mirror. "A red jump drive?" he asked with a huff.

"That's right," she said, sounding a little surprised.

"Fuck," Nicola spat. He was dead dog tired and wanted nothing more than to go to sleep. Looking at his watch, he wiped the stubble forming on his face. "Can you hang on to it until tomorrow?"

"Sure thing," she said, preoccupied with her work.

"Thanks, Amy."

"No problem."

With that, he hung up the phone. He knew that in the back of his mind, he would be preoccupied with the jump drive all night, but he desperately needed to rest.

Dialing Johnson, he waited.

"Yeah," Johnson said, answering on the first ring.

Nicola spoke up louder even though he didn't want to wake up Ivy because of the background noise from Johnson's phone. Evidently, he was out partying. "Twist had my jump drive in his stomach," Nicola said, hoping Johnson might go down and get it right then.

"He swallowed it?" Johnson asked.

"Yeah," Nicola said yawning.

"What do you think is on it?"

"Evidently more than I gave him," Nicola said, wondering if he didn't need to go on and go himself. It was only a twenty-minute drive.

"Well, good. Maybe all isn't lost," Johnson said, moving to a quieter place. "So we should go down and pick it up tomorrow morning, after the news conference."

"Shit, I already forgot about that. Thanks for reminding me. Yeah, we need to do that."

Johnson paused to watch a woman walk past him. "I'll hook up with you after Amway's thing."

"Alright. I'm going to hit the sack."

"I'm going to get a lap dance," Johnson said in a matter-of-fact tone.

Nicola shook his head. "See you in the morning, man."

8

The smell of early morning eggs scrambled with real butter and then covered in three cheeses left a lingering fragrance of a well-balanced breakfast sorely missed in the air as Nicola finally rolled over in bed and realized that he was alone. His hand raked over the goose down comforter before he pushed his head up and looked over at the nightstand. 8:45 a.m.

Dammit. He had overslept again.

Grabbing the remote, he flicked his wrist at the television embedded in the wall and turned to CNN. Don Lemon was reporting on the situation in Afghanistan, while outside of Nicola's large Victorian windows opened to let sunlight through the white plantation blinds, the drizzling rain subsided and blue skies peeked past patches of dark rain clouds.

He turned his attention back to the television.

"On another note, Memphis, Tennessee is still in the headlines as they race to find the serial murderer and rapists of elementary children in the area. They are calling these the Baby Boy murders. So far there have been four young male victims ranging in age from six to nine, including two twin boys from Idlewind Elementary school only a couple of blocks from the West Precinct of the Memphis Police Department. The outcry from community has reached fever pitch. A joint news conference with the mayor of Memphis and the director of the Memphis police department is scheduled for later today. Dave Hammond is in Memphis with more. Dave," Lemon said as the video cut to a backdrop of the police station downtown in Memphis where a man stood with a microphone.

Nicola grunted and changed the channel.

Great. That was all he needed - more press meant more pressure.

Of course, the media was portraying the department as less than competent in finding the person or persons responsible for the baby boy killings, when in fact every resource available was being used to put an end to this continuing massacre. Unfortunately, the department's public relations department was not nearly as aggressive about controlling the message as the national media was.

Pictures of the dead and missing children had gone viral on several underground blogs and Twitter; radio shows across the nation were discussing the case and interviewing the parents and every family in the city was scared to death to let their children out of their sight.

Ivy was right. This was going to be a media circus. He had participated in news conferences before, but none had been this high profile.

Evidently, he'd need to wear a suit today.

***

Ivy turned off her television, picked up her folders off her well-organized desk and headed to the conference room to meet with her 9:00. Assistant in-tow, she made her way down the elaborate halls of the upscale marketing firm she had worked for since graduation through the glass doors of the conference room of the hall and greeted her boss.

"How are you today, Ivy," Mr. Letiwich said, raising his head from the executive summary that Ivy had submitted.

"Doing great, sir. How are you this morning?" she asked, pointing at her assistant to set out the portfolio folders with the integrated strategy that she had been working on for the last three weeks.

"Just doing some damn-good reading. This is thorough. The client will be happy. Sorry that I couldn't read it before and give you feed back. I just got back in town from D.C. early this morning. Plus, I knew that I could count on you."

"I'm happy to lighten the load, sir," Ivy said, pleased that he was pleased.

"How's the family? How's the husband?" he asked, taking off his reading glasses and setting the brief in front of him. His well-manicured hands brushed over the leather cover.

"We're great, but Nicola was just assigned to the Baby Boy murders," she said so with a certain amount of pride in her husband and frustration that such a case even existed.

"Wow, high profile," Mr. Letewich said, wheels spinning. "Sounds like Amway needs a PR firm to help back him on this one."

"You have his ear," Ivy said, sitting down. "You should give him a call."

"Wouldn't be a conflict of interest in anyway, and this firm thrives off crisis communications," he said, talking himself into the call.

"Yes, sir," Ivy answered, unsure of what else to say.

"I'll give him a call this afternoon. Tell Nicola congrats for me, will you. That's a big case. If he solves it, which I'm sure he will, there will be a significant promotion involved, I imagine."

"Hopefully something that puts him behind a desk," Ivy said half-hearted.

"Well, either way. You and Nicola and me and Barbara need to get together for dinner soon. It's been a while," he said with finality.

"Absolutely. I'll have Marsha check your schedule," she said, cueing her assistant to make a special note to do that today.

Ivy's assistant placed a cut of hot green tea in a simple white mug in front of her and stepped away. The steam billowed out and wafted up to her nose.

"Thank you, Lisa," Ivy said softly.

Letewich continued. "Now, on to the other piece of business, the Blue Top Brewery is scheduled for 9:00. What do you have in store for them besides this amazing executive summary?"

"A fully integrated strategic plan ready to implement after they select us from the RFP pool and some superb mock-ups. Also, I had Warren develop a possible App for them," she said, ready to pitch.

"We've got a few minutes. Run it back to me," he said, motioning at his assistant, who sat in the corner quietly, to close the door.

***

Nicola hated news conferences. Everyone had to stand around each other listening as the speakers read their notes from the podium and the news cameras watched them like a hawk with their nosy lenses. After which, they were bombarded with a hundred questions and then the media took all the coverage back to the studio and twisted it all up.

As he stood quietly in the holding room with Johnson before the infamous news conference with the mayor and director, he listened to the communications director go over the order that they were to speak in, the questions that they could and could not answer and the time limits. Honestly, he could not see how Ivy did this every day. It was annoying. Too much talk, too little action.

In fact, he felt like they were wasting time by the minute. The time that they were spending talking to the cameras, he should have been tracking down leads, starting with the jump drive the coroner pulled out of Twist's stomach.

May Upton, the communications lead, fully dressed in her official blue police uniform looked over at Nicola and waved him over from the corner where he stood by the refreshments. He stepped across the room quietly, past the mayor and his people, Director Amway and his people and half a dozen other suits and took the paper that she handed him.

"Okay, Agosto. We have a simple statement for you to read. Here it is," she said, waiting for him to look at the paper.

"I have to talk out there?" Nicola asked, immediately wanting to leave.

"Yes, you're the lead detective on this case. The public will want to hear from you," she said in a stern tone as if saying *don't even think about trying to get out of this.*

Nicola pursed his lips together.

"What? You nervous?" she asked with a smirk.

"I don't like speaking in front of cameras," Nicola protested.

"Tough, you're doing it. The mayor and the director's office want you to speak. You're speaking. It's real simple. You just say what's on that paper, no more, no less." She watched his pensive stare as he snatched the paper open and read it. She couldn't help but admire his statuesque, carefree swag. He wore his black suit with poised grace. The fabric fell over his rippled muscles, cut to show the perfection of his tanned, perfect body.

"This is it?" he asked, trying to make sure that he wasn't expected to say anymore. He looked up at her and saw her eyes snap from his wide shoulders to his eyes.

May blinked hard. "That's it. Any questions will be answered by Director Amway or the mayor," she said, patting him on the back. She had to get away from the man with his faint but sexy cologne and his black locks. It was a sin for a cop to look that good and be married.

Johnson walked over, eavesdropping the entire time. He had forgone the suit and wore dark jeans and a black t-shirt with his badge hanging on his chest.

"Nothing for me to say?" he asked May before she could get away.

May huffed, suddenly put in a very sour mood. "Not dressed like that. This isn't a rap video. Just stand where I tell you and keep your mouth closed, Johnson." She rolled her eyes at him. "You'll do fine, Agosto, just read those lines" May said, walking off.

Johnson scratched his neck and turned to watch her walk away. "She's just mad that I never called her back.

Women, boy. I tell ya. They do know how to hold a grudge."

"You slept with May," Nicola said, shaking his head. The guy was incorrigible.

"Once or twice. She's got a beautiful little body under all those clothes," Johnson said, raising his brow.

"I don't want to know," Nicola said quickly. "So, when we leave here, we go straight to the coroner."

"Yeah, yeah. Sure thing," Johnson said, checking his phone. "Are you going to ditch the suit, because you're cramping my style with the GQ Versace look? I run into some chicks, they're going to think this is CSI: Miami."

"Yeah, I'll ditch the damned suit. I've got my clothes in the truck. Hey, who are you always texting," Nicola asked, sucking his teeth. "You're not married."

Johnson looked up from his phone. "A woman," he said flatly.

"A *real* girlfriend?" Nicola asked cleverly.

Johnson clammed up. A little tent of red color formed on his cheeks. "Just a friend," he said, putting his phone away.

"That's what I said. Six years later, she's still *a friend*," Nicola said with a smirk.

"Man, I'm never getting married," Johnson said, ready to end the conversation. "That shit is for the birds. Checking in, giving away half your check, fucked up schedules…"

"Cool your heels there, chief. I haven't proposed yet," Nicola said, walking over to Amway.

The entourage of assistants and directors split down the middle as Nicola made his way to see his boss. Engulfed in his script, Amway looked up from his notes and waved him over. The crowd disbursed, giving them a small gap of privacy. "How are you?" he asked, pulling off his glasses. He looked Agosto up and down. "You clean up well. I'm glad. Johnson didn't get a clue and put on a fucking suit."

They both looked over at Johnson who had made his way back to the refreshment table and was stuffing his pants with granola bars and shook their heads.

"Thanks for the compliment," Nicola said, shocked that a three-year old suit was garnering so much attention. "Just wanted to let you know that we've got a good lead," Nicola said, shrugging. "He's just dead."

Amway's eager face quickly turned into a severe frown. "You've got to be shitting me."

"Well, the good news is that he may have left some evidence in his stomach," Nicola said quietly.

Amway stepped closer to Nicola and lowered his voice. "I don't want to know until you can confirm that it's evidence. If you get a viable, hard, concrete lead, call me day or night. My cell is still the same. I want to shut some of these city councilmembers, especially Ferris, and these nosy, raggedy-ass reporters up once and for all. I've got a town hall meeting tonight with more families who want to know 'what the fuck' and I'm quoting them verbatim. Plus, the mayor is ready to crucify me and this entire department. We've got to turn up something now. And I'm counting on you to do it before the FBI steps in and makes us all look like a bunch of backwater hicks...and I hate backwater hicks."

Nicola nodded, swallowing down the mounting pressure that Amway had just thrown on him. "Of course, man. We're in this together."

"Excuse me gentlemen. Let's get you out to the staging area. We're ready to begin the news conference. Please either turn your cell phones off or on silent," May said, ushering people out of the room.

"Alright, see you out there," Amway said to Nicola before he was escorted out.

Nicola walked back over to Johnson and picked up a bottle of water sitting on the table in front of him. He wished at that moment that it was a jack and coke.

"Not everyone can just *talk* to the director," Johnson said, curious again. "What's up with that? Are you all boys?"

"We've known each other forever," Nicola said, taking a sip of the water.

"So, your ass isn't riding on this case then."

"He's still my boss. The mayor is still his boss and the city council still has us by the short and curlies. My ass is right beside yours," Nicola said, pulling out the paper one last time.

"Yeah, but it's different, right?" Johnson said, with a shrug. "You're in good with the big man. That's gotta count for something in the grand scheme of things."

Nicola rolled his eyes at Johnson. "It doesn't mean shit in our position."

***

In the middle of Ivy's meeting, the owner of the Brewery, Mike Hayes, brought up the subject of the Baby Boy murders and how worried it had both he and his wife for their children. She sat at the end of the table flabbergasted. Everyone was talking about this case - in kitchens, classrooms, boardrooms and locker rooms. Her husband's case was the talk of the city.

She could feel the tightness in her gut when her boss looked down at her and nodded.

"Our Ivy's husband is the lead detective on the case," he said proudly. "He's an excellent detective. You might remember him from a few years back. He was best friends with K.C. Brooks before he passed. The guy was a legend. If anyone can solve this case, he can."

Mike looked over at Ivy impressed by her affiliation. She hadn't used that as a selling point yesterday when they had lunch. Most publicists would have.

Ivy smiled and rearranged the papers in front of her like she was suffering from OCD. All eyes were locked right then on her, especially Mike Hayes.

Hayes was a middle aged, caramel-skinned black man who had worked his way from selling beer for a national brewery to forming his own brewery in less than ten years. Ivy was responsible for vetting him and finally getting him to sign the contract that sat in front of him and his lawyers now. He was a bit militant and completely against going with a white/Jewish firm, but Ivy had sealed the deal. He liked her as soon as he met her. She had ambition and passion - two things he would need to make his campaign work.

Mr. Letewich quietly urged Ivy to jump in on the discussion. She picked up on his cue quickly and sat up in her chair.

"Yes, Nicola has been working day and night on this case," she said with a smile, even though she wanted to scream at that very moment. "I doubt that there is anyone more dedicated to solving this than my husband."

"There is a news conference going on right now," Mike said, looking over at the large flat screen mounted on the wall. "Do you mind, Carl?"

"Not at all. We've got time," Mr. Letewich said, turning in his chair to face the television.

The young assistant was quick. Before the salt and pepper gray man could even ask for the remote, he had it in the palm of his hand.

He turned on the television and switched to a local channel broadcasting the news conference live.

Nicola was in the shot, looking tall and dashing. As soon as Ivy saw him, a smile crept across her face. She turned from her paperwork and watched the story unfold.

"That's her husband there," Letewich said to Mike, pointing at the television.

"On the left of Director Amway?" Mike asked, scooting closer to the table.

"No, the man standing directly behind him in the black suit. The…white guy," Letewich blurted out.

Mike swallowed hard as he kept his eyes planted on the screen, but Ivy could see his disapproval.

The white guy.

She looked down at the paper and took a deep breath. She had been through that before too. Black men who didn't want to see a successful sister with a white man. She wanted to stand up right then and give a dissertation on why she was fed up with the "sell-out" response from men of color. Instead, she swallowed down her pride. After all, she had worked too hard to get there. Forget his personal views of her family. Judge her or not, she just had the man sign a $500,000 public relations deal over the next year.

"Interesting," Mike finally said, twirling the pen in his right hand like a baton.

Just then on the television, Nicola stepped up after Director Amway and spoke into the microphones on the podium with cameras flashing and nearly blinding him.

Ivy could see her husband's nervousness. He hated being the center of attention, no matter the venue. She stared intently at the television, waiting on his every word and critiquing his every gesture. She was after all in marketing and public relations. And from his first word, she knew that he needed a ton of media training. Still, she had to admit, he looked amazing in his suit. He stood out like a sore thumb, striking and foreboding.

***

Nicola felt his stomach wrench with nervousness. There were not only reporters and cameras. There were dozens of families, some of them the parents of the victims, with signs demanding justice. They held up pictures of the children and stared at him like his words somehow would help ease their pain or give them comfort. Sadly, he knew that his words would not. In fact, his words might only insight more anger. Promises meant nothing to the grieving. Action was the key. And there could be no action on his part if he was here right now talking into a damned microphone.

"You're on," May said, motioning at the podium. He stepped up to it and placed his paper among the litter of station microphones around the podium. Sure that every station in Memphis and a few nationwide would pick up even his slightest breath only made him more nervous.

"My name is Lt...," he paused. "Excuse me, my name is Sargent Nicola Agosto, and I've been assigned to the Baby Boys Case. I can assure you..." Nicola nervously cleared his throat and started again, this time with a stronger more authoritative voice. "I can assure you that I am dedicated to this case and the families of the victims. We are working tirelessly, using all resources at our disposal to solve this case and racing against the clock to prevent more murders. We are still leaning on the public for any information that you might have. Please call (901) 528-Cash with any information that might help us solve these murders and bring justice to all four of these children." Raising his head from the paper, he looked out at the crowd.

"Hanna Tomley from the Commercial Appeal. One question, Sgt. Agosto," one of the female reporters from the most popular newspapers, *Commercial Reveal*, in the crowd said. She pointed her recorder towards him, eyes glazed over with a bit of intrigue by the handsome man and his extreme humility considering his high profile position in the biggest case to hit Memphis in decades. The readers would love his face. Her photographer moved in for several good shots of his easy-on-the-eyes face. "How close are you to solving this case? And what can you tell us about the type of person or persons that we should be looking for?"

Nicola looked over at Amway and waited for him to respond. After all, May said that he didn't have to do *questions*.

"We'll be taking questions at the end," May interjected from the side of the platform. "We'll be happy to address your concerns at the end."

Nicola nodded and stepped back, straightening his black tailored suit as he did, happy to pass the limelight on to someone who knew how to handle it.

The woman gave a frustrated sigh but kept her eyes locked on Nicola Agosto. The story was definitely the Baby Boys case, but he would be the star, if she could only get to him.

***

Ivy turned back from the television and looked at Mike with a sort of confident glare, like she was looking past him judging her, like his opinion suddenly didn't matter to her at all.

"My husband is devoted to this community in all aspects. Race is not an issue. He just wants what's best," she said as if reading the man's mind. "We have four of our own." *And one on the way*, she thought to herself as she rubbed her stomach covertly.

"Good to hear," he said, brushing off her validation of what he considered to be Memphis's attempt at another great white hope. "No offense, Letewich, but few white men in his position are culturally sensitive to our community, yet they continue to put them in our communities to police us - the exact opposite of the community policing concept. These guys bust in like gangbusters and highjack our kids, throw them in prison and then go home and have good ole' American pie with their snow white house wives."

Even Letewich was thrown by the statement. He found himself sitting with his mouth gaped wide open. Shutting it and readjusting in his chair, he focused. *Money talked.* "Well, enough of Memphis politics and current affairs. We're here to make this deal the best thing that your brewery has ever entered into," Ivy's boss said, determined to get back on track.

And what community do you live in? Ivy wanted to ask. She was certain that he didn't live in the projects and from her research on him, she'd found that he had grown up in a middle-class suburb. His grotesque dismissal of her presence made her want to stab him in the eye with her pen and piss on his contract, literally, but instead, she caught Letewich's silent plea to not ruin this deal.

Ivy again held her tongue, though this time, she wanted so badly to share her views on *community* and his own help in demonizing his own people through the sale of alcohol.

"Right, gentlemen," she said, clearing her throat and giving Letewich a stern look that let him know that she had reached her boiling point. "Let's talk strategy."

9

As soon as the new conference was over, both Nicola and Johnson bailed, making a b-line for the front doors of the police headquarters and out into the grueling summer sun.

Nicola could not wait to get the hell out of 201 Poplar, away from all those fake politicians and hungry reporters and get on with his day. In just the few short hours that he had spent grab-assing with the brass, he had missed two calls.

He walked with Johnson quietly down the sidewalk past dozens of people who stood waiting for their court time, talking to lawyers, begging for money or just being bonded out of jail by the bail bondsmen who had shops up and down Poplar Avenue.

"Where'd you park," Nicola asked, phone to his ear.

Johnson scratched his brow. "Damn, it's hot as hell out here. Got to be at least a hundred degrees." He pointed directly across the street in front of a lawyer's office. "I'm right there. You want me to ride with you?"

Nicola held up a hand, halting Johnson from talking or moving. "Wait."

The voice on the other end of the message was a black female from what he could tell. She sounded flustered, maybe even scared.

"Sgt. Agosto, my name is Roxie. I was Twist's…contact. I was supposed to meet him last night but then," she paused. "Well, you know what happened. It's a damn shame what they did to him." Swallowing hard, she smacked her lips. "Look, if you wanna meet, I'll be at the Peek strip club on Winchester at 4:30 today. Just go in and sit down. I'll be the girl who offers you the lap dance." She smirked. "Well, I'll be the right girl to offer you *a* lap dance. From the look of you, you might get offered a few, but you'll know me when you see me. Everybody does. Twist said that you could offer me some kind of protection, maybe get me out of town. I hope that's the case. If you don't show today, I'm getting in the wind. Things are getting too heavy here."

Nicola looked to see if there was a number but it was blocked.

"Dammit," he said, going to his next message.

"Baby, you did great," Ivy said. "Your posture was a little off, but we'll work on that. Anyway, call me when you get this. Love you. Bye."

Johnson stood waiting for Nicola to say something. Shrugging, he looked at him. "What? What is it?"

"That Molly dealer that Twist was going to connect me to just called. Missed it because of that fucking news conference." The mounting frustration was evident on Nicola's face. "I've gotta meet her at 4:30 at Peek."

"Well, let's get to the coroner," Johnson said, pulling out his keys. "Then, let's hit the strip club."

"Why don't you run over and get the jump drive for me. It doesn't take two of us, right? Meet me back at the office when you're done. I'm going to see if I can run down anything on her," Nicola said in a huff. "She says that she's going to blow town if I don't show."

"The dealer's a woman?" Johnson said surprised.

"Yeah," Nicola said, stuffing his phone back down in his pocket. "Fits now that I think about it. The female bodyguards. Female dealers. What can I say? Twist liked the ladies. Poor bastard." Nicola never mourned the death of a drug dealer, but everything else aside, he liked Twist. He wasn't an asshole like most of the dealers he ran into.

"What's her name?" Johnson asked. "The dealer?"

"Roxie. She didn't give a last name."

"My boy has been trying to get in on this case. Mark Flowers from narc…you know him?"

"Just by name. He's a little young on the force for my taste," Nicola said with a raised brow.

"Well, if you want me to give him a call, I can check if he knows any girls named Roxie in the business."

Nicola nodded. "Do it. I'm going to head on over to the office. I'll see you in a few."

Johnson quickly jetted across the two lanes of traffic and jumped into his car. Before he could even buckle his seatbelt, he was already on the phone.

Nicola headed to his truck, determined to make the meeting with Roxie at 4:30 and try to put together all of the missing pieces of his puzzle.

As soon as he pulled out into the streets, his cell rang. It was Johnson. "Yeah."

"You won't believe this," Johnson said, voice fairly excited.

"Believe what?" Nicola asked.

"I called Mark and coincidentally he was trying to get in touch with us. Narc just busted a crack house in South Memphis. Get this. One of the guys in there swears that he has *sensitive information* regarding the case."

Nicola paused. "Where is he?"

Johnson knew that Nicola would bite. "I had my boy hold him. But you have to be quick about picking him up. They're getting ready to roll out with the wagon soon."

"Where is he?"

"Your old stomping ground. 400 Walker Avenue. About two blocks south of the college."

"I'm on the way."

Nicola flipped a U-turn in the road and turned on his flashers. Siren erupted as he pushed past the traffic. This was his first possible concrete lead and it had his stomach all knotted up. A crack head with Intel? It was hard to believe, but he had seen some strange things in his time on the force.

Ten minutes later he was in front of an impoverished old, broken down two-story home that used to be something back in the day. He knew because Brooks had owned the property and used it as a half-way house for guys who were trying to get a new start on life after serving time. Now, however, since Brooks' death, the place had fallen prey to the elements and the environment.

His old unit, Narc, had an impressive line of habitual abusers lined up on the sidewalk, arms behind them, handcuffed and Mirandized. Everyone knew him when he pulled up. Both the perps and the cops looked his way. Evidently, it had not been that long since he had been out here cleaning up the streets, because the drug dealers who were standing by the cops started shaking their heads and curse, like definite trouble was coming their way.

"Agosto!" the lead guy on the Narc unit screamed out. "Come over here."

Nicola laughed and closed his door. "Another day at the office, huh?"

"Shit. You know how we do it," Sgt. Cruzan said, taking off his black Rayban shades. "I was told to hold a gift for you."

"I was told to be grateful," Nicola answered, shaking Cruzan's hand.

"The little shit is separated from the others. Started crying like a little bitch when I slap the cuffs on him."

Nicola looked around. "Where is he?"

"In the unmarked across the street. The motherfucker should be grateful. The rest of us are sweating our balls off out here. We put him in the car with the air running so he wouldn't pass out before you got here."

"You know him?" Nicola asked.

"Yeah. He's low level Gangster's Cross. He was getting high on meth when we raided the shit hole."

Nicola chuckled. "He's on that white-boy drug, huh?"

"Looks like it." Cruzan waved at the cop standing beside the unmarked down and screamed over. "Hey, let Agosto have the snitch." Cruzan looked back over at Nicola. "His name is DeMario Washington. He's got a sheet two miles long."

"I'll remember that," Nicola said, wiping sweat off his brow.

Cruzan cracked open a water bottle. "So, how did the news conference go today? Are you a superstar now?"

"Shit, I hope not. It's pretty hard to do my job when everybody knows my face."

"Maybe they are prepping you for a nice cushiony desk job. No more working the field," Cruzan said with a raised brow.

"Don't say that shit, man. I'd die on the desk," Nicola said with a frown. The thought had never crossed his mind before.

The officer leaning on the hood of the car across the street nodded at Cruzan and went to the back of the car to pull out Nicola's prize.

DeMario wasn't much to look at. Barely six feet tall and skinny, he had long black dreads, jean shorts sagging under his dirty white boxers and a half-torn, filthy wife beater on that showed his less than muscular physique.

Nicola walked over to the perp and grabbed his handcuffs. "Walk with me," he said, nodding thank you to the uniformed officer.

"Eh, man, you ain't gotta snatch me like I'm some kind of bitch," DeMario said, pulling away.

"One more yank from you, and it'll be resisting." Nicola turned him around and looked down into the young man's dilated eyes. "You want to resist me?" he asked with a growl in his voice, brow furrowed and chest stuck out, showing the broadness of his concrete chest.

Suddenly, the boisterous perp didn't like the conflict. He immediately changed his tune. "I don't want no trouble, man. Hey, I called for you." The stench of unwashed arm pits wafted up. "I'm trying to help you out," he said, revealing a tarnished, gold upper grill.

Nicola stepped back as his smell permeated the corner. "Help me out by not talking or raising your stank ass arms until we get to our destination then."

"Oh, I see you one of them funny cops," the man said, rolling his eyes.

"I'll be here all week," Nicola said, giving him a shove. "To my truck. Let's go." Raising his arm, he thanked Cruzan. "Appreciate it," he screamed across the street. His baritone voice boomed over the officers loading the wagon with offenders.

"Any time," Cruzan yelled back.

***

The rank smell of the perp handcuffed in the backseat was getting to Nicola, even though he had smelled a hundred dead bodies. Letting the windows down a quarter of the way to filter good air in, he also turned up the AC and drove quietly to his off-site interrogation center. Every once in a while, he would check his rearview mirror to see what the guy was doing behind him, but he doubted much.

"Aye, man, these handcuffs are hurting my hands," the guy complained.

"If they are hurting your hands, then I wouldn't be good at my job. They are hurting your wrists," Nicola corrected.

"Whatever. You know what I mean," DeMario said, rolling his eyes. "Where are you taking me anyway?"

"Don't worry about that."

"I know my rights, and I ain't new to this shit. You're supposed to take me downtown to 201," the man said, looking out the window.

"Well, if you know so much, then why are you asking me questions?"

The perp got quiet for a minute and then sat his head back anxiously looking at the roof of the truck. "This your ride?"

"Yep."

"Why don't you have to drive an unmarked like the rest of the pigs?"

Nicola didn't answer his question, but did ask one of his own. "So, why did you ask for me?"

The perp cracked a smile. "Cuz I know shit." His lip turned up as he cut his devious, red eyes.

"You *know shit*, huh. Let me get you to the location, and you can pour your little heart out," Nicola said, following protocol. There was no way he was going to mess up good Intel by letting him talk before he could get him in a confession hole.

Evidently, Nicola must have hit a nerve with the perp because he looked back out of the window and pursed his chapped lips together. "How far are we away, because I gotta piss?"

"Hold it."

"So you don't care if I piss in your truck?"

"You piss in it; you clean it."

There was a long pause as if the man was thinking hard about something. He watched the streets as they passed by them and took a deep breath.

"Aye. You're Nicola Agosto. *The Agosto*, right? The motherfucker who popped Caesar?" he asked.

"The one and only. Don't' worry, pal. I've popped a few more since then." Nicola checked his mirrors and moved carefully into the right lane.

"Yeah, I know your ass," the man taunted.

"What do you know OG, triple OG?" Nicola asked, unmoved by the man. He couldn't wait to hear this.

"I know you live at 4673 Peabody with Ivy Winters," he said with a grin on his face.

"That information is public and can be found on the internet," Nicola said with a huff. "Good try though. Clever actually." He smiled into the rearview mirror at the man.

There was a brief moment of silence where all that could be heard was the sound of cars passing and wind blowing through the windows. Nicola settled back into the drive and thought no more of the man's taunts.

But the perp wasn't satisfied just yet.

"Maybe I should rephrase my statement," he said, when he'd finally built up the courage.

"You live at 4673 Peabody with Ivy Winters and four bad ass kids. Then there is one on the way, right? I know that the dead cop, Brooks, has a baby with Ivy's best friend. I know that you spend most nights on a fucking case and that yo' bitch don't like sleeping alone. And I know that if you don't stop barking up the wrong tree the same thing that happened to the Naples brats is gone happen to yours. Bound. Gagged and fucked. That's gone be all you, dude. And yo' wife is gon' find out what *number three* feels like. Who knows? It might just be better than what you're doing? That tripped me out though. Your wife has only been with two men? You really believe that shit? Man, that bitch probably don' been with a whole set of niggas. Lined up taping that ass like a ho at frat house, you hear me." He laughed, this time sure that he had gotten Nicola's attention.

Nicola's foot let up off the gas as he heard the words. "What did you just say?" he asked as a car blared its horn behind him. Incensed, he rolled the window down and waved the car past him as he turned on his blue siren quickly to let the woman know that she was two seconds from getting shot today.

As the car drove slowly by, Nicola pulled over to the side of Union in front of the Kroger's grocery store and turned around in his seat. His eyes were clouded with death and destruction.

"Yeah, I bet I got your attention then," the perp said with a clever grin. However, his nervousness was apparent. Still, he pushed Nicola further. "Not so bad now, are you?"

"Who are you working for?" Nicola growled.

"That's the last of your worries," the perp said, sucking his teeth. "Just tell me this, how did a greasy head pig like you end up with a black woman that fine? Man, I know you ain't hitting it right. I don't' care what they say."

"Who is *they*?" Before Nicola could ask the question, his hand was on the handle of the car door, opening it as he barreled out.

As if without thought at all in a mechanical motion, he snatched open the back door and pulled the perp out by his skinny, sweaty neck. Slamming him against the side of the truck, he pulled out his side arm and pointed it at him.

"What the *fuck* did you say about my wife and kids?" Nicola asked, pushing the gun into the perps right eye socket. "I'm waiting, bitch. You got something else smart to say or you wanna start talking?"

"You gone do me right here?" The perp smiled, toothy and cocky, feeling safe now that he was in full view of the public. "Fuck you, nigga. You ain't gone do shit. You ain't shit without that badge, and you ain't got do a motherfucking thing but lock me up, so fuck you."

"Oh, I'm not going to do shit, huh," Nicola asked, cocking his gun. Onlookers slowed down to watch as Nicola shoved the gun into the man's mouth and broke out his two front teeth. "I will blow your fucking worthless ass head off right here. So help me God, I swear that if you don't start talking, I'm going to lose my job right after you lose your life." His hands were shaking with anger. "Now, I know that your stank, nasty, broke punk ass didn't just find that information out. You're working for someone. Who is it?" He pulled the gun out of his mouth, just long enough for him to answer.

The perp swallowed a gurgling breath and spit out thick blood and broken, jagged teeth. "It doesn't really matter what you do to me. You should be worried about your kids. Trust that. They are going to end up in garbage cans too. You can add them to the Baby Boys case list. Take the count from 4 to 8." He laughed even in writhing, excruciating pain.

The pictures of the children that Nicola had pulled out of the darkest, dingiest places in Memphis flashed through Nicola's head, and before he knew it, he was beating the man with the butt of the gun.

"Who do you work for, huh?" Nicola screamed. He hit him again. "Who the fuck do you work for?"

The perp fell hard after the heart stopping blows to his face and skull, but Nicola picked him back up and slammed his head against the side of the truck. Blood splattered as he cracked the tinted window glass.

The fragile man buckled under the pressure of Nicola's blows.

"Get your punk ass up!" Nicola screamed snatching and tearing his dirty t-shirt. "Get. The. Fuck. Up!!!" His voice echoed across the street as he pointed the gun at the man's head.

The entire front grill of the perp's mouth was gone and thick red blood spewed out.

Nicola ignored the man's state.

"I'm going to ask you one more time, and if I don't get an answer out of you, I'm going to start breaking shit right here, right fucking now! Who are you working for, who sent you to me with this shit?"

Again, the man said nothing.

Nicola snatched him up again and hammered a quick, dead on punch to the gut that made the man double over again, this time out of breath and panting.

By now, Nicola was in a rabid trance. Putting his wide forearm on the man's throat and pushing into his Adam's apple, he penned him against the truck.

"Talk," Nicola growled.

Barely able to speak, the man held his secret. "I ain't saying shit to you," the man said with a crooked, pained grin. "You already did what I wanted." He gave a blood, stomach-curdling smile. "You fucked up."

Just as he said the words, two police cars pulled up beside Nicola's truck and jumped out. "Put your hands up in the air!" all four police officers screamed.

"I'm a cop," Nicola said, refusing to let the man go. With one hand pushing the perp's neck into the broken glass, he used the other to lift his badge. "Step off. I am interrogating this prisoner." He turned back to the perp. "Who sent you?" Nicola asked again, choking him out with the deadly grip he had on his neck. "Who sent you?!!"

"Help me!" the man screamed to the other police officers. "Please help me. This cop is crazy. He called me a nigga and beat the fuck out of me because I told him that I had to piss, man. Help me!"

"Shut your lying ass mouth!" Nicola screamed. "Unless you're going to tell me who sent you…"

"Sir, let go of the prisoner and put your hands in the air!" the white, female uniform cop screamed, weapon pointed. She stepped closer, both hands grasping the handle of her department issued Glock.

"He's in my custody," Nicola said, watching him start to black out.

"Not anymore, sir. Let him go now!" she ordered. "My lieutenant is on the way. You can square it with him when he arrives, but right now, I need you to step away from the prisoner.

"Or what?" Nicola seethed at the woman. "You are a fucking beat cop."

The woman stepped closer. "And you're being recorded, sir," she said, moving her gaze across the street. "We've received several 911 calls. You have to release him to me."

Nicola turned to look at the audience that he had acquired in the short time since he had pulled over. Onlookers stood on the sidewalk recording with their phones, others stood with their hands over their mouths as cars slowed to watch the spectacle. It was then that he realized that he had let his emotions get the best of him.

"We're nowhere near done," Nicola promised the man with a snarl. "If it's the last thing you do, you're going to answer me."

Releasing the man from the chokehold, Nicola let the perp slide down the truck and hit the pavement, nearly unconscious and gasping for air. Immediately, the uniform officers rushed over to help.

"We need a bus!" the female officer screamed out as she bent down and checked his pulse. "Hold on, sir. Help is coming."

"Help?" Nicola asked appalled. "Fuck him. He just threatened my family." He walked back to his door and flung it open.

"Sir, where are you going?" the female police officer asked Nicola.

"I'm going to check on my family," Nicola said, getting inside of the truck. "I don't need your fucking permission."

"Sir, you cannot leave the scene," the male officer said in his most authoritative tone.

"Is there a crime here?" Nicola asked, hearing the perp convulsing on the ground.

The female cop was shocked that he even asked. "Sir..." she paused in disbelief at the scene. "Look at him." Her brow furrowed. *Was he serious?*

"Detective Agosto, you cannot leave," the male officer said, turning around to see another unmarked squad car pull up. "Step out of your vehicle."

It was Detective Johnson.

Nicola stepped out slowly, fighting his urge to flee.

Johnson jumped out of the car and ran up. "What the fuck, Agosto?" he said, hand on his gun. He stopped and looked at the guy on the ground. "Shit, he needs a bus."

"Already called one, sir," the female officer answered.

"Can you handle this?" Nicola asked Johnson, grabbing his cell phone. He dialed Ivy.

"Where are you going?" Johnson asked Agosto. He grabbed Nicola's phone and hung it up. "No calls. Nothing. Nada, you hear me. Fuck, Agosto!"

Nicola wasn't hearing Johnson. "I gotta get home. This guy just threatened my family, and he knows *very* personal shit about my wife and my kids. They aren't safe." Biting down on his lip, he kicked the tire of his truck and ran a frustrated hand through is hair.

Johnson gave in and passed him the phone. "You can't fucking leave, Agosto."

"Yeah, yeah," he said dialing Ivy. Her phone went straight to voicemail. His voice quivered in sheer worry. "Baby, it's me. When you get this call me back. But look there has been an emergency. Go and get the kids and head to your parent's house. Leave work. Trust me on this okay. Do what I ask and call me as soon as you get this message. Love you. Bye." He hung up in a huff.

"Dude, you can't go," Johnson said sincerely. He put his hand on Nicola's chest to stop him. Nicola quickly pushed his hand off his chest.

Trying to reason with Agosto, he stepped back with open hands, palms out. "Trust me. You don't want to leave the scene of this shit." He looked over at the perp on the ground. "Is the bus on the way?" he asked the female cop tending to the guy.

"It should be pulling up," she answered, checking the perps pulse. "Stay with me, sir."

Johnson sucked his teeth. Normally, he would have accused her of being overly dramatic, but this time, it was warranted. He turned back to Nicola and shook his head. Lowering his voice, he pleaded, "Man, look you gotta come up with a story," he whispered to Agosto, making sure no one heard him. His eyes were urgent, his voice tense with emotion. "You got a drop gun on you or something? I've got one in the car…"

"No," Agosto growled. "I didn't do anything wrong." He shook his head emphatically.

There was a low chuckle of disbelief from Johnson, despite the brevity of the situation. "Agosto, you just fucked that dude up so bad until he needs a bus. There is going to be blow back from this from the heads…" Johnson sighed. "From everyone. Shit, you got people recording this on their phones across the street."

They both looked across the main thoroughfare at the crowd, growing by the moment and screaming out for justice for the man who appeared to have been beaten by a cop for no apparent reason.

Nicola could feel his stomach turn. He was being set up, and he had actually fallen for it, taken the bait like an idiot. For that, he wanted to go over and finish the perp off.

"Nine times out of ten, someone over there in that lynch mob is going to have the ass beating you just gave this guy on YouTube before he even gets to the hospital. Then the calls from the NAACP are going to start." Johnson tried not to panic. "This is bad. This is fucking disastrous."

"How many times do I have to say it? The guy just threatened my family and you're talkin' to me about being sued? I could give a flying fuck about being *sued* right now. I want that bastard's head on a silver platter!" Nicola's voice rose.

Johnson looked Agosto in the eye without blinking. "No man, I'm not talking about you being sued. I am talking about jail time."

The thought slightly snapped Agosto out of his rage. He looked back at the perp again. "If I am going to have to do jail time, then I should have killed his ass."

"Think about what you're saying," Johnson whispered. He gripped Nicola's shoulder. "If you don't do it for yourself, do it for your family. How are you going to keep them safe, if you're locked up?"

Nicola began to think clearer. "It's already done. It can't be undone and..."

"Give me a minute," Johnson said, walking over to the other side of Nicola's SUV. He opened the back door and looked around. "Hey," he screamed out to the male officer tending to the man. "We've got a weapon over here. Looks like a shank or some shit."

Nicola turned around and walked closer, but Johnson threw up his hand. "Detective Agosto, I'm going to need you to stay on that side of the truck. This is evidence."

The male officer walked over to the other side of the truck beside Johnson and looked into the truck where a handmade shank was thrown on the back seat. He looked over at Johnson and shook his head, understanding what Johnson meant.

"Yeah, sir. You need to stay over there," he said, barely looking Agosto's way.

"Looks like the detective was just protecting himself," Johnson said with raised brows at the officer. "True, it may have gotten a little out of control, but there was obviously a concealed weapon on the guy. He probably tried to get loose, get to his shank, resisted arrest, blah, blah, blah," Johnson said, rolling his eyes.

"Johnson that's not what happened," Agosto said, quickly denying the false story.

Johnson's eyes grew larger as if to tell Agosto to *shut the hell up*. "Well, how did this shank get here? I didn't put it there," Johnson said, turning to the cop. "Did you?"

"No, sir," the male cop snapped.

"You're just shook up right now. You lost your head for a minute. Stay over there and cool down. T*hink* a little." Johnson pulled out a cigarette and lit it as he did the same. Only, he was thinking of how to cover Nicola's ass, not his own.

10

News swept through the city like wildfire about the beating that Nicola Agosto had given to an unidentified man whom he was transporting, possibly about the Baby Boys case. Five of the people who had witnessed the assault had already posted their video to YouTube or handed over footage to the local media. The videos that had been uploaded to YouTube had already received over 500,000 hits. It played in college rooms, board rooms and living rooms across the country. People watched on in disbelief as they witnessed what was being called the new Rodney King video of the 21st century.

COP BEATS PRISONER NEARLY TO DEATH was one of the video titles.

WHITE COP LOSES CONTROL AND KICKS BLACK MAN'S ASS was another title on YouTube.

Facebook pages all over the internet posted the video to share with their friends. Responses ranged from outrage to pride to indifference.

Twitter exploded with the story of Nicola Agosto. By evening, he had his own hash mark.

#NICOLA_AGOSTO was used over 50,000 times by seven that evening.

While the recordings were crude, it was evident that Nicola had used excessive force. From every vantage point of the footage, people saw that the victim was still in handcuffs at the time that the assault took place, and it was clear that he did not fight back. The only thing that people did not know was why any of it had happened.

So far, the Memphis Police Department had not issued a statement except the incident was "currently under investigation."

News reporters from every station were broadcasting live from not only from the police station where Nicola was being interrogated by Internal Affairs but also from the Med where the victim was being treated for his injuries and in front of the Kroger's grocery store on Union where the assault had taken place. People who witnessed the crime also spoke with the media, visibly upset from the scene and baffled by the entire situation.

One woman cried on camera begging for the Memphis Police Department to "please do something to stop this kind of blatant racist brutality of the African-American community."

Since CNN was already broadcasting about the news conference earlier in the day, they also seized the opportunity to use the footage from Nicola at the news conference to package the breaking story of his alleged brutal "beating of a local gang member." His backstory was flashing across national news outlets, everything from his credentials to his previous cases and relationship to fallen officer K. C. Brooks.

In just a few hours, the entire city of Memphis was buzzing with chatter. People in offices and homes called in to local talk radio stations, tuned in to local programming where Nicola was being lauded as a broken hero or accused of being a closet racist.

National human and civil rights groups had already issued statements on their websites and their social media outlets. The NAACP, Rainbow Push Coalition, several grassroots groups and legal associations were demanding Nicola's head and justice for the victim.

A white cop in a city known for its divisiveness had publicly humiliated, beaten and brutalized a young black man, not for his actions but allegedly for words. The new story for prime time that evening was not just the Baby Boys case, it was also about the now instantly famous Nicola Agosto.

***

When Ivy received the text from her husband, she was still in a meeting with Mike Hughes and her boss. She nearly dismissed it until it buzzed several time. Nicola was not known for long texts. If it was more than just a few lines that he had to type, he simply called. He had always said that texting was not for him, yet she insisted that they do it to keep from interrupting each other's work schedules.

Baby, I need you to drop whatever you are doing and get the kids and get to your mother's house. Don't go home. I've done something horrible. I'll explain it later, but right now I just need to know that you are safe and that you received this. I love you and I'm very sorry, he had texted to her.

After reading the text, she immediately pushed away from the board room table and stood up interrupting the conversation taking place. Her face was void of color and her eyes watering.

"Excuse me, gentlemen. I'm afraid something has happened…a family emergency." She gathered her paperwork in her arms and without waiting for a response darted out of the room.

"Is there anything we can do?" Mr. Letewich asked, confused by Ivy's sudden mid-stream change. The meeting was going so well, and it was most unlike her to leave in such a dramatic way.

Ivy stopped at the door and looked back at her boss. "I don't know," she said, shaking her head. "Mr. Hughes, I apologize for my need to leave. Please don't allow this to reflect on the firm's ability to…"

"Family comes first," Mike said, thinking that a family member must have been ill based upon her behavior.

It took only minutes for Ivy to make her way out of the office. Dropping her things on her desk, she quickly grabbed her keys and purse and headed to the parking lot.

The first thing that she did when she was out of the earshot of colleagues and clients was call her husband back. Unfortunately, all she got was his voicemail.

"This is Nicola. Leave a message."

She hung up the phone and cursed. "Damn it, what is going on?" she asked as the phone rang.

It was her mother. Heart thudding against her chest cavity, she answered. "What's wrong, Mom?" she asked.

"Have you seen the news?" Sadie asked, turning down the television.

"No, what has happened?" Ivy asked, worried about Nicola. "What happened?"

"Honey, Nicky beat someone…a prisoner he was transporting. The reports aren't good. Have you spoken with him?"

"No." Ivy stopped in her tracks. Running a hand through her hair, she looked around the packed parking lot. "He won't answer his phone." Tears formed in the corner of her eyes. "Who did he beat?"

"A boy. A black boy. The reports so far aren't good. You should come home now, Ivy. Whatever that is going on at that office can wait."

She walked up to her reserved parking spot. Her heels clicked on the concrete ground echoing in the hollow area. "I'm on the way now. He told me to get the kids and come to your place," Ivy said, hitting the fob on her keychain to unlock the doors of her car.

"Where are you?" Sadie asked.

"In the parking garage of my office," she said, getting in the car.

Sadie's heart skipped a beat. "Listen to me, get out of there and get here now. I've sent Madison after the kids at the camp already. Just come straight here," Sadie said worried. "And don't tell anyone where you're going."

***

Several hours after the assault had hit the news and spread like wildfire, Nicola was still locked in an interrogation room of the MPD's headquarters, giving his statement about what had happened. Two of the Securities Squad's toughest bulldogs were unleashed on the case per hardliner Councilman Ferris's demands of the police department, which were also leading the news at the top of every hour.

Nicola didn't know how bad things had gotten. As soon as his lieutenant made the scene, he was immediately escorted out of public view and thrown in a room without a window. Only he wasn't particularly concerned about theatric Gestapo tactics as he was about the safety of his family.

Sergeant Sandy Newton, a blonde, athletic bomb-shell with piercing blue eyes stood in front of Nicola with a piece of paper in her slender fingers. She was statuesque and perfectly put together in black slacks that fit her long legs and blue oxford that fit her perky breasts. Her gold badge rested on her hip on the oppo-site side of her gun. One could tell just by looking at her that she loved her job, loved being in charge and being presumed to be a certifiable bad ass, but her act was quickly lost on Nicola.

Placing the paper on the table, she put her hand flat on the document and slid it roughly over to him. Her eyes penetrated through his daze and willed him to pay attention to her.

"Sergeant Agosto," she said in a husky southern drawl.

He looked up from the table, hazel brown eyes glazed over and blinked hard like he had just woken from a deep sleep.

She continued when she saw that getting any more statements out of Nicola for the moment might take an act of congress.

"You've been charged with excessive force and conduct unbecoming of an officer. You're relieved of duty pending an investigation. This suspension is paid until your hearing. You are to turn over your badge and gun immediately and not speak to the press regarding this matter. Do you understand?" She tilted her head as she stared down at him, waiting for a response.

Nicola looked back down at the paper in front of him and read it slowly. After three hours of an intense investigation of both he and Johnson and both uni-formed officers who made the scene, he simply saw more bullshit on the document. There was no need to read anymore. It would only make him angrier.

Swallowing hard, he took the pen offered up by her less than impressive partner, Sergeant Wilford, a skinny pale man with dull brown hair, bushy eyebrows, an unmistakably wide gap in his front teeth and sloping, unformed shoulders.

"Yes, I understand," he said, pushing back from the table. Taking off his shield, he placed it carefully on the table, rubbing his fingers over the brass one last time, before he quickly pulled his department-issued Glock 19 off his hip and set it on the table. It was hard to see his life's work on the table, under scrutiny yet again, especially in a climate where the only thing keeping this city safe was cops willing to put their lives on the line.

It was sickening. After everything, this was the thanks that he received.

Sergeant Newton looked surprised that he didn't have much to say. He was expecting an outburst of some kind - at least a plea to reconsider, but Nicola remained quiet, if not composed. Everyone else in-volved from Johnson to the cops on the scene were screaming that he was innocent, yet he didn't seem to want to fight for his job one way or another.

"Do you have any questions at all before you are excused?" she asked, watching him head to the door.

Nicola opened the door and looked back at her. "No," he said sternly, walking out. The door slammed loudly behind him as he headed down the hallway. Officers and detectives watched with a myriad of expressions on their faces. Some wore sympathy others wore disdain.

As he hit the elevator to head down to the lobby, Johnson came down the opposite hall yelling for him.

"Agosto," he said, running to catch him.

Nicola turned around and gritted his teeth.

"How did it go?" Johnson asked, chewing on gum and looking around. "These motherfuckers hounded me in there, but I think everything is cool."

Before Nicola could control himself, he had Johnson's shirt in his hands and pushed him hard up against the wall.

"What the fuck!" Johnson gasped, trying to push Nicola off of him.

"You were the only one that I told that Ivy was pregnant. No one else knew," Nicola growled.

"You think I had something to do with this?" Johnson asked with a frown. "Man, get the fuck off of me."

Nicola didn't budge.

"You'd be in fucking cuffs, if it weren't for me. How the fuck would I have anything to do with it, huh? I told you to beat the shit out of that guy? I lost the only lead we had?" he was dumbfounded by Nicola's thought process.

"He knew very specific information about me, most of which, you knew!" Nicola seethed.

"And the other shit I didn't know?" Johnson asked, trying to keep his voice low. "I'm going to only tell you one more time to get your hands off of me." He looked down at Nicola's balled up fists clenching his black t-shirt and breathed heavily through his nostrils. "Well?"

Nicola still didn't budge. "If not you, then who?" His eyes were ablaze with suspicion.

"We won't ever find out if we both end up in the fucking hospital, and that's where we're headed if you don't let me down," Johnson said, looking Nicola in the eyes.

Sliding him down the wall, Nicola stepped back a few feet and gathered his fleeting composure.

Everyone within in earshot looked at them, waiting to see what would happen next but did nothing to separate the two.

The peeping of the elevator opened drew Nicola and Johnson's attention.

"Let's go talk *alone*," Johnson said, looking down the hallway at the hordes of cops.

Nicola stepped inside of the elevator after Johnson and the doors closed quietly.

"What would make you think that I'd have a reason to be a part of this?" Johnson asked, keeping his eyes on the doors of the elevator.

"You knew about Twist. He showed up dead. You knew about Ivy and suddenly so does the perp. You knew where I lived and how to get to me. You knew about the girl…"

Johnson threw up a hand. "Let me stop you right there. Yes, I knew, but why would I sabotage this case?"

"Maybe you're on the take," Nicola said, looking over at him.

"I should shoot you in your fucking face for saying that shit. What? You think you're the only good cop on this force?" Johnson huffed and straightened his clothes. "Whoever is setting you up wants you to fall apart."

"Well, it's working," Nicola said as the doors opened.

"You're blowing this case," Johnson said, stepping out into the quiet hallways of the lobby. "I don't know if that means anything to you, but it should."

There was a chuckle in his voice. "This case *is* blown in case you haven't noticed," Nicola said, pulling his phone out. "Look, I need to get to my wife."

"Is she at the house?" Johnson asked alarmed.

"And why would I tell you anything at all?" Nicola said with eyes narrowed.

"Because right now, I'm the only one on your side. Because I'm the guy who showed up to cover your fucking ass and I'm owed more respect than being accused. Hey, I don't know you. You don't know me, but I'm here. If I wanted you off the case, if I was working for someone else, then I wouldn't need you anymore, now would I? I'd be gone on about my business. Instead, here I am like a fucking bug up your ass, trying to stick it out because it could have easily been me," Johnson snapped.

"Bug," Nicola huffed. He wiped a hand through his hair and shook his head.

"What?" Johnson asked confused.

"When I asked if she had told anyone about the baby, Ivy said that she hadn't told a soul even though she had spent all day on the phone with her sister-in-law. They were talking about my ex-partner." Nicola gritted his teeth and lowered his voice. "My house is bugged."

"You think?"

"What else?" Nicola said, shaking his head.

"Look, I've got a tech guy we can call to come and check the place out for us."

"Can he get out there tonight?"

"Yeah, sure. He owes me," Johnson said, pulling out his phone.

As they were about to head out the front doors of the building, they saw media swarming on the stairs waiting for Nicola to come out.

Stopping in their tracks, they turned around.

"Shit, we better go through the back," Johnson said, feeling sorry for his partner.

"Ivy tried to warn me," Nicola said, under his breath.

"What?" Johnson asked.

"Nothing," Nicola said. "Let's get out of here."

"Well, one good thing came out of this," Johnson said, pulling the red jump drive out of his pocket.

"You got it?" Nicola said in relief.

"And made a copy, but I haven't been able to review it yet."

"Well, we better not do it at my place," Agosto said, feeling for his gun. Shit, it felt weird not having it or his badge on his side.

Johnson saw Nicola's hand run over his hip and instantly felt bad for him. "You're going to get reinstated," he said in a matter-of-fact tone.

Nicola chuckled again, this time it oozed with sarcasm. "You don't know Memphis very well, do you?"

11

Music boomed in the background as patrons continued on with their evening completely oblivious to the treacherous events happening in the back of the club in the owner's office.

Cane slammed his meaty hand down on the desk of the strip club owner, Big Yummi, and spit into the bloodied man's face blurring his sight even more. "Where the fuck is the bitch? I know that you know where she went!" he said as his men held the middle-aged black man down in his black chair. "Just gone and tell me now, and I'll let you go."

Blood shot out of Big Yummi's mouth as he coughed. "I told you, man. I don't know shit. She came in here earlier for a minute, waited around and then left. I haven't seen her since," he said, gasping for air through his broken nose.

"Where did she go?" Cane asked, wiping the sweat from his red forehead and then slipping back on his John Deere cap.

"If I knew…"

Cane reached across the table and slapped the man across his face, making sure to crack him hard across his battered nose. "Don't you fucking lie to me. I know you know something. All you pimps keep up with your hoes. And all you fucking niggers stick together."

"She wasn't my hoe," the man tried to explain. "She just worked here for Twist. That's it. The bitch rarely even made pay out."

He writhed in pain, trying to break free from the two men who gripped his shoulders.

"He's pretty fucked up, boss. If he had known something, he would have said by now," Cane's number two, Sammy said, leaning against the table also. He watched on disgusted by how badly Big Yummi had been beaten. He had known the guy for years, picked up cash for Twist and Cane from him, drank with him. Now, he was approaching having to put a bullet in his head. It just didn't sit right.

"And who the fuck asked you when I should stop?" Cane asked Sammy in a huff. He knew that Sammy was right but still enjoyed beating the hell out of the man. "Did you get that surveillance shit out of the cop's house like I told you?"

Sammy sucked his teeth at the question. When had he not done what he was supposed to do? "Yeah," he said, standing up. "We got it out right when the setup was going down with DeMario."

"And did you get to DeMario yet?" Cane asked, spitting snuff into a Styrofoam cup beside him.

Sammy looked at the cup first and then up at his boss. On more than one occasion, he had seen his boss throw the contents of that cup into a man's face. A disgusting action that he didn't want done to him. "We tried, but cops are everywhere. He's impossible to get to right now at the Med," he said, shaking his head.

"The media is thick down there right now and so the attention. We weren't banking on that."

Cane was unmoved by the roadblock. "Well, then get *our* cop to do it. I want that motherfucker dead before the police have time to shake him down and find out that we set this shit up. I am not going down because of no fucking meth head. You got me?" He grabbed the cup.

Sammy nodded, watching Cane's hand. "We'll get him, boss."

Cane paused for a minute and then spit into the cup again. Setting it beside him, he looked back over at his current project.

Cane cracked a smile and pulled out a syringe. "Do you know what this is, Yummi?"

"Man, I ain't never did a fucking drug a day in my life. No one is going to believe that I started at 54 years old," Big Yummi spat on the table and tried to sit up. If he was going to die then he was going to do it with a certain amount of dignity.

The men quickly pushed him back in the seat.

The booming base of music and loud conversations from the main area of the club clouded the room.

"This ain't about who believes what," Cane said, taking the top off the syringe. "This is about sending a message to everybody who needs telling." There was a devious smile on his chubby face.

"Yeah. What they need telling you fat motherfucker?" Yummy asked, snarling.

Cane smiled. "Isn't it obvious, boy? There's a new boss in town."

***

Roxie checked her phone one last time for any message from Agosto before she boarded a Greyhound bus headed for the only place that she knew that she would be safe.

Tulsa, Oklahoma.

The only person whom she'd ever told where she was truly from was Twist, and she knew that he wouldn't have told a soul. Plus, it had been a while since she had gone home to the family farm to visit. They would gladly welcome her back with open arms without asking a hundred questions. And less questions ensured more safety.

She was hoping for a different end result than having to leave town suddenly. She hadn't brought anything with her. She left her apartment with only the clothes on her back. She'd burned all of her documentation, destroyed all of her technology, save her phone, which she ditched before she got on the bus and parked her brand new BMW on the long-term parking lot at the airport. For extra safety, she had also cut her hair, colored it and slapped on a pair of reading glasses.

She had to disappear, never to surface again if she was going to stay alive.

When it was obvious that Agosto wouldn't show, she knew what she had to do. Before he was brutally murdered nearly in front of her, Twist had already warned her to only trust the cop, and the news said that he was hemmed up something fierce for beating the hell out of some gang member.

It didn't take a genius to see that this was all related. At least from her standpoint.

Maybe the gang member knew too much, just like she did. Or maybe, this Agosto guy wasn't someone that she could trust after all.

Either way, she was headed out of Memphis and taking with her any hopes in solving Twist's murder.

***

For nearly a decade, Nicola had driven a department-issued, carpool vehicle nearly every day of his life. It was as much a part of him as being a cop. In fact, he hadn't put over 1,000 miles on his newest personal car in the last year and half since he bought it.

Even through the trouble that he had managed to get into down through the years, he had never been stripped of his amenities, simply because even on suspension, everyone knew that he would be back after his days were cut and sometimes his salary was lowered. This time, however, he was not only asked to turn in his badge and gun but also the keys to his city-owned Escalade. And that shining confidence that he had once had inside the department was suddenly lackluster. Before he could even get out of the precinct, people were whispering that this time would be the time that he was fired.

Nicola wasn't sure that they were wrong.

Even after accusing him of being a mole and jacking him up at the headquarters, Johnson still was willing to give Nicola a ride back to his house in his a shitty little, Ford Taurus unmarked. On the way, Johnson turned on the radio and let down the window to smoke a cigarette.

Nicola's natural instinct was to complain, but he held his comments tight to his chest and simply breathed in the carcinogens.

The talk show host, of course, was talking at about the misconstrued beating that Nicola had given DeMario earlier.

A right-wing, conservative Republican with extremely far-right ideals had a huge following and it seemed that everyone was weighing in on the discussion.

"Our phone lines are lit up today. Hopefully, we'll be able to get to your comments or questions, but if not, feel free to go to our Facebook page and make yourself heard," Yuman said, ecstatic that his ratings were shooting through the roof.

Johnson reached for the radio to turn the station, but Nicola stopped him.

"No, I want to hear what they have to say," he said with a huff.

"Are you sure about that?" Johnson asked. "You've been locked down at 201, but out here, man…" he paused. "People can't stop talking about the video."

"I haven't seen it yet," Nicola growled, reaching for his phone.

"Do me a favor and look at that once I drop you off," Johnson asked.

Nicola put his phone back in his pocket. "That bad, huh?"

"You Rodney King'd his ass."

Yuman sighed into the microphone and chuckled. "You know, it's odd that this guy was just all over the news promising the public that he would do everything in his power to keep us and our children safe. So, I find it ironic that he is now only hours later being brought up on charges for a brutal beating of a black man. I mean, are we really getting the entire story here? Was this man a possible suspect in the Baby Boy murders? Some are saying that it's so. This is the kind of thing that divides our already divided city more. What are your thoughts?"

Nicola knew that he was being sent to the slaughter.

"Caller, you're on the air," Yuman said, trying to sound concerned.

"Hi, Yuman, I don't normally listen to your station, but I tuned in today to share another perspective. You all are taking his side inadvertently, suggesting that just because this black man is a supposed suspect that that gives this white man the right to beat the shit out of him. I saw the video. Excessive is not the word for it. Here we are in the 21st century and still making every excuse under the damn sun to protect white bigots with badges."

The phone went dead and Yuman immediately began his rant.

"To call this man a bigot is a bit premature, don't you think? We don't even have all of the facts. All we know is that he is being investigated…."

Nicola changed his mind. Turning off the radio, he looked out of the window. "So that's how they plan to paint me." He was suddenly sick to his stomach.

"Don't let that shit get to you, man. Everyone who knows you, knows you are definitely not a racist," Johnson said with sudden passion. "The guys on the force will speak up for you."

Nicola chuckled as though the idea was preposterous. "You haven't been on as long as I have. Race is one issue that divides even the blue blooded."

"This is not the 1900's."

"I was born in the 1900's. So were you. It wasn't that far back that lynching's were taking place right over on Auction Avenue, before the condos and mixed income living." Nicola rubbed his aching head. "People have long memories."

"But you didn't do it because he was black."

Nicola couldn't tell if Johnson was asking or simply saying. He swallowed down his frustration and said the words aloud. "I did it because he threatened my family. I would have done the same thing no matter what color the guy happened to be."

"So find a way to get that out. Hold a news conference or something."

"You know the protocol as well as I do. I can't say a word until this investigation is over." Nicola rested his head back on the seat and looked out of the window.

"Well, look. First thing first. We clear your name. If we find wiretaps or bugs at your place, then it will just prove what you've been saying. Someone is trying to sabotage this investigation."

Nicola nodded. "Proof is the key. The fucking burden of proof."

***

Four hours after sweeping every inch of his 5,500 square-foot, colonial house unsuccessfully for bugs and wiretaps with Johnson and his "bug" guy, Nicola finally gave up on his futile pursuit.

Johnson screamed down from the attic as he wiped sweat from his brow. "Nothing up here either." He ducked his head out of the attic stairwell at Nicola who walked up to the stairwell with a beer. "Figured as much," he said with a tired, low treble in his deep voice. "Come down and have a beer with me."

Johnson's eyes lit up at the sight of the chilled Bud Light. His reward for a job well done. "You don't have to ask me twice. Yo, Deeds, get down here, man. Let's have a cold one before we get out of here."

"On the way," Deeds, the bug guy, screamed from the other side of the attic. "This place is huge."

"Tell me about it," Johnson said, making his way down the attic steps. "How much do you pay for utilities with this monster?"

"Had the entire place updated with more efficient appliances and had some installation changes done a few years back. It's not as bad as you might think."

Nicola led the way down to the den on the first floor, where he turned on the television and sat down on the sofa. It was the first time since this morning that he had really exhaled and it hurt something awful. His chest cavity burned as it deflated.

"Mind if I fix a sandwich to go with this beer? I'm starving," Johnson said, making a b-line for the kitchen, which was adjacent to the den.

"Help yourself," Nicola said, tuning in to ESPN.

The bug guy sat quietly on the other side of Nicola and rested back on the sofa as well.

Nicola turned to the guy and passed him a beer. "How much do I owe you?" he asked, reaching for his pocket.

"It's on the house," the bug guy said, taking the beer. "Courtesy of Johnson."

Nicola didn't like hand-outs. "I don't mind paying. You can't work for free."

Johnson stuck his head out of the door as the microwave warmed up leftovers he had found in the refrigerator. "Keep your money, Nicola. At least on this one. Just think of him next time you need some work done."

The bug guy nodded in agreement and passed him his card. "You call that day or night anytime."

Nicola took the card and put it in his wallet. "Will do."

"Don't you want to see the news?" Johnson asked curiously. "I mean, I know it's painful to hear them lie on you, but how are you going to defend yourself, if you don't know which lies their spewing?"

"I'm sure the same lies that their telling tonight will be on first thing in the morning. Right now, I need a break," Nicola said, running his tongue against his gums.

"Well, we at least need to figure out who set you up," Johnson said, determined to get something out of Nicola tonight before he left.

Nicola sucked his teeth. "I'll focus on all that tomorrow."

"Or you just don't want to brainstorm with me, because you still don't trust me," Johnson said with a growl. "Look man, it wasn't me."

"We've established that." Nicola looked over at Johnson with a cool-it-look on his face. "But I've worked on enough shit to know for a fact that we have a mole. Someone, somewhere in this department is on the take and they are working hard to keep us off the scent, and off the trail that leads back to whoever is responsible for the Baby Boy murders."

"So let's make a list of everyone we've come into contact with since the beginning of the case and use that list to make a list of possible suspects," Johnson urged.

He shoved the sandwich of meatloaf and salad wrapped in a whole-wheat bun into his mouth.

Nicola looked over at the bug guy and smiled. "Don't take offense but I'm not 100% sure of your work, so I won't be doing any planning whatsoever in this place."

"I guarantee my work," the bug guy responded, nodding his head.

"Do you guarantee it for five to ten? Because that's what I'm looking at if I'm charged with beating the shit out of that kid."

The bug guy was suddenly quiet.

Nicola smirked. "Hey, I wouldn't guarantee that either.

"So do you want to meet somewhere?" Johnson asked Nicola.

"Why don't you just focus on trying to solve this case, and I'll worry about saving my ass," Nicola said, resting back.

12

With Al Green's greatest hits playing softly on the stereo, Nicola sat outside of his in-laws' house in his LX Lexus truck, smoking a cigar and drinking cognac straight out of the bottle with his window half down and the air blasting. The cool midnight breeze provided a temporary calming backdrop for his chaotic thoughts and helped circulate the robust smell of his fine Cuban cigar out of his new vehicle.

He had a hundred problems to solve and in no particular order they flooded him like crashing waves against the rocks of a battered coastline: where was Roxie? How long had his house been bugged? Could he trust Johnson? Was there a mole? How did Cane fit into the murder of Twist? What was the common link between Twist and the Baby Boy murders outside of the drug, Molly? How was he going to go about solving this case? How was he going to keep his family safe until he did solve the case? Would jail be more likely than just being fired? Did he have a case to fight for his job? What was he going to do about his unborn child?

He was in the eye of a major storm in his life and all that he could do was brace for impact.

The questions kept multiplying in his head, yet the answers seemed so distant from him. If he were to prioritize his concerns, even for a second, the most important thing would be to keep his family safe. But it would be a lot easier to do that if he only knew who he was looking for in the first place. Ivy wouldn't be receptive to staying home from work until he found out, and she really wouldn't be receptive to leaving town and staying with his family in Miami until it was all over. So, he had to figure out a way to maneuver around her so that she didn't feel that he was watching her every move, even though he would be. He had no choice.

The thought of hurricane winds ripping through a seaside city crossed his mind. That's how he felt at that moment. Like he was being ripped into. But it wasn't guilt for his actions; it was anger that he hadn't done more. He should have pushed the man to a confession, especially since now he was in critical condition. He should have pushed him to a cliff and dangled him over, offering him death for silence or life or answers. Pity that he didn't get enough time.

As Nicola sat in deep thought staring out of the window of his truck, more hyper alert than he appeared, he noticed a figure emerge out of the front door of his in-laws' house.

At first, he figured that it was Ivy, but then he noticed a tall, muscular bald man closing the door behind him. Madison. Ivy's father. One of the most militant black men that he'd ever met in his life. The retired military colonel probably had an earful for him. Madison had always stomached Nicola, but he was never really sure that he liked him. He was a quiet man who normally only showed affection to his grandchildren and the women in his family. Still, he had always given him respect. And in turn, Nicola had done the same.

Making his way to Nicola's truck in pajama bottoms and a red Marine Corps t-shirt with a beer in his hand, Madison opened the passenger door and slipped inside. With a nod, he closed the door and settled down in the seat.

"So, do you plan to stay out here all night?" Madison asked, looking over at the cigar with envy. *Sadie never let him smoke anymore.*

In quiet understanding, Nicola moved his gun off his lap and put it carefully on his console between them, then reached across his father-in-law to his glove compartment. Pulling another cigar out, he passed it to him. "Consider it an early Christmas gift," he said, sitting back.

Madison took the cigar in his hand and ran it under his nose, inhaling the aroma. "Real Cuban, huh?"

"Oh, yeah. Only the best." Nicola grunted and shifted in his seat. "How's Ivy?" He could barely look at Madison.

"Not well. She's been a basket case since she received your text earlier." Madison huffed, frustrated with the entire situation. He had received call after call all day about the boy. People wanted to know what Nicola was thinking. *Like he knew.* He wasn't a damned mind-reader, just the boy's father-in-law. Even Nicola's father had called him. Evidently, Nicola's twin brother had seen the story and alerted everyone in Miami.

"Is she pissed at me?" It seemed like nothing else really mattered in the world at that moment. Nicola just wanted to know that she was still by his side. If she was, then he could find a way to handle everything else.

Madison frowned. "Angry? No. She *is* confused. We all are. You went from a press conference being backed by the mayor of Memphis to a damned police brutality beat down *that will go down in history* in less than an afternoon." He looked over at Nicola for an explanation. He had known the man long enough to know that whatever had brought all of this on had to be major. Nicola had grown to be a level-headed man, devoted only to his family and his job.

"Cops get threatened every day," Nicola began. He almost laughed. "I remember the first time someone threatened my mom. I was fresh out of the academy and working with my FTO. This guy promised me that when he got out, he was going to find her and sodomize her."

Madison cringed.

Nicola smacked his lips at the fleeting thought. His tone was even and low. "I wanted to kill him, but my FTO just told me to shake it off. He said that it was one thing that I could get used to… being threatened because of my job. Shortly after that, I saw what the FTO was talking about. Someone was going to fuck me up, kill my family, and screw my wife even before I had one, every single day that I made an arrest." He looked over at Madison to make sure that he was following him.

"So what was different about this arrest?" Madison asked.

"What was different?" Nicola looked out of the window and clenched his jaw. "Every cop worth his salt knows the difference between idle threats and the real thing. *This was the real thing.* He…the perp…threatened my family for real." Nicola bit down on his lip. "He knew about Ivy being pregnant. He knew about Brooks' death and the baby. He threatened my kids…said they would end up like the others. Just like the boys I pulled out of the fucking dumpster not even a week ago."

Madison winced as if hearing the words hurt him to his core. "Do you think he has the capability?"

Nicola shook his head. "I don't know if he does but someone he works for sure in the hell does." He rolled his eyes and gripped the steering wheel until his knuckles turned white. "I don't know anything anymore, except that I did what any man in my place would have done. I showed him that my job was not the most important thing to me…my family is. And anyone who threatens them won't get another chance to do so as long as I'm around."

That brought up another point for Madison. "I hate to risk sounding like a prick, but how long do you think you'll be around? The news said that if you're brought up on charges, you could go to prison." Madison hated to say it, but it was true. They had to think ahead, at least starting now.

"I doubt if I'll go to jail, but I don't think they'll let me be a cop anymore." His voice broke in disappointment. All he'd ever known was being a cop. *If they took that away, who would he be then?*

Madison turned to Nicola. This was an area that he truly understood. He had retired from the military after devoting his entire adult life to it. Nothing was stranger than acclimating after. It was a hard pill to swallow to go from being saluted every day to being ignored by the person right in front of you. He touched Nicola's shoulder in sympathy. "You're a damned fine cop. They aren't just going to throw you to the wind, *but if they do*, you have other options. You're educated. You come from a damned fine family with opportunities they'd love to share with you. And you have your skills, no matter what. Just remember that you have to keep your cool. Getting fired isn't the worst thing in the world. There is life after." He shook his head and turned back around, fearful that he'd shown too much of himself. "As far as the family, you know that you'll have my help. Ivy is my little girl, and my grandchildren mean the world to me." He chuckled. "You I could do without."

Nicola snickered and took another sip of his cognac. "Sorry, old man. You aren't getting rid of me that easily."

"Tell you what…why don't you give me that bottle and go in there and see after Ivy? I'm sure that she's dying to talk to you. And I'm not going to lie, she needs consoling. Your mother and I tried, but she only wants you. The kids are finally asleep. It took a hell of a lot of work. I don't see how you two do it every single night. And the idea of another one…" His face lit up. "I can't lie. That's great news, but I hope it's a girl. You're just a few shy of a damned football team."

"You didn't know she was pregnant?" Nicola asked.

"No, she still hasn't said a word," Madison said under his breath. "I imagine that with everything that happened today, she wouldn't want to talk about that."

"Do me a favor and don't say anything yet," Nicola asked sincerely.

"Mums the word." Madison zipped his lips.

Nicola passed Madison the bottle and kept his quiet shock to himself. This was the first time in their marriage that Madison had ever been so open and so intimate with him. "For what it's worth, I appreciate you," Nicola said, opening the car door.

Madison nodded and picked up the lighter. "I'm going to sit out here and enjoy this cigar before I go back into the wife and let her rip me a new asshole for smoking."

"Bring the gun in with you. I've got another one on me," Nicola said, raising his shirt slightly to show another Glock packed closely to his side.

"Beat you to it," Madison said, tapping his side.

***

As quietly as he could, Nicola slipped upstairs to the guest bedroom where he found Ivy laying on the bed, curled up tightly in a ball. As soon as the door opened, her head popped up and crocodile tears ran down her face. She wiped them quickly and sat up in bed.

"Nicky," she said exasperated, eyes wide.

"I'm sorry that I couldn't get to you sooner," he could barely look at her.

"Are you alright?" she asked as he walked up to her. She checked him for scars, roaming her hands all over his body. With a careful eye, she checked him thoroughly. "Did he hurt you?" the frown lines in her face creased harder as she tried to understand.

Not a scratch on him? Not one bullet. Not one stab wound. What could have made him do what he had done?

Nicola took her hands in his own and huffed. "I'm fine," he said, truly afraid of how she might see him.

"But the video…" she sat back. "What happened that made you beat that man like that? They're calling you a racist…a bigot…"

He calmed her with fingers over her soft, pouty bare lips. "I did what I had to do." He prayed that she believed him.

"Why did you have to do it?" she pushed. Her nostrils flared as she tried to make reason of her husband's actions.

Nicola sat down beside her and looked her in her eyes. "He threatened us. He knew sensitive, personal information about our family and our children, and I just lost it."

"How personal?" she asked, heart thudding in her chest.

"He knew that you were pregnant." Nicola paused, questioning if it was wise to share everything with her.

As if reading his mind, she gritted her teeth and grabbed him by his face. "Nicola, don't shut down on me now. I have to know everything in order to protect you."

A smile crossed his lips. Here he was worried about how to protect her from physical harm and she was still worried about protecting his image. He guessed that was why he loved her. She was always *all in* for him, even when he didn't deserve her.

"He knew where we lived, about Brooks and the baby, about where our children went to school and their teachers' names. He knew how often you and I made love." Nicola could see that she was turning pale. Holding her hand tighter, he continued. "Maybe you were right. Maybe I did need to see a shrink and get some of this shit off my chest, but it was too late by the time that I came in to contact with this guy. He threatened our children, said the same thing that had happened to those other kids would happen to my kids."

"Is he the Baby Boy murderer?" she gasped, hand over her mouth.

Nicola rolled his eyes. "No, he was sent by someone to get me off this case. I was just too wrapped up in the moment to see that."

Ivy's posture sunk into a sloping curve of grief. "Good god, Nicola."

"I don't' feel bad about it, Ivy," he confessed.

Ivy looked over at him as he fidgeted with his wedding band and looked down at the floor. "I don't feel like putting that punk in the hospital was such a bad thing. He's alive right now, because I didn't kill him. And after making the threats that he did to the only people I love in this world, he should be kissing my ass right now that he's not dead. I could have killed him." He looked over with an icy stare at his wife. *I wanted to kill him*, he thought to himself.

Ivy was lost for words but she knew that she needed to console her husband. "We'll figure this out together. Whatever happens, we'll do it together. You did what you felt was right." She shook her head as she gained more clarity. "I would want you to support me if…"

Nicola laughed suddenly as he tried to picture Ivy beating the hell out of anything but bloody steak on a counter. "Don't worry, baby. I don't think that you'll be in a brawl anytime soon." He touched her chin softly and whispered. "All I care about is you and my kids, Ivy."

His eyes, while red from exhaustion and worry, were clear with honesty.

She leaned in to whisper the words only inches from his mouth. "I love you too," she said with the faintest of smiles.

Crooning to her soothing tone, he closed his eyes. "I love you," he said, pushing his lips up against hers.

The softness of their soft flesh mingled together as his strong arms wrapped around her, gently pulling her from his side up in the cradle of his lap. There was a varying reaction in Ivy's body, both excitement at his physical touch and worry in her heart. A wave of emotion washed over her face even as she melted into him.

"I love you so damn much," he said again, running a hand over her shoulder and down her arms.

The soft curves of her body showing through her pink cotton nightgown slowly heated his desire pooling below. Even the frumpy pajamas did little to hide her voluptuous figure. The intensity of his fever pitch gaze made her bite her lip. He could never hide when he wanted her…and she could never hide how much that made her want him in return.

"The kids are sleep?" he asked, looking at the closed door.

Ivy nodded, running her hand down his rock hard chest. The taut muscles in his chest were bulging and wide. The crease down the middle of his chest was like a valley through a mountain.

"No one will be up to check on us?" he asked, slowly unbuttoning her nightgown. Control and domination laced his words.

Ivy nodded again. She knew what was coming and she wanted it as much as him, maybe more.

"Have you ever made love at your parent's house?" he asked with a wicked grin. He pulled her nightgown off her shoulders once it was unbuttoned to reveal rigid nipples at the tip of full, melon-like breasts.

His mouth watered at the sight. She was absolutely beautiful and after all these years, she was still absolutely his.

Maybe it was just pheromones, but Ivy felt a sudden mix of heady lust overtaking her. "No, but I have a feeling that you're about to change that." She arched her back and rested her hands on his wide set legs. "Let me make you forget about it all, Nicky," she said, voice husky. Her eyes met his and locked him into a trance.

"You already have," he said, pulling her to him. Searching her mouth with a harder, more passionate kiss this time, he nestled his hands into her hair before pulling her into the full-sized, sleigh bed with him.

He laid her flat on her back and was quick about pulling his shirt off. With an impatient hand, she reached for the buckle on his jeans and snapped the clasp. He pulled them and his black briefs down obediently to his ankles and then kicked them off with his boots on the floor.

In the darkness and silence of the room, he moved on top of her and pushed her loose strands of hair from her face. Kissing her cheek, he slipped a hand under her thigh and lifted it slightly. She felt the tip of him at the door of her sex. A slight brush of skin against her own caused a shudder. Goose bumps formed on her skin. Raking nails down the side of his wide back, she arched her back for him to enter.

A cold hand grabbed her by the waist and then pulled her further down into the bed. Slipping his head into the fold between her neck and shoulder, he pushed into the warmness of her body and gasped.

They had to be silent tonight.

No sounds beyond a whisper.

Her mouth flew open as he filled her. Swallowing down a moan, she wrapped her arms tighter around his neck.

"Ivy," he whispered. Her name floated off his tongue like a melody.

"I'm right here," she said, holding him tighter. "I'll always be right here."

He lifted his head and looked into her eyes. The connection panged in his heart. "I need you," he whispered into her mouth. "I need you now more than ever."

"I'm not going anywhere. None of us are. We're your family." She moved his hand down to her stomach. "All of us."

He looked down at her hand, and still inside of her, pushed again. "You're all I've ever needed. As long as I have you, I'll make it."

She wrapped her legs tighter around him and undulated under his body. The heat between them began to rise.

"Then you'll make it," she said, kissing his lips again.

She tasted like sweet nectar. Dipping his head, he kissed her back, deeper and deeper he lapped at her wet until he pushed her down into the bed. All reason had gone from him then. He emptied all of his emotions into her with each and every slow, powerful pump into her body. Slipping his knuckle into her mouth for her to bite down on so that she wouldn't scream aloud, he wrapped his other arms around her lower back and pulled her in.

She was locked into his warm embrace, a prisoner of his touch, and she loved every moment of it. Although tonight, he was more urgent. She could tell that making love to him was healing him in ways that words could not. There were wounds there that she hadn't noticed before, invisible to the eye, but to the touch…she could feel it there, torturing him. The murder of all those children, the pressure to find their killer, the worry of protecting his family.

Holding him tighter, she whispered, "I love you."

It was then that she felt him grow harder inside of her. "I love you," he whispered. "I love you so much."

13

Johnson threw a black bag of garbage into the can in the backyard of Carmen's house and instantly thought of the twins he had pulled out of the dumpster near the zoo. Flashbacks were just a byproduct of his profession, but it didn't mean that he had to like them. He hated, in fact, the constant reminders of all the children who had gone missing and come up dead on his watch. Quietly he committed to seeing this case solved, but he had to keep better composure than his partner had. Damn, Nicola had lost his shit on a historical level. So much so that even he had to dodge reporters. Everyone wanted a piece of him, wanted to get the inside scoop. Even the guys on the force were stalking him. They all wanted to know what really happened.

Only he couldn't tell them, because he wasn't there. Not for the stuff that mattered.

Closing the top to the nearly-full garbage can, he turned around and wiped his sweaty brow. It wasn't even nine in the morning yet, and it was already scorching outside. *Memphis had a way of putting people in a bad mood early in the day, so by nightfall they were innately ready to kill someone.*

He looked up at the clear blue skies above the evergreen trees in the yard and yawned at the serene beauty. It was time to get ready for work. Time for enjoyment to be over and for hell to begin again. He had been

lounging long enough. He and Carmen had had breakfast together, rolled around in the bed a little more and
taken a shower. It was time now to meet the reality of
the day. His fantasy was slowly coming to an end.

In a casual stroll, still taking time to enjoy the sound
of chirping birds perched up in the towering trees on the
tranquil lane, he contemplated how to handle his
current situation.

This was the third night that he had spent at Carmen's house, and while she was great company, he
knew that he was wearing out his welcome. It was time
for him to go home and have another look at things.
Besides, he was still on this investigation, and if he
stayed too long he might bring trouble to her doorstep.
Still there was a part of him that was severely paranoid.
If Agosto's house had been bugged, his could have
been too. Of course, he had the place checked, but he
still didn't feel comfortable. Although, he doubt that he
ever would feel comfortable again until this case was
solved.

The pressure was ramping and he felt like he was at
a standstill. Maybe that's what whoever was behind this
wanted.

They knew that media frenzy would ensue and the
road to solving the murders would turn to complete
gridlock.

Going through the back porch of the old bricked
bungalow style home, he kicked off his running shoes
on the mat and walked into the kitchen where Carmen
was pouring more coffee. She turned from the mug and
smiled at him.

"Fixed you another cup," she said, tugging at her
short, powder pink terry cloth robe.

Johnson walked up behind her and kissed the nape of her neck. "Thanks," he growled. "I can never get used to seeing you in pink." Wrapping his arm around her waist, he pulled her closer to him and nearly picked her up off the ground.

"Why?" she laughed.

"You always wear black slacks, blue top, boots and a gun for starters. Cops don't wear pink." In truth, he liked it. He liked seeing more of her than just the tough exterior she had to put on when she was on duty.

"Some days I wear a black top instead of a blue one. I try to mix it up," she joked.

Carmen was a busty brunette with startling green eyes and full pink lips. Her body was a thing of beauty built in the gym and hard, long hours in the field. Her Italian heritage was evident in the warm tones of her olive hue and huskiness of her sultry voice. She was in fact the most beautiful woman that Johnson had ever seen.

Having worked her way up the ranks on her own despite her father, Deputy Chief Magnelli's efforts to influence her career, she had drawn a hard line between work and family. At home, Magnelli was her father, but at work, she regarded him with distance and only came in contact with him a few times out of the year.

Because of her last name, Carmen had been a prize sought after by many officers either looking to climb the ranks or with ulterior motives. Hundreds of bar bets had been placed in her name and thousands of cheesy lines had been used to get her attention over the years. But she had steered clear of anyone who even remotely seemed anxious. She knew that many of the officers that her father had burned over the years saw her as a trophy, something to dangle in front of the old man's face in an effort to stick it to him where everyone knew it would hurt most. But Magnelli had taught her well, making her privy even as a young girl to men and their devious intentions. Plus she was no angel.

Once she had fallen prey to a man on the force, a Sergeant that she had fallen in love with on Delta Shift at the Tillman precinct. Her father had been petrified at the union and in complete disapproval of the man's background. Their affair had spawned a rollercoaster relationship that had resulted in one beautiful child and one ugly divorce. However, being on center stage had taught her one lesson. It was always best that she keep her affairs private. She had done so since the divorce, dating inconspicuously or not at all.

And then one night after partying downtown with a few of her closest female cop friends, she stumbled upon Johnson in the wee hours of the morning at Alex's Tavern, a dank, dark old cop hangout that was thick with cigarette smoke and greasy burger residue. It had been a cornerstone of the department for decades and the only place in town to get a cold beer at four in the morning.

Johnson was sitting by the jukebox with his feet propped up on the table having a beer with a few other off-duty cops. He was laughing about something. His voice so loud and dominant that it rumbled in her chest. She remembered that his dark jeans had fit his muscular legs so inappropriately until when he leisurely shifted she tried to sneak a peak in between his thighs. The tattoos that ran down his arms seemed to make his large muscles bulge that much more. His skin was glowing tan even in the darkness of the room and his face was chiseled to perfection, every detail a mirror of perfection from his thick eyebrows to his perfectly shaped nose, his squared, wide jaw and the irritatingly sexy dimple in his chin. His thick neck led down to cascading muscles from his shoulders to his pecks to his flat stomach, all taut and rippling, begging to be touched.

Eye contact was immediate.

In mid-laughter, he had sat up erect in his chair and watched her as she made her way across the room with her friends.

The Eagles were playing on the box. Hotel California set the mood for something sinister. Highlights of the Lakers vs. Grizzlies game were playing on the television across from him. But at the moment that they spotted each other, the room went silent.

She had tried to ignore him, ignore the devilish grin and wide playfulness of his naughty mouth. His eyes sparkled like a deer in headlights and his wreaked of unadulterated sex.

And that was all that she thought that she wanted from him. Pure, animal-like, lust-filled, hardcore, heart pounding, sweat pouring, candy-laced sex.

Johnson had not disappointed. In fact, he more than performed.

They had spent the morning talking and the afternoon in his bed. The evening was spent asleep, trying to recover from the best sex that she had ever had.

The rest had been downhill since then.

She had figured Johnson for just another cute cop with a huge cock that she could easily discard when she was done playing, but he had not been so easy to get away from. There was a part of him that though guarded well was genuine and undeniably special. He made her laugh, made her think and worst of all, he made her dream.

But Carmen was a smart woman. She had kept their sordid affair a secret, never leading on that he was the only one, the singular person in her mind and her heart. She could not bear to reveal such a thing to him no matter how he confessed a desire to be with her and only her.

In fact, she encouraged his indiscretions. As long as he was in another woman's bed, he couldn't be stealing her heart....or at least what was left of it.

Taking her from her thoughts, Johnson sat down on the stool by the island and leaned his large arm on the counter. "You know what I mean. Nothing about you is *girly*."

She took offense. "You just don't know me well enough." She hated herself instantly for saying it. It just opened up the door for an unwanted conversation.

He looked up from the hot, steamy mug and bit his lip. "I want to know you better but you won't let me." He broached the subject again for the hundredth time.

Carmen huffed and sat down beside him. "Johnson."

"My name is Luke," he corrected. "We're sleeping together. I think you can call me by my first name. It's been months."

"*Johnson*," she said, ignoring him, "you and I have two things in common that I like in a relationship." She counted them off on her fingers. "One - we're both cops. So we know the score. I don't have to worry about you complaining that a case is ruining our relationship or that I'm gone too long. Two-we both believe in a casual relationship to save each other from getting hurt. Now, there is only one of those two things that's a double-edge sword and that's the part about us both being cops. I was married to a cop for five years." She should her head emphatically in disgust. The memory of the man made her want to gag.

"How many times do I have to say that I'm not him," Johnson protested.

"It was the worse five years of my life *except for the birth of my daughter*. You haven't been married. You have no idea. Okay. I know how these things go. Our relationship will interfere with our careers and our careers will then interfere with our relationship. Let's just keep it simple. We see each other when we see each other and that's that." She swallowed down a deep breath with her well-covered lie.

Johnson picked up the coffee cup and sipped it. "It's not that simple for me."

"When I met you, Johnson, you were a certified, four-legged dog straight out of the pound looking for a bitch in heat. You have slept with half of the heterosexual women on the force. You're part of an initiation for goodness sake. You're like that board that football players jump up and hit before they run out of the locker room onto the field."

Johnson coughed. There was one thing about Carmen. She was definitely hard around the edges. He tried to stay focused on the key point instead of allowing her investigative tactics to cloud the conversation. He knew that she wanted to unnerve him. She was good at providing diversions, but they wouldn't work on him this time. "Go on and make jokes if it makes you feel safer. The point is no matter how many women that I've slept with, I've finally found the one for me. I'm serious. So serious until I think that we should tell your father. I think that's the only thing holding you back."

"My father would hate you, but no that's not the reason."

"What's the reason?" He looked her dead in her eyes.

"I just told you the reason." She looked back and raised her brow. "No matter how many times you ask, it's not going to change."

"Carmen, why are you so afraid of me? You've obviously got all of the control." His tone was low and serious. The words were so clear, so filled with meaning until she knew that it was not a lie.

His tone caught her off guard. "I don't want control," she answered, wing-like lashes flapping.

"You want a toy? Do you like playing with my heart?" he asked with a frown.

"No and no." She rolled her tongue around her teeth. "What if lack of control is the only thing that has you here? What if once you gain that control, you go right back to being the Johnson that everyone has always known?"

"What if I don't? What if I want to settle down, have a relationship, move in and do monogamous shit together?" He tilted his head. "What if it just you that makes me a better man?"

Carmen rolled her eyes. Now he was just being a drama queen, trying to win an argument and have the last word. She had to remember that. "What makes you think that you care about me anyway? Because you stayed more than one night at my house? Because I saved your number in my cell phone?" Her neck rolled as she made her point, brow raised to an extreme point.

Johnson refused to give up. "Hey, I know my own feelings. A man doesn't feel like this every day. You're different from the others and you make me different. I like being around you and *Laila*." Why was he having to argue this point? In his entire life, he had fallen in love just this once and she was making it as hard on him as she could.

Carmen folded her arms. "Don't bring her into this." She hated to discuss her daughter or use her as a pawn in their relationship, but she knew that her five-year old was crazy about Johnson, especially after he had volunteered to take her to the father/daughter dance when her ex-husband cancelled on her the night of the event.

He pulled at Carmen's arm. "Don't do that."

"Do what?" she asked, guard up now. Ever so slightly she edged a centimeter away, but even with just a minor shift in their proximity, Johnson could feel it. She was his magnet.

"Shut me out." He swallowed down his pride and the coffee. "Are you sleeping with someone else then?" He didn't quite know how he'd handle it if she said yes. Still, he had to ask the question in order to make the point if the answer was in his favor.

"No, I'm not," she said quickly. "But that doesn't mean that just because it's just you *for now* that I want to complicate my life with a committed relationship."

His eye twitched. "Especially for me, right?" Even he had to admit that he didn't think he was good enough for her, but women like her were never attracted to the guys who were *good enough*. They liked bad boys; guys who barely returned a text the morning after and *never* stayed the night; guys who drove fast, flashy cars and spent countless hours in the gym to get a woman's attention but never took the time to notice any woman he had been with.

No, they didn't like good enough.

They liked worthless.

Women complained continuously about the kind of guy he was, but they couldn't stay away from him. They wanted to be fucked within an inch of their lives, made to feel as though there was no one more important or beautiful on the earth besides them, made to feel as though the bad boy couldn't live without them and then cry and moan when they were discarded days if not hours later.

And in the past, that was him down to the last detail.

Even now with other women that was still him, but with Carmen being the bad guy, the worthless *all wrong* choice wasn't an option anymore.

Too bad she didn't believe him.

Too bad she might very well like him the way that he used to be.

Too bad he couldn't change back.

Carmen rolled her eyes again at the sight of him sulking but relaxed her shoulders at his confession. She knew that she was being too hard on him, but she also knew that she was dealing with a reforming player…basically chopped liver. "It's not that. I just…I can't go back to that life, Johnson. It made me want to pull my hair out. All the fighting and the drama." She unfolded her arms and touched his face. "What we have now works." Her voice pleaded for his understanding.

Johnson flashed his amber eyes her way. "For you?"

"For us," she said, standing up and snaking around him. Wrapping her arms around his shoulders, she kissed the tip of his nose. "Besides, you're too sexy to pout." Playfully, she made a sad face. "And there are so many other things we could be doing right besides fighting."

He rubbed her lower back and rested his hand on her bottom. "You know, you can't always change the subject with this," he said looking down the front of her robe at her ample breasts. He licked his lips. "I mean…I might forget for a minute but it's going to come back up."

She kissed his ear and bit his lobe. "What's going to come back up?" Pushing in between his legs, she ran a hand down his black gym shorts and felt his erection.

"Sometimes, I think you only mess with me because of him," Johnson said, biting his lip.

Carmen chuckled. "Well *he* is ten very thick inches of…steel."

"A girl's best friend," Johnson said, standing up. "Come on. Let's go upstairs."

Just then, his cell phone started to vibrate on the table. Picking it up, he cursed under his breath before answering.

"Hello," he said, watching Carmen walk in front of him and drop her robe to the floor. Completely naked, she made her way to the back stairwell that led upstairs and turned to look at him.

"God," he muttered.

She smiled and pulled her hair down out of its ponytail.

He rubbed his growing erection and pushed his phone closer to his ear. "Yes sir. I'm on my way."

Hanging up the phone, he walked pulling down his shorts to reveal his gorging manhood.

"I thought you had to go?" she asked, holding on to him as he scooped her up in his arms.

"They can wait ten minutes," he said firmly.

"Ten minutes?" She frowned.

"Beggars can't be choosers," he said, carrying her up the stairs.

14

On the twelfth floor of 201 Poplar, the headquarters of the Memphis Police Department, beyond the reach of the hungry reporters, who were camped out below, Johnson's lieutenant sat patiently waiting for him to arrive while he listened to Director Amway speak firmly with someone on the phone.

When he had come in, Amway was on the phone and had remained occupied, waiting on Johnson's arrival. All he wanted was a minute to ask what the meeting was about. He didn't like going in just as blind as the men that he commanded. A little Intel would have been nice…a common courtesy that any high-ranking officer would have expected.

Still, he was made to wait.

He tried to act as if he wasn't paying attention, but the tone of the conversation between Amway and the mysterious caller had taken on such intensity that it pulled him out of his thoughts and propelled him to move closer to the bathroom door. Amway was inside, holed up and sounding like he was ready to tear his own hair out.

Abruptly, the call ended, and from what the lieutenant could tell, it did not end well. He stepped quickly away from the door and made his way over to the window.

Amway stepped out of the bathroom and wiped his brow. The discussion had obviously gotten the best of him. Sweating profusely, he went over to his desk and dug through some paperwork until he found what he was looking for. Clutching a card in his hand, he looked up as Deputy Chief Magnelli knocked and entered the office.

"Sorry that I'm late," Magnelli said, making his way over to the coffee pot percolating in the corner. Dressed in a golf shirt and khakis, he looked at Lieutenant Thomas and nodded. "How are you, Bill?"

"Fine, sir," Thomas answered quickly. He swallowed hard, realizing that this was a meeting of top brass and for the first time, he was a part of it.

"Is Johnson on the way?" Amway asked shortly.

"Yes, sir. He should be here any minute," Thomas said, looking at his watch.

"I need to remind Phyllis to order me some more damned cards," Amway said absently. He grabbed a pen and wrote something on the back of the card that he had fished off of his cluttered desk.

"Damn, your office looks like when you were a detective," Magnelli joked with Amway.

Thomas smirked, but didn't dare make a sound. He knew that he was mostly here just to observe.

"Lately, I've been feeling like that's where I'd prefer to be. Do you know since this shit went down with Agosto, I've given out more cards, gotten more fucking emails and phone calls from people who want to weigh in on the situation." Amway rolled his eyes. "It's ridiculous. And I just got off the phone with the mayor."

"He wants an update?" Magnelli asked.

"No. He wants the case solved. He wants Agosto's head on a plate. He wants Memphis' name cleaned up and he wants it all done today," Amway answered, irritated again.

"He wouldn't be the mayor if he wasn't asking for the world," Magnelli said, revealing his politician-like demeanor.

"Where are you coming from, the golf course?" Amway asked Magnelli after he finally noticed his attire.

"Damn near drove off the green in the cart straight to the office," Magnelli answered.

"Well, I wouldn't know what that's like. I haven't had an off day since Agosto made the news."

Magnelli's chest immediately swelled. He knew that his boss was implying that if he hadn't taken a day off, neither should he. "Sorry, I don't make your salary. A day off is the only way that I keep my sanity."

Amway's eyes narrowed. "You make enough to skip a day on the green so that we can solve this case, I'm sure. And the pay never matches up to the fucking responsibility around this place. When was the last time that the mayor called you bitching, complaining and making demands."

"I meant no disrespect, sir," Magnelli said with his nose turned up. Quietly, he wanted to spit in Amway's face. The audacity of the young director made him sick. He had put in years to be able to take off without hearing from some snot-nosed, black boy from the LeMoyne Gardens, who only got tapped to Director because the mayor wanted another dark-face in the administration.

Amway could sense the animosity. Turning around, he looked over at Thomas. "Lieutenant, when was the last day that you had a day off."

Thomas held a breath. Dear God, he didn't want to be pulled into this brass pitching match.

Realizing both men were waiting on an answer, he finally spoke. "I can't remember."

"Even with a four percent cut in pay that the city council just took from us, you still feel the need to put in the work that citizens need?" Amway said, looking over Magnelli with an insinuating glare. He shrugged his wide shoulders. "Well, I guess that some of us get it."

Thomas sucked in a breath, trying to hold on to some oxygen as all the air left out of the room. Talk about intimidating. This was warfare that he really didn't want to be involved with.

The rebuttal was almost immediate. Eye twitching, Magnelli opened his mouth to say something but Amway quickly put the conversation to bed. "End of discussion. I didn't bring you here to discuss this shit."

An interruption came with invited arms. Johnson, in his usual shirt and jeans, opened the door and closed it behind him.

Amway looked over from Magnelli and waved Johnson over. "Have a seat and let's get started." He walked over to his circular work desk where the men were to convene their meeting.

Johnson nodded at Magnelli and immediately thought of Carmen. The old man would have a heart attack if he knew that he was seeing his baby girl. Too bad she wouldn't let him tell him. He could probably convince him that he wasn't a bad guy.

"Do you own anything other than jeans and t-shirts? Shit, Johnson grow up," Magnelli said out of the blue.

Johnson audibly clucked his tongue against the bottom of his mouth. "Didn't know it mattered," he said, looking down at his clothes. "Their clean, freshly washed." By your daughter, he thought to himself.

"The next time I see you, I want you to have a suit on," Magnelli said with a point.

Johnson didn't answer. Maybe Carmen was right. *He would hate him.*

In the middle of the table were newspapers from across the country. The local paper sat atop the pile with Agosto's picture, A1 above the fold.

"Gentlemen, we are way behind the eight ball on the Baby Boys case. Agosto's untimely and very *fucked up* situation has all but buried us in a media hell that we won't likely dig ourselves out of for quite some time. I have people picketing outside downstairs, as you could clearly see on your way up. They are demanding jail time for a man that I'm not even sure is guilty of anything except getting caught. I have news reporters covering every inch of this man's life and begging me for a statement. I have parents demanding something be done to find the killer or killers, according to Agosto and Johnson's report." He huffed in frustration as he passed the newspapers around the table. "The public relations firm that we have hired to help us in this has recommended several steps in a crisis communications plan. I'm looking it over. But I need action now on this case. We have to find a way to control the message and get back to our job." Even as he gave the directive, he hated sounding like a politician. It wasn't who he was at all, but it was a title that he had to come to grips with or be swallowed by the very people who hired him.

"It would be a lot easier to *control the message* if Agosto hadn't lost his cool," Magnelli snarled angrily.

"Be that as it may, I brought you here to help me make a final decision on either letting Johnson move forward on this case alone, or assigning him a new partner." Amway looked over at Johnson. "Now, normally, this decision wouldn't include you at all, but considering that I did handpicked Agosto, and considering that we need to work extremely hard on the case, I'm going to take your suggestions into consideration."

"Who did you have in mind?" Thomas asked, finally feeling comfortable enough to enter into the discussion. He knew his team well and there were only a few people that he would even consider teaming up with Johnson.

"Detective Cory Hamilton and Lt. Kat Steele come to mind," Amway said, looking over at Magnelli.

"One OCU member. One homicide." Magnelli sat back in his chair and took a deep breath. "My bet would be on Steele. She's sharp, and she'd be able to handle the media."

"I don't think either one would be a good fit," Thomas said, biting his lip. He tilted his head and looked over at Johnson. "I think he can handle this alone."

"Alone?" Amway shook his head. "No offense, Johnson, but at this point, this case is too big for one person."

There was an ally in the room. "Having to catch someone up on this case is going to slow things down.

Plus, Johnson would still be the lead," Thomas defended.

"I'm worried that he might not be mature enough to handle this alone," Amway added. His reservations were evident in his tone.

Johnson frowned. "In what way?"

"Johnson, you're a good cop but I mean you did come to a news conference in jeans and a damned t-shirt. I need someone who can represent the police department and build confidence in the citizens."

"Agosto wore a suit to the news conference, right?" Johnson asked, feeling Thomas's eyes burning through him. "And yet, here he is on the front of the paper, sir."

"Steele is solid, and she has 15 years on the job. Getting her up to speed won't be a problem," Magnelli said, tapping his pen against the desk. He ignored Johnson's rebuttal altogether. "Plus, she has an unblemished record."

"I guess that it helps from a PR standpoint that she's a woman," Amway said, flipping through her file.

"And it also helps that she's black," Thomas blurted out. He looked around the room at all eyes on him for his obviously awkward statement. Being a southern white guy with blue eyes and graying brown hair, he instantly felt uncomfortable again. *Was black a bad word now?*

Amway turned the page in the file and smirked.

"This case isn't about PR," Johnson said, after he had heard enough. He had to get them to see the bigger picture, but he felt like he was losing them to some popularity contest.

"I don't need to be reminded what this case is about, Johnson." Amway gave Johnson a stern stare. "Where are you with leads?" he asked. "What do we know so far besides the fucking obvious?"

Johnson hesitated. He didn't necessarily mind sharing with Amway but Magnelli rubbed him the wrong way. He simply didn't trust him.

Picking up on his concern, Amway rolled his eyes. "Please don't tell me that you think you've got a mole." He pushed back in his chair and dropped his pen.

Johnson raised a brow and stared at his boss. "That's what I'm telling you."

"This is just great," Amway seethed sarcastically. "Have you reported it to the Securities Squad?"

"No," Johnson said quickly.

"Reason being?" Amway asked.

"I don't have proof and I don't have a name. I'm working on hunches."

"The public already has me literally by the balls. I'm pissing opinions in the toilet and wiping my ass with national newspapers. And you're telling me that not only do I have to deal with this Agosto bullshit, but I now have to deal with another dirty cop on my watch?" His voice reached a high pitch in utter frustration. "I've got cops beating the hell out of gang bangers...one last week busted for running hoes down to the fucking casinos in tunica...two shaking down drug dealers on duty...."

Magnelli interrupted, "Don't forget that dumb shit, Patterson, who got caught having sex on duty."

Amway shook his head. "Yeah, I've got his ass and about 15 more, front and center fucking up for all of Memphis to see and trying to make a damn mockery out of this department. But that's nothing...all that shit is moot if you're telling me that you think there is a cop in on these murders." He had to take a deep breath. The room began to close in on him.

"Well, whoever the bastard is, he's not in this room, so please enlighten us on the specifics of this case," Magnelli said, frustrated. "Maybe we can help you in some way. Closed mouths don't get fed."

Johnson sighed. "We think that the murders have less to do with a single psycho killer and more to do with drugs. Molly was found in the system of each child and then after Agosto leaned on Twist, Twist ended up dead. Cane is a subject of interest but we can't prove anything definitively right now and he's in the wind."

"So you're saying Molly dealers are killing kids? Why?" Amway asked intrigued.

"There is a connection there but we have to find out what. The night that Twist was killed he had a jump drive in his stomach. He swallowed it."

"What was on the jump drive?" Amway asked.

"Well," Johnson narrowed his eyes. "Agosto gave him the FBI's profile report to review. He wanted to find out if one of Twist's dealers knew someone who fit the bill."

Amway rolled his eyes. "Does anyone outside of us know that he was that stupid?"

"No," Johnson said, looking over at Thomas. He hadn't even told him about that part of the investigation.

"And we recovered the jump drive?" Magnelli asked.

"Yes." Johnson wouldn't look at him. "There was another file on the drive when we got it back. It was a WMV file of something, but it was corrupted."

"Are we trying to recover that information?" Amway asked.

"Yes," Johnson answered reluctantly. "But we haven't gotten anywhere yet."

"Call our friend over at the FBI and see if they can help us out," Amway said, writing down a number. "Tell him that I need this favor done quietly."

Johnson took the number. "Yes, sir." He pushed the issue. "The fact that we met with Twist that morning and asked for his help and then he was killed that evening with this thing in his stomach, makes us certain of the connection."

"It's circumstantial at best," Amway said, looking over at Thomas. "So, what makes you think a cop is involved?"

"The perp, DeMario Washington, was planted at the trap house. When he was arrested, he asked for Agosto specifically. Before he…umm…got put on his ass…he told Agosto that he had done what he came to do. Get him off the case."

"And you think DeMario was planted at the crack house by a cop?"

"Yes," Johnson answered directly.

Amway raised a brow. "Why?"

"Someone knew that the place was going to get busted. That someone would have had to be a cop. The NARC unit had been planning that bust for a minute."

"So, it's presumably someone on the NARC Unit?" Amway asked disgusted.

Johnson turned up his lip. "Could be."

The thought disturbed Amway more than he showed. The one thing that he hated most in the world was a dirty cop.

"So, Thomas, Steele or Hamilton?"

"Hamilton," Thomas answered. "This is still a homicide."

Amway looked over at Magnelli. "Steele for you?"

Magnelli shook his head. "The fact that Twist and Cane are involved only drives home the point, don't you think?"

Amway raised his brow and looked at Johnson. "And you want to work alone?"

"I could get more done," Johnson said. "And what if Agosto is cleared?"

Magnelli chuckled facetiously. "Did you see the video, boy?"

"Last time I checked, the MPD didn't hire boys," Johnson snarled at Magnelli.

Amway liked Johnson's spunk but he also knew that he didn't need another hot-head let loose on the city without supervision. "Johnson, I have a meeting in twenty minutes with Councilman Herbert Ferris. You know the name?"

Johnson frowned. "Yeah, I know the asshole. He was the one who suggested the four percent cut in the first place. Plus, he's been gunning for Agosto's head."

Amway nodded. "Well that same asshole has also demanded a civil rights violation investigation from the FBI on Agosto. Needless to say our brother in blue has enough problems of his own just based on the public fit that Ferris has been throwing to prolong his fifteen minutes of fame. Even if Agosto doesn't get fired…he's off this case."

Johnson shook his head in disgust and looked down at the newspaper. *What ever happened to protecting your own?* It sounded to him like they were preparing to stone Agosto in the court square.

"Hamilton worked for Agosto at some point, right? He had him undercover working the Medlov investigation." Amway looked over at Thomas to confirm.

"Yes, sir," Thomas replied reluctantly.

"That case went nowhere, simply because the Medlov clan has more money than God." Amway rolled his eyes. "We were dipped in shit and handed over to the lawyers to feather us every single time that we went after Dmitry. Thank God he finally left the city to go and wreak havoc somewhere else."

Magnelli cleared his throat and tried to act like it disturbed him to have to give his report. "He's back actually, sir. Dmitry and several members of his family arrived back in Memphis about two days ago on a private jet."

Amway hit the table. "Can anything else go wrong?" He took a deep breath and closed his eyes. Several seconds later, he re-opened them. "Alright, that bastard will have to wait. It's going to take a lot more than one detective to infiltrate that shit anyway. I want all eyes on helping Johnson solve this case. We give him all resources that we have and all access. I've got the mayor, the governor, the city council, the county commission and citizens of Memphis on my ass. I need answers and I need results now." He looked at his watch. "Hamilton is a no go, Thomas. I just thought about that. I don't want any close relationships that can be further scrutinized in the public eye. Let's go with Steele. Bring her in and get her up to speed today. You and Magnelli's lieutenant can work on that."

"On it sir," Thomas answered quickly.

"So, I was brought here for what?" Magnelli asked.

"You're staying on for this Ferris meeting. I figure that I need to combat one asshole with another," Amway said, standing up. "Alright men. Let's go."

As Johnson stood up to leave, Amway walked up to him. Offering his hand, he nodded. "Good work, Johnson. Keep focused. We're counting on you."

"Yes, sir," Johnson said with a nod. He felt a card in his hand as he shook Amway's.

"Give that to Agosto for me, will you?" Amway asked in a lowered voice. "And after that, I don't want you to see him anymore until this shit is cleared."

"Yes, sir," Johnson said, putting his balled up fist in his pocket. Quietly, he left the office right behind Thomas. As he opened the door, he saw Councilman Ferris waiting in the common area.

It was going to be a long day.

15

Five days had gone by since the police department had relieved Nicola of his duty. The Securities Squad was in the middle of a very thorough investigation, digging back in Nicola's career and private life from the moment he assaulted the perp until the moment he became a police officer.

In the meantime, he was adjusting to home life. Normally, he always had something to do, somewhere to be. Now, he was at home with his four sons and his wife.

Every news station in the city had been to their home begging for an interview, a statement, an answer to just one of their questions; reporters from the press were hiding out in bushes to get a photo of him as he lurked quietly around his home taking out trash, cleaning the lawn and nailing down windows. The unwelcomed and unwanted traffic had gotten so bad until he had to put up a sign in the front yard warning that trespassers would be *shot on sight*. It did little to build confidence in the community around him. The public saw the sign as his continued use of cruel, brute force to protect his own private interests.

Nicola saw it as the only way to keep people from just popping up on his doorstep with cameras to shove down his throat in the name of good journalism. Plus, he couldn't be sure that someone posing as a reporter might not be someone sent to kill him or his family.

Since they had come home a few days ago, Nicola had gutted their original security system and put another in its place. He had also put in cameras of his own throughout the entire house where he could monitor everything. Huge motion lights had been placed around the perimeter of the house and the few friends he had left on the department sent cars to heavily patrol the area.

Essentially, they were living in a prison. Although it was a nice prison with all the trapping of luxury, it was still a prison.

But he had to keep things tight. He was both prisoner and warden.

As expected, Ivy was going crazy. She had promised not to go into the office for a few days and work from home remotely, but sitting around watching every local station in the city and most of the major networks across the nation cover her husband's story with no regard for the truth was making her insane.

Ivy reminded him constantly of her profession. She knew PR. She knew crisis communications. She had begged him to release a statement. He would not.

She had begged him to do one interview with one of the stations in town she had a good relationship with. He would not.

She had asked him to call in and do talk radio with the most controversial man in radio, because she was certain the public would see his side. But Nicola refused.

He told her every time that she asked that he was waiting on the investigation to be over. According to him, *the police had a gag order until then*. But Ivy felt that by the time that this was all over, his silence would have destroyed his image and any chances of a career forever.

She pleaded with him daily, he said no to all of her suggestions and even a few of her demands.

The kids had been taken out of summer camp and were confined to the house also. Just the thought of the perp making good on his promise to hurt the children and then leaving them in a position to be vulnerable was simply out of the question for Nicola.

They would stay where he could protect them at all times.

Buried in buttermilk biscuits, salmon croquettes and bacon at the moment, he sloshed around the kitchen swinging cabinets open and closed while the boys argued at the table.

"I didn't eat my booger," Madison yelled at his twin brother. He slammed his small fists against the table. "I don't eat boogers. It's gross!"

"Yes, you did," Adamo said emphatically. His eyes narrowed like his father's and brow furrowed. "I saw you eat it. You munched it up and then swallowed…" He quickly played out the gross action with his finger, sticking it into his mouth. Nicola had always said that Adamo would be a cop when he grew up. He was always the one that Nicola could depend on to give an even, accurate account of any situation - how something was broken, what happened to a toy, who did what. The boy seemed to be unable to tell a lie.

Their little brothers laughed at them as they became more heated, but Nicola ignored them all. With is ear buds pressed tightly in his earlobes he fixed six plates of breakfast food, deaf to the war brewing at the table. He had learned not to get enthralled in what he called kiddie politics.

"Take it back *booty* head," Madison demanded, throwing a fork across the table and hitting his brother in the forehead.

"Ouch! I'm not taking it back, but I am telling Mom, cootie breath. She told you to stop eating your boogers."

The smaller twin boys laughed again. They recited the words in unison. "Cootie breath, booty head." With a naughty snicker, they pointed at both of their big brothers, gazing out past their heavy, curled lashes and green, sparkling eyes. It was exciting to them to watch the Titans of their childhood fight for dominance.

"Well, if you tell Mom that, then I'll tell her that you snuck and watched Cartoon Network after bedtime," Madison snarled. "And you'll be in as much trouble as me you little snitch."

Adamo sucked in his frustration and thought hard for a moment. Finally, he squared in on his brother. "Fine, then we'll both get in trouble, but I'm telling," he promised.

Pulling the ear buds out of his ear, Nicola looked over at the table and surveyed his sons. "What's going on here?" he asked, knowing without knowing that something was wrong.

Both boys pointed at each other and began to tell.

"Adamo snuck and watched Cartoon Network after bedtime," Madison yelled first.

"Maddy won't stop eating his boogers," Adamo screeched.

"Save it for your mother," Nicola said, putting the plates in front of the boys. "Eat up. You're too skinny."

"We're not skinny," the youngest said. His voice sounded like a mouse as he squeaked at his father.

Nicola cut a smile and looked over his boys. The sight of them, carefree and happy made him proud.

Despite the war brewing outside of his door, his boys still loved him. They were still happy, still unaware of how loathed their father had become.

Grateful for the moment, he ran his hand over each boy's head. "You are skinny sticks, boys. You won't be men until you've eaten."

The sound behind him let him know that Ivy had entered into the kitchen. He turned around and looked over at her. She was wearing her normal loungewear of pink running shorts and a green Nike t-shirt with her hair pulled into a ponytail.

"Are you off your conference call?" he asked.

She looked in the refrigerator for a bottle of water and cut her eyes at him. "It's ridiculous that you won't let me go to work."

"You are working," he said, shaking his head.

"I've got my own career to think of, Nicola." She slammed the door and turned to walk back out of the kitchen.

"I've cooked your favorite," he said, drawing her back in.

She stopped in her tracks, stomach burning to its core.

"I'm not hungry," she lied.

Nicola walked up behind her and kissed her shoulder. "Are you sure about that?" He ran a hand over her stomach. "If you're not hungry, maybe she is."

Despite her many frustrations, Ivy couldn't help but smile. "Flattery won't get you anywhere this morning, Nicky. I want to go to work." She stopped. "Scratch that. I need to go to work."

"Is it so bad being here with us?" he asked playfully.

"Horrible," she said sarcastically.

"You go back tomorrow. There is no need to pout today," he said, pulling at her arm. "Now come eat with me and the boys. We miss you. You've been locked in that damned room working all day."

Unable to deny all of her men at the same time, she turned on her heels and followed her husband to the kitchen table where the boys waited.

As soon as they sat down at the table by the beautiful morning view of blue skies and chirping birds outside of the bay window, Nicola's phone dinged with a text.

Ivy raised a brow immediately, forbidding him to even look at it. He hesitated at first, his gut telling him that it was important. But the urgency of her snarl made him question if he would survive the aftermath of digging in his pocket for it.

"Let us pray," Nicola said with a smirk.

The children and Ivy bowed their heads and clasped their hands together.

Nicola began, "Lord…"

The phone dinged again.

Nicola sighed. "*Please* Lord, bless us for this food that we are now about to receive…"

The phone rang.

"Shit!" he exclaimed.

"Nicky!" Ivy snapped.

He put up a finger. "Baby, just hold on one minute." He reached down and pulled out his phone. He was about to turn off the ringer when he saw the text. "DeMario's mother and lawyer are holding a news conference at The Med right now. Turn on your television." It was from one of his friends, Cory, in his old unit.

"Damn it," Nicola said, standing up. "Where is the remote?"

"Probably in the counter drawer where it always is," Ivy said, frowning. "What's wrong?" She turned in her chair to watch him, her fingers clasping the back of the chair.

"The perp is having a news conference," Nicola growled, walking over to the counter. He opened the drawer and pulled out the remote. Turning on the television in the nook near the table, he leaned against the counter and smacked his lips.

As soon as the television clicked on, DeMario's mother appeared on the screen standing beside her lawyer while her son sat in a wheelchair. The live shot was a horrid reminder of what the media was capable of.

"Look at him up there like a fucking victim," Nicola said, feeling his blood boil.

"Oooh, Daddy," Adamo said, shaking his head. "You're cursing."

Nicola turned up his lips into a smirk. "Thanks for stating the obvious there, chief."

"Shh!" Ivy said, leaning into the television. "Turn it up. I can't hear."

"It's all lies anyway." Nicola pressed hard down on the remote with his thumb taking out his frustration on the button.

DeMario Washington's mother was barely 16 years older than him. Standing at the podium with her lawyer with crimson red streaks in her well-curled mane and false eye lashes that extended nearly an inch out from her face, she nervously read from the paper that had been prepared for her.

"My name is Marquetta Washington. My son, De-Mario Washington, was a victim of police brutality suffered at the hand of the Memphis Police Department," she opened. Her voice quivered as she spoke. Grabbing the microphone to pull it closer, she cleared her throat. "He was beaten within an inch of his life by Sergeant Ni...Nick-cola Agusta, a Vice detective from one of the investigative bureaus ran by the Memphis Police Department under Director Amway."

Nicola bated an eye. "Well, maybe it's not me that's in trouble here. We should be going after Agusta, whoever the fuck that is."

Ivy rolled her eyes but said nothing.

Marquetta took a deep breath and wiped a tear from her eye. "He beat him because of bad intelligence from another police officer that somehow he was the Baby Boy killer, when in fact, he just wanted to share the information that he thought might help solve the case. After a ten minute beating caught on tape by onlookers, my son, DeMario suffered broken ribs, broken teeth, a cracked jaw that had to be wired, multiple abra... abrasion to the face, head and chest. He has a hairline fracture to the skull and a bruised kidney."

Ivy looked back at her husband and frowned. "Did you really do all of that?"

Nicola sighed. "I thought I did more. I guess I'm losing my touch."

"There are reports that my son was carrying a weapon, but he was not. There are reports that he somehow intimidated the Sergeant with information about his family, but my son had never met him before the beating. It comes down to a man in power taking advantage of the disenfranchised because of his skin color and his socioeconomic status." She looked up from the paper. "And we want justice." She looked back down at the paper and gained her composure. "How many of our sons, husband and fathers have to be nearly killed by white officers who hate young black men simply because they wear their pants low or listen to a certain type of music? Why are our children not safe from the very men and women who are trained to uphold the law when no one else will? Sgt. Agusta is a prime example of what the broken system looks like. Letting him walk away without the loss of his job and his freedom for his crimes will be an injustice to all of us. We are humans, not animals. Our children are people, and they deserve to be protected from bigots who look to make examples out of them just because they can't comp...competently do their jobs and find the right people responsible for their cases."

"Oh no she didn't just..." Ivy said, eyes narrowed on the screen.

Nicola turned the television off. "I've seen enough."

She spun around in her chair. "But Nicola we need to watch this to prepare a sound rebuttal through our channels," Ivy said, going into work mode.

"I don't want you involved in this, Ivy. How many times do I have to tell you?" he said, turning around to face the counter to hide the sheer anger in his face. He clutched the marble end with his hands until the white in his knuckles began to show and bowed his head.

Ivy stood up from the table and looked over her children, who watched on confused and mortified. "Babies, will you excuse us?" she said softly with a painted on smile. Walking over to Nicola, she put her hand on his back and led him into the adjoining entertainment room.

"Nicola," she said, taking his face into her hands. "Nicky, you have to let me help you. I can," she pleaded.

He shook his head. "No, I don't want you anywhere near this. Everyone who gets close is going to get burned." He slipped her hands into his own as he tried to talk softer.

"I'm your wife. If anyone should be standing beside you..."

"I know you mean well. I do, but you don't understand what's happening here. This isn't something that can be cleaned up with a media statement and news conference. This isn't something that's going to just go away."

"You don't think that I don't know that?" she asked, eyebrows spiked. "But you can't go at it alone. Now, I can..."

His stance was now protective. "Ivy, you're my wife," Nicola said, eyes blazing, voice in command mode. "I'm responsible for you and for my sons. And I'm telling you that you are not to get involved. I don't want one camera in your face and I don't want one statement out of your mouth. I don't want anyone to know who you are. Do you understand me?"

Ivy blinked hard.

"Do you?" Nicola growled. His voice rose. He wanted an answer now.

Ivy's eyes watered at the sheer roughness of his tone. He hadn't spoken to her like that in so long until she had forgotten what his truly angry tone sounded like.

Shaking her head, she stepped back away from him. "You're a real bastard, you know that? You put us in this position and then you turn around and tell me that I can't do anything about it? That we can't defend ourselves? That we can't tell people that I'm not married to a racist bigot like everyone is accusing you of being? Yes, I understand you. You're setting this entire family up for failure," she said, turning away from him.

Nicola was left speechless. Swallowing down words meant for a harsher audience, he humbled himself.

"Ivy, I'm doing this for your own good," he said, reaching out for her.

Her shoulders went slack as she heard the pain in his voice, still her temper flared with irritation. The conflicting emotions made the room too small to stomach. "Have you ever given consideration to the fact that you can't know what our own good is without allowing us to weigh in on it?" she asked, shaking her head. Walking away from him, she headed up stairs to be alone where she could cry in peace.

Nicola pounced down on the side of the sofa and wiped his tired face. "I know what's best," he answered her. "And as long as I keep you safe, I don't really give a damn about being a bastard."

It was a sign that he was truly angry. Nicola only talked to himself, answered others and formulated plans audibly when he was beyond himself, and only one woman could do that to him.

Drive him crazy.

Make him question everything.

Make him regret.

He heard her feet upstairs as she stomped into the bedroom and slammed the door.

That only meant one thing for him.

The damned couch.

As he heard a slap of a small hand against bare skin from the kitchen, one of his sons began to cry. He was about to go in and check on the boys, who were known to break out in fights, when the doorbell rang.

"Really?" Nicola growled.

Stalking through the hallway to the front door, he peered out to find Johnson, unannounced and unwelcomed again.

He opened the door quickly. "You know that if you get caught here, then your ass is just as suspended as mine, right?" Nicola asked, pulling him in and looking around outside before he slammed the door.

Johnson looked towards the direction of the kitchen as he heard a child crying. "Is everyone okay?"

"I forgot, you don't have kids," Nicola said, locking each metal latch on the wooden door back. The clicking sound of steel echoed down the hall. He rolled his eyes as he turned to Johnson and led him towards the noise. "If they aren't screaming, crying, laughing, eating or making a mess, then normally something is wrong."

Johnson raised a brow. "Sounds like fun."

He could not keep the obvious sarcasm out of his voice. He listened closer and realized that he heard multiple cries coming from what sounded like a football team of children.

They walked into the den, where Nicola took a seat in his favorite reclining leather chair. Johnson sat across from him on the sofa and pulled out the card that Amway had given him.

"The Director told me to give this to you," Johnson said, looking at the name on the back of the card one last time.

Nicola took the card and flipped it over. Reading the name, he released a long exhale and nodded. "Okay," he said, biting down on his lip.

"What the fuck does that mean?" Johnson asked, intrigued.

Nicola looked at his watch and stood up. Walking over to the small bar carved into the corner wall and poured himself a shot of Gentleman's Jack.

Johnson watched his partner as he poured a second shot. "Hey, I'm not opposed to an early morning drink. Don't get me wrong. But I at least like to know what I'm drinking to."

Nicola brought the shot glasses back to his chair and sat down. Passing one to Johnson, he raised it. "Here's to a great fucking career."

Drinking the alcohol down quickly, he rested his head back on the chair.

Johnson was even more confused now. After taking the shot, he put the glass down on the coffee table beside him and rested his elbows on his knees. "Your career? I don't understand. What does Tate mean?"

"Lt. Craig Tate, a damned fine cop, lost his job after he beat the shit out of the State Senator's son. Keep in mind that this cokehead had it coming, but the powers-that-be went after his job, and there was nothing that he could do. After the police department fired him, he tried to sue and get his job back, but the guy was just out on his ass. He lost his pension and everything. End of story. End of career." Nicola smacked his lips together and gave a crooked half grin. "Amway just let me know what I've thought all the while. They are going to fire me."

Johnson's face mirrored his disbelief. Shifting in his seat, he quipped his mouth to say something but was lost for words. Taking a deep breath, he ran a hand over his head and looked at Nicola. "So, what are you going to do, man?" His voice was low and even as to not alert anyone who might pass by the doorway.

That was the million-dollar question for Nicola. What was he going to do? For the first time in his life, he felt like an outsider to the only thing that he had truly felt a part of except his family. The Memphis Police Department had shunned him.

"I have to take things into my own hands," Nicola said finally. His eyes glinted with malice.

16

At near dusk, Carmen closed the back door of her Jeep Cherokee after her daughter, Laila, had slowly slipped out with her teddy bear. Locking hands, they walked up the long drive to her father's house. It was Thursday night, and her mother had planned their normal bi-weekly dinner to get everyone together for something other than police work.

With Deputy Director Magnelli and Carmen both on the police department, their schedules conflicted on a regular basis, so Sunday dinner had long gone out the window. But Mrs. Magnelli was getting older and wanted to be around her family more, especially with her granddaughter growing so fast.

It had taken some finagling, but she had gotten them to agree, despite their differences, to cancel all plans once every two weeks to see each other and catch up on things outside of the police department.

As soon as Carmen opened the front door, she inhaled the aroma of a feast slaved over by her mother for hours, maybe even days before. Her daughter, happy to see her grandparents, went running, while Carmen slipped her purse on the knob of the entryway door and made her way back to the den where the family was congregating.

She came into the den, dragging slowly to the couch. Laila was already giggling and twisting into her grandmother's embrace. "Hey, you guys," she said, leaning over to kiss her father's forehead. "What are you old people up to?"

He looked up and grabbed her with one arm. "Hey, princess," he said, happy to see his daughter. "Just getting older, I suppose."

"Ma," she said, walking over to kiss her mother, who was already in the throes of hugging her granddaughter.

"Hi, sweetie," Mrs. Magnelli said with a smile.

"Dinner smells good. I can't wait to dig in," Carmen said, looking over at Collin. "What brings you out?" she asked, eyes narrowed.

Collin was the black sheep of their small family—an indiscretion from her father's early years on the force.

"Just figured that I'd come out and see you guys," Collin said, standing up from the chair in the far corner.

"I can grab a chair from the other room," Carmen said, bidding him to sit back down.

"Don't be silly. I don't mind," he said, offering the last seat in the room. "I'm good. I was just going to the bathroom anyway."

Excusing himself out of the room, Collin could feel his stepmother's eyes on his back. She still hated him after all these years, resented him for existing.

Carmen took the seat and looked over at her father with a what-the-hell glare on her face.

Without acknowledging his daughter's unstated question, he scratched under his double chin and growled. "Well, now that we're all here, we can probably start dinner. I don't want to keep everyone out all night, Bobbi," he said to his wife.

Mrs. Magnelli nodded and stood up. Taking her granddaughter's hand, she smoothed out her skirt and went to put out the last of the food on the table.

"Why don't you help me, Laila?" Mrs. Magnelli said, trying desperately to keep her attention on the one positive thing in her life at that moment. She gratefully held on Laila's small hand and walked out of the room, hoping not to run into Collin as she headed into the kitchen.

When Carmen was sure that her mother and half-brother were out of ear shot, she pushed towards the end of her chair and whispered loudly. "Daddy? Why is he here?" she asked.

Her uncle and aunt kept quiet, though their faces told her that they too knew the strain Collin's presence presented.

"He called and said that he wanted to see us," Mr. Magnelli answered without lowering his voice. "The boy is part of this family."

"I never said he wasn't, but Mom…" Carmen looked over at the doorway again. "Mom is going to throw a fit later and you know it."

"Your mother will be fine," Mr. Magnelli said, voice sterner now. He stood up from his reclining chair and turned off the television.

Carmen curled up her lip and dropped the conversation. "If you say so," she added as one last stab at him.

"I just said so," Mr. Magnelli said, shaking his head.

Rolling her eyes, Carmen threw up her hands and followed her father out of the room. Quietly, they walked into the dining room where all the food sat waiting on them.

"Mom, this looks great, but you didn't have to fix so much," Carmen said, pulling her chair out.

"I'm going to take some over to the McKinney's tomorrow. Albert has been sick for a week now and poor Marge is exhausted from taking care of him," Mrs. Magnelli said, setting a final dish on the table.

"You're a saint," Carmen professed sincerely. She looked over at her father and hoped that he knew the same. Her mother slaved day-in and day-out to give him the best home life that she could. Traditional to her very core, her mother, Bobbi had been devoted to her father since the day that they were married. And still their marriage had been rocky, mostly because her father had a wandering eye…among other things.

Collin entered into the dining room with a smile on his face, looking at the food on the table.

"Looks great, Mrs. M," he said, pulling out a chair.

"Thank you, Collin," she said, making herself smile. "Well, let's not stand here looking at dinner. Honey, why don't you say the prayer so we can eat."

Mr. Magnelli quickly bowed his head, wanting to get this night over with quickly. "Let us pray," he said, making the sign of the cross.

***

There uncle and aunt announced their goodnights as Collin thanked Mrs. Magnelli after dinner for pouring him a cup of coffee as he sat with his father and sister at the dinner table, full and ready to end the evening. With her granddaughter behind her, she quickly excused herself to the kitchen to start the clean-up process that always took the rest of the night.

Unbuttoning his pants and resting back in his chair at the head of the table, Mr. Magnelli looked over his children and did what he normally did after Thursday night dinner. He divulged confidential information with them in the hopes that they could use it somehow to further their careers. It was the way that family on the police department did things. Shared. It was an old custom, but a tried and true one.

Despite his promise to Director Amway, Detective Johnson and Lt. Thomas, he clasped his hands together, twirling his thumbs around each other and sighed, preparing to get into the details that only three men should have known.

"So, have you all run into any leads that might be helpful with the Baby Boys case? As you've heard, it's all the Director in his infinite incompetency can think about, like there is no other crime in the city." He said it with the true disgust that he had for the darkie. Amway was too young for the position that he had been assigned to and way to inexperienced. The job should have gone to him. And he may no qualms about saying so in private settings.

Carmen cringed. She liked Director Amway and more than that, she respected him. "I don't think that's all that he cares about. I think that's what the city is urging him to make a priority and rightfully so, Daddy," she said, picking up her coffee mug and blowing the contents thoughtfully.

Mr. Magnelli pursed his lips together at his daughter's statement. She continually stayed neutral regarding most of his statements concerning MPD leadership and would not take a hard stance on the things that he most worried about, specifically her buddying up to some of the darker fellows on the force.

He had heard rumors through his many spies, although his daughter had never uttered a word. Ever since she was little she had been a pacifist. He blamed it solely on her mother and her treat-everyone-equally philosophy on life. If the woman had been on the force as long as he had, then she'd know better. There was no such thing as equal treatment or equal rights. Everyone was judged according to their rank, in life, in their jobs, in their community and the lower a person rank's was, the more they paid for their choices.

Mr. Magnelli looked over at his son, a brooding, muscular mutt of a boy with more genetic code than a database. Collin had become a cop to please him, but he had been born and raised in a lowly neighborhood off Jackson Avenue. His mother had lied to him when they were together, told him that she was older in hopes of getting her hoods buried deep down in him and being saved from her shot-gun home and waitress job.

It had almost worked. Her bright blue eyes and wide hips nearly convinced him to leave his Bobbi. Nearly. He was pulled back into his senses, however, by his father, *God rest his soul*, who reminded him that he was a Magnelli and the Magnelli men did not run off and leave their wives for non-Italian white trash.

He didn't get out completely Scott-free, however. Collin had been born amidst an excruciatingly painful part of his marriage and a trying time on the force. The boy's existence damn near cost him everything. And even after 29 years, his face was still a sore reminder of 18 years of child support, countless years of marriage counseling and still very little true trust between him and his wife. Maybe that was why he never legitimized him until after Amylyn's death when it was necessity.

Although it had been hard on Collin, Mr. Magnelli was glad and relieved when his mother, Amylyn, had overdosed on heroine. For the first time ever, he happily took the boy in and raised him for his last few years of high school before he quickly sent him to the military hoping that he'd never return.

Collin did, however, return. He came home after receiving a medical discharge and joined the police department.

Now Collin worked on the DEA task force - a job that he had to secure on his own. He was one of the MPD contacts on the team and a quiet worker bee. Collin was never lauded and praised or reprimanded. He simply stayed out of the way and did his job.

Mr. Magnelli, however, did every once in a while throw him a bone, in the form of good Intel, and he would in turn suck up all the information that he could get from his children.

He waited now for some response, but Carmen, normally the first to talk twisted up her lip and shrugged her shoulders. "I haven't heard a thing, unfortunately. Are they going to put Agosto back on?"

Mr. Magnelli had no clue that his daughter was the one sucking up information for once. Nodding his head with a frown, he confirmed her suspicion. "Amway said that he's out. The official decision won't come down for a few days but the investigation is basically over."

Collin's eyes lit up. "Wow, they are really going to can him, huh?" He finally took a sip of his coffee. "Does he know it, yet?"

"I think Amway sent word through that hooligan mutt Johnson."

"Why do you call him a hooligan?" Carmen asked protectively.

"Because he is. The damn boy has never heard of a decent suit. He always walks around in jeans and t-shirts, but he wants someone to take him seriously," Mr. Magnelli huffed. "He's the type, you know. He watched too many of those fucking Die Hard movies as a kid and thinks that he's one of the cool ones."

"He seems smart," Carmen said with a frown. She tried to readjust her wording, worried that her true emotions for her pseudo-boyfriend might show. "Everyone says that he's worked his ass off on this case. He's given 100 percent."

"What is this, a Friday night ball game? We're not talking about a person's personal best here. We're talking about dead children and the possible connection to a drug dealer name Cane and his dead business partner."

Collin's eyes narrowed. "Rodney Cane?" he asked.

"I'm sure that you've heard of him," Mr. Magnelli said, turning to Collin. "And I don't have to tell you that this is confidential…"

"When have I ever said a word?" Collin interrupted. "I just wonder if I might be able to get you some info on the guy."

"Unofficially, Amway wants Johnson to bring him in and get some answers on his whereabouts the night the other dealer was killed," Magnelli said. "Do you happen to know where he might be?" His eyebrow raised in sarcasm.

"I can definitely put a filler out and see if anyone might know," Collin said with a pliable voice.

His father could not give an ill response to the boy's suddenly cooperative nature.

"Do that," Magnelli said, backing off. "It just might be helpful. But only tell me."

"I get it," Collin said with a smirk.

"This isn't going to go over well on the force," Carmen said concerned. "No one believes the man should lose his job. I mean sure, he should get some days cut…"

"He damned near killed that boy," Collin interrupted.

"He kicked his ass. He didn't almost kill him," Mr. Magnelli said with little emotion. "Anyway, it is a damn shame, but there is very little that can be done about it now. It seems that Lt. Kat Steele is coming aboard to help iron things out."

Carmen rolled her eyes. She hated Kat. "I wonder who she had to sleep with to get that job." She looked at her father accusingly.

"Amway suggested her. So maybe he did," Mr. Magnelli lied. "The city is at the point of a riot. If the administration doesn't do something, then Memphis will turn on its fucking ear."

"And firing a good man is the right course of action, I suppose," Carmen said infuriated.

"This is the way of the world," Mr. Magnelli answered. "Do yourself a favor and don't pick a man thoroughfare to kick someone's ass on while you're on duty and don't get caught on fucking camera doing it. The guy was an idiot."

"Would you have done something if a man knew the most intimate details of your life and threatened to kill us?" Carmen turned the tables on her father.

It didn't take Mr. Magnelli but a second to respond. "I would have driven him out to the river, tortured him and put a bullet in his head."

With that Collin stood up. "Well, folks. It's been a blast, but I've got to be up early in the morning."

"Don't we all?" Mr. Magnelli asked.

Carmen glared at her brother with a suspicious eye.

A smile tugged at the right side of his mouth. "And I have to go and see a nice young lady who is waiting for me for a night cap," he said more to his father than his sister.

"The truth will set you free," Mr. Magnelli said, nodding. "See you later. Call me if you hear anything."

"Will do," Collin said, bolting out of the house.

As soon as he was safely in his car and pulling out into the streets, he used his track phone and dialed the number he had memorized three weeks ago.

"Yeah," Cane answered on the first ring.

"Agosto's out. You don't have to worry about him anymore," Collin said with an evil grin. "But the bad news is that they want to bring you in for questioning about Twist."

"Find the bitch, will you," Cane growled. "And get to DeMario. Christ! How hard is it to get to a fucking meth head at a hospital? I want him dead before he trips up."

"I'm working on it. I'm going to need your boys to get it done though," Collin said, pissed that the news hadn't changed Cane's attitude towards him.

"Good. Now that Agosto is no longer a boy in blue, we'll get to his ass too. No more loose ends. This deal is going down in a couple of weeks, and I don't want it fucked up by a renegade cop, a snitch whore or some meth-head gang banging nigger. Do I make myself clear?" Cane asked, nearly screaming on the phone.

"Crystal," Collin answered, hanging up the phone.

***

Cane slammed the phone down and sucked his teeth. Without even looking across at his business partner, he knew that the middle-aged black man was seething over his nigger-comment. Picking a bag of newly manufactured pill in the weighed baggy, he passed it carefully over to the man as an unspoken peace offering.

"We don't have much time to pull this off, Ferris. I hope that you took heed to our previous discussion and will only use this shit on the adult-persuasion," Cane said, looking over at Councilman Ferris.

Councilman Ferris took the small baggie and pushed it down into his suit pocket. "This won't be used at all for the time being. I'm stockpiling for a rainy day," he said with arrogance in his voice. "Outside of the loose ends so aptly discussed on the phone with Magnelli, are we on schedule for this thing to actually happen?"

"There is one other thing. I need guns…well more guns," Cane corrected himself.

"Why do we need more guns?" Councilman Ferris asked, irritated by the amount of his own resources he had been forced to use since their partnership took effect.

"I'm about to take over the entire Molly drug operation for six states. We've got this huge fucking facility to run out here in the damn sticks and I need to be able to protect our investment."

"So, what's your plan?" Ferris asked, unamused so far.

"There is a guy," Cane said, wiping his hands before he walked away from the conveyor belt. Ferris walked beside him with the bodyguards following closely behind. "His name is Anatoly Medlov. He's a fucking Russian."

Councilman Ferris stopped in his tracks. "He is the fucking Russian. I don't know a damned thing about organized crime except that this scheme of yours is going to get me elected Mayor in the upcoming primary. But even I know that the Medlov family doesn't make good bedfellows. Do you not remember the damn fiasco a few years ago? They reportedly blew up and/or burned down half of downtown in a crime war. Plus, word was that he was gone."

"Well, he's back," Cane said, unmoved by the councilman's skittishness. "And I've coordinated a meeting with him for tomorrow. I need to make a deal for some clean weapons. And he's the only game in town, so they say. The son-of-a-bitch done ran out everyone else, 'kept this up and coming good ole boy from Tipton county. I heard his prices are higher though. If Medlov and I can't see eye-to-eye, I'll go to him."

"Why would his prices be higher than Medlov's? Seems like the smartest way to enter into a saturated market is to make your prices cheaper. But maybe that's redneck logic," Ferris said, getting back at Cane for his earlier comment.

Cane snarled. "I guess it would be because he can't get them as cheap as the commy can. So, he's got to still make a profit. I don't know why I'm talking market price with you anyway. All you're here to do is rape boys and get elected our next Mayor. Do your job and keep the powers that be occupied and off of my trail."

"Well do your job and get these loose ends tied before the entire operation goes up in smoke," Ferris said, walking out of the door. "By the way, I won't stand for one more of your racist comments, okay? The way I see it, when I'm mayor, I'll be the only thing between the cops and your short and red curlies. And one other thing, the boys like what I do, especially after they've had their medicine. It's all about coming to an understanding."

Cane spit on the ground and adjusted his itching balls. He didn't give a damn one way or the other. "An understanding, huh?" he said, eye twitching. "Call it whatever you want. I just don't want to have to send my boys to clean up anymore of your messes when you have those uppity pedophile parties."

Incensed by Cane's tone, Ferris stormed out of the re-enforced barn door and let it slam behind him. When Cane was certain that he was gone, he turned to his bodyguard and frowned. "How the fuck does that sick bastard know that my ball hair is red?"

17

On a small parcel of property in the heart of downtown Memphis that was neither of Memphis or the US, there was a place that only the most sinister of organized crime bosses dwelled. It was deceivingly attractively with intricate designs that spoke to old world opulence and newly acquired money. Outside of the three-story, black-bricked building with smoky-colored bricks and rod-iron enclosures, there hung black awning over authentic Tiffany windows bearing block-style, red lettering that simply said *Mother Russia*.

Nothing foreboding or intense radiated from the space; in fact it was extremely inviting to tourist and local Memphians seeking authentic Russian faire. But it wasn't just the foreign cuisine or the top-drawer service that brought people to the restaurant; it was the urban legends that surrounded the name. Only a few years back, a blood war between the two Medlov brothers erupted onto the streets of downtown, killing tens of men, some of which were police officers, others who were mob bosses. The singular event caused the family to flee for years in order to repair the damage that was done. However, even in silence, the story only grew both in whispers and online. Photos of the Medlov men were plastered online, claiming ties not to the many businesses that they owned and their billion dollar-empire but to the Russian mafia both in the US and abroad.

Tourists stood outside taking photos of themselves in front of the restaurant and occasionally taking a photo with the Russian-only staff just to boast later about being at an authentic mob gathering. Coincidentally, it also was a cash cow for the Medlov family bringing in more money than any other restaurant in the city. And for that reason, it remained open.

Because of the spectacle that the place had become, most assumed that nothing illegal ever happened at Mother Russia anymore, but it was in fact still the place where most conversations took place. Checked daily by former Spetznaz soldiers and seasoned bodyguards for any and all forms of surveillance and wired with all the latest technology, Mother Russia was the safest place in the city for an illegal transaction. Every single room was wired for sound, filed with cameras watched 24 hours a day by Medlov staff and protected by some of the most dangerous men in the world. It was Dmitry Medlov's personal fort, nearly impenetrable by the law.

When Cane and his bodyguard pulled up to the front of the building and parked on Main Street, he looked across the street at the restaurant and people sitting out on the street tables eating lunch and enjoying the unseasonably breezy afternoon. The first thing that he noticed was the well-placed bodyguards and security men who were mixed with in with the actual patrons.

Sitting under black umbrellas sipping beverages and eating, they watched from all vantage points, dressed in jeans and t-shirts and hiding weapons. The tattoos that lined the arms of some of the men spoke to their mafia ties, specifically the Vory v Zakone. Most of the men were tightly-muscled, in top-shape and seem to all carry a distinctly Eastern European look.

"Is this Medlov a homo? All of his men look like fucking butt-models," Cane said with a hint of resentment in his voice.

His bodyguard chuckled and opened the door. Stepping out, he nodded across the way at one of the men who stood instantly as they made eye contact. "Homo or not, there is a lot of them, boss."

"Don't shit your shorts just yet," Cane snarled. "There is quantity and then there is quality. This guy may have quantity but Ronny up in Tipton has quality."

His bodyguard was not convinced, but quieted down. He knew that his boss was used to being the big man in the room and although he had never seen the Medlov men, he gathered very quickly that today they were surely out of their realm. He had heard things about the Medlov men, things that people in their circles didn't whisper if they didn't carry some truth.

Cane slid on his shades and walked with his men across the walkway of the cobblestone street. "If these commy bastards try to waste my time, we are out of here in ten minutes flat," he told them under his breath.

"Sure thing," his bodyguard answered, noticing two more men who rounded the corner of the building as they approached. These two were even taller, even bigger, and even more Russian. His confidence waned with every step towards the restaurant. He felt as though they were entering into a hornet's nest and that maybe his boss might need to be more careful with his words, though he dared not say so aloud.

One of the men lurking towards the front opened the door for Cane and smiled menacingly as they walked past him. "Welcome to Mother Russia," the man said, voice a deep, raspy baritone.

"Yeah, thanks," Cane said, taking off his glasses. Normally, he was a bit of a sucker for hospitality but coming from this lot, it just seemed off.

The air was chilled in stark contrast to the sticky humidity of Memphis summer weather outside. The aroma of hot, delicious food filled the building. The interior walls were black brick and the floors were black marble. Each of the tables were black wooden with black chairs and red linen table cloths. Each table was topped with votive candles and a single red rose. On the far wall was a picture of Putin and two flags - one American and one Russian. He looked around the restaurant and realized it was much bigger on the inside than it appeared from the outside. Russian music played while redheaded waitresses made their way quickly to tables in black uniforms of pant and black tops. It extended very far back and had rooms carved out for special events. Unlike anything in the city, this four-star restaurant was what others had accused it of being. It was old world and full of mystery.

"Someone will be right with you," the hostess at the front said with a thick accent and cunning smile as the door closed behind them. She was a tall woman, very shapely with fire red hair and crimson red lips. Her blue eyes were like sparkling gems glinting at him. Simply put, she was devastatingly beautiful, more beautiful than any hostess he had ever seen.

"He sure knows how to pick them," Cane's body-guard said as he watched the woman walk away. "I wonder how much it would cost to have her served up on a plate."

"She'd probably cut your fucking throat before you could blink," Cane answered seriously. "The bitch is packing. Did you see the bulge behind her shirt? They're all assassins. The whole lot of them," he said narrowing his eyes at the other women. "He thinks he's the only one who arms his women. Shit, Twist and I were doing that shit before it became cool."

The bodyguard raised his brow. Their women were nowhere near as beautiful as the Medlov women. And nowhere near as well-mannered. Cane and Twist had hired old battle cats, but these women were femme fatales, someone who he wouldn't mind being shot by. Looking over behind the bar in the far right corner, he saw a sign that instantly made him laugh. No guns allowed. He found the sign rather amusing considering the place was front for illegal gun running activity.

A wide-chested, muscular man standing-6'4" walked out of the double doors of the kitchen in a black suit and a low buzz haircut that barely showed the blond in his hair. With blue eyes that matched the hostesses' but a dead glare that rivaled any of the worst criminals that Cane had met, the man approached in a slow, intentionally stalking stride. Almost theatric, he approached the men and then pointed at the bodyguards who flanked them.

"Are you Cane?" the man asked, trailing his gaze over the bodyguard.

His look sent a chill up the man's spine.

"In the flesh," Cane answered with intentionally more southern drawl in his voice. "And you are?" he asked, insinuating that he was not at all intimidated by the man.

The man turned his lip up and tilted his head. "I am Vasily," the tall man answered almost as if he were shocked that Cane had asked. He paused for a minute and then gave a clever smirk. "Come with me," he said, turning on his heel.

"I'm 'bout done with this shit already," Cane said as he walked with his bodyguard and the group of men down the middle of the restaurant to a hallway that led into a private dining room in the back. He thought this little outfit to be Mickey Mouse. After all, they hadn't even bothered to pat him or his man down for weapons or wires. No wonder they had nearly been run out of town.

The room was enclosed by two double doors that were also covered in Tiffany glass. Vasily opened them quietly and stepped to the side for Cane to pass. As his bodyguard walked into the room behind Cane, Vasily put a hand out and placed it square on his chest. "Why don't I take you into the next room and get you a bite to eat," Vasily said, eyes narrowed.

Cane looked back at Vasily and his man and rolled his eyes. "He's with me, big guy."

There was a man sitting at the large dining table reading quietly. Putting down his newspaper, he cleared his throat. "Which one of these men is going to pay for this proposed transaction?" he asked, voice a deep, foreboding Russian baritone that made Cane look over.

"I'm paying for this transaction," Cane answered. Locking eyes with the blond man, who seemed too tall for the table that he sat at, he quickly changed his aggressive disposition.

"Then you are the man that I would like to talk to," the man said with lighter tone. He motioned towards the chair across from him and then picked up his shot glass. "Vasily, bring us a bottle of vodka, will you?"

"Yes, sir," Vasily said, hand still on the man. "Would you mind coming with me," he asked the bodyguard again.

The bodyguard nodded, realizing that the request was really a command. Stepping back from the door, he watched as Vasily closed the door behind him and escorted him to the adjoining room. "You can sit here," Vasily said, snapping. A hostess quickly came in with a menu.

"Welcome to Mother Russia," she said with a gentle smile. She quickly set the menu in front of him with silverware wrapped in a red linen napkin. "I'll be your waitress for today. Should we start you with something to drink?"

"Order whatever you like. It's on us. I'll be back to collect you once the meeting is over," Vasily said, closing the door behind him. Two of the Medlov bodyguards quickly took their post standing at the door. He stopped and looked at his watch and then leaned into the men. "If he comes out of that room and heads towards the boss, kill him," Vasily ordered.

"Da, da boss," the men answered in unison without taking their eyes off the wall in front of them.

Sure that Vasily had made his point, he walked toward the kitchen.

***

There was something very regal about the man in the linen suit sitting in front of Cane. With the air and grace of Lord, he sat relaxed and sure of himself, like the entire world lay at his feet. His demeanor only pissed Cane off more. He hated Euro trash.

"So, I am told by my men that you requested an audience with me," Dmitry Medlov said, running his large hand over the smooth surface of the table.

Cane sat straighter. "Yeah, I need guns and I was told that you were the man to see."

Dmitry smiled proudly. "I'm the only man to see."

Cane turned up his lip. "I wouldn't say the only…"

Dmitry raised a long finger, interrupting Cane. "I am the only man to see," he said again. It wasn't his words that corrected his visitor but his tone. While still gentle, there was a hint of aggression. "Some people confuse what is with what they want it to be. But I would just say this…reality is something that can't be changed just because one wants it to. It has to be changed with action. And in the world of arms dealing, the only action is where I say it is." His eyes were cold like eyes and his tone softened again.

Cane bit down on his lip. "Look, I don't know a hell of a lot about arms trafficking, but I do know a little something about drugs. And they tend to go hand-in-hand."

Dmitry raised his brow. "They can. I've found that weapons tend to go with everything…drugs included."

"So if we were to move away from your first point to why I'm here…" Cane said frustrated.

"But how can we, when they so closely align?" Dmitry looked over as the door opened and Vasily brought a bottle of vodka and two shot glasses. Setting them down on the table in front of the two men, he opened the bottle and poured a shot for both.

"Thank you, Vasily," Dmitry said, lifting his shot glass. "To good health."

Cane realized the threat but still raised his glass and took the shot. The strong contents burned as they slid down his throat, wrenching his esophagus. "Back to what I was saying. I'm looking for guns, military grade."

"Are you preparing for war?" Dmitry asked.

"War? No, you could call it occupation." Cane sucked his teeth. "I want to buy about 500 to 1,000 semi-automatic weapons from you. AKs if you gottem." He scratched his nose and waited.

Lazily, Dmitry looked up from his glass unimpressed. "That's an awfully small quantity for an occupation," Dmitry said with a grin.

"Well, I can always take my business elsewhere," Cane snarled. He didn't like the smug Russian nor his insinuations.

Dmitry smiled. "How is Twist?" He picked up the bottle and poured another shot. "I liked Twist, but I heard a dirty rumor that he was...dead."

"Yeah, Twist got himself shot," Cane said, locking eyes with Dmitry. "Evidently, he pissed off the wrong guy."

"Evidently," Dmitry said, raising a naturally arched brow. He pushed closer to the table with his elbows. "And have you found the person responsible for the murder of your friend. As I understand it, you two were so close, you lived together."

"We lived on the same property. And yes, he was my friend, but no I haven't found the fuckers responsible yet."

"But you are looking?" Dmitry asked. "I only ask this because you said that you were preparing for an occupation not a war and if someone had killed my best friend, I would be preparing for war." Dmitry wiggled his nose. "But that's me."

"Two things bother me about what you just said. One, it sounds like you accused me of being a homo. Second, you accused me of being a coward. Now, where I'm from we don't try to offend potential business partners on the first meet."

Dmitry chuckled. "And where are you from?"

Cane didn't answer.

Dmitry sat back in his seat and looked at Vasily. "Is Anatoly still working?"

"Yes, boss," Vasily answered.

"Good," Dmitry said, standing up from the table. "I'd like to take my friend to meet him." Dmitry looked down at Cane. "Anatoly is my son, but I'm sure that you already know that. He's just downstairs with another gentleman who is in our particular industry of arms dealing. Shall we go and talk more about our possible transaction."

Cane stared at the man in awe. Dmitry looked tall sitting at the table, but standing up, he was an absolute giant. At seven feet in height and nearly three-feet wide with bulging muscles that lined his tailored suit, the Adonis sucked all of the air out of the room with his uncompromising presence. Twin chrome Glocks with pearl handles peaked out of his suit jacket as he motioned towards the door.

Suddenly, Cane didn't want to go downstairs. But he knew that walking out at the moment would only speak to his growing intimidation. He stood from his seat. "Yeah, sure. Lead the way," he said, realizing that the men had not checked him for his weapon. Stealthy, he felt for it.

"There is no need to feel threatened. If I wanted you dead, you'd be dead. If I felt you a threat, you'd be dead. If I felt you a complete irritant, you'd be dead. Right now, I simply want to continue the conversation downstairs. You have my word that no harm will be brought to you," Dmitry said, walking toward the door.

"Course not," Cane said, following Dmitry.

Vasily and his men walked behind Cane on his flank, only inches away. They passed by the room where his bodyguard sat and headed down a steep flight of stairs to an elevator at the end of a dark hall.

Stepping inside, Dmitry made room for Cane. They all stood silently in the elevator for the short descent to the lower floor.

As soon as the elevator opened, Cane heard a man screaming in pain.

Dmitry stepped out first, and slipped his large hands into his pants pockets. "Don't worry. That's not your bodyguard, friend," Dmitry said with a smile.

Cane didn't want to step off the elevator but Vasily was right behind him. He was certain that if he didn't move forward on his own, the man would surely push him forward. He held his composure and followed Dmitry into the sterile room where the screams became louder.

Dmitry stopped at a table near the door and picked up a handful of grapes and cheese on a platter. "Would you like some?" he asked Cane.

"No, I'm good," Cane answered. Ready to get whatever was waiting on him behind the wall.

"I will preface what you're about to see with this statement. Earlier, I made the point of saying that I am the only man to see about weapons. Well, evidently this gentleman out of Tipton County didn't get the memo. You see, if I'm not directly selling the guns, then I'm getting a cut from the guns being sold. That's for every weapon that exchanges hands within a 500-mile radius. Now, my reach goes a lot further than that, but I believe in protecting home first. And the rule is one must pay to play. If they don't," Dmitry shrugged his large shoulders. "Then I have to make an example out of them. You understand this, right. After all, you said you were involved in the nasty business of drugs. It's never been my forte, but hey, everyone can't be me."

Cane swallowed hard as he heard the man in the back scream again as what sounded like a whip slash against his skin.

"My son, Anatoly, has very persuading tactics in the field," Dmitry said, walking towards the loud screams.

Cane followed, knowing that he wouldn't like what he saw behind the wall, especially since he had an idea of who was behind it.

"Anatoly," Dmitry called.

"Da," Anatoly answered shortly.

"We have a guest," Dmitry said, stepping around the wall.

Cane waited, but Vasily urged him forward. He turned the corner to confirm his suspicions. The gun runner from Tipton County was naked and bloody, tied to a chair sitting atop plastic covering the ground. A halogen lamp lit the dark corner with unforgiving light, showing ever lash that Anatoly had inflicted on the man's wounded skin.

Anatoly Medlov stood a few feet away from the man clasping a bullwhip in his hand. He was 6'1" but had the same yellowish, golden hair as his father and the same piercing blue eyes. He wore dark jeans and a black t-shirt, hugging to his taut muscles that were embellished with many tattoos.

Three bottles of vodka sat atop a table right behind him. Turning towards his father, he motioned toward Vasily to take the whip while he put out his cigarette.

"Who is this?" Anatoly asked, blue eyes blazing at Cane like he wouldn't mind putting him under his whip as well.

"This is our friend, Cane. He's interested in buying some military grade weapons from us. Just a small quantity, right?" Dmitry asked, looking over at Cane. "In my opinion it's about both quality and quantity."

Cane caught his breath. The bastards had him under surveillance from the moment that he pulled up. Evidently, their equipment was good enough to pick up even the slightest mumble. He smacked his lips in total supplication.

"So what did he do to deserve to be treated like this?" Cane asked.

Anatoly rolled his eyes again. "I think he's being treated quite well, actually. I believe the words that he used to describe us were commy bastards, if I recall correctly." He spit on the floor. "That's enough in my mind to carve out his liver."

Behind Anatoly, Vasily reached back and unleashed another lash right into the man's chest and across his legs. The man screamed out in agony again, begging for the torture to stop. Tears filled, the blood and gurgling cries filled their ears.

"His pain seems to bother you," Dmitry said, watching Cane closely. He didn't flinch in the man's agony. In fact, he seemed unbothered by it all together.

"I know him," Cane answered, stomach turned.

"I'm sorry. I can't hear you above his screams. What did you say?" Dmitry asked.

"I said that I know the fucking guy," Cane said, unable to look at the beaten man.

Vasily unleashed another unforgiving blow. This time the man begged to be killed.

Dmitry smiled and bit his lip. "I tell you what. I'm a pretty fair man. To be honest, I had plans on keeping him here until his flesh began to rot off his bones. You see, he was attempting to break into the market without my permission. And he was gaining quite the momentum. In fact, it was his growth that caught my attention. Certain people were suddenly not coming to me for their weapons. And I knew that they had to be getting them from somewhere."

The man screamed again as Vasily whipped him, this time across his face.

Cane gritted his teeth.

"But I'll do this for you," Dmitry said, nodding. He narrowed his eyes at Cane. "I'll let you kill him."

Cane snarled.

"If you're not up to it, then he can stay here with me," Anatoly said with a grin. "I like his company."

"Vasily, did you check him for weapons before you allowed him into the restaurant?" Dmitry asked, not taking his eyes off of Cane.

"No. He's got one at his back and one on his right leg," Vasily said, picking up a bottle of vodka. He walked over to the man, pulled the cork out of the bottle with his teeth and poured the contents on the top of the man's head. He screamed out in agony, alcohol seeping into all of his aching wounds.

Cane shook his head. "Fine, I'll do it." He reached under his shirt and pulled his pistol out.

"Smith and Wesson," Anatoly said in approval.

Vasily's men pulled their weapons and pointed them at Cane just in case he decided that he wanted to shoot their bosses instead of the man.

Feeling the weapons and their red scopes on him, he walked up to the man and pointed the gun at him.

"Thank you," the man said, nodding. His mangled face bore the resemblance of a beaten, bloody steak.

Nodding, Cane pulled the trigger three times, ensuring the man was put out of his misery. Stepping back, he quickly put away his weapon and looked up at Dmitry.

"Now it seems that I truly am the only man to talk to," Dmitry said with a grin.

"So 1,000 AK-47s…automatic," Cane snarled.

Dmitry lifted his brow. "Once I check your references."

"My references?" Cane asked infuriated. His voice echoed throughout the room.

"You didn't think that this was where you got to interview me, did you?" Dmitry shook his head. "It's quite the other way around. I never sell to anyone that I don't feel absolutely comfortable with." Turning his back to the man, he popped another tender grape into his mouth. "You'll be hearing from us on our decision."

18

Nicola's old office was covered with papers from the Baby Boys case and a hundred other cases he was either actively pursuing or building upon. Sticky notes, napkins with hand written messages and business cards covered the walls, pinned to corkscrew boards along with photos of people and places. It was a time capsule locked in criminal perpetuity and to most who might see it, a depressing doom of misfortune.

Lt. Kat Steele moved aside a large pile of files from the center of his oak desk, a piece of antique history that he must have had brought in because it didn't fit anything else in the office, and sat down a box of her own personal items to make the space her own, especially now since she would be taking over his old position, including the case of the century. Her mouth watered at the opportunity. This was any detective's dream.

She pushed back his black leather chair and sat down, relishing in joy of her well-deserved appointment. Hmm. This felt good. Running her hands over the armrest, she stopped for a moment and looked at the picture in a wooden frame of Agosto with four small children surrounding him while he sat and a black woman in a yellow sundress on his flank. It appeared that they were aboard a fine yacht off a coast.

Picking the frame up, she looked closer, digesting every detail. To her surprise, all four children were biracial with mocha skin, curly hair and blazing eyes. And they all looked like their father, handsome and stocky, proud and strong. And his wife was extremely beautiful, a bit on the regal side like maybe she'd been highly educated and came from a good family. And Agosto, a man who was normally full of snide remarks and serious policing, was all smiles. Yes, he was actually happy, not just content the way many men she knew were.

Wow. The rumors must have been true.

Nicola Agosto, *the world's newest bigot according to every news outlet in the world*, was married to a black woman. From her vast experience in the dirty south, extreme racists normally didn't do that sort of thing. She found the idea curious and extremely disturbing. Why wasn't Agosto going public about his family? Why wasn't he defending himself against the media and Ferris? Then it hit her. He'd rather go down than expose his family to any more hurt or harm. That was a sobering thought. That made her see him completely different.

She hated a bad man no matter what good he tried to do in the world, but she hated even more a good man being persecuted for a bad choice.

She had heard that definitively, Agosto was out for good. There would be no suspension. He would be kicked out on his ass literally and forgotten by the Memphis Police Department like so many before him. Every case he solved would be forgotten. Every perp he chased, caught and bled to track down will be forgotten.

Every good deed that he did instead of exploiting his position will be forgotten.

Word was also that the Director was extremely troubled about the entire thing, not just because he and Agosto were friends but also because he didn't believe in letting one good man go. In a department where cops were running cars up poles, raping women, having sex in their squad cars, intimidating private citizens and stealing drugs on busts, they needed every, competent good cop that they could hold on to.

However, this was a tricky situation to navigate around. If Amway stepped in and tried to save Agosto, the city would turn on him as well, maybe demand his job. Plus, Councilman Ferris was leading the charge against Agosto, and that was a death sentence in itself. Everyone loved Ferris. He was black, elitist Ivy Leaguer who fought for children's rights and civil rights both as a lawyer and as a politician. Every day he was on the television demanding action like he really cared. The masses of uninformed rallied behind him blindly, unaware of his ulterior motive, but she saw it as clear as day. Ferris was just using this as another opportunity for him to get in the limelight.

Glancing up from the photo and her thoughts, she noticed that out at the desks her new subordinates were whispering and talking. Huddled up together, they shared rancid rumors of how she had gotten her new assignment and chuckled under their collective breath about her private life. Lifting her head and brow at them, she gave one of her seriously intimidating glares, making them disperse without a word.

Nosy bastards.

It had been a long-running consensus on the force that Lt. Steele had climbed the ranks of the MPD one incredible blowjob at a time. And because of her uncanny good looks and truly promiscuous lifestyle, the rumors were believed to be the gospel, negating her stellar record and stats, which rivaled her male counterparts on any given day. However, where other women would have clamored into a ball of insecurities, it only drove her to aim higher, work harder and at the end of the day, rub her successes in everyone's face.

Yes, she fucked whomever she wanted, but she also did her job. So, as far as she was concerned, how was she different from 99% of the male cops on the job? No one had been able to answer that yet. Instead, they judged and they judged harshly.

Getting back to pulling her what-not's out of her box, she took her stare from the masses outside of her new office and focused on trying to organize the messy world of Nicola Agosto into cohesive clues and leads to solve this case. With her head down and her mind now shifted back to its rightful place, she didn't notice Deputy Director Magnelli enter into the office, but the other detectives did. They quickly scattered like rats to their seats, nodding his way as the *Big Brass* came down the aisle in full uniform, shaking things up with every step.

If he was the guy who had appointed her, then she was here to stay. Magnelli was a top cop, a tough cop and respected man and to have his blessing was the biggest of deals.

Stepping into the office, he tapped the door to get her attention and then closed it behind him.

Lt. Steele looked up surprised and broke a sly smile. Quickly, she pushed away from the desk to stand up. "Sir," she said with extreme reverence.

"Don't get up," Magnelli said with a warmness in his voice that spoke to their ongoing relationship. He raised his right hand slightly to halt her.

Lt. Steele tilted her head. "Don't you think it would look odd if I did not?" She stood up anyway and made her way over to shake his hand.

He grabbed it gently and caressed her long fingers. "Are you getting settled in?" he asked. Her heart-shaped lips covered in a red-matte lipstick stole his attention.

"I am," she said, holding his hand longer than she knew that she should have.

Releasing her, he took a seat in front of her desk and watched her as she made her way behind it again. Seeing her long, limber body neatly tucked into her black slacks and white oxford with her gun and badge hoisted securely on her hip, made him incredibly hard. He licked his lips and made a mental note to see her later that week for a *private encounter*, one that had been on the books for weeks but unable to be satisfied because of their hectic work schedules.

"Do you have everything that you need to hit the ground running?" he asked, sweeping her body with another insinuating glance. Damn, he wanted her bad. Maybe it was her sweet perfume or her cat-like brown eyes staring at him like she wanted him as badly as he wanted her, or maybe it was her perfect features, her caramel skin, her thick perfect brows or pouty mouth, the curve of her chin or the snooty little tip of her nose. Kat Steele was an angel to look at but a devil in the sack. Voluptuous and athletic, a hellcat to fight and an even bigger hell cat to dominate, the woman before him was all that he had wanted in a woman, pity he couldn't have her for real. For now, they simply satisfied each other's needs as often as they were given the chance.

"I do have everything. Thank you. I won't let you down on this case," she said completely professional. "I'm meeting with Johnson as soon as he arrives. I want to go after this Cane fellow today and start to beat the streets until someone talks." She sat erect in her chair, breasts pushing at the fine cotton of her shirt. "Plus, I want to have a word with DeMario."

"DeMario?" He didn't like the sound of it.

"He was accused of having pertinent information to the case. I want to know what that is. I'll make sure that it's cordial…kid's gloves and all that. But the man has to be interviewed. If he knows something, then we need to know it."

"Just make sure that his lawyer is present," Magnelli said nodding. "One look at you and he might not mind answering a few questions."

"That's the idea," she said, unashamed that she used her looks in the field to get farther with interrogations than the men.

"Good," Magnelli said, assured that she'd do a good job. "Amway and I have confidence that you all will solve this case and put the department back in a good light with the public."

She nodded. "That is my intention."

"Should you get any push back from Johnson or any of the men, you call me. I'll see to it," he said, protectively.

"Don't worry. I know how to handle myself."

"Yes, you do," he said with a sexually frustrated sigh. "What does your schedule look like later in the week?"

"Open," she answered with a devilish slow grin. "Just call me. We can meet at our normal place."

Chills ran down his arm and goose bumps formed. Suddenly, he was imagining her naked and coiled around him again.

"Good," he said, standing up. His hard-on outlined his pants. "Then, expect a call for an update." Pushing down his pants discreetly, he nodded and stuck out his hand. "Lieutenant."

"Before you go…" she said with a frown. Taking the photo, she passed it to Magnelli. "Did you know about this?"

Magnelli took the photo and looked at it. "Know about what?"

"He's married to a black woman," she said, stating the obvious.

"Of course I know." He sat the photo down and looked at her, clearly seeing how the fact that he was Italian and she was black had some bearing on how she saw Agosto. "It's not my decision any more than it's yours, Kat." He rubbed a hand over hers. "Stay focused and get the job done, okay."

She nodded, even if she didn't like what she was hearing. "Okay."

"Good girl. I'll see you later this week." With that, he turned on his heels and headed back out of the door, airs back on and broad chest back out. She watched him as he disappeared out of sight and then deflated against her chair.

***

Nicola had been on the phone with his parents for nearly an hour. He listened to them as they argued with each other on the phone and then tried to talk to him. Wanting to run his head into the wall, he sat down on the top stair of the staircase and looked down at the first floor.

"Dad, what would I do at the company?" he asked, running a hand through his wild hair. It felt oily from not showering. Rubbing his fingers together, he made a note to shower and while he was at it…shave.

"You have an MBA for goodness sake," Mr. Agosto said, hitting his newspaper on his large granite desk. "There are a hundred things you could do here." He looked out the windows of his corner office at the Miami bay.

Nicola tried to reason with the man. "I have a degree that I've never used. I'm a cop."

"Marketing is common sense," Mr. Agosto argued back.

"Ivy is the one with the brains for that kind of thing anyway. I don't even know how to Tweet or twit or whatever." He sighed into the phone as he heard small footsteps run past him at Mach speed. "Stop running!" he yelled out without even turning around.

"Your father's right. There is nothing there in Memphis for you and those people….have you watched the news? They are making you out to be a monster," his mother Liz said in a high octave.

Nicola shook his head. His mother was an emotional worrywart, and the last thing he wanted was to get her involved in the conversations about what he planned to do post-PD.

"Well, have you spoken with the press at all?" His father asked.

"No," Nicola answered shortly.

"Why not? This is getting ridiculous," Mr. Agosto growled.

"I am waiting for the final findings from the Securities Squad," Nicola explained.

"But you just said that unofficially you're out," Mr. Agosto's voice growled. "That city never deserved you anyway, son. You have given everything. And for what? You could have been making millions just like your brother, Santo. He's made quite a good life for him and Arin here."

The last thing that Nicola wanted to talk about was his brother's success, not that he was jealous of it, but considering his own situation, it wasn't exactly helping his morale.

"How are the kids?" Liz asked. Worry laced her small voice. "I haven't spoken to them since last week. Normally, Ivy calls me, but with everything that is going on and the fact the poor thing is pregnant…" She cringed at the thought. The news of a new Agosto was supposed to come with gleeful and joyful celebration, not hampered by a murder investigation.

"Really, son, you should think of your wife," Mr. Agosto said, intending a guilt trip on Nicola. "Maybe living in Miami would be better for her, especially in her state."

"Ivy is fine. She just went back to work today after being off for over a week. She was about to go crazy in this house. You don't know how she is. Once she sets her mind to a thing, it's done. It would be easier to try to re-write the constitution. Plus, she loves her job.

She's been there for years and she's moved up. And the boys are fine. Hold on and I'll get them for you and you talk to them until you're blue in the face," Nicola said, standing up. He could hear his sons rolling around in the playroom fighting and scuffling down the hallway. He had a mind to tear into their asses.

Ignoring his son's statements, he continued. "We need someone to run our operations at the company. We've expanded and..."

Nicola cut his father off. "Dad, once I know something, I'll give you a call about job opportunities, but right now, I need to focus on staying here. Ivy's job means a lot to her, and I doubt that she'd be interested in just walking away from it because of me."

"Well, we need a new marketing exec too," he said, willing to compromise in any way possible to get his family closer to him in his old age.

The doorbell rang, saving Nicola from a continued conversation.

"Hey, there is someone at the door. I'll have the kids call you back, okay?" Nicola said, walking slowly down the stairs.

"Okay, we love you son," Mr. Agosto said sincerely. "If there is anything that you need..."

"I'll call. Promise. Love you guys too," Nicola said, hanging up the phone.

The doorbell rang once more before Nicola got to the door.

"Coming!" he said, looking through the peephole. It was a woman. Probably a desperate reporter.

He eyed his gun, sitting on the top rack of the hat shelf, tucked under a scarf, before he opened the door, just in case. To his surprise, it was Mrs. Naples, the mother of the twin boys who had been murdered. She looked even more worn down than the day that he had broken the news to her about her boys. In a pink cotton t-shirt and a pair of jeans with her hair pulled back in a loose ponytail, she appeared to have aged dramatically within a few weeks. With cracked dry lips and no make-up on, she tried to smile when she saw his face.

"Lt. Agosto," she said, eyes red and puffy like she had been crying for days.

"Mrs. Naples," Nicola said, opening the door wider. "Please, come in." Quickly, he stuck his head out of the door and looked around, praying that no media was lurking around.

He closed the door and tried to straighten his clothes. He didn't look much better than her in his black Nike jersey shorts and his sleeveless, orange Nike t-shirt.

"Please come and have a seat," he said, walking her to the living room.

She looked around his house in surprise. Even in the mist of her trauma, her face was awash with the same curiosity that most people had when they visited his home for the first time.

"You have a very lovely home," she said, following him into the perfectly designed room.

He offered her a seat on the sofa and moved a toy police car on the cushion. "Thanks," he said, hearing his kids running upstairs. "Can I offer you something to drink?" It was odd, but the sound of his boys laughing and playing made him feel guilty.

"No, I'm fine," she said, trying to smile again. "Your house looks like it fell out of Southern Living."

He grinned. He had heard it a hundred times before but he could take absolutely no credit for it. "My wife has what some people call *an eye* for that type of thing." Unsure if he should sit or stand, he walked over to the fireplace and leaned against the mantle. "So, what brings you to my home, and how did you find it?"

"I could have easily found it on the County Assessor's site, but it's available online as well on a bunch of forums. There are tons of people rallying to…" she didn't finish her sentence. She didn't want to tell him that people were suggesting going to his house in protest.

Nicola raised a brow. "Well that's disturbing."

She reached into her purse to pull out something and Nicola quickly stopped her. "I don't mean any harm, but sudden movements make me uneasy," he said, face pensive.

"It's just a photo of my boys," she said, slowly pulling out two pictures of her twins. "I know what they are accusing you of, but I don't believe it."

Nicola didn't know what to say. He walked over and took the pictures. Running his hand over their faces, he put down his head. "I never meant to let you down, Mrs. Naples." He sat down beside her and scratched his head. "The other detective you met, Johnson, is working hard to find the persons responsible for this."

"But you made me a promise," she said, eyes watering again. "And I could see in your eyes that you really cared."

"Daddy!" Adamo exclaimed, barreling down the stairs. "Can I have some ice cream?"

"Not right now, Adamo," Nicola said, standing up. "Go back upstairs."

His words were too late. His son hit the last step of the stairway and headed straight for him.

Mrs. Naples eyes lit up as Madison followed. Twins. Just like hers. She swallowed hard and nodded at the boys. "Hello," she said, voice cracking.

"Hello," Madison answered first. "Who is she, daddy?" he said, turning towards Nicola.

"Someone daddy worked with," Nicola answered, putting his hand on their heads. "Why don't you boys go upstairs and after I'm done, I'll be up."

"But…" Madison prepared to protest. His emerald green eyes were bright as he begged. "We want a snack."

"Later," Nicola said sternly.

Sulking they both headed back up the stairs as quickly as they had come.

Nicola turned around and tried to smile. "My boys…well half my boys. I've got two more upstairs and one on the way." He didn't know why, but he felt comfortable telling her that.

"And they are bi-racial?" she asked.

"Yes," Nicola answered. He went back to her and sat down. "I really want to help you. I do."

"You made a promise. And in my heart, I believe that you are the only one who can do this. I had a dream about you yesterday, Lt. Agosto. You were in front of a plume of smoke and there were children all around you. I think it was a sign that you would lead them out of this hell." Tears ran down her cheeks.

Nicola's heart broke for her. "They are not going to give me my job back."

"Even if we beg for it. I've gotten with some of the other parents and…"

Nicola cut her off. "It won't matter. With all the bad press, they have to take another course of action." He heaved a frustrated sigh. "This is my fault, I know, but trust me. It was something that I had to do."

"I believe you," she said with sincere understanding in her voice. "But you have to find a way to solve this case."

With the photos still in his hand, Nicola rested back on the couch. His long, muscular body was tense with frustration. Running a hand over his stubbly beard, he tried to figure out a way to tell her that there was nothing that he could do.

He was five minutes from not being a cop any longer.

"Mrs. Naples…" he said, closing his eyes. He didn't want to break her heart or take hope from her but he had his own family to think about. Right now, he needed to be thinking about job options and how to take care of his family, not trying to take care of someone else's misfortune.

The jingle of keys at the front door interrupted him in the middle of yet another statement. He rolled his eyes, feeling as though his cell phone and his front door had become his biggest enemies. He knew that it had to be Ivy, but looking at his watch, he knew that it was way too early for her to be home.

Having been married for years, he realized that there was a woman in his house, *regardless of the reasoning behind it*. He tensed up tighter as he heard her heels click against the hard wood floor. Dropping her bags on the bench in the foyer, she called out for her husband.

"Nicky," she said, voice echoing through the large airy rooms. In just one word, it was obvious that Ivy wasn't happy.

"In here, babe," Nicola said, looking over at Mrs. Naples, who heard Ivy's voice and also tensed a bit.

The woman of the house had arrived.

Ivy turned the corner in a navy blue tailored business suit and yellow Brooks Brothers oxford. With pearls around her neck and on her ears and her matching navy blue pumps, she looked every bit of the part of executive. She eyed her husband first, sitting on the couch in his lounge wear and then the white woman sitting beside him.

"Am I interrupting something?" Ivy asked, looking to her husband for an explanation as she took off her suit jacket. She laid it across her arm and walked over to the arm chair by the sofa where Mrs. Naples was and took a seat.

"This is Mrs. Naples," Nicola said, watching his wife closely. "I'm sorry, Mrs. Naples, I don't know your first name, but this is my wife Ivy Agosto."

Mrs. Naples pushed to the end of the sofa and offered her hand. "It's very nice to meet you."

Ivy shook her hand with a frown on her face. "It's nice to meet you too."

"You're home early," Nicola said, finally standing up.

"Yes, I know." Ivy cut her eyes at her husband. "I was let go today. Something about too much negative publicity."

Nicola bucked his eyes. "What?" He growled. "You've been at that firm for nearly a decade."

"We'll talk about it after Mrs. Naples has left," Ivy said, turning her attention back to the woman. "So, what brings you to my home in the middle of the day?"

Mrs. Naples took the pictures that Nicola had laid on the coffee table and passed them to Ivy. "My boys," she said with finality. "I was hoping that Lt. Agosto wouldn't give up on trying to find their killers."

Suddenly extremely more sympathetic, Ivy took the pictures slowly. She had never met one of her husband's cases. He wouldn't allow it. And now she knew why. Staring at the photos of the twin boys who were no doubt her children's ages brought tears to her eyes.

"I'm sorry for your loss," Ivy said, looking the woman square in the eyes.

"I saw your children," Mrs. Naples said. "If anyone understands what this has done to me, you all do. In some ways because of what is happening to your own family, we are connected." She tried to smile. "Lt. Agosto made me a promise to find whoever was responsible for taking my reason for living from me." Shaking her head, she pulled her purse to her body. "I just wanted to know if he planned to keep that promise."

Standing quietly and watching, Nicola saw Ivy's range of emotion as she tried to take in what she had truly just walked into. His wife met his gaze with a determined look, but for once, he was not sure what she would say.

"He can't give you an answer on that, Mrs. Naples," Ivy said finally, handing the pictures back to her. "You're asking him to be your personal vigilante and you're asking him to forget the needs of his own family." Ivy stood up as if to tell the woman that her visit was coming to an abrupt end.

Mrs. Naples stood too.

Nicola stepped out of the way, amazed at how graceful his wife could be. He watched his wife put a loving hand around the woman to comfort her, even as she walked her to the front door.

Ivy leaned into her and in a low voice said, "And if he were to do that, you wouldn't want to know about it. Now would you?"

Mrs. Naples looked in Ivy's eyes with a grateful smile. Nodding, she mouthed thank you. "No," she answered aloud. "I wouldn't want to place you in that position. Thank you both for your time." Looking back at Nicola one last time, he heard the two of them mumbling words before the door closed and Ivy came back around the corner alone.

"Well, this Baby Boys case has truly come home to roost, hasn't it?" she said, walking up to him.

Nicola looked down at her and rubbed her cheek with his thumb. "Baby, I'm so sorry. I didn't mean to…"

"Finish this, Nicola," Ivy said, cutting him off. Her eyes blazed with anger and disgust. "We've lost nearly everything. Our jobs. Our friends. Our life. If what you say is true about being set up, then this was all orchestrated by someone. And for all we know, they aren't done with us. So, finish this before they do. Finish this for our family, for those children and for yourself so that we can move on with our lives. I don't want my baby coming into this mess, and I don't want my other babies suffering anymore."

Nicola nodded. "Thank you," he whispered. To finally have his wife's blessing, took a weight off his shoulders that he could not explain. "I will. I promise you. I'll finish it."

19

Johnson slammed the door of his dusty, unmarked squad car and headed quickly up the stone walkway of Carmen's house, ready to confront her for what he considered high treason in a relationship. Ten minutes before his illegal, blue-light dash across town to her house, he had gotten a text from her on his private cell saying that they should *spend some time apart at least until the case was over.*

Complete and utter bullshit.

He knew that it all stemmed from the night before, when while drunk and guard finally down, she had told him that she loved him. And in turn, he had told her the same. At last, he felt like they had turned a corner. He went to bed with her curled into him and his mind finally at ease. However, the next morning, he had awoken to an empty bed. She had ditched him at his place and headed off to work.

That would have been fine if only the text five hours later had not been so damn cold. Intending to get to the bottom of things, he beat on her front door with his fist and rang the doorbell like he was serving a felony warrant.

Frustrated, she snatched the wooden door open and stared out at him with a scowl. "Johnson, what are you doing here?" she asked.

Her question seemed ridiculous to him at the moment. In fact, it only infuriated him more. "I need to talk to you," he said, trying to push his way in. "I'm tired of this cat and mouse game."

She planted her hand on his wide chest. "This isn't a game," she said, refusing to let him in. "I've had time to think about it, and I just don't think we should do this right now."

Johnson stepped back and got composure of himself. Narrowing his eyes on her, he asked, "Is there someone else in there?" His concrete chest swelled. Radiating tension, he looked around to see if there was another car parked closely around.

"No, there is no one here," she said, shaking her head. "God, you just don't get it, do you?"

"What is there to get?" his deep voice echoed in the quietness of the tree-lined street. He lowered his voice and snatched off his shades. "Did you mean what you said last night?" He swallowed hard and the motion caused a jolt of his Adam's apple in his thick neck.

Carmen looked away, rolling her eyes. She had to tell him the truth. He deserved that much, but somehow exposing even the truth could be a way for him to develop a better lie. "Johnson, you're just going to hurt me, if I let you get too close. And I can't afford to do that again."

He repeated himself again. "Did you mean what you said last night? That's all I want to know."

Carmen folded her arms and stood her ground but said nothing.

After an awkward moment of standing there in chaotic silence, Johnson shook his head and threw up his hands. "Alright." Stepping up to her, he bent and whispered, "I meant it. I meant every *fucking* word. And you know what, until now, no I haven't been with a woman that I actually gave a damn about. But with you and your daughter, I could be that guy…the one that you need so badly. I could be anything that you want me to be because I know that you're what I want. But it's you getting in the way. You're getting in the way of what we could have because you're afraid. And I can handle a woman who comes a little damaged, someone who's a little angry, but I can't deal with a coward." Stepping back, he spit out his gum and turned on his heels for his car.

Carmen watched him leave her. And suddenly, the worry that she felt turned quickly into loneliness. She knew that he made her happy, and he made her safe and that was what scared her. However, actually seeing him walk away for good made her the most afraid.

Digging in his pocket for his keys and trying to hold back hot tears, Johnson heard Carmen scream from the door.

"Yes, okay. Yes, I meant it!" she said, stepping on-to the walkway. She scratched the back of her neck and wiped a tear. "But at what cost, Johnson?" Her voice had lost all authority. Now it only sounded desperate, much like she felt inside.

He looked up from his car door and wiped his face. "Everything," he answered. "For both of us."

She walked closer as the sun burned her olive-skin. Golden streaks of untamed hair danced in the dry wind. Putting a hand over her eyes to shield the glare, she looked out at him.

There was something very vulnerable about the way that she appeared at that moment to Johnson. Standing there, eyes wrought with need, heart open as a fresh wound, fear emanating from her very being. He knew that if he went to her now, he would need to be with her forever, and for once in his life, that feeling exhilarated him.

Stalking back up to her, he picked her up in his embrace and kissed her passionately as if for the very first time. Their body armor prevented the feeling of hearts beating against each other, but they could feel the pulse of their love through their touch. He stroked her face with the back of his knuckles as he set her down. "I'm not going anywhere, Carmen," he promised. "I'll be here with you for life. All you have to do is just let me be. Don't be afraid to feel something real." He wasn't sure if he was talking to himself or her.

"For life?" she asked, as if hearing the words soothed some hidden pain.

"Till our last breath," he answered sincerely. "From this moment on, I'm done with every other woman. I'll change my number; I'll move; I'll take your last name…"

Carmen laughed. "Are you trying to give my dad a heart attack?"

"Well the last name might be a bit much, but hey…you could always take mine." His brown eyes sparkled in the sunlight and sent a zinger through her heart.

Carmen gaped at him. Was that a proposal? She swallowed down all need to be sarcastic and simply allowed herself to just be in the moment with him for once. "I do love you," she said in a whisper.

"Good, because I love you…so much." Johnson knew that he was supposed to be meeting his new partner/boss in less than thirty minutes, but there was no way in hell he was going to leave this house without making love to her.

Grabbing her by the hand, he led her to the door.

"My lunch is over," she said, looking at her watch. "I just came here to grab a bite and then get back."

Johnson opened her screen door for her and waited.

Stepping into the house passed him, she watched him carefully close and lock the door behind him. Like a predator eyeing his prey, he kept his eyes on her as he approached, nearly salivating at the thought of having her again, even though it had only been hours since their last encounter.

With one carnivorous gaze, he pushed her roughly against the wall and pressed his body up against hers. Hands against the wall, covering her like a web, he attacked. The act was electric. He picked her up off the floor and wrapped her legs around his waist. At the apex of her sex, he nestled his aching hardness as he kissed her open mouth, sucking at her tongue and moaning at the thought of what he would do to her.

Her body convulsed as he moved his kiss from her mouth to her neck. She raked her nails over his bald-head and down his neck as he kissed her.

With his hands on her breasts, massaged over where he knew her nipples were under the Kevlar and then ripped her oxford open. The sound of buttons hitting the floor and rolling around on the hardwood floor mixed with the heady moans and groans of anxious lovers.

Returning the favor, Carmen happily tore off his grey t-shirt, knowing that he had a hundred more like it upstairs in her bedroom. Tattoos and muscles rippled before her. Pushing back up to her body, he kissed her mouth as he ripped off her yellow lace bra and found her nipples between his fingers, but his mouth watered for the taste. Picking her back up off the floor, he suckled at her breasts wildly as she clawed at his shoulders and back.

She held him close, taking in the aroma of Cool Water cologne and cigarettes.

Within a minute flat, they were both naked. Bullet-proof vests lined the hallway, clothes lined the entry way to the living room and Johnson had Carmen thrown over the sofa table.

Her naked body was arched over the table and her arms rested on the sofa. Behind her, Johnson bent between her legs and sucked at the inner folds of her womanhood until she began to shutter. Knees buckling, she tried to stand but felt herself weaning with his every kiss.

"Yes," she panted. "Oh…yes," she said again as she heard audible licks to her swollen clitoris.

"Come on, baby. Let me taste you," he said, lapping his tongue against her violently.

She tried to crawl away from him, but he pulled her back down.

With both hands on her plump bottom, Johnson opened her wider and slipped his fingers inside her slickness. In slow evolutions, he moved in and out of her as she began to moan louder.

Unable to take anymore, he stood up and grabbed his shaft, rock hard and pulsing. He was about to explode at just the sight of her athletic build. Pushing into her, he grabbed a fist of her hair and pulled her to him while he slapped her behind. Redness quickly formed when he moved his hand. Muscles tense and taut, he bent his knees to lower himself deeper into her and growled.

"Fuck," he said, as he pushed into her.

"Johnson," she screamed, feeling her body began to pulsate.

Watching her wide, muscular legs part to brace herself, he pulled her head back further and planted a kiss on her open mouth. "Do you love me?" he asked, moving in and out of her.

"Yes," she whimpered.

"Say it," he said, grabbing her by the waist with both hands. Slamming into her body, he watched as she began to climax.

Bending down on her body, he reached around and put one hand on the front of her aching vagina and the other on her bobbing breast.

"I love you," she whispered.

His blows became more powerful.

He growled. "Say it louder." Still ramming into her, he grabbed her by her neck and pulled her into his chest.

"Ahhh, I love you," she screamed. Holding on to the sofa table, she tried to absorb his powerful thrusts. "Fuck me," she ordered.

Looking down at his penis as he penetrated her, he felt himself begin to tense up. "Not yet," he said allowed, turning her over. Picking her up, he pushed her against the wall and picked her back up.

The painting beside them fell on the ground.

Laughing, he kissed her mouth as she held on to him. They moved in a synchronic dance of love making until he felt her tense. Locking her legs around his sweaty back, she began to moan louder.

"I'm coming," she said, looking him in his eyes.

Johnson gritted his teeth. She would never know how badly she turned him on. "Yeah?" he asked, bucking his body harder.

"Yes," she whimpered. "Yes," she said, eyes rolling.

Gritting his teeth, he felt the strain in down in his groin. Throwing her on the rug in the middle of the floor, he turned her over and buried himself in between her legs. As she held him close, he felt them both reach a powerful climax.

Sweating and exhausted, he rested with his head down on her breasts and his naked body on her rug. Listening to her heart beat, he closed his eyes.

"Don't go to sleep," Carmen warned. "We have to get back."

"Let's just lay here for a minute," he said, sucking on one of her nipples.

Carmen licked her lips. "Just a minute," she said, closing her eyes. "Then we have to get up."

"Sure thing. Then tonight, when we get off, I'm moving in," he said, looking up at her to see if she would protest.

Smiling, she ran her hand over his shaved head. "I'd like that," she said softly.

"Yeah? Me too," Johnson said, laying his head back down.

***

By the time Johnson arrived at the office four hours after first showing up at Carmen's doorstep, Lt. Kat Steele was absolutely incensed. Sitting at her new desk with a file locked between her fingers, she watched him with a close eye as he entered into her office. He breezed in with a carefree grin and closed the door behind him.

"Sorry that I'm late," he said, standing in front of her.

She looked at her watch and then stood up from her desk. "Late?" Walking behind him, she gazed over his body. He was an extremely muscular man, tall and confident, but most of the guys in this unit were. It was an asset in the field to be attractive and aggressive, but it was a necessity to be well-built. Theirs was a job for fighters, not negotiators.

Stepping closer into him, she inhaled his scent. He smelled of soap and cologne...freshly showered. To make her point, she audibly sniffed him. Her voice was sweet and sultry. "Have you been *fucking* today, detective?"

Johnson bucked his eyes. That was completely out of left field, but he had heard about Lt. Steele before. She was supposed to be a ball breaker. "Excuse me, ma'am?" he asked, running his hand over the bridge of his nose.

She lowered her voice but made sure that her words were perfectly heard. "Have you been fucking, detective," she asked even slower.

Johnson kept his eyes on the window in front of him. With his legs in a wide stance, he locked his hands in front of him. "As of when, ma'am?"

"In the last four hours. Because you smell like soap and in this hot ass Memphis weather, I really doubt that would be possible if you've actually been working like the rest of us. While I sat here, waiting to get on this case, were you out somewhere using that oh so popular dick of yours? Because if you have, I have to tell you that the families who are patiently waiting for the person or persons who are responsible for their children's rapes and murders won't be impressed."

The overt aggression of his superior officer emanated around the room like a thick fog.

And unintentionally, it turned Johnson on a bit. Not enough to chase, just enough to notice. Smacking his lips, he huffed. "No, I was actually tracking down the contents of a jump drive that was given to me by Director Amway. It took longer than expected," he said with a snicker. What did he care if she had a suspicion of him; it wasn't like she could prove it. Hell, he couldn't even prove it, and he was there.

Plus, it wasn't a complete lie. He had actually gone by the federal building before he ended up at Carmen's house. Unfortunately, after their sex session, they had both slept a little over three hours instead of five minutes.

"I know that you think that you're hot shit, Johnson," Steele said, looking at his tightly formed ass one last time before she made her way back around to the front of her desk, "but to me, you're just a guy. So leave the stereotypical, bad-boy, fuck machine image out in your city-issued Charger. When you come in here, you come in here on time and you come in here ready to work."

"Absolutely," Johnson said, smirking.

"Is something funny?" she asked seriously.

"Just the *fuck machine* part," he answered. "And for the record, I'm a one woman man."

"And why would that need to go on the record?" she asked with a frown.

Johnson shrugged. "Just in case, you got the wrong idea of who I am," he said, finally putting his gaze on her. Shit, she was beautiful. He took his eyes off her again and stared back at the window where it was safe. He was in a relationship now, and he was happy. There was no reason to rock the boat.

"Johnson, look at me. I want you to hear me when I say this," Steele said, resting her hands firmly on the desk.

Johnson looked back at her. "Ma'am?"

"You showed up four fucking hours late to our first meeting. The wrong impression was made then, okay. Everything that I think of you subsequently is right on the money."

"Yes ma'am," Johnson said, biting his lip.

Rolling her eyes, she finally pushed the file over to him. "I see that we haven't spoken to this DeMario yet. I want to do that today."

Johnson relaxed. "Do we have permission from the powers that be?" he asked with a frown.

"Leave that to me," Steele said, slipping on her black suit jacket. It was cut to perfection, highlighting every curve that she had in her slim shoulders, huge breasts and small waist. She caught him staring at her backside when she turned towards him. She hesitated at first but continued. "And I had time while I was waiting on you to get your *jump drive* to review the file on Cane. I want to find him and get him in a hole for questioning today regarding Twist's murder. If we can't find him, then I want to drag in his guys until someone squeals. But first thing first, I want to see that piece of shit lying bastard at the hospital to find out exactly what Intel led him into Nicola Agosto's truck." Grabbing her suit jacket, she slipped it over her gun holster and walked passed him. "Well, let's get a move on, lover boy."

"On it," Johnson said, following her out of the office.

***

Leaving the pool of reporters outside of the hospital, Councilman Ferris made his way out of the sweltering heat up to the private room where DeMario was being held. Tapping on the door before entering, he gave a warm smile to the man's mother, who was sitting beside him watching the television on the opposite wall.

"Councilman," she said, standing up. The look in her eyes was that of complete trust considering he had been there since the first moments of the attack to rally the community and be by her side.

"How are you today?" he asked, extending his arms.

She hugged him tightly and inhaled his expensive sent. "Each day, he gets a little better."

"Good. You'll be happy to know that we've got over 300 confirmed participants for tomorrow's rally at the police station. I have insider information that Agosto will be present at a closed hearing to determine action against him at 3:00 p.m. and we will be there to let them know that the community is watching."

"Well, what did the FBI say?" she asked, stepping back and folding her arms.

The councilman heaved a frustrated sigh. "Unfortunately, they felt that they had no case. So, they have closed the investigation."

"But his rights were violated," she said with tears in her eyes. "Just look at him." She pointed back at her son.

"I understand your frustration and we are going to do everything in our power to remedy this for you. This lawsuit will be paid by the City and I'm certain that Agosto will face some form of jail time."

With the sudden raised voices and ruckus, DeMario opened his bruised eyes and looked over at the councilman. "What's up, man? Glad you're here. I wanted to talk to you," he fought to say. His mouth was still severely swollen and covered in lacerations and bruising.

The councilman looked back with a nod. "Ms. Washington, would you mind if I speak with DeMario alone for just a moment?" he asked. He was tired of speaking to the woman. Every day it was the same damn thing. She wanted justice for a son with a rap sheet longer than his driveway. They were becoming irritants for him though he built the very foundation for his campaign upon their unknowing backs.

Looking back at her son, Ms. Washington turned up her lip and nodded. "We can talk later, right?"

The council reached down for one last piece of civility. "We sure can. I'm always here for you."

As she excused herself out of the room, Councilman Ferris locked the door and took off his suit jacket. Placing it on the chair beside the bed, he took a seat beside DeMario and pushed up to the bed. He looked down his nose at the young man covered in gauze and tape and tried not to directly inhale any of the man's scent.

"Man, you said that he might bruise me up a little bit. You didn't say that he would put me in the fucking hospital."

"This will all be over for you soon," he said with a double meaning. "There is no need to complain. Even like this, you are better off than you were before. All your…sins have been wiped clean."

"Whatever," DeMario said, rolling his eyes. "I've been thinking that this money we're supposed to be suing for ain't gone come overnight."

The councilman raised his brow. "You already knew that."

"Yeah, well, I'm gone need some more money up-front."

"We gave you ten thousand dollars cash. Where is that money?"

"It's gone," DeMario said in a matter-of-fact tone.

"Well, you didn't do anything to help your family out with it. I just paid your mother's utility bill last week to keep your sisters and brothers from living in the dark." He found their way of life to be disgusting though he would never lead on to it.

"I need more," he said in a lower voice.

Councilman Ferris bit down on his bottom lip. "How much more?"

DeMario blew a stinking breath out of his mouth that made Councilman Ferris sit back in his chair. "I'm thinking a hundred thousand. You can have it back from my settlement."

"You expect me to give you a hundred thousand dollars?"

"You. Cane. The city. I don't give a fuck who gives it to me. All I know is that I'm owed it. You hear me? Man, I'm sitting in here all fucked up. It's the least that you can do. After all like y'all niggas said, I was the cattle in this thing."

The councilman corrected. "The catalyst."

"Look, you know what I mean. I need some money. Now, you gone do that or what? I mean, I could always get paid by telling the other side what really happened. That I got busted by that cop Magnelli on the DEA Task force and flipped and was introduce to you and Cane, and was told to set up Agosto to take him off the case."

Councilman Ferris refused to give DeMario an ounce of pushback on the matter and he would not let him see him sweat. Pulling a few pills out of his pocket, he cupped them in his hand. "Do you have visitors? I can't very well bring the money up myself. And there is no way that we want you on the other side of this thing. So we'll do what we have to do to keep you."

DeMario's eyes relaxed. He knew that the man would see things his way once he let them know that he knew how important he was to this entire investigation. "Yeah, my boys come back and forward to see me."

"Good, we'll imbed someone who looks like your boys. They will bring up a package for you. Although, I wonder how you're going to spend it in your position."

"I've got ways," DeMario said, happy with himself.

"I'm sure that Cane can get you the money, but it may take a day or two."

"You've got two days," DeMario said with a bit of grit in his haggard voice.

Councilman Ferris. "Fair enough." He raised his hand and showed the red pills in his hand. "I thought you might be able to help the pain with a few of your little friends."

DeMario's eye twitched at the sight of the Molly pills in Councilman Ferris's hand.

"Now that's what I'm talking about. I haven't been able to get high once since I landed in this hell hole."

The councilman reached over DeMario and dropped them in his open mouth. Like a fish, DeMario swallowed hard without water and licked his cracked lips. "Thanks, man."

"We do what we can," the councilman said with a grin. "Don't forget. The guy you don't recognize is the guy with the package for you."

"Don't think about sending someone in here to pop a cap in my ass. There are cops everywhere," DeMario said, settling in for the rush that would soon come cascading over his body.

"I wouldn't think of sending anyone to kill you," the Councilman said, standing up. "Well, I'll leave you to enjoy your evening and unlock the door for your mother to come back in."

"Thanks, man," DeMario said, looking back up at the television.

"Anytime," the councilman said in a low soothing voice. "You deserve it."

***

Johnson hated the fact that Lt. Steele wanted to drive. Although it was a very short drive, he found her sitting behind the wheel a reminder that she was going to try to emasculate him as much as possible during this investigation. With his eyes locked on his cell phone, he texted Gabriel, his code name for Carmen. Evidently, she had gotten some shit for being late back to work also, but like him, she had felt it worth it.

Steele pulled into the hospital parking lot and parked the car. Looking over at him, she pursed her lips to say something that appeared to be kind but then she stopped herself.

"What is it?" Johnson asked with a frown.

"Nothing," she said, rolling her eyes. Opening the door, she got out of the car and slipped on her shades and suit jacket. "Have you had the opportunity to talk to DeMario at all? Does he know who you are?"

Johnson closed the door behind him and laid his large arms on the top of the dusty car. "He knows what I look like, yeah. I made the scene. But I haven't interviewed him at all."

"Well, let me lead this. I know you don't want to but trust me, it's for the best," she said, walking towards the building.

Johnson rounded the car and caught up with her. "Why you?"

"I'm easier on the eyes," she said with confidence. "Wouldn't you agree?"

"No comment," Johnson joked.

Johnson and Steele pushed their way through the reporters mulling around downstairs waiting on a chance to talk to Ms. Washington or better yet DeMario. So far, Councilman Ferris had been controlling the interaction the family had with the media in order to ensure that they were only seen with him. Recognizing both officers, a few of the reporters started in trying to get a statement but the two kept their lips shut until they got out of the lobby.

"Fucking parasites," Johnson bit out. "They'll do anything for a story."

"They are just doing their jobs," Steele said, sure that she still wasn't out of earshot of the media. Inwardly, she felt the exact same way as Johnson, but she had a show to put on. People passed them in hoards as they waited on the elevator. As soon as they got on it and the door closed, she looked over at him.

"So, are you friends with Agosto?"

"You could say that," Johnson said with a frown. "Why?"

"Did you know all along that he was married to a black woman and had bi-racial children?" she asked, unable to let the thought go. "I mean, you hear the allegations every day just like I do. They think that he's a hate monger. Why didn't you ever say anything or stand up for him?"

"I guess you think that a gag order is something to play with," Johnson said as the doors to the elevator opened on the fourth floor.

"I would have found a way to get the right information to the right people if he had been my partner," she said, stepping off the elevator as a nurse ran past her. "What's going on up here?"

"And what if your partner told you not to, would you still do it?" he asked seriously. He already knew her type. "Or do you know what's best for everybody *even* beyond their own wishes."

Their conversation was quickly cut short. A woman's voice echoed down the hall as she screamed out for her son. DeMario. As soon as they heard his name, they bolted towards the screams. Following the sound of alarms beeping, they walked up on a team of nurses and doctors trying to resuscitate DeMario in his room. His mother was standing outside of the door where she was being held at bay, crying and screaming. Her eyes were red and covered in mascara that dripped down onto her cheeks in black dots.

Johnson quickly walked up to her. "Ma'am," he said, getting her attention. "Tell me what is going on? What happened?"

"He just started to convulse," DeMario's mother cried. "They said he looked like he was overdosing, but he has been clean since he got in here. We both have."

Johnson looked over at Steele, who was trying to squeeze her way inside the room to see what was going on, but some of the orderlies were blocking the door. "I'm a cop!" she screamed as if they actually cared.

Johnson used the opportunity to find out as much as he could before she came to her senses. "Who has been here today that could have gotten him drugs?"

DeMario's mother sobbed loudly as Johnson held her by the shoulders. "His cousin Mooky came by and Councilman Ferris. That's it!"

"Mooky have a real name?" Johnson asked.

The sound of DeMario flat lining made Johnson turn around and look towards the door. He walked up slowly, watching the nurses press the defibrillator against his boney chest.

"Clear," the nurse nearly sitting on his chest said.

The sound of electricity shocking his body was undeniable.

"Overdoes my ass," Steele said, pushing the chest of one of the larger orderlies as she tried to look inside. "Someone had it out for him." She stepped back and kicked the wall. "Fuck!"

"What?" DeMario's mother said enraged.

"Does Mooky have a real name?" Johnson asked, pulling out his note pad.

"DeFarious Washington," she said, wiping her eyes. "Tell me what is going on," she demanded.

20

The golden sun had begun to set on the blue horizon by the time that Nicola put on his running shoes. Stepping outside, he checked his back to make sure that his weapon was tucked carefully under his shirt and in his shorts, he slipped his ear plugs in his ears and then hit the pavement hard. Running like he was charging toward someone, he headed down the drive and onto Peabody Avenue like he had done so many times before when he needed to sort things out in his mind.

Quietly, Ivy watched him from the upstairs bedroom window as he disappeared from site. She knew that he was beyond angry and that worried her more than he could ever know. To their surprise, one of the sergeants from the Security Squad had been around just an hour ago to officially serve Nicola with papers for his hearing on the investigation. They had beat on the door like they were going to knock it down and served him with his son in his arms.

Nicola took the paper and closed the door quietly, then sent the children upstairs. They had stood in the foyer for a few minutes in silence before he finally opened the envelope and read the papers. Afterwards, he had passed them to her and told her that he needed to get some air.

He had told her a few nights before that he was out, but up until then she hadn't realized that he was actually holding out for hope.

His disappointment broke her into pieces. She held back her tears only for him, because inside she was screaming.

For Nicola this hearing meant a finality to his entire life's work, where for Ivy it meant the beginning of a chance at a life together. No more late nights of worry and wondering if someone would show up at her door apologizing for her loss.

She knew that tomorrow, the powers that be were going to fire her husband. And she knew that the world would be under the assumption that it was because he was a bigot, when in fact he had given everything to the entire Memphis community and he had done it selflessly not for her but for them.

And while she could handle a lot of things - Nicola moving forward with this investigation without the authorization to do so, the constant angst, and losing her job because those ungrateful shits cared more about their image than their employees—she could not handle her husband's name being dragged through the mud and that's why she had to do what she had to do just like he did. She only hoped that he understood.

Grabbing her cell phone, when she was sure that he was gone, she dialed a friend at the local television station. Her hands literally shook as she dialed. Nervousness made her nauseated and a bit light headed or maybe that was the baby.

"Terra, hey it's me," Ivy said, opening the curtain to look again. Her voice quivered. Suddenly, she was incredibly paranoid and afraid. This sounded like a good idea earlier today and now she was having second thoughts only because she was afraid of how Nicola would react.

The reporter sounded relieved to hear Ivy's voice. "Oh, shit, girl. I didn't think you'd call. I've got my guy ready. We are just waiting for your signal." Papers shuffled in the background.

"Look, he won't be gone that long. You have to get over here right now with the camera if you want an exclusive. Drive something other than that big ass van and park towards the back of the drive." Hanging up the phone, she took a deep breath. "I can do this," she said aloud. "I have to do this."

***

Nicola felt the weight of the world on his shoulders as he ran. Part of him wanted to cry; the other part of him wanted to scream. There was no part of him, however, that felt like giving up and that's all that mattered to him.

Nearly sprinting, he got just a second of clarity and realized that he was not alone. Someone was running behind him, and they were gaining on him. He turned down a quiet lane off the main thoroughfare and sped up. The other runner did the same.

Turning quickly down an alley, he ducked behind a tree and caught the guy as he passed it. Pulling out his gun, he pointed it at the head of the man wearing a hoodie in the summer heat.

"Stop right there," Nicola said, walking up closer. "Turn around."

The man did as he was told, holding his hands up in the air where Nicola could see them. As he turned towards Nicola, took the hood off his head and slipped off his shades, Nicola lowered the gun. "Shit, Amway, you scared the hell out of me."

"Obviously," Amway said, looking around.

"What are you doing here?" Nicola tucked the gun back in his shorts.

"I couldn't call, but I needed to talk to you. Figured you would do the same shit you always do when you get pissed off. Go for a run."

Nicola wiped the sweat from his brow. "Yeah."

"Look, I have to make this quick, but I wanted to let you know man to man that the decision was not made lightly." Amway walked up closer to him. Getting control of his breath, he wiped his mouth with his hand. "In fact, it was one of the hardest decisions that I've had to back."

"I'm no racist," Nicola said quickly.

"You don't think I know that?" He put his hands on his hips. "We busted our ass together trying to clean up these streets. You had dinner with my folks, and Cara and I ate your wife's nasty ass ravioli."

Nicola smirked. "It is God awful, isn't it?"

Amway laughed, happy that he still had a sense of humor. "If you had done anything else, I could have found a way…" He took a deep breath. "I've got the entire city against me right now, and I'm doing everything that I can to hold the department together. I had to support this. With the video and the facts, there was no other way. But I'm man enough to tell you that I had to weigh in, and I'm man enough to tell you that I'm sorry but it had to be done."

Nicola shook his head. "Yeah, I know."

"I know you. Don't pursue this case. Just…take care of your family," Amway urged.

"I can accept that I just lost everything because of my own choices, but I can't accept that whoever is responsible is just going to get away with it."

"He didn't get away with it," Amway said, cutting him off. "DeMario overdosed today at the hospital. I'm surprised that you haven't seen the news."

"I'm sick of watching television," Nicola said, unsure if he was relieved about DeMario's death or more angered by it. "Johnson didn't call. That's not like him."

"He's chasing ghosts right now. Steele is the lead on this…"

Nicola bucked his eyes. "Steele?"

"Yeah, Magnelli backed her play," Amway said with a smirk.

"Is he fucking her?" Nicola asked, shaking his head. Unbelievable.

"Probably," Amway said, looking at his watch. "But she's a good cop. No matter what, she'll do her job." He glanced around the alleyway again, knowing that he'd been there too long. "Tomorrow, you're going to lose your job, but that's it. You won't lose who you are and you won't lose all that you have done. If you need anything…"

Nicola scratched his head at the words and growled. "I'll call you if I do." He stuck out his hand. "Thanks."

"Take care of yourself," Amway said, shaking his hand.

"You too," Nicola said, watching him as he slipped back on his hoodie and ran back the way that he had come.

Watching his boss and his old friend run away from him was a sign on so many levels for Nicola. It symbolized the end of an era in his life. Everything that he had known would change. Everything had already changed. Before, he was a cop off duty dealing with demons. Now, he was just a guy on a run with a gun on his person. He had no one to call and no one to back his play. Everything that he did would be up to him.

"Alright," he said aloud. Knowing what he had to do, he put his ear buds on and decided to take a longer run than he had at first planned. He was headed to see an old friend from his past, someone he knew could help him beyond the strict lines of the law.

***

By the time that Nicola arrived at the Medlov compound nestled comfortably in the luxury homes community off of Walnut Grove, he was utterly exhausted. Leaning against the high brick fence that kept the world out of the lives of the world's most private crime family, he caught his breath and tried to get his thoughts together. Before he could stand, an armed guard rounded the corner. After speaking into his head piece, he walked up to Nicola.

"Keep moving. You can't stop here," the man said with a Russian accent.

"This is the sidewalk," Nicola said, standing up. "It's public property, asshole, and it's paid for by my tax money."

"Your tax money is about to pay for you to get fucked up," the man said, stepping closer.

Another guard rounded the corner quickly. "He's a cop," he said to the other guard.

The guard stepped back. "What do you want?" he asked Nicola.

"I need to talk to Dmitry." Nicola looked through the wrought iron fence and saw that a quarter mile up the drive there were five black SUV's parked in front of the house.

"Mr. Medlov is not available," the nearest guard said sternly as if Nicola's mention of his boss's name was blasphemy.

Nicola forced the point. "Tell him that I'm here. He'll give me an audience." He walked in front of the camera on the side of the gate so that the guard watching could see his face.

"I don't relay messages from pigs," the guard answered quickly. "Now, take your tax paying ass down the street."

Nicola bit back his immediate reaction and instead insisted again, this time with a lower voice. "I'm not a pig," he said, eyes narrowed. "Now do yourself a favor and get on that earpiece and tell him that I'm here."

The guard watched Nicola's intense body language and stepped back. Turning his back on him, he spoke in Russian over his earpiece to the person on the other end of the receiver. A few seconds later, he turned back around and sucked his teeth.

"Follow me," the man said, visibly agitated.

The large, elaborate gate opened and the three men began their trek up the long drive past other guards who were out on the grounds. Nicola watched the men carefully, making sure to mind the gun pressed to his back.

All the men watched him as he made his way up to the house. Many of them knew exactly who he was and his reputation in Memphis, not only with the police department but in pursuit of their boss. They found it odd for him to be here now, walking no less. Curious eyes gazed out at him from all over the property. They walked in pairs with fully automatic weapons in black tactical gear. All of them Russian, all of them killers.

When Nicola's foot hit the top step of the Medlov's palatial mansion, the doors opened and a butler ushered him in quickly. He spoke in Russian as well, telling the guards were to take Nicola.

The mansion made his colonial-style home look shabby. He had been there a few times before, once to arrest Dmitry Medlov. He had come in with a team in the middle of the night and slapped the cuffs on him, but not before he had also pulled his beautiful girlfriend out of the tub naked and arrested her too. None of the laundry list of charges had stuck. In fact, Dmitry walked the very same night.

He was certain that Dmitry had never forgiven him for that, but here he was anyway, about to ask for his help. The way that Nicola saw it, the most the man could do was turn him down. But he had the distinct feeling that he would not.

"This way," the guard said, walking out of the elaborate foyer down the left corridor. Nicola followed the man and the other guard followed Nicola. Their footsteps echoed on the marble floor. The ceilings were tall, nearly twenty-feet high and every few feet there were grand original paintings from all over the world. This man, Dmitry, had built a decadent life for himself on the back of hard work, but his labor had been in arms dealing and the underground world of the mob. He was the king of criminals, royalty of killers and thieves. Yet, his world seemed better than most. The sound of children playing somewhere in the house could be heard along with the laughter of young women. The smell of fresh flowers in expenses vases filled the hallways with fragrant aromas. And all around him was the distinct feeling of contentment. Such strange bedfellows for under lords.

It seemed to pay well to be on the other side of the law. It seemed to be more rewarding. At least from the outside.

The guard leading them opened the door at the end of the long hallway and stepped to the side. Nicola walked into the study, another elaborately decorated room of dark wood, leather chairs, antique furniture, expensive rugs, art, books and large monitors that gave different vantage points around the compound. A huge bay window with the view of the grounds in the backyard gave a picturesque view of a well-manicured lawn, masterful gardens of flowers, a white gazebo covered in Ivy and low hanging trees.

"Sit there," the guard said, roughly. He pointed toward a small sofa in the corner.

Nicola didn't bother to answer the man with a smart-ass comment. The guy was just a worker, not even worth the extra effort. But he did give him a look that let him know that he would have loved to punch him in the face.

Taking a seat, he watched the guard close the door and stand in the corner of the room quietly waiting.

Nicola smacked his lips and sat back on the sofa. *Here it is. Rock bottom*, he thought to himself. Taking a newspaper off the end table, he looked at the story A1 above the fold and read more about how he was a horrible person and a racist cop. *Utter bullshit.* He rolled his eyes and threw the paper down. Whoever said 15 minutes of fame was exciting didn't know what it was like to be in his shoes.

Just a few minutes later, he heard footsteps marching down the same hall that he had been ushered down. Evidently, Dmitry was a gracious host who didn't believe in keeping his guests waiting, even if they were cops. Inwardly, he appreciated that considering he had such a long run home. Plus, he wasn't quite comfortable leaving Ivy and the kids alone for any extended period of time. *Always on borrowed time.*

The door opened and the second guard moved out of the way to let Dmitry Medlov, his son Anatoly Medlov and the newest addition to the organization, Dmitry's nephew, Gabriel Medlov into the room. It was a parade of giants. While Dmitry and Gabriel towered physically over all they lorded over, Anatoly was a man with a reputation bigger than life in a not so colossal body.

The Medlov men were quite the enigma when people first saw them. Dmitry was the patriarch of the family. He was an exceedingly tall man, blond, blue-eyed, immaculately dressed and well spoken. His grey pant suit fitted him perfectly, more than likely because they were tailor made. His dress shirt was cut to show the wideness of his bulging chest and his small waist. And his perfect smile was designed to put people at ease.

He was a man who appeared approachable at first glance, until one looked him in the eye. It was then that anyone with sense realized that he was a predator, plain and simple. All of his charisma and beauty were mechanisms to lure people into his trap, and then when they were adequately ensnared in his vicious web, he pounced on them, leaving no remains to waste.

Nicola knew Dmitry well and over the years they had had their share of run-ins, but there was also an unspoken respect between them. Dmitry respected Nicola for his integrity and devotion to the department, and Nicola respected Dmitry for the way that he handled his men and his business. It was never sloppy. No one ever stepped out of line or disobeyed his orders. Few had ever been stupid enough to cross him. As a result, Nicola couldn't even count anymore how many bodies that he had picked up over the years because of Dmitry. Yet, nothing had ever stuck. Money and power had a way of doing that. And Dmitry was nothing if not thorough.

Then there was Dmitry's son. He was a completely different man.

Anatoly was also a blond. A little over six feet tall, wide and muscular, brooding and dark with icy blue eyes that belonged on a painting, the young man was pure hate incarnate. He wore dark jeans, weathered brown boots and a navy blue t-shirt that looked like he bought it off a rack at Wal-Mart. Russian tattoos ran the length of his muscular, vein-filled arms down to his hands and up to his neck. He always seemed to have a chip on his shoulder, more than likely because he was always being discussed in some circle or another. Like his father, Anatoly was from Moscow and had lived in the slums there before he ended up in the states. After working like a slave for his father, he had been selected to serve on the council and made a leading member of the Vor.

Over a year ago, Anatoly found out that a woman he was seeing was an undercover cop that Nicola had sent to infiltrate their organization. When he discovered it, Anatoly made her witness to a flawless murder before he drugged her and put her on tape while they had sex in front of countless people in a pool at his summer home in South Beach, Miami. Ultimately, the incident had cost the girl her badge, reputation and fiancé. However, she rebounded by writing a bestselling memoir detailing everything from his opulent lifestyle to the size of his penis. The last time that Nicola had heard anything about her, she lived in L.A. now and was working on a movie deal.

Gabriel Medlov was a bit of an enigma to Nicola. He was a curious character that gave off a different vibe from his other family members. Raised in private schools, college-educated, and a former DEA agent, no one knew just how good or bad the man was. After a stint undercover, he too had turned for the family and had never looked back. In his early thirties, he was a black haired, green-eyed beast of a man, nearly seven feet tall and while slimmer than Dmitry, he was exceedingly brawny. His dress was a little less menacing. In jeans and winter green polo, he was something of a hybrid of the two men. The word in law enforcement was that Gabriel reported to Anatoly now, and that Anatoly reported to his father. The familial hierarchy was designed to be impenetrable.

Looking at the three men now, Nicola felt the same. They *were* impenetrable. After all of the years of chasing them, it only took one glimpse after he was unshielded by the badge to really realize that the only thing that could bring these men down was themselves -

one man's greed, one' man's lust for power, one man's arrogance. They were a triad of destruction that had become a force of nature in their world. And as long as they stuck together, no investigation would ever succeed.

Dmitry sat in the corner of the room with his legs cocked open and his elbows on his knees, an unusual seated position for such a normally poised man. But in truth, he was sort of unnerved by the impromptu meeting. From his experience, Agosto didn't bend, didn't ask and didn't negotiate.

Gabriel watched from the corner of the desk, leaning against it with his legs crossed at the ankle. Participating in this meeting was only born from curiosity for him. He was confused about why the guy in front of them was so damn important to his uncle. Dmitry was global, yet here he was entertaining a local cop. To Gabriel, this was just one more example of why his uncle was such a complicated man. He saw use in everyone, where others didn't.

However, the most scrutiny came from the ever-paranoid Anatoly, who sat behind the desk, fingers threaded and eyes as pensive as ever. The sunlight coming in from the window behind him shined in on the top of his head and made him appear to be wearing a golden halo with his tousled blonde locks. *Such a deceptive thing.* It was obviously a trait bestowed upon him genetically by his father, because his body language told a different story. Nothing angelic radiated from Anatoly. In fact, all he wanted to do was launch across the room and attack the man for all of his past troubles.

Finally, Agosto spoke. "I'm sure that you've seen what happened," he said, taking off his shades.

"How could we miss it? You made national news and started what could be a citywide riot. Have you watched TV? Hundreds are camping out downtown for your closed-door hearing tomorrow. If you walk, analysts are saying that the city will burn." Dmitry stood up and walked over to the bar. Running his fingers over the many crystal decanters filled with a hosts of different spirits, he looked back at Nicola. "You still drinking Jack and Coke?"

Gabriel and Anatoly exchanged a quiet glance. *Dmitry was actually going to drink with this man, like he was an equal?* They found the idea preposterous.

"Yeah," Nicola said, sitting back on the sofa. "Funny how shit happens, right?"

"Really fucking funny," Gabriel said, finally re-membering who the guy was after Nicola pulled off his shades. "You're in deep shit. Why did you do it? Beat that guy up like that?"

Nicola looked over at Gabriel, face stoic and said, "He deserved it. Trust me. He was threatening to harm my children…sexually."

Dmitry snickered. "You'll have to forgive my neph-ew. He hasn't gotten acclimated to brutality yet. And trying to teach him is like trying to teach wine to be water." After pouring him a drink, he walked over and passed it to Nicola as a sign of respect. "Here, this should take some of the edge off."

"Thanks," Nicola said, taking a big gulp. His breaths calmed instantly. *Wow, did he need that.*

"So, you're off the force?" Dmitry asked, sitting back down, closer to Nicola this time.

Nicola nodded.

With a half grin, Anatoly leaned back in the chair. "Wow, I never thought it would end this way," he said relieved.

"Oh, it's not fucking over," Nicola said quickly. "That's why I'm here. I need your help. There is a child sex ring right here in the city, and if they think just because they were able to destroy my name that they can stop me from coming after them, then they have another fucking thing coming. No, this only means that I get to take the gloves off. And I will get them...all of them, even if it kills me. I will make them pay."

Dmitry listened carefully to Nicola the entire time, reading every one of his facial expressions, hearing the inflection in his voice, watching the tenseness in his body. The man wasn't lying. He sat back in his chair and crossed his legs. "*Da*, let's talk."

Anatoly took a deep breath and rolled his eyes at his father. *He was actually going to entertain this guy now? Great.*

"I need some guns, some help locating a girl and a few of your men to track down this drug dealer name Cane. I think he's responsible for not only the murder of a guy named Twist, but also some kind of way has a connection to the Baby Boys case. I'm locked out of the police department and my partner is under a hawk eye. So, he can't help me." Nicola looked Dmitry in the eye. "I know you have guys on the inside. I need their help to access the databases once I turn something up and get it back to me."

"Why don't we throw in a few million dollars to sweeten the deal?" Anatoly said sarcastically. "Papa, don't listen to him. Send him out…better yet…kill him."

Dmitry raised a brow at his son to silence him and then turned to Nicola. "In exchange for what?"

That was a good question. "What do you want? I don't have much to give," Nicola answered sincerely.

Anatoly sucked in a breath. "I should warn you. Normally, conversations like this don't end well for the person asking that question."

Gabriel chuckled but did not speak.

"You and I have been playing the game of cat and mouse for quite some time," Dmitry said grimly.

Nicola swallowed down his pride. "We have," he said in a low, flat voice. He knew that the cost of coming here would be high, but he wasn't sure how high.

Dmitry nodded. "A man like you could have significant worth to a man like me. You are honest, *far too honest*, and you are good. Therefore, you are trusted in circles that I can't necessarily sway because they don't care about money and power."

Nicola shrugged. "Maybe once I was in those circles, but not anymore."

Dmitry leaned closer. "It might not seem like it at this moment, but you are still a very valuable resource. And I want to use you."

"When?" Nicola asked. "How?"

"This is the tricky part. Not now. Not sure how. Just when I call, you have to answer and what I ask, you must do." Dmitry twisted up his lips considering how this might be perceived by Nicola. "It is not easy to be in your position, but you must play the cards that you have been dealt."

"I don't believe in turning on my former fellow officers just because I got booted off the force. I still have my self-respect."

"A pig with respect," Anatoly huffed. "Bullshit. Men like you only have power because someone appointed it to you. You didn't work for it. You don't deserve it. And when it's taken from you, you realize that you are less than nothing."

Gabriel did not laugh at that. He was a law enforcement officer once and could appreciate the man's delicate situation. He cut his eyes at his cousin.

Dmitry ignored his son, promoting Nicola to do the same. "All I ask is that you are a phone call away…"

"And you'll give me what I need?" Nicola asked. "Why?"

Dmitry winked at him and grinned. The dimple in his jaw emerged. "I could give a few reasons. *I don't like pedophiles.* I don't like Cane. I don't like missing an opportunity when I see one. Even though I have millions…well a lot more than that…I still believe that human capital is a man's best and most valuable asset, not money."

"How do you know that you can trust him?" Anatoly interrupted when he saw that his father might actually consider Nicola's request. "He's spent years chasing us and now that we finally have an opportunity to get rid of him, you offer him amnesty? Papa, this isn't right."

Dmitry smiled. "I love my son. He's so full of passion, but he lacks in his youth the ability to see the bigger picture."

"I lack in my youth to see the point in playing games with people who have become obsolete in purpose," Anatoly snarled.

Nicola's eyes narrowed at Anatoly. He had endured just about as much as he would with the little shit. "You think not having a badge will keep me from jumping across that desk and whooping your narrow ass?" he asked with lips curled and muscles tense.

Dmitry laughed aloud and slapped his knee. "Real men. I love it. Alpha males. True to the death." He sighed. "I can trust him, Anatoly, because once he enters into this agreement with me, he understands what he's risking."

The veins in Nicola's neck bulged. Taking his eyes off of Anatoly, he looked back at Dmitry. "It's already at risk. Why do you think that I'm here? It's only a matter of time before they come after my family. My wife doesn't fully understand that, but I do and you do."

Dmitry nodded. "I do."

"So, if I'm going to deal with devils…" Nicola said, shaking his head.

"Then you had better deal with the biggest ones," Dmitry said, nodding. "Call in Vasily."

Anatoly grunted and motioned at the guard. "Bring him in here now."

Dmitry looked at his watch and realized that the conversation had taken him from his guests longer than he expected. "Good then. Why don't you come around day after tomorrow, after you have received your official walking papers from the police department and we can get started? Anatoly and Gabriel will assist you from this point on. I'm an old man. I'm sure that you don't really need my direct assistance. But these young men can be my eyes and ears and most importantly, my mouth to get you the things that you need."

Vasily, Anatoly's personal guard came into the room, and closed the door behind him. Standing six-four, he looked more menacing then all the rest with a bald head, crooked nose and a dark tan. "Boss?" he asked, respectfully.

Dmitry stood. "Nicola, what is this girl's name that you were trying to locate?"

"She goes by the name Roxie. She was a stripper at The Tie. I think that she skipped town."

"Do you have a photo?" Dmitry asked.

"I can get you one," Nicola said, unsure how this man could track down the girl when he could not.

"Good, get Vasily a picture of her. When do you need her here?" Dmitry said, clasping his hands together.

"I need her back here immediately. She saw something, and I need to know what," Nicola answered.

"Vasily," Dmitry said, turning towards his subordinate. "Find her and bring her here to me. Nicola," he turned back around. "I'll see you day after tomorrow. We will have some party favors for you and we'll introduce you to one of my teams of men."

"Your team?" Nicola asked.

"You wanted into the real police department. You got it," Dmitry said with a smile. "My men will assist you in getting what you need. Now, if you'll excuse me, I have to get back to my wife and my guests. We are getting ready for a wedding."

Nicola looked confused.

Dmitry smiled. "It would seem that Anatoly isn't always such an asshole after all. He actually got a good girl to not only love him but make me a grandfather." With that, he nodded and bowed out of the room gracefully, leaving the other men behind.

When Dmitry was gone, Anatoly stood up from behind the desk and shook his head. "Please fuck this up, Agosto. Please." Walking to the door, he slapped his captain on the chest and whispered. "Put a tail on him. Where he goes, we go."

Vasily nodded and then followed his boss out, leaving the door open as a sign that he wanted Nicola out of the house.

Gabriel stood up and smiled. "After you," he said, pointing at the door. He followed Nicola out of the room with his fists down in his pockets. "We'll see you in two days," he said when they got to the end of the hall. With a smirk, he disappeared into the house while the guards saw Nicola outside to the porch.

21

DeFarious Washington, AKA, Mooky was an easy person of interest to locate. In the heart of the poor but proud community of Binghamton was a small housing project called the Hampton Gardens. The fifty-year old complex was packed with people out on their weathered stoops, watching the cars as they drove pass on the main thoroughfare.   Small pockets of drug dealers posted up on the corners, walking from place to place as they flagged down cars.   Uniform police officers patrolled the area with their windows down and their shades on and kids ran back and forth on their bikes ignoring the absolutely dismal environment that they were being raised in.

Johnson and Steele parked on Tillman in front of the complex and stepped out into the lava-like heat. Their presence was immediately recognized.   Those who were up to no good simply disappeared into the many small cracks and crevices of the area, praying that they were not there for them. Johnson took the lead, walking up the dirty pathway to the small exposed black door of the apartment complex, he looked around before he beat on the door.

"Police," he said, putting his badge up to the peep-hole.

He could immediately hear scrambling behind the door. Beating at it again, so hard that the dust accumulating on the edges fell off, he looked back at Steele, who pulled her weapon and walked toward the side of the complex.

"Police," Johnson said again, voice booming like thunder. The people sitting on their stoops and chairs looked over at him, but said nothing. Finally, the door opened and a small teenage girl with her hair half braided looked out at them.

Johnson bit back irritation just long enough to follow policy and procedure. Showing her his badge, he looked past her into the dark house. "I'm looking for Mooky," he said, eye twitching. Sweat ran down his brow.

"He ain't here," the young girl answered.

"Where is he? Has he been here?" Johnson asked. The smell of marijuana wafted to his nose.

"No," the girl said with hesitation. "I haven't seen him." She tried to close the door a little more.

Johnson knew that she was lying. Placing his hand on the door above her head, he pushed it open. "Do you mind if I come in?" He stared at her. "You sure about that?"

"Yes," she protested. "Like I said, he ain't here." She rolled her eyes.

"You're right," Steele answered from behind Johnson. "He's right here." Her voice sounded a ragged. Pushing Mooky forward bound in handcuffs, she adjusted her belt and wiped the dirt from her jacket. Mooky appeared to be in pain, evidently from a serious struggle and his lip was bloodied. She pulled out her iPhone and pulled up a picture of Mooky. "This is the same guy, isn't it?" she asked Johnson smugly. "Or did I just beat the wrong man's ass?"

"No, that's our man." Johnson cracked a smile at how Steele had handled herself. Again, her reputation preceded her. "You wanna invite us in now?" he asked the girl, turning back around.

***

Mooky's girlfriend sat by him in a pair of jean shorts that barely covered her more than ample behind and applied a homemade icepack to his swollen lip while he sat on the small cloth sofa with his hands cuffed behind him. Rolling his eyes at Steele, who stood by the door with her arms folded, he mumbled under his breath.

Johnson stood on the opposite side looking into the kitchen and monitoring the window where Mooky had tried to escape from earlier. "So you gone play ball or what, Mooky? I don't have all day," he said sternly.

His girlfriend instantly gave Johnson a dirty look.

"Man, look. Like I told this Herculean bitch you brought with you, I don't know what happened to DeMario. My lil' nigga was fine when I left him this morning." Mooky winced at the pain of his bound hands and tried to adjust himself.

Johnson huffed. "Only you, the nurses, Ms. Washington and Councilman Ferris were in that room today. One of you slipped him something."

"If someone slipped him drugs, then who said that he got it today?" Mooky asked, quite intelligently.

"We believe that he did," Steele said, stepping forward. "And call me a bitch one more time and I'll do more than bust your lip and ribs. I'll cut your dick off."

Mooky pushed back in his seat. "Keep *her* away from me, *please*." He looked to Johnson to restrain his partner.

"Next time, don't run," Steele quipped. "So, who would be interested in killing your cousin?"

"Probably the same cop who tried to kill him before," Mooky snapped. "Why are y'all in my ass? I don't know shit."

"Why were you there visiting him today?" Johnson pushed.

"I just came to see how my cousin was doing, man. I just got out of jail, and when I heard what had happened, I wanted to go and see for myself. I could barely recognize my dude, man. Y'all should be arresting that pig that did that shit instead of chasing down his folks beating the hell out of them." Mooky fidgeted with the cuffs. "These damn things too tight."

"They aren't meant to be comfortable." Steele wasn't convinced. "Who else would want to hurt your cousin?" She walked over and kneeled down in front of him. She locked on his eyes and softened her voice. Immediately, she could see the change in his demeanor. They always changed when they really looked at her. They were men. "I'm not here to arrest you. You tell me what I want to know, you walk. It's that simple. I want to find whoever is responsible for killing your cousin. Don't you? You said yourself that you went to see him. Tell me who might have wanted him dead."

Mooky smacked his lips. "I ain't saying shit."

Johnson eyebrow rose in sudden interest. So the guy did know something. Instead of intruding on the interrogation, he watched Steele work. She stood up, took out her cuff key, leaned into his body so that he

could smell her intoxicating perfume and unlocked him.
Stepping back only a few inches, she put her hands on
her hips. "Then his killer will get away, and you'll be a
coward."

"I ain't no punk," Mooky snapped again.

"Then tell me what I want to know." She pushed
him harder.

"So, I can get killed to?" Mooky shook his head.
"Man, please."

"It's off the record," Steele promised. "I just want a
lead."

"Off the record," Mooky laughed sarcastically.
"Every motherfucker in Binghamton knows that you're
here....*off the record my ass*."

Steele folded her arms again. "I'll give you a get
out of jail free card one time and one time only. Just
tell me what I want to know and I'll walk out of here
and act like I never heard a word."

"And if I don't," Mooky asked.

"Resisting arrest, assault on a police officer...." She
started to count the charges out.

"Bitch, I didn't touch you!"

Johnson couldn't help but chuckle. "I saw otherwise," he lied.

Mooky's girlfriend got up to move out of the way.

"And I smell marijuana. Did you have time enough
to get rid of it?" Johnson asked the girl. "You didn't
did you? So, I'm sure if I toss this place, and I have
reasonable suspicion now, I'll find something. You
already got a jacket, sweetheart?"

"Leave her alone," Mooky growled.

"How sweet," Steele said with a grin. "Mooky, I'll
lock her ass up too."

"Tell them, Mooky," the girl said afraid. She knew that there was more than enough marijuana in the small apartment to get federal time. Shaking her head at him, she urged him quietly to tell them what they wanted to know so that they would leave.

Mooky put his head back on the couch in frustration. "Fuck!" he exclaimed.

Steele waited. She knew that he was on the verge of telling her what she wanted to hear.

"DeMario got mixed up with some cop and some politician. I don't know who. They paid him ten grand to set up that cop, but they couldn't put the money into an account, so they gave him cash. I was holding the money for him for a while, but the little nigga just blew threw it on that shit. I took the last little bit to flip some more work and make some more money, but I got pinched. So…"

Johnson's mouth watered. "What cop? What politician?" He had at least one person in mind. "Councilman Ferris?" he asked. Did he say that it was Councilman Ferris?"

Steele looked back at Johnson stupefied.

"I don't know one from the other. He never told me no damn names. All he said was that he'd be getting paid when it came time for his lawyer to sue the police department." Mooky rubbed his dusty hands over his face.

"Does anyone know that you know?" Steele asked. "We can place you somewhere if you testify."

"You ain't putting me nowhere. And I ain't saying that shit before no judge or no jury or no damned district attorney. You said that if I told you, you'd let us go. We about to bounce."

Johnson pushed the issue. "Do you at least know what color the cop or the politician is?"

"He said it was a white cop and a black politician. That's all I know."

Johnson looked at Steele. "We gotta go."

Steele nodded. "Get out of here," she said, turning back to Mooky. "Now, and don't come back if you know what's best for you."

Walking back out into the sunlight from the dark, dingy apartment, Johnson slipped on his shades and shook his head in disgust. The pieces were starting to fall into place now and it frustrated him to know that if it were Councilman Ferris that he had been orchestrating this entire farce right from city hall.

"These are very serious charges," Steele said, closing the door behind her. She looked up at Johnson and saw the determination in his face. "We have to be very careful about this."

"I'm not stupid, Steele," he answered, walking towards the car. "We're just going to ask him to come in and answer a few questions for us that might help us track down who slipped DeMario bad drugs."

"What we think are bad drugs," she corrected. "We haven't heard back from the hospital."

"How long have you worked with narcotics?" Johnson asked Steele, more as a point.

"Ten years," she answered.

"What did that look like to you?" Johnson opened the driver's door of his car and slipped onto the hot leather seats.

"I know what it looked like from five, ten feet away," Steele said, closing her door. "But we need confirmation first."

Johnson was tired of the bullshit. "Fine, call him and tell him that we want to talk to him."

"Don't fuck this up, Johnson," Steele warned. "You're already too close to this. Let me do the talking."

"You can do whatever you want to do. If I find out that smug bastard is responsible for all this shit, you might as well just take my damn badge, because I'm going to kill his ass."

***

Councilman Ferris in a fit of rage and fear, slammed down the phone on his Carpathian elm power desk at his office and stood straight up. Wiping his face, he looked around for his satchel and eyed it hanging on the back of his door. The women outside in the main area of the office space looked in quizzically as he stalked over to his bag, grabbed his track phone and closed the blinds to his office.

Cane answered on the first ring.

"Yeah," he said preoccupied.

"Your plan failed miserably." Ferris lowered his voice and went to the window to look out at the city.

"What are you talking about? I just saw the news. DeMario is dead. Just one more pill head to add to the coiffeurs."

"Unfortunately not just one more. I just got off the phone. Johnson and Steele are now investigating his death and want me to come in and answer questions tomorrow morning about what I was doing there."

"So lie." Cane didn't see the problem.

"Do you really think that they would call me in for questioning if they didn't possibly have something,

Cane? Think about this." Ferris voiced raised in frustration.

"It's just questioning. Some homicide bitch pulled me in for Twist's murdered a day and a half ago, and they couldn't hold me. I had an alibi for that night that he was murdered. I was at the basketball playoffs."

"Well, good for you. Unfortunately, I was right there in the same room. And I don't know if you remember the specifics of our arrangement but everyone goes down with the ship. So, if I burn…"

Ferris didn't have any idea how badly Cane wanted to kill him but he also knew that if anything happened to the pedophile, proof would surely surface. "So what do you want me to do about it?" Cane finally asked.

"I want you to do what you do. Handle Johnson and Steele before they unearth this entire operation."

"You're not thinking straight," Cane said, walking into another room where there was more privacy. "If you don't think that the police will figure this out. You have another thing coming. Killing some cop the day he gets ousted from the force is one thing, because he ain't no cop no more. But you want to kill two of the most high profile cops on the force tonight?"

"Cane, this is a deal breaker. Do you understand that? Now, I did what you wanted me to do, what you couldn't seem to get someone else to do. I took care of DeMario. I need you to take care of Johnson and Steele. I do not want to have to answer about today. I told you that at first."

When Cane was sure that Ferris was absolutely serious, he changed his tune. "Look, I've already got my hands full with this thing going down on Agosto tomorrow. We don't have the resources or the time to chase down two more cops. Are you crazy?"

Ferris didn't budge. "I want this done. I can handle the fall out."

"Fine. Fine. We'll get Magnelli to do it," Cane said.

Now Ferris was really pissed. "Magnelli has never killed anyone. In fact, he is a horrible cop. Why else would he need us? I heard that he should really be a P2 but they felt sorry for him and moved him to the DEA Task force."

"Beggars can't be choosers. Besides, it's time for him to get his hands dirty. Everyone else has had to. I had to kill Twist; you had to kill DeMario among others. It only makes sense. And to make you feel better, I'll send some of my locals with him, but it will be up to him to get it done."

"I'm not convinced that's a good idea."

"Let me be the first to tell you that this is a bad idea. Killing these two pigs could spook Agosto tomorrow and then I've missed my opportunity and paid these assholes for nothing."

Ferris snapped back. "Agosto has a hearing tomorrow come hell or high water. He will be a sitting duck. There is no option here."

"Are you scared to be questioned? I mean you are a politician. You guys lie all the time."

"I'm worried about how this looks. Perception is everything, Cane, especially in my line of work."

That sealed it for Cane. "Then you've got Magnelli. He'll do it. He has no choice."

Ferris felt like he was getting the short end of the stick but also knew that considering the short window he had to get this done, he'd have to work with whatever he could arrange.

"Get it done tonight," Ferris ordered.

"Both of them?" Cane asked.

"Yes, both of them," Ferris said with unfiltered arrogance.

Cane laughed. "And to think. You actually are going to be our next mayor. Fine. Consider it done, but Ferris your tab is growing. I just hope that you can pay it."

"The polls don't lie. I'm a shoe-in for mayor behind this madness, but not if I'm implicated for the death of the same man that I've been advocating for. And for your information, I don't care about creating more chaos. I'd rather deal with uncertainty and confusion then a clear case of homicide."

"Just remember that when it's time to pay me in favors," Cane said seriously.

"Trust me, based upon our relationship, I doubt that either one of us will ever forget each other in any respect. Just do it, tonight, please. Thank you." He hung up the phone abruptly.

22

There were loose ends to clean up all over town for Cane, and it was during the eleventh hour of the biggest move he had ever made by himself. There would be no more room for error. Becoming the most feared Molly dealer in Memphis would be his legacy, not anyone else's. He had worked the streets with his men and built the client base. He had busted his ass. He had done the legwork. And now it was only right that he reap the benefits. It was his time.

Now that DeMario was finally out of the picture, he had to get rid of Agosto, Johnson, and Steele, find that bitch, Roxie, and eventually get rid of Ferris. Too many loose ends.

But things had gone way too far to turn back now, even if he wanted to. Twist was dead. He had killed him, something that he had never thought he'd be force to do. As a result, he had to kill half his old staff, those only loyal to Twist, especially those bitches he had called his bodyguards. He and his men had to put bullets in the back of their little blonde heads and bury them way behind the horse stables.

His new supplier would be arriving in Memphis tonight with the first large shipment of Molly and he still needed to get guns to prepare for the war he would have with their old supplier out of Miami.

Still, sitting in the old den of their ranch home where he and Twist had plotted and schemed for years, he felt a sudden emptiness. Killing his best friend had been his only choice. The man had left him no options.

Twist had held them both back by not seeing the bigger picture of what they could accomplish in Memphis and beyond. Twist was content with what they had accumulated, but not interested in really cornering the market. Twist was the one that everyone liked, the attractive one. Twist had the women, rules and morals that didn't align with what they were trying to do. The list had been long for years. *Don't sell to teenagers. Don't set up operations in high schools. Don't sell to pregnant women. Don't, don't, don't!* They were drug dealers for fuck sake. They should not have been worried about the fall out. But Twist had a sense of responsibility that had pushed them into a corner.

So when Cane was approached by his contact in New York, he had to take the offer. And he had to get Twist out of the picture.

Joining up with Ferris made the most sense. Ferris had no rules. All he cared about was winning and getting rich. He wouldn't hold him back with nonsense or try to reason in a game where there was no reason. True, the sick fuck liked elementary boys and used their first shipment of Molly to desensitize his prey, but the man also delivered results. He had money to back his investments, power to protect him from the cops and juice in the community to sway opinion. Only, now he didn't see how he needed him. Ferris wanted to be mayor. The investment that Ferris had made with him for the new product would be returned through the campaign in the form of a well-funded pact and long-term revenue. It would make him untouchable in the races. He'd be able to buy air time, bill boards, minimize his need for fundraisers and run on the promise to clean up the department, drugs in the street and protect the children of Memphis.

Cane found that hilarious.

A pedophile was going to clean up Memphis.

But the people bought it hook, line and sinker.

Just like Ferris had said it would happen, it had happened. The guy was a master-strategist. No one was even looking his way right now and he was plotting right under their noses.

Of course the entire Baby Boys situation was a by-product of the initial plan, which was only to take over the Molly market. No one knew the drugs would kill the children and no one knew how insatiable Ferris's appetite for that kind of sick shit was. He had gone through four children in a matter of a month, and he seemed to have no conscious about it.

Consequently, neither did Cane.

His biggest concern, as was everyone involved, was not to get caught. So when Agosto got assigned to the high profile case, they knew there would be trouble. Agosto was a fucking boy scout and the guy never let up. Just as Cane had be concerned about, Agosto went straight to Twist about the Molly in the dead kids, and being the soft ass that Twist was, he started digging around and asking questions.

Digging around would only mean that Twist would eventually find out about the deal that he had made with his contact in New York. So the plot thickened quickly for Cane. He bumped up his timeline and got rid of Twist during a nasty altercation, chase and shoot-out.

The only loose end in Twist's murder was his side-piece of ass and best Molly dealer, Roxie, who got away during the shoot-out and had been missing ever since. Sammy, his right hand bodyguard had been charged with scouring the city for her, but hadn't turned up one damn lead. The girl was a ghost. Her apartment had gone untouched. She hadn't shown up in any of the places that she normally frequented and no one had seen her. All he could hope for at this point was that she stayed that way. Otherwise, she'd be killed on sight.

Then they had to set up Agosto to get him off the case and off their ass. Agosto had a long history of busting dealers. He had snitches on the street. Eyes everywhere and no real weaknesses outside of his family. They couldn't buy him and couldn't deter him from solving the case. Only they knew that just getting him thrown off the case or even off the force wouldn't be good enough. They'd have to kill him. Otherwise, he'd just help Johnson solve the case.

Johnson was never a real threat to Cane before De-Mario's death. He was hoping for no direct link between any of it. But now, with Ferris freaking out about being called in for questioning, yet another couple of cops would have to be killed. Hopefully, they could get rid of everyone before anyone had an opportunity to put it all together.

After Cane had spoken to Ferris earlier that day, they had gotten together later to discuss just how all of this would take place. The plan sounded solid. Cane originally thought about cutting all of his ties. He wanted to get rid of Ferris and Magnelli too, but there was a hitch. Ferris was not the type of man to get caught with his pants down. He was sure the bastard had concocted a way to make sure that if anything happened to him, the entire operation would be found out. So, instead of having Magnelli and Ferris killed, he opted to just keep them close…for now.

Besides, Magnelli was just a greedy bastard on the DEA Task Force that could smell an opportunity a mile away. He was also in too deep to turn back. In the past, Magnelli had turned his head a hundred times before to let deals happen in the city just as long as his hand was greased. However, when Ferris told Cane that they needed a permanent man inside the police department that he could trust and eventually tap when he became mayor to be the director, Magnelli seemed the perfect choice. He had the credentials, the greed and the spinelessness they needed to make things happen. Also no one could deny that the man had serious issues with his father, problems with managing money and a big ass chip on his shoulder. He sort of reminded him of himself.

Cane hadn't always been the way that he was now. He honestly had tried to live on the other side of the law, but it never paid. His father had promised him his pharmacy but reneged when he found out that he was selling prescription drugs to the locals. So to pay him back, he had burned the place down using a Molotov cocktail and leaving his father's battered body inside. It was the first murder he had ever done and he had gotten away with it. From there, it was all downhill.

Now, many years later, about to finally be his own boss - running the city the way he saw fit, and no one was going to stop him.

Tonight would be the end of all of the loose ends and the beginning of his new life.

"Boss, you ready?" His head bodyguard asked, sticking his head through the door. In the hallway, a small team of guards waited in full tactical gear to escort their boss to the meeting between him and the New York contact.

Cane pushed the weight of his heavy body up off the sofa and stood up. "Is everyone in place or what?" he asked, sticking snuff down in the lower jaw of his mouth.

"Yeah, everyone's ready. Just waiting till you say move," Sammy answered. He stepped completely into the room and rested his hands in front of him.

Cane picked up his red plastic spit cup off the coffee table and slipped on his John Deere cap. "Move."

***

The darkness of the Mississippi river was calming after a long day. Peaceful winds cooled the night air and crickets chirped in the thick grass around the edge of the bay. Under a full moon, Cane and his men quietly made it to the dock where the barge with their shipment had arrived on the banks of Arkansas.

The men on the boat quickly unloaded packages labeled produce onto large 18-wheel trucks while Cane and Sammy went to meet with his New York contact.

Two black Yukon Denali trucks were parked near a warehouse near the loading dock. Men stood outside in suits with ear pieces and guns. Escorting the men into the musty dank building, they took strategic places waiting for the meeting to begin.

Cane was quiet and somber tonight. With so much on his mind, he wasn't his normal arrogant self, which made Sammy nervous and uncomfortable. He watched over his boss, occasionally looking around to monitor the men who were monitoring them.

After a few moments of being alone, the door to the warehouse office where opened two tall, muscular, Puerto Rican men in suits stepped out before a well-dressed woman followed. She was average in looks. Black hair and olive skin toned with a large nose set on wide brown eyes. However, it was her demeanor that made her beautiful. In a St. John's black suit and pearls with heels that made her stand over six feet, she sauntered over to the table wear Cane was sitting.

"Very nice to see you again," she said, passing off her clutch purse to her bodyguard.

"Yeah, same here, Ms. Santiago," Cane said, standing up as a sign of his respect for her.

"I gather that since you are here everything is in place?" she sat down and crossed her long shapely legs.

"Yeah, we got everything in place. We got a farm house on the outskirts of town ready to set up and start manufacturing. All we were waiting on was the materials from you. I've got girls ready to work, and I've got a fucking shit load of orders to fill."

Ms. Santiago seemed pleased, but her face was hard to read with the long scar down the side of it. It was old, from many years before and ran from her left ear down to her chin. The jet-black bob haircut that she wore hid some of it, but it was absolutely noticeable. Cane thought it made her look even sexier. A serious business woman with a past. He liked that. He liked her.

"And your previous supplier in Miami? Has that been a problem?" Her eyes locked on Cane.

He knitted his meaty fingers together and leaned over on the table. "I've got a connection I'm waiting to come through on some guns. But no, I don't think that will be a problem. My men are ready to battle if it comes to our doorstep, but we are going through with this partnership because you can give me what I need. Those other fucks were loyal to Twist. I don't want nothing to do with them."

Ms. Santiago cut him off but did so only with one raised finger. "My only concern is that you'll be able to produce for me, Mr. Cane. We, meaning your organization and mine, have agreed on a quarterly dividend that you have to make good on, otherwise you leave me in a very curious situation."

"I've always made good on my debts on time." Cane sucked his teeth. "What makes you think I'll stop now?"

"I'm sure that you won't. Just let me know in advance if there is push back from Miami. I need to be able to protect my investments."

Now Cane was just insulted. However, he tried to hide his disdain for her statements considering the fragile nature of their budding relationship. "If there is pushback from Miami, I'll handle it. I don't' need Yankees coming down here to my territory trying to fix things for me. It just don't look right. Like I said, I'm working with someone to get more guns and equipment, just in case there is problem."

"And this person would be?" she asked with a soft voice.

"Anonymous," he answered with a tilted head.

Ms. Santiago smiled. "Everyone knows that there is only one organization you can buy from here, Mr. Cane. He's a son-of-a-bitch isn't he?"

Cane rolled his eyes. "Yes, he is, but like I said, I'll handle it."

Ms. Santiago smiled. "I'm sure that you will, Mr. Cane. I have faith in you. Now, shall we get down to it? As we speak, my men are loading your trucks. Once we have payment, they can drive off and I can fly back to Manhattan."

"Do you take checks?" Cane asked, as Sammy placed a large container of money on the table and turned it towards Ms. Santiago to open.

She smiled softly. "Unfortunately no." Her body-guard opened the case to reveal bundles of hundred dollar bills wrapped and ready for her. She ran her hand over the cash and then sat back in the chair. "It's a pleasure doing business with you, Mr. Cane."

"The pleasure is all mine," Cane said, spitting into his cup. "You sure you don't want to count it?"

Her bodyguard picked up the case and stepped back. As he did so, the machine gun under his coat showed.

Cane looked up at it and narrowed his eyes at the man.

Ms. Santiago offered her manicured hand to Cane and he shook it graciously. Standing up from her chair, she pulled out a cigarette and lit it. "Oh, I trust you, Mr. Cane. Besides, I know where you live." With an evil smile, she turned on her heels and followed her men out of the warehouse as quickly as she came.

"That was short and sweet," Cane said, standing up. "Get them boys on the road. I want the supplies at the warehouse in an hour so we can start production."

"Yes, boss," Sammy said, following Cane out of the warehouse.

Cane stopped at the door. "And that other thing?" he asked as his truck pulled up with his men waiting for him to load in.

"It's all going down tonight," Sammy answered. "That's why we have you going to the crawfish festival. It'll be plenty of people there who will see you. You'll have an alibi."

"Good. Let's get this shit done. I'm tired of having to think about it."

23

Alex's Tavern was packed to capacity. The little pub buried in the obscurity of homes and businesses on the quiet side of Jackson Avenue played Led Zeppelin on the jukebox and was filled with smoke and cigarettes. A mix of college students, on and off duty police officers, couples cuddled up together hiding from their spouses and men watching the baseball game on the flat screen televisions mounted on the wall gave the small place a clandestine atmosphere.

Downing another beer under dim lights, Johnson went over his notes one more time with Steele, who sat on the other side of their booth eating a burger and fries. They had been chasing ghosts all day. Following up with as many insiders as they could, they tried to track down any cops who could possibly be on the take with local politicians. No one had anything promising. Without any idea if the politician in question was a councilman, commissioner, clerk, state representative, congressman or a hundred other positions, they were walking in the dark.

"Shit," Johnson said, pushing back from the table. "It just doesn't add up. My gut tells me that it is Ferris, but why would he want DeMario dead? And he doesn't roll with cops. No one can put him with anyone."

Steele pushed her MacBook Air to the side and sighed. "In the past, Ferris has not been a friend of the department. He has proposed cuts to salaries, layoffs, everything short of public executions. Plus, he's always been after Amway. Everyone knows he's lobbying for him to be replaced."

"Yeah, but so has two or three other city councilmen," Johnson answered reluctantly. He rubbed is aching head. "Let's go through his businesses. Maybe there is something there."

"The guy owns shit all over town," Steele said, rolling her neck. Pulling up the Assessor's website, she put in his name. "He owns a restaurant, some parcels of land, it looks like three child care centers, an apartment complex…"

Johnson stopped her. "He owns child care centers?" The wheels in his mind started to turn quickly.

Steele ran a query on Google and pulled up the website. "Yes, Happyland Daycare Centers. They are for before and after care of school aged children along with toddlers." She looked over at Johnson and cringed. "Are you thinking what I'm thinking?"

"I wonder where his central offices would be located," Johnson said, finishing his beer.

"His management office is off of Walnut Grove across from the main library," she said with a glint of hope in her eyes.

Johnson pushed up to the table. "We'd never get the chance to access those files the legal way, Steele. You know that. But if we were to break in tonight and look around for ourselves. We could probably get something."

Steele shook her head. "I was afraid you would say that, Johnson. It's illegal. It wouldn't stand up in court, plus we could lose our badges."

"We could save lives, Steele. Think about it. What link does the Baby Boys case have to him outside of children? Nothing. Now, he lives alone. He's not married. He's been accused of being gay."

"Just because a man is gay doesn't make him a fucking, murdering pedophile," Steele protested.

"I agree. But what if he isn't gay. What if he's just a pedophile? What if he's our guy?" Johnson hit the table with this fists. "Steele, we need to do this. If we can find any records that prove that these children all went to Happyland, then we have a reason to legally access his files."

"Then let's go and talk to the parents of the victims," she said, trying to reason with him.

Johnson's voice strained. "Are you fucking kidding me? He's been in contact with all of them. They call on him all the time. They think he's their advocate. They will tip him off. We have to do this quietly."

"Aren't you supposed to be moving in with your girlfriend tonight or something?" she asked, hoping that they could do this later and give him time to sleep on his insane idea.

"She can wait. She's a cop. She gets it. Trust me. But this can't wait. Every moment that we sit around here holding our dicks, we get closer to losing the opportunity to get this guy."

"If he's the one," she said interjecting doubt. She wouldn't comment on the *holding our dicks* statement. In just the few hours that she knew Johnson, she had discovered that he was less than sensitive.

He pushed her further. "Let's just go and check the place out. It can't be too hard to get into."

"What if there is an alarm?"

Johnson smiled. "I've got a way to get around that too. We all used to patrol. You can't tell me that you don't have a few friends who still walk the beat. One of my boys will have my back. Now, let's go."

"I don't know, Johnson," Steele said, unconvinced.

Johnson offered his hand. "Trust me, please. I'm telling you that this will work."

***

The private office space off of Walnut Grove was completely deserted. No cars were parked outside of the many one-floor bricked buildings. Johnson and Steel parked a few blocks down and then walked over to the back of the buildings. Scaling the fence facing the back of the office buildings, they went to the back window of Ferris's building and stuck a crowbar under the window to shimmy it open. As expected, the alarm sounded.

"Just wait," Johnson said, grabbing Steele by the arm.

"I told you that it would be an alarm," she said, pissed that she had even followed him into his hair-brained scheme. "We're going to get caught!"

"No, we won't. Trust me," Johnson said, pulling her back into the shrubs beyond sight.

They nestled back into the trees and waited for a uniform patrol car to pull up. It was only minutes later a car pulled up with blue lights and got out. They could hear him on the radio reporting in to the dispatcher. Following protocol, the officer walked the building and checked it. Once he was done, he walked to the back of the building and shined his light into the trees.

"Okay, let's go," he said, coming out of the shrubs. He nodded at the officer and then crawled into the window.

"What if there are cameras?" Steele asked, still not convinced.

Johnson pulled out two masks. "Put this on."

"Johnson, this is stupid," Steele protested.

Johnson sighed in frustration. "Hernandez is on duty tonight. He's the burglary detective. He owes me like a hundred fucking favors. If there is video, it will come to him first. He'll get rid of it."

"How can you be sure?" Steel asked, slipping on the mask.

"Because he's done it before," Johnson answered. "Now let's go."

They crawled into the window and landed right behind Ferris' desk in his private office. Quickly, they pulled out their small flashlights and surveyed the room.

"What are we looking for?" Steele asked.

"Files from the childcare center. He wouldn't keep them there," Johnson answered, using a utility knife that he kept with him to bust open Ferris's desk. He passed her the knife. Get the file cabinets open and search for anything that can tell us if those kids went to his child care center."

Steele opened the door and went out into the office building. She looked around for cameras but didn't see any. One of God's small favors. Quickly finding the file room, she found a large row of archive files labeled Happyland. Just as Johnson had done, she used the knife to open the cabinet.

She had studied the boys and their parents' names a hundred times since the case had landed on her desk. It only took a few minutes to pull every file for all four boys. The reality was sobering. Not only had Johnson been right, but it was more than possible that they had finally cracked the Baby Boys case open and found their killer.

Johnson walked into the room behind her, shining the light on her face.

"Did you find anything?" he asked with hope.

Steele nodded. "All four," she said angrily. "How did we miss this?"

"It doesn't matter. Let's just get them and go. Wipe down everything you touched. We've got one minute."

When they were done, they crawled back out of the window and signaled with the flashlight to the officer walking to the perimeter. Nodding, the police officer got back on the radio.

"We've got a possible break in. There appears to be a window open in the back," the officer said over his radio.

Johnson and Steele headed over the fence quickly the same way that they had gotten in. Walking quickly to their car with the files in hand, Johnson looked over at Steele and smiled. "We may have gotten the mother-fucker."

* * *

As a part of protocol, Ferris was immediately notified when the alarm to his office went off. Paralyzed with fear when he got the call, he jumped out of his warm bed and started to get dressed. Calling Cane on the track phone as he grabbed his keys, he went out to his three car-garage and jumped into his Mercedes-Benz.

"Someone was at my office, Cane. Why do I have the feeling that it was Johnson and Steele? Aren't they supposed to be dead?" he shouted.

"I don't give a fuck who was at that office. Send your office manager. That's their job. Tonight, you have to stay in the house if you want our plan to work," Cane growled back at him. The sound of music and people drowned out his voice.

"Where are you? I can barely hear you?" Ferris exclaimed. "I have to go and get to the office."

"And what are you going to do?" Cane protested. "Whoever was in there, got what they came for. You need to stay at the fucking house where we agreed that you'd be. Go down in that fucking wine cellar and wait. Or all of this is for nothing and I swear to God, I'll kill you myself!" Realizing that he was drawing attention to himself, Cane lowered his voice.

"Those files are there. I kept them there so that it wouldn't look suspicious, but now that they've broken in, I know that they've got them. They know, Cane. I'm telling you that those snooping bastards know. That's why they wanted me to come in for questioning tomorrow. They fucking know!"

"Would you just calm down?" Cane said, scratching his head in frustration. He looked around at the people walking, talking and laughing around him at the festival and closed his eyes to center himself. "They will be taken care of just like we planned, tonight. But you have to pull your shit together and wait."

Ferris looked out of his rearview mirror and cursed. "Fuck!" Turning his car back off, he put his head down on his steering wheel. "You have to take care of this Cane."

"Then let me," Cane answered. "Go back into the house. In thirty minutes, go down to your cellar and wait. By morning, this will all be over and you'll have another 15 minutes of fame in front of all those fucking cameras that you love so much. Go and work on your speech or something."

Ferris raised his head and took a deep breath. "You've gotten what you want. The meeting happened tonight. The supplies for the drugs are here. The money is the in bank. Why would I trust you?"

Cane chucked. "Because motherfucker, there is no one else to trust. Now, if I had plans on killing you, would I tell you to go down to your cellar? Would I even let you know what I planned to do? I'm trying to watch your ass and mine too. I know you have something on me. I'm not stupid. Your life is my security."

Ferris sucked in a breath. Cane evidently knew him better than he thought. He did have something on him. Something heavy. But he didn't want to use it unless he absolutely had to. He calmed himself to the point of cool arrogance again. "Fine," he said, getting out of the car. "I'm going back into the house. Just get this done, please. I'm ready to move past this."

"You and me both," Cane said, hanging up the phone.

24

Johnson and Steele sat in their unmarked police car in the driveway of Steele's Cordova home reading through the files. Every single child that had gone missing had been in the care of Happyland at least two years before they had gone missing and ended up dead. While there was still no direct tie to Ferris, they knew that all that was needed was to start an investigation in the morning and then ultimately connect him to the children. With formal questioning of the families and Ferris, they could establish a motive and start to dig into his private life.

"We finally have his ass," Johnson said, staring off into space. Even as he spoke, he could see the faces of all the children he had unearthed in the last few months.

"You did it," Steele said, reaching over to rub his hairy, muscular arm. Her voice was warm now like a wool blanket.

Johnson cracked a smile. "No, I didn't." He turned to her and shook his head. His voice croaked low. "Agosto did. If he'd never had the balls to sacrifice everything by beating the shit out of DeMario, then we wouldn't have found dick."

Steele paused. "Well, his sacrifice won't be in vain. We're going to nail this guy. Maybe we can even get his job back."

The thought brought Johnson comfort. "He's a good cop. And he is not hate monger. He has a family..."

Steele cut him off. "I know."

Johnson nodded and let the moment go as quickly as it had come. "I'll take the files with me, just in case. Possession is nine-tenths of the law. In the morning, we'll question that fucking bastard and nail his ass to the wall. Get some rest. Go see your family or whoever is in there waiting on you."

Steele raised a brow. "No one's in the house. My son spent the night with his friends tonight. They are probably up right now playing video games. I'm just going in to crash. You get some rest too. I'll see you in the morning," Steele said, opening the door.

Getting out, she meandered slowly up the walkway to her large-two story contemporary home, waved at him before finally slipping inside. Closing the door, she turned on the porch light as Johnson pulled off.

For the first time in months, he felt like he had actually accomplished something. The Baby Boys case was wearing him down, and there were many times during this process where he wondered if he would even be able to solve the case before the FBI came in and took everything over. But now, he felt certain that he could put all the pieces together.

Checking his phone, he realized that he had missed a call from Carmen. Dammit! The hours had passed by quickly and he was certain that she'd be pissed at him. He was supposed to be moving some of his stuff into her place tonight, but he hoped that considering the circumstances, she'd understand. Dialing her number, he waited.

She answered on the first ring.

"Hello." She folded his jeans and laid them on the bed.

"Baby," Johnson said, glad to hear her voice. "I'm so sorry."

"It's okay," she said, grabbing his night bag.

"What are you doing?"

"Packing your things."

His heart skipped a beat. Was she getting rid of the things that he had left at her house after one night of not checking in?

"Am I already in the dog house?" he asked.

She chuckled as she picked up a beer and sat at the end of his bed. "No, I'm at your place, silly. I figured that I'd get started since you were running late."

He let go a sigh of relief. "Oh, good."

She paused. "You sound exhausted."

"I am, but I think we cracked the case."

Carmen smiled. She knew what that felt like. "I'm so glad, baby. You need this. Hey, I got an idea. Why don't you grab a pizza and we can just chill out at your place tonight. We can move tomorrow."

That sounded perfect to Johnson. "I love your beautiful mind. I'll stop at Papa Joe's and grab a pizza, get some beer and head there."

"Alright, see you in a few."

"Alright, love you." He let it slip out before he had time to think about how she would react. Sure he had said it before, said it just that day, but this was a casual sort of recognition that he'd never attempted before.

"Love you too," she said with a snicker in her voice

***

Collin Magnelli parked a block from Johnson's condo and waited. He knew that he'd be home at some point and chose this location to do the job. This wasn't Magnelli's forte and it was never part of the agreement with Ferris and Cane, but evidently it had to be done. He sat quietly in the stolen car with illegally deep tinted windows and a bad tag that Cane had provided and waited with another man from Cane's camp with his lights off. Everyone called the man Butter, for what reason, Magnelli didn't care, but he was a specialist when it came to house hits. Butter was a tall white man with a bald head, bad hygiene and too many tats and scars not to be a career criminal. Every time the man spoke, his breath was like fog fouling the air more than likely because of the rotten teeth in his mouth.

"How long are we supposed to sit here?" Butter asked.

Magnelli lowered the window just enough to circulate clean air and not vomit. "As long as it takes," he said, wishing that Johnson would quickly pull up so that he could get this done and get out of here.

He took no pride in killing cops, but it was also torture to be in the car with the bad breath heathen. Under normal circumstances, he'd be locking bastards like this up, not planning murders with him.

Rubbing on his balls through his jeans, Butter reached for the radio to turn the channel.

"Leave it," Magnelli said rolling his eyes.

"What's up your ass?" Butter asked.

Magnelli looked over at the man and rolled his eyes. "Look, we're not here to talk about our *feelings*, okay? Let's just get that straight. We're just gonna sit here quietly and wait. When he gets in the house and gets settled, we do it. It's that simple. Not fucking rocket science and there's nothing to talk about."

"Why don't we just clip him when he gets out of his car? It's easier." Butter didn't understand why there was a need to make things complicated. He'd been doing this a long time and it was always best to not let the mark get inside of his home.

"I was told that you follow directions well, Butter." Magnelli gritted his teeth. "And before we left, I'm certain that Cane gave you directions. He wanted things done a certain way. So just follow them."

"Abso-fucking-lutely," Butter said, sucking his teeth.

A few minutes later, Johnson pulled up to the front of his condo and got out with a backpack, a hot pizza and a six-pack of beer. Closing the door to his car with his hip, he looked around but missed their vehicle, parked so far away. Quickly, he made his way up to the door, unlocked it and went inside.

"I thought this guy was supposed to be a damn player. It's a Thursday night and he's going home alone to eat," Butter joked. "Guess we're his only date for tonight." He pulled out his AK-47 and checked his magazine.

Magnelli ignored Butter's continued attempt to get on his nerves. Checking his own weapon, he slipped on his mask and checked the backseat where four Molotov cocktail bombs waited to be lit and thrown.

"So how long you thinking 'bout waiting?" Butter asked. "Until he goes to sleep?"

"Give him a chance to get settled. Then we do this," Magnelli said, feeling butterflies erupt in his stomach. While he wouldn't dare tell Butter the truth, he felt like he was going to be sick.

***

Johnson looked around his condo and realized that Carmen had cleaned. All the clothes that had been thrown over the sofa throughout the long week had been picked up. The papers scattered on the counter in the kitchen had been organized. It smelled like air freshener and felt like a woman had been there. Not like a girl or a chick he was screwing but a real woman. That was an odd but comforting feeling.

The television in the living room was on the news; the kitchen smelled like Pine-Sol and bleach; the garbage had been taken out. And his washer and dryer were running. Strangely, he liked the feeling. Throwing the pizza on the counter, he quickly dropped his bags, took off his gun and headed up stairs to find Carmen.

"Baby?" he said as soon as his foot hit the top step of the second floor. "Where are you?"

"In your room," she called out in a low, sexy voice.

He walked in his bedroom to find candles burning and her lying in the dark room naked on his bed. A smile formed on his lips. Closing the door behind him, he pulled off his t-shirt and walked over to the bed.

"Damn," he said, licking his lips. "Now that is what a man is supposed to come home to."

Carmen grinned, sitting up in the bed against his pillows. Her long hair washed over her shoulders and down to the rigid tips of her rose-colored nipples. Crawling to the edge of the bed to meet him, she tugged at his belt.

"Why don't you go and jump in the shower and then we can celebrate your break in the case," she said, kissing his lips gently.

The smell of perfume and mint transferred to his lips from her. Johnson moaned at the taste of her and grew hard in his pants. Grabbing her by the shoulders, he pulled her to him and kissed her deeper. One of his large hands curved around the round globe of her warm breasts. "I'm not going anywhere," he said, helping her unbuckled his pants.

"So you're just going to come to bed funky?" Carmen joked.

"You won't notice," Johnson hissed, pulling his pants down. He was commando and ready to go. Rubbing his hand over his manhood, he watched her with a sharpened expression of lust and need.

She looked at his rock hard penis, pointing up towards his navel and reached out for it. "I want you inside of me now," she ordered.

Johnson stopped her abruptly. Throwing her back on the bed in one easy overly practiced move, he grabbed her by the back of her knees and pulled her towards the end of the bed. Her liquid hair dragged behind her. "Not before I taste you," he said, bending to lick the folds between her thighs.

She closed her eyes and rested her head back. Undulating under him, she opened her legs wider to let him in. Her nails raked over his head and down his neck as she guided him towards her sweet spot.

He kept his eyes on her, enjoying each and every reaction to his touch. With every intimate kiss and lick, he drove her wilder and wilder.

Rising up with his mouth wet with her essence, he finally pulled her shapely hips toward his own. He couldn't' take it any longer. He had to be inside of her right then. Wedging the head of his throbbing penis inside of her, he leaned into her body and kissed the side of her neck.

She gasped and then relaxed to let him fully enter.

"That's it, baby. Let me in," he said, using one hand to grab her by the waist and pull her in further.

"Luke," she whimpered. "Oh, Luke."

Johnson's head flung back as he clenched her thighs in his hands. Pumping into her while he stood, feet planted into the carpet, he finally let out a growl. "I've been wanting to do this all day," he whispered. Biting his lip, he looked down at her beautiful body. "Shit, you're beautiful."

She opened up wider and pushed against him.

The sight of her complete enjoyment only made Johnson want her more. He crawled into the bed on top of her and ran his fingers down the side of her body. Still inside of her, he stopped for a moment and looked into her eyes.

"I meant it, you know," he said, fighting the snugness of her tight fit.

"Meant what?" she asked, finally opening her eyes.

"That I love you."

Rubbing her fingers over his stubbly five-o'clock shadow, she smiled. "I love you too."

***

The pizza was cold by the time that Johnson and Carmen came sauntering back downstairs together. He only wore his boxers with no shirt. While she opted for one of his black MPD t-shirts. Exhausted and starving, Carmen crawled up on the stool in front of the bar while Johnson walked into the kitchen and fixed her plate.

Johnson smiled at her and passed her a beer. "I can admit that I could get used to this."

"Really?" she asked, taking a sip. She shrugged her slim shoulders. "Well, so could I." They locked eyes again, feeling a sense of euphoria between them. She finally found words to speak before they ended up on the floor making love again. "So, tell me how you broke the case."

Johnson grabbed his backpack and pulled out the files. Throwing them on the bar, he nodded. "I can't tell you how I got these, but I will just say that there is a connection between all four children."

She looked down at the files and opened them. "Happyland?" she asked with a frown. "Isn't that the childcare centers that are around town?"

"Bingo," Johnson said, giving her a nod.

Carmen flipped through the papers. "I can barely see in the dark."

"Good point." He walked over to the wall by the refrigerator and flicked on the light. "That better?" he asked.

"Yeah, thanks," Carmen said without taking her eyes off the paperwork. She looked up at him confused. "So are you suggesting that the *politician* involved is Councilman Ferris and that he's wrapped up in drugs?" Her mouth dropped open. "The same guy who is on the news everyday demanding something be done about the Baby Boys murders?"

Johnson knew it was hard to fathom. "One in the same. Help yourself to some easy reading while I warm the pizza," he said, slipping a few slices onto a plate and sticking it in the microwave.

As soon as Johnson's finger hit the keypad, a loud explosion erupted behind him. His heart constricted when he heard Carmen's blood curdling scream. Turning to see a spray of bullets impact with the walls, through the furniture and into the kitchen, he ducked behind the counter just in time to save his own head.

"Carmen!" he screamed. "Carmen!"

There was no answer.

More bullets slammed into the walls, knocking chunks of drywall and hanging paintings onto the floor and chipping away at Johnson's position curled below the counter behind the dishwasher. He could literally feel bullets jamming into the back of the appliance. It was only a matter of time before the bullets made their way through to the other side and in to him. He had to move.

He waited for what seemed like minutes but was only seconds for the shooters to reload. When the bullets stopped, he raised up from his crouching position to find Carmen.

The lights above him flickered on and off, shattered by the shooting and hanging out of the ceiling. Sockets popped with electricity around him.

"Baby," he whispered, knowing that he only had seconds. Shattered glass cracked under his feet, tearing into his sensitive flesh. "Where are you?"

He looked over the bar to see her twisted body lying on the floor. Blood oozed from her gaping chest wound and out the side of her mouth. A hole was blown through her back and out of her rib cage.

Stunned, he stood there looking at her body a second too long. The shooters reloaded and began the second wave of their assault. The bullets came again, this time concentrated on his position instead of all over the condo.

Seeing his gun on the end of the counter, he grabbed it and his backpack and got behind the counter again.

Shaky fingers made it nearly impossible for him to dial 911, but he managed. As soon as the dispatcher answered, he screamed into the phone past the sound of the thunderous clap of ammunition.

"I need an ambulance at 312 Florida. Officer down. The shooters are still on site. My badge number is 9898. I repeat, officer down. I need a fucking bus now!" He didn't care about himself as much as he cared about getting her help.

Dropping the phone without hanging it up, he heard footsteps at the front door. A kick sent the door off its hinges and the men quickly stepped inside. Flanking each other, they moved closer to Johnson.

He could hear the operator asking questions on the phone and the sound of glass cracking under the men's boots. But he stayed deathly quiet.

"120 seconds exactly," Magnelli said, looking at his watch.

"Who's the bitch?" Butter asked, moving closer to-wards Carmen's body. From about five feet away, he looked down at her lifeless limbs. "Nice ass too. Such a waste."

Magnelli was across the room, scanning the living room for Johnson's body. "There wasn't supposed to be anyone else here. Is she alive?" He could barely see through the mask. Irritated with the situation and short on time, he dismissed the girl. "Dead, check her and find our primary target."

Butter aimed his weapon directly at Carmen's body to shoot her one final time, but as he did, Johnson inhaled one low breath and then stood up quickly from behind the counter. There was no time for Butter to react. Years of training mixed with the chaotic adrenaline rushing through his veins, gave Johnson a dead-on hit. Exhaling, he pulled the trigger as soon as Butter saw him and shot the man directly in his neck.

Instinctively, Butter grabbed his neck, dropping his weapon to apply pressure to the gushing wound. Blood spewed from his mouth and hit the floor, flapping like a fish.

Magnelli turned and began to shoot widely in Johnson's direction, though he could not get a direct hit because of the wall.

Crouched again, Johnson waited before returning fire. Raising his hand just a little above him in the direction of Magnelli, he pulled the trigger blindly shooting.

Magnelli ducked behind the sidewall leading out of the dining room into the living room and dropped his duffle bag. Hearing sirens out of the shattered windows and seeing onlookers starting to come out of their homes, he started to panic.

Shit! They had taken too long to do the hit. Time had run out.

Kneeling down while still keeping his eyes on the corner as Johnson returned fire, he pulled out the Molotov cocktail bombs from the bag and placed them on the floor beside him. Sticking the muzzle of his weapon around the corner blindly, he shot again, but this time hitting Butter in the back.

The man gurgled out his last painful breaths and went limp on his side.

Glancing quickly around the corner, Magnelli cursed. "Fuck!"

Johnson crawled around the corner of the kitchen quietly, biting down on his lip as he cut his knees and hands on the broken glass. Blood trailed behind him as he made his way to Carmen's body. Putting his fingers to her neck, he felt for a pulse. Nothing. He was about to pull her back behind the kitchen wall with him when Magnelli stepped out to throw the homemade bomb at him.

Without words, Johnson tried to cover Carmen's body. Pulling her by her broken chest, he wrapped his arms around her and lowered her head to brace for the impact of the fire.

Magnelli stepped closer, hoping that his eyes were deceiving him.

He stepped closer with the bottle still in hand. The rag inside of it was lit and ready to be thrown.

"Carmen?" Magnelli said in disbelief. His voice trailed off into an abyss of terror at what he had done.

Johnson looked up, confused about why the masked man had stopped.

Realizing that he had no choice but to cover his tracks, Magnelli raised his hand to throw the bottle, but Johnson had his weapon tucked under her body. Stealthily aiming it, he shot at Magnelli as he raised his hand.

Throwing the bottle only a few feet away from him, Magnelli ran out of the door the way that he had come.

Fire quickly consumed the area, nearly blocking Johnson from the entranceway. He struggled with

Carmen's body, blood covering his hands and naked chest. Picking her up in his arms as the fire spread around them, he jumped through the flames with her in his embrace. His legs burned as he ran out of the door. Hearing screeching tires in the nearby distance, Johnson knew that whoever the hitter was had driven off. As soon as he was outside in the night air, he dropped onto the dewy grass and rolled hard, putting the fire out on their bodies.

Sirens rushed towards him. Blue lights pulled up on his lawn in front of his condo and police officers poured out of their cars to help them.

Still holding on to Carmen, Johnson looked on as everything that he had ever owned went up in smoke.

"Sir, are you alright?" an Asian male officer asked, running to Johnson and dropping to his knees.

"It's not me. It's her," Johnson said, voice cracking.

The officer put his hand to Carmen's neck as he pulled her out of Johnson's arms. Looking over at the other officer standing a few feet away, he nodded. "She's gone," he said, recognizing her face.

25

After a long day, there was nothing better than the peace and tranquility of a clean home. Since she was alone for the night, there was no need to cook a big meal, so Steele had settled for leftover Church's chicken and a bottle of chardonnay. A little tipsy after her second glass, she sauntered into her downstairs master bedroom, sat on the edge of her king-sized bed and kicked off her black boots.

An instant sigh of relief escaped her as soon as her tired feet were free. Damn, she was exhausted. Resisting the urge to crawl into bed without cleaning herself, she grabbed the remote and turned on her stereo.

Disc one. Track three.

Stevie Ray Vaughn's Tin Pan Alley came on.

Swaying to the sound of down home blues, Steele walked into her bathroom and sat on the edge of her two-person garden tub. Twisting the knobs, she turned on the water as hot as she could get it and poured in bath salts. The aroma of cherry blossom rose to her nose, creating bubbles in the tub as it filled to the top.

After a few more sips of wine, she finally started to peal out of her clothes, one slow layer at a time. With each layer removed, she felt more and more relaxed, even though involuntarily she played the day's event back in her head.

Four dead children.

DeMario.

Councilman Ferris.

Mooky.

The mysterious cop.

Agosto.

She took another sip of her wine and rolled her eyes. The police didn't pay her enough for this bullshit. She should have stayed in the military. By now, she'd be a fucking Lt. Colonel and preparing for retirement. Instead, here she was chasing idiots on the street who didn't even deserve the freedom that others had died to give them and for half the pay.

What a life she had chosen for herself and her son. Her mother would be proud.

Walking to her medicine cabinet, she pulled out her PTSD medicine, dropped a pill in her hand and washed it down with another sip of wine.

That should do the trick.

Looking at herself in the mirror naked, she pulled her hair down out of the ponytail and wiped her hands under her eyelids, wiping away the extra mascara. Brown eyes stared back at her, red and tired. Black hair fell over her chocolate shoulders, stopping at her defined collarbone. Full breasts flowed down into a six pack of muscle and expanded back out at wide-set hips encasing a bushy secret of pleasure and traveled down to muscular, thick long legs in need of a good shaving, wide calves and finally manicured feet.

She looked at herself in the mirror like this every night, as if she expected something to change. And yet, nothing ever did.

Getting on the scale, she looked at the digital calculator as it populated. 162 lbs. She had been that weight for ten years. Stepping off the scale, she cursed under her breath again when she thought about the case and prepared to get in the tub when she heard a creaking sound even beyond her music. The hardwoods floors in her hallway right outside of her bedroom had not settled yet. She had just had them replaced the week before. Any steps over it made a distinctive sound. She even heard whoever it was stop when the noise startled them.

Flicking off the light in the bathroom very carefully, she pulled her Glock from behind the bathroom door, hanging in her shoe rack and put a pink, terrycloth towel over it. Laying it and the towel on the side of the garden tub, she slipped into the water under the towering bubbles as they rose with the water still running and stilled her movements. Holding her breath, she waited.

At that very moment, Stevie Ray Vaughn's slow melodic song ended and the entire room was suddenly eerily silent. She could hear footsteps in her bedroom, invading her space. Two sets of large feet.

Without a question, she knew that it wasn't her son, because she had just talked to him a few minutes before, and he was at his friend's house across town, playing video games and sucking down sodas. And no one else had a key.

This was an intruder. *Intruders to be exact.*

The water only magnified the footsteps. She heard them and her own heartbeat as they got closer and closer. Holding her breath, she waited.

The footsteps entered into the bathroom and then someone turned on the light. Steele went deathly still, praying that her entire body was covered by the bubbles and running water. Unable to see anything, she kept her eyes open in the hot water, batting them occasionally only because she couldn't help the natural reaction, but she denied her body the ability to breathe.

A man's deep baritone voice rattled the silence. "I thought you said that the bitch was downstairs?"

Another man answered. "She was." He walked to the closet and pushed her clothes aside. "I don't know. Maybe she went upstairs or in another room."

"How could you miss her? Go look under the bed again," the man with the deep voice ordered.

"There is nothing under the fucking bed," the other man protested. "I'm not looking again. Come on. We're wasting time. Boss said to do her and get back pronto."

Steele could feel her strength waning. Closing her eyes, she waited as the words *do her* repeated in her head.

"Turn the light back off, so that she won't know that you've been in there," the other man reminded.

The two men walked out of the bedroom, searching for Steele, not knowing that she was right under their noses the entire time.

Quietly, she raised her head out of the water to listen for their footsteps as they walked across the hardwood floors again in the hallway. Sure that she had enough time to get out, she slowly crawled out of the bathtub and grabbed her Glock from under the towel.

There was no time to dry off or even think about how she looked. Inching from the bathroom to the bedroom, she slipped on the panties that she had laid on the bed and threw on the bulletproof vest she had laid over the chair.

She could hear them moving about down the hall. They were searching for her now, certain that she had gone hiding.

Pressing her back up against the wall with her gun clenched between her fingers, she calmed her breaths. Wet hair hung down on her shoulders, dripping water on the musty vest and down the cracks of the vest to her exposed breasts. This would be a horrible way to go.

To die at the hands of two fucking idiots while taking a damn bath.

Then a thought hit her. Her shotgun was right behind the dresser. Sneaking quietly over to it, she pushed the dresser up, grabbed the loaded weapon and went back to the door as fast as she could without making a noise.

Sticking her head out quickly, she locked their positions. One was on each side of the hallway, both carrying weapons, neither wearing vests. She tried to memorize their characteristics. One white. One black. They both wore masks, both were right handed based on how they handled their weapons, but the dumb asses had forgotten their gloves.

Good, she'd have finger prints later.

The hard part for now would be to rack her weapon without giving away her position. So, in essence she had the element of surprise only for a second and then she'd be forced to either kill or be killed.

Making the sign of the cross over her chest and head, she looked over at the picture of her son and then racked the shotgun.

The sound so distinct in nature that it instantly alerted them, they turned around guns pointed but couldn't figure out which door it had come from.

"She's got a gun," the deep voiced man warned.

"You think," the other man sneered.

Realizing that she couldn't let them out of her sight, she stepped out from her position beside the entry of the door. Pointing the gun directly at the tallest man first, she pulled the trigger. Buckshot splattered, hitting the man dead square in the chest and throwing him five feet down the hall and into the entryway of the other bedroom.

The other man immediately began to send rounds her way. Slamming the door shut, she moved out of the way of the bullets that tore through the wooden door and impacted into the far wall and window of her bedroom.

She prayed someone heard that and was calling the police immediately.

Stepping back, she racked the gun again. Throwing her gun holster over her shoulder, she backed into the opposite wall and pointed the gun directly at the door.

As soon as she thought she saw someone through the large holes in the door, she shot again.

"I can do this all night, motherfucker!" she screamed, racking the gun again. "Or at least until the cops get here. And yes, I already called them. You can stay and die, go to jail or you can be smart for once in your life and get the hell out of here. But one thing's for sure. You come through that door and so help me God, you'll never leave out of it."

More rounds entered the room through the door in response and blowing holes into her bed, nightstand and lamp. Ducking down she shot back again. Finally out of bullets, she dropped her shotgun and started to shoot her sidearm. Moving out of the corner as she shot, she quickly ran to the opposite side of the room, where he couldn't see her and grabbed the Glock she had put down for her shotgun earlier.

Anticipation of what was to come drove her crazy. She waited for more men to come barreling through the door, even though she had only seen two before. Stilling her breath, gun pointed, heart pounding, sweat pouring, hair wet and nearly naked, she listened.

Minutes passed.

Still she waited in the same position, frozen into a protective stance.

Finally, she heard the door. A shot at the doorknob left a gaping hole. He kicked the door open. A bottle flew into the bedroom and landed on the floor on fire. Then another flew in and landed on the bed setting it on fire. Then a third. Each one was thrown into different parts of the room to ensure that it burned from every side.

On the opposite wall, hidden from view of the door, she pushed herself up in the corner and grabbed the picture from behind her of her son when he was a baby. Throwing it into the bathroom to make a noise and distract him, she crouched down.

Wood crunched under the man's heavy boot as he walked in, gun pointed aiming towards the bathroom. The flames had begun to consume the room. Immediately, he began to shoot everything but as he turned, Steele was waiting.

Shooting him first in the stomach, she watched him as he pulled the trigger one last time, barely missing her head and leaving a hole in the wall only inches above her. She stood up, drywall in her hair, hands shaking and pointed the gun at him. Stepping out of the corner, she unloaded into his body - legs, arms and finally one final shot to the head.

"I told you motherfucker. You can come in, but you can't come out."

Leaving his bloody body to burn, she turned and ran out of the bedroom door as fast as her feet would take her to call for help.

26

As soon as word got back to Cane that not one but both attempts on Johnson and Steele's lives had failed miserably, he immediately stopped managing the inventory of the supplies to begin manufacturing the drugs at the new warehouse and called Sammy into a private meeting. Cursing and spitting, he ordered the hit on Agosto to move from tomorrow after the hearing to tonight, knowing that the police would be on full alert.

"Do I have to do everything myself?" Cane screamed, hitting the desk. "What is so hard about shooting sitting ducks?"

Sammy couldn't answer. He wasn't there. With this hands placed in front of him, he stood legs spread, waiting for an actual order.

"That boy-loving bastard Ferris. Agosto could be dead right now, and I could be on to the business of moving this shit, if I weren't out cleaning up his fuck ups!" Cane rolled his neck and sat down in the chair behind his desk. "Okay, this is what I want you to do." He looked up at Sammy, whose eyes were as red as his own from sheer exhaustion.

"Take our best guys, get some guns and those cock-tails and *you* kill Agosto tonight. Do you hear me?" He pointed his finger at Sammy. "Don't mess this up, Sammy. It's one man, a pregnant woman and four kids.

That's not a tall order. Hell, I'd do it myself, but I've got shit to do here. And I don't want any of this drive-by shit either, which I told Magnelli was a bad idea in the first place, and I don't want two-hitter teams that will get clipped by some GI-Jane wanna-be. Get ten guys if that's what it takes, but you get in that house and kill them all. I want bullets in the back of their skulls by daybreak. Am I clear?"

Sammy didn't flinch. "Crystal," he said flatly.

"Good, then get out of here and go do it," Cane said, grabbing the whiskey bottle beside him on the desk. Pouring him a glass, he looked at the clock on the wall as Sammy walked out and closed the door behind him.

***

Ivy wanted to tell Nicola about the interview, but when he came in from his unusually long run, the children were running wild, and she had to get dinner on the table. Wrapped up in that and the hundred calls that were coming in from her family, his family and their friends regarding his hearing the next day, she thought it would be better to break the news to him once the kids were put down for the night.

However, quickly her plans changed when a promo from the station that she had just interviewed with ran a clip of her defending her husband's innocence flashed across the television and drew Nicola's attention as he walked past the media room. All the lights were off. The kids were upstairs. Ivy was listening to the radio while she cooked, singing along with Beyoncé like she didn't have a care in the world.

Hearing Ivy's voice coming from the television, he stepped quietly into the room and stood in front of the television. There she was on screen, a perfect close up of his beautiful black wife declaring his innocence in their living room.

"He's innocent," Ivy told the reporter. "And as far as him being a racist," she paused, eyes watering. "Well, how do you explain us?"

The promo ended telling viewers that the full interview would air tomorrow at five. Turning the television off, he went into the kitchen and leaned against the counter. She looked up from chopping green bell peppers on her favorite dark cherry cutting board and smiled innocently at him.

Nicola smiled back but then turned up his bottom lip. "So, what did you do today while I was gone?" he asked, brow furrowed.

Ivy stopped chopping and put down the knife. "I…" She looked up at him and swallowed hard. "I took care of a few outstanding things."

Nicola had to give it to her. She could find a way to lie without lying. Probing deeper, he shrugged. "What things? If you had told me that there was something that you needed done, I could have handled it for you. I know how hard the first trimester is for you. I don't want you over exerting yourself."

Ivy's shoulders dropped. "It was something that I felt that I needed to do," she said, unsure if he knew or not.

"What was it?" he asked, voice as soft as a whisper.

Ivy cleared her throat. "I…um…I did an interview with a local station about the allegations against you."

"Why, Ivy?" Nicola asked, shaking his head. "I told you…"

She cut him off. "I had to."

"You had to?" Nicola asked. His voice rose. "What did we just discuss?"

Ivy snapped. Voice quivering, she tried to stand her ground. "We haven't *discussed* anything, Nicola. You've been telling me what to do and how to do it, since this all happened. You never trust in me to know that I actually can help." Her eyes watered.

"How can you help me, when I don't even know what you're doing? You're sneaking behind my back and talking about me not to your family or your friends but to the entire Mid-South. Yeah, that's being a real team player."

"Okay, Mr. Team player. Where were you today?" she asked, wiping the tears from her cheeks.

"I had a meeting," he said, walking over to the refrigerator. Opening it, he pulled out a beer and twisted the top off.

"So, it's okay for you to go off and do whatever but for me, there is a different standard," she said, eyes blazing.

"How many times and in how many ways do I have to explain to you that it's more important for me to keep you safe and out of the public eye then it is for me to worry about what people think who have never put food on my table, clothes on your backs or a roof over your head?"

"Don't even start with that shit," Ivy countered. "I have helped put every dollar into our house."

Nicola pointed a finger at her and shook his head. There was no way that he was following her down that rabbit hole. "That's not what I mean and you know it. You're just avoiding the point."

She snapped back. "I am not avoiding the point!"

"You are!"

Ivy screamed as loud as she could at her husband. With all her frustration boiled down into heated words, she spat them at him like burning daggers. But Nicola caught them all, every single insult and turned them back on her. He was too angry to be civil at the moment. She had betrayed him, betrayed their family and his wishes even after he had told her how important it was to remain silent.

"How could you be so selfish?" he asked, voice raised. It echoed through the house. "I told you that I didn't want to see you on the television or anything else until this was over, and what do you do? You give an exclusive!"

"You don't always know what is best, Nicola. I do know some things. And I know that someone needed to speak out about the accusations." Tears ran down her eyes but she refused to back down.

"And what difference would it make besides putting you in harm's way?" he screamed back. He slammed his hands down on the counter and huffed. His wide back expanded. "Dammit, Ivy!"

Across the room, Ivy crossed her arms. "It makes a world of difference, Nicola. That's how PR battles are won."

Nicola laughed sardonically. "Is that what you think that this is about?" He turned his angry eyes on her. "This isn't about a PR battle. This is about keeping you and my sons alive!"

Ivy immediately protested his argument. "And what real threats have come of this? Huh? None."

Nicola put his hand over his head. "You don't know how fucked we are because of that. There are people who want my head. But they'll take yours instead. And now, you've given them a face to go with the name."

"And what makes you think that they don't already know my face?" she asked.

Nicola was done with this. "You had better not do one more damn interview with one more fucking reporter!" he screamed at the top of his lungs.

Ivy walked across the room and slapped him in the face. "Don't you dare talk to me like that," she said seething.

There was complete silence suddenly and they stood looking at each other.

The phone rang, drawing them out of their insanity.

Nicola wiped the blood from his mouth and walked over to the cordless phone on the dock. It was his old friend, Moss. Answering it, he rolled his eyes at her and walked out of the room. "Yeah," he answered with a growl.

"Agosto," Moss said quickly. "Are you alright?"

"Yeah," Agosto answered. "I guess. Ivy's up my ass, but it's nothing I can't handle. Why?" He figured that Moss must have seen the promo also.

"There was a hit on Johnson and Steele, not even an hour ago. It went bad, thank God. But Carmen Magnelli got killed at Johnson's house tonight. Shit is bad out here, man. You need to be careful. Lay low."

Agosto went into the bathroom in the downstairs hallway and closed the door. Locking it, he sat down on the toilet. "Why was Carmen Magnelli at Johnson's house? She isn't on this case?"

"You'll never believe this. She was dating Johnson. They were supposed to move in together tonight. A two-man team shot the house up, burned it down with Molotov cocktails and in the process, killed her." Moss made sure to keep his voice low. Walking outside of his house, he closed the door and looked up at the stars. "It seems that it's open season on anyone who is on this case. The way I see it, they could also be after you."

"With DeMario dead, it's going to be hard to find out who's responsible for this." Agosto cradled his head in his hand. "Dammit, man."

"Look, if you need anything, you still have friends here…brothers in blue that you can count on."

Agosto appreciated that. "If I need you, I'll call you. Just keep me informed man. I need to keep my ear to the ground."

"Will do. Keep a lookout over your family," Moss said concerned.

"I plan to," Nicola said, standing up. "I'll talk to you soon." Hanging up the phone, he looked at himself in the mirror. Tired eyes, a beard and wild hair covered the face that he once knew. And the chaos of his life was ruining things with Ivy. He had to fix it.

Nicola walked back into the kitchen were Ivy had turned on the television. "Baby?" he said, preparing to apologize.

Ivy stood with tears in her eyes and her hand over her mouth.

Nicola thought that it was because of his outburst. "Baby, look I'm sorry, okay. But we need to talk."

Ivy turned from the television and shook her head. "There's been a shooting. A female officer was shot. They think it had something to do with the case."

Nicola sighed and looked at the television. "It was Deputy Director Magnelli's daughter, Carmen Magnelli. I was reporting to him before I was pulled off the case and suspended."

"Do you think it's all somehow connected?" Her eyes were wide with fear again.

Nicola nodded. "I'm sure it is."

"Nicky, I'm sorry." She wiped her face. "That could have been you. That could have been me." Reality set in, and suddenly, she wasn't sure that she had done the right thing.

Nicola walked over and put his arms around Ivy's trembling shoulders. "Now do you understand?" He lifted her chin and made her look at him. "I have to keep you safe."

She nodded with tears running down her cheeks. Burying her face in his chest, she held him tight. "I didn't know, Nicky. I just didn't know."

Nicola kissed her forehead and hugged her. "It's all this pressure. It's being locked in this house, and being robbed of our jobs and worrying about our children..." He kissed her again. "But it's not us. It's not us."

"What are we going to do?" she asked.

Nicola looked at his watch. "Go upstairs and pack some clothes. I have to get you out of here."

"Do you think that's wise?" she asked. "Where will we go?"

"Tonight, I'm going to take you guys to your parents' house. Tomorrow, I'm getting you out of the city. It's best for you to go with the kids to Miami for a while. My folks will keep you safe there." He closed his hands around hers. "You have to trust me."

***

Earlier that day, when Agosto had shown up at Dmitry's compound asking for his help, Anatoly Medlov

only knew one thing. He didn't trust him. Agosto had
been a thorn in his side for years and for the life of him,
he couldn't understand his father's decision to help
him. Still, his father was boss and what he said was the
law. However, just because Anatoly didn't immediately order one of his men to kill the man as soon as he
was out of his father's sight, he did send three of his
best men to keep watch on Agosto at his home. The
order specifically was to keep surveillance on the man
until otherwise notified.

Doing what they were ordered, three men from
Dmitry's camp sat quietly watching Agosto's home in a
black Land Rover. Hidden by the dark night and the
huge oak trees that lined the street, they talked among
themselves and casually passed around food and an
IPad.

Suddenly, a suspicious black van pulled up on the
opposite side of the street and parked, immediately
triggering their interest.

"*Chto za huy*. Who is that?" the driver, Marat,
asked in a thick Russian accent. He had only been in
the states for a little over a year now but had been
handling *business* for Dmitry in Sochi, Russia for
several years. His techniques were unorthodox but
results-oriented, a thing that Dmitry found very useful
in situations like this.

"You're asking me like I know," Nestor, the man in
the passenger seat answered. He also was Russian but
had lived in the states for nearly a decade. However, no
one could tell with his broken English. Pulling out his
binoculars, he got a better view of the men inside the
van. "Looks like fucking hitters to me. The man in the

passenger seat just cocked a big fucking shot gun." He put down his binoculars and looked over at his partner.

"Shit, radio back to Boris, while I call back to the house and see what Boss wants us to do," the driver said. Getting on the phone, he dialed on his cell phone quickly, while the other man got on the radio to the third man in their party, who was parked in a black BMW several houses away.

***

The help was about to serve the second course of their five-course meal when Anatoly's cell phone vibrated in his pocket. In the middle of the elaborate, authentic Russian dinner in his father's formal dining hall, he expressed his frustration for being interrupted. "What?" he growled into the receiver.

The other guests immediately stopped talking and looked over at him.

Marat wasted no time. "Boss, there are hitters here. It looks like they are about to pull down on Agosto. What do you want us to do? Watch or counter attack?"

Clasping the phone between his ear and shoulder, Anatoly pushed away from his dinner with his family and his soon-to-be family. "I'm sorry, baby," he said to his fiancée, sitting beside him giving him an evil eye. "I have to take this." He gave a fake smile.

In return, she gave him a sincere scowl that he ignored. Kissing the head of his newborn baby girl, cradled in his fiancée's arms, he disappeared through the tall double doors of the dining hall and went out into the dimly lit hallway.

But Dmitry, who was sitting at the head of the table, continued his entertaining conversation as if nothing had happened. He genuinely smiled as he explained the difference between Beluga and lower-quality caviar to his guests, while he sent a flirting wink at his wife at the other end of the table.

As soon as Anatoly exited, on cue, Gabriel stood up from across the table, excusing himself from his girlfriend and followed him.

"What's the matter?" Gabriel asked, checking his cell phone. He had an unrelated message from Miami, telling him that an expected shipment had arrived without problems. He was glad to be able to report that back to Dmitry after dinner.

Anatoly's Russian accent was thick now as his frustration grew. "Someone is at the pig's house to finish him off. The men want to know what I want to do," he said, as if the decision was too difficult for him to make alone.

Gabriel frowned and quickly responded. "Tell them to stop them." He didn't see what there was to grapple with.

"Do we really want to?" Anatoly asked. He propped his foot up on the back of the wall and wished for a Menthol cigarette. He would much rather had been playing with his dogs out in the backyard or doing the hit himself instead of being bogged down with traditional wedding preparation. It only added to his growing annoyance.

"According to your father, we do," Gabriel answered. He hid his downright disdain for the attack on a policeman and his family for fear that it might just push Anatoly to do the wrong thing. "No one knows your father's mind like you do. He obviously has plans for the man. Otherwise, he wouldn't be helping him in the first place."

Anatoly rolled his eyes. As usual, Gabriel had a point. Putting the phone back to his ear and pushing unmute, he gave his answer. "Stop them," he said, looking up into his cousin's pensive stare.

"Then what, boss? He doesn't know that we're even here," Marat said, nodding at Nestor.

"Well, I guess that he'll know after, won't he?" Anatoly responded sarcastically. With a huff, he turned from Gabriel who watched his every move and shook his head. "Fine, bring them here and put them in the guest wing. We'll figure out what to do with them once you arrive. For now just fucking handle it, *da*. You're ruining my evening."

"Yes, boss," Marat answered.

"There, are you happy?" Anatoly asked Gabriel as he hung up the phone.

"Very." Gabriel opened the door for his cousin to enter back into the dining hall. "You should be happy. It's not often that you get to save lives with a phone call. Most often you're ending them."

"And what's wrong with that?" Anatoly asked completely missing Gabriel's point. Agosto was a cop and not just any cop - the biggest thorn in his side on the Memphis Police Department.

"Nothing," Gabriel chuckled. "My point is that you're doing the right thing for once." He patted him on the back.

"Glad to know that I have your approval," Anatoly said, sucking his teeth.

***

The night's air was still and silent on the quiet street of Peabody. Luxury homes were illuminated with landscape lighting, protected by complex security systems, high gates and fences and prowling, vicious dogs. The ornate streetlights lit up the rows of foreign cars parked up and down the sidewalk behind the many rows of oak and magnolia trees. In all, it was a picturesque view of an upper-middle income southern community ill prepared for what was about to happen.

Sammy and his men were packed in their van like sardines, ready to unleash hell on the Agosto family right in the comfort of their plantation-style home. His orders while grotesquely savage were simple. Kill the entire family. Sammy found it even more disgusting that Cane knew that Ivy Agosto was pregnant and still chose to hit her. They had all listened to the conversations between her and her husband, heard the audio of them making love and fighting, cringed at the wild children running about and playing, snickered at the remarks. In essence, they had gotten to know this family, just to kill them better.

"Boss, I can kill the cop. No problem, but I don't know how I feel about popping four kids," one of the men in the back said, cocking his gun.

"There are six of them. There are six of us. I don't care how we do it. Just do it," Sammy ordered. "Or the next family to be killed could be your own."

The men stiffened at the threat.

"I'll do it," one of the other men in the back said, wiping his running nose. "The way I see it, a kid is just an adult in training." His green eyes were ice cold.

Sammy tried not to cut his eyes at the man. After all, only a true sociopath should get into their line of work. "Sounds like we have a fucking volunteer then." Looking at his watch, he swallowed down his disdain and thought of his own two children. When it came down to it was either Agosto's family or his own. "Are we clear on what we're doing? I don't want any fuck ups. If this doesn't go down, you might as well just put a bullet in your own head."

The men answered in unison.

Still, Sammy went over the details again. He'd rather be safe than sorry. "The back of the house is fortified by the fence, the lights and the damn dog. So, we go through the front door. It's going to be risky, but even if he has a weapon, he won't be able to get to us all. Three go upstairs, three down. Check every room, kill everyone on sight. I don't care if it takes five bullets a piece to put these people down, Cane wants one bullet in the back of each head. Once the job is done, drop the cocktails, burn the bitch down and get out. We have exactly ten minutes to do it all." He turned and looked at the men. "Are we clear?"

The men nodded again.

Turning back around, Sammy opened his passenger door. The other men quickly followed. With black ski masks on and guns pointed, they came up the drive quickly, moving across the lawn in a two-by-two flank formation. As soon as they got to mid-point on the plush lawn, the security lights came on. Without pause, they continued advancing towards the house, anticipating every possible move that Agosto could make.

Marat got out of the Land Rover undetected by the crew right down the street and made his way to the back of the truck. While Cane's men were armed with sawed off shotguns, a new order of AA-12 fully automatic shot guns had just arrived and Dmitry had stocked each car with several for his "runs" around the region. Spitting out 300 round per minute with a range of up to 575 feet, he was certain that when he did fire his stainless steel new-age tommy gun, everyone on the street would know it. Grabbing one for himself with a full magazine and one for Nestor, he closed the trunk quietly.

Nestor threw his cigarette out of the passenger window and scooted across to the driver's seat. Letting down the window, he pulled the large weapon inside from Marat and laid it across his lap.

Quickly Marat, put his black boot on the foot rail of the truck, slung the strap of the gun over his wide shoulder and slipped his tattooed hand inside the handrail to ride the side of the truck up to the front of the house.

***

Nicola had a bad feeling after the call from Moss. It wouldn't be likely that Johnson and Steele had found out any more than he already knew in such a short time. Whoever was cleaning house, wouldn't just stop at them. He gathered the most important things, social security cards, birth certificates, credit cards, identification, etc. and threw them in a bag. Slipping on his gym shoes, he screamed out of the bedroom door to Ivy.

"Baby, just get some clothes on them," he said, hair suddenly standing on his arms.

"Don't I need to get them some clothes and toothbrushes," Ivy screamed back from the oldest twins' room."

"No," Nicola said, looking at his watch. "We're leaving this house in five minutes. We can buy what we need."

Urgency boiled in his veins with each and every passing minute.

Hearing the strain in his voice, Ivy hurried. Wiping the sweat from her brow, she pushed back tears and fear to focus. Bending down to put on Adamo's shoes, she realized that he didn't have on socks.

"Where are we going?" he asked, sensing her worry.

Running a hand through his curly hair, she tried to smile. "We're going to see grandma and grandpa. You love it there. Don't you?"

"But it's late," he said, wiping his tired eyes. I want to go to sleep, mama." He looked up at her with a pouty mouth that made her feel guilty.

Ivy finished tying his shoes and stood up. Feeling dizzy, she braced herself on the nightstand. "You can sleep in the car, baby. I promise."

Turning around, she saw Nicola at the door with the two smallest boys in his arms. "Let's go," he said more of an urging than an order.

With protest, she grabbed her boys by the hands and hurried out of the room. They walked quickly down the long hall. More silent than they'd ever been both she and Nicola contemplated what their next move would be.

"I need my purse," she said as they passed the master bedroom. She looked into the inviting warmth of the tranquil room and suddenly felt like she'd never see it again.

"I'll grab it," Nicola said, walking into the room with the kids. "Where is it?" He looked around quickly.

"On the doorknob of the bathroom."

Walking to the bathroom door, he grabbed the purse and headed back out. "Got it. Let's go." This time his voice was more of an order.

As soon as they headed down the long stairwell together with Ivy and the boys leading, a large boom came from downstairs startling everyone. The wooden front door flew off the hinges and two men came quickly inside with shotguns. Both sets of twins and Ivy screamed, falling back onto the stairs.

Quickly Nicola snatched them up the stairs. Pulling behind them to shield them, he heard guns shots ring out right by their head. Blowing a hole into the wall beside his head and knocking down a large painting, he threw everyone on the floor.

Covering their heads, he pushed them back up into the hallway. Grabbing Ivy's face as she screamed frantically, he looked her in the eyes. "Get them to the back bedroom!" Pulling a gun from the back of his jeans, he gave it to her. "Get in the corner of the room and turn the lights off. Shoot anyone who comes through the door."

"Nicky!" she screamed. Shaking, she took the gun.

"Go!" he said, pulling the other gun from under his arm. "Go now!" he pushed her.

As soon as he saw Ivy and the children crawling out of the path of the mad gunfire, he dove over into the doorway of the master bedroom where he could get a clear view of the stairwell. He counted at least four.

Returning fire with his large Desert Eagle, he pointed at the man coming up the stairs and pulled the trigger. The bullet went straight through his head and exited out the back. Blood splattered against the wall and stairs and the man fell backwards down the stairs. But another was right behind him, shooting directly at Nicola.

Shards of wood and drywall exploded as the man unloaded towards Nicola, trying with all his might to kill him quickly. Diving back behind the doorway out of the path of the bullets, Nicola looked down the hallway at Ivy and the kids as they went into the back bedroom and closed the door.

He knew one thing and one thing only. He could not under any circumstances let anyone up the stairs.

The sound of the bullets impacting into the walls from every direction was deafening. Taking another glance out, he lowered his body and shot again, this time, hitting the man behind the one that he had just killed in the leg. The man fell but returned fire again, this time sending a bullet that barely missed Nicola by only centimeters.

Hiding behind the mangled wall for a second, he took a breath and then stuck his body halfway out of the room to send another round into the man's chest as he tried to stand.

Suddenly, a large glass bottle with a dirty rag was launched from downstairs up to the door, exploding with fire. It quickly fed on the paint, burning the walls and entryway.

Nicola dove out of the door and into the path of fire toward the other side of the hallway to keep a view of the stairwell. Returning another couple of shots, he felt the heat of the flames as they grew.

Another man determined to fix the mistake of his departed, advanced up the stairs past the dead bodies shooting as cover, but Nicola stood up with the bullets whizzing past him only half covered by the balcony low wall and made one good shot that sent the man diving back down the stairs to safety.

Panic started to rip through Nicola at the thought of running out of bullets before every man in there was dead. In his head, he counted his shots. He had to protect his family. He was the only thing that stood between them and death.

Adrenaline coursed through his veins. Heart pumping, mouth dry, he crouched back down behind the balcony wall as bullets and fire surrounded him in death.

"Please God," Nicola said aloud, praying as he returned fire again. "Help me." All he could think of was the five people hidden down the hall who were depending on him. Nothing else mattered.

Boris pulled up quickly to the front door in the BMW, shredding the immaculate lawn under the tread of his tires. With his hand on the trigger of his weapon, he popped out of the car, leaving the door open. It sounded like a full-on war inside, just his type of party. Gunfire rang out in rapid bursts from at least three different directions. He could also hear Nicola returning fire from the top of the stairwell on the second floor with a distinctively loud cannon of a weapon. He guessed it to be a Desert Eagle.

All the men were now inside and completely oblivious to the fact that Nicola had re-enforcements. Without bothering to look behind them, they fired up the stairwell at Nicola as black smoke started to billow out of the front door and filled the house. It gave Boris perfect cover and distracted the men inside.

Making sure not to get in full view of the open door, he quickly mapped out their locations inside of the house. One was in the living room, using the door entry as cover. One was in the dining room doing the same. Each was on opposite sides of the foyer. In between shooting, they also launched more handmade firebombs up the stairs. It was only a matter of time before the smoke and fire consumed the upstairs and his goal of getting Agosto out safely. He had to move quickly.

When he was certain that he wouldn't get Agosto or his family in the crosshairs, Boris stepped back a few feet from the porch light, cocked his weapon and unloaded without prejudice. Before he could drop one magazine on the ground and slide in another, Marat was already beside him, shooting at the house.

The quiet night had suddenly been interrupted. From a far neighbors, afraid for their lives watched on from their windows while they waited for the police as Marat and Boris emptied round after explosive round into the house.

The bullets were so powerful until they knocked off chunks of brick from the exterior of the house, went through windows and pierced straight through several walls, furniture, and paintings inside of the house all while lighting up the night's sky.

Shells hit the ground by their feet as they advanced.

Both Marat and Boris had extensive experience in professional hits. In synchronization with their powerful weapons, they strategically covered every inch of the front of the house. Large bullet holes covered the entire first floor. Glass shards hung from the busted windows. The piano in the parlor leaned over on the floor missing two legs. The furniture was blown to bits. Glass vases with flowers lay cracked on the rugs, family photos were destroyed and the distinctive smell of gas came from the kitchen.

And among all the rubble as they advanced inside of the house flanking each other and clearing the area, they found the two men riddled with bullets.

Laying in bloody pools full of bullet holes, Cane's men never knew what hit them. Marat stepped over one of them, kicking away his guns as he examined the body. *The boss didn't like leaving witnesses.* Stepping back to prevent getting splatter on his clothes, he shot the dead man in the head again, just to make sure.

"That was easy," he said, nodding across the foyer at Boris. He didn't see why it took three of them to kill two amateur hitters. And it looked like from the bodies lining the staircase that Agosto was capable of handling himself.

"Da, that's the thing about these Southern American boys," Marat said, walking into the room with him after he had done the same thing to the man on the other side of the house. "They're all soft...like...girls," he chuckled as he looked at the mess that Boris had made.

While Boris and Marat were securing the front of the house, Nestor had driven the Land Rover straight through the back gate and pulled up to the back of the house. Getting out of the truck, he was met by a huge dog barking and trying to bite him.

He pointed the gun but thought twice. He was a serious dog lover and if his boss, Anatoly, found out that he had shot a dog in the midst of the battle, he might just shoot him. He would have done better to accidently shoot one of the people he was in charge of saving.

Shooting over the dog's head, he scared him off, shot the doorknob off the back of the house and entered carefully. The thick fog smelled of smoke greeted him.

Bullets from Dmitry's powerful guns had found their way all the way to the mudroom and blew out some of the windows in the sunroom.

As he turned the corner to check the bathroom, he found Sammy inside the shower taking cover.

"Don't fucking move," Nestor said with a grin. He motioned for his new captor to step towards him. "Slow," he ordered in a low voice. "Who is with you?"

"No one," Sammy said, more frustrated than afraid. He raised his hands and dropped his gun, knowing that he was completely outnumbered.

"If you're lying to me, I'll make your death very painful," Nestor promised.

"I'm not lying. No one is with me," Sammy repeated.

Boris and Marat continued checking each room in the back and came to the restroom where Nestor was holding Sammy.

"We've got to get to the cop and get him out of here now," Marat said, hitting his watch. "I'm surprised the pigs aren't already here, considering he's one of their own."

Pushing Sammy in front of them, they headed back toward the stairwell. Nicola had already gone to get his family. Running as fast as he could, he screamed for Ivy. "Baby," he said, hearing his children crying.

"In here!" Ivy screamed back. Her heart lifted when she heard her husband's voice. Wiping tears, she stood up out of the corner.

As he opened the door, Ivy put down the gun and ran towards him. Never before had she seen a better sight. Hugging him tightly, she cried. "Are we safe?" she asked, reaching for her children.

Nicola picked up his youngest two boys and Ivy held Adamo and Madison's small hands. "I don't know," he answered. "We've got to go. This place is going to go up in smoke."

As he turned around, he saw Boris enter the room with his gun. Nicola knew that he was out of bullets and it was too late to grab the weapon that Ivy had set down. His heart constricted in fear for his family.

Before Nicola could say a word, Boris put up a hand. "The boss sent us," he said, sucking his teeth. He looked at the large family in confusion. *Why was this man so important to the Medlov organization?*

Nicola's shoulders relaxed. Tension eased out and the reality set in that Dmitry Medlov had actually saved his life. "I need you to help me get them out," he said, looking over at Ivy, who was totally confused.

"Who are these men?" Ivy asked Nicola.

Nicola didn't respond. An explanation at this point would take too long. Shaking his head, he walked towards the door with his family in tow. Clutching his children, he nodded towards Boris. "Thank you," he said quietly.

"Thank my boss," Boris said flatly.

Pulling the comforter off the bed, Boris passed it to Ivy. He could sense her fear, see her visible trembling. "Cover up. We have to go now." There was a slight warmness in his voice, though he tried to cover it as quickly as the words left his lips.

27

Ivy held her sleeping children tight as she rode silently in the back of the mysterious Russian man's Land Rover. All four of her boys had been so frightened during the fire fight until they passed out as soon as they got inside the SUV. *But were they safe?* Even she couldn't really answer that question. Looking down at them pooled around her, all fighting for a piece of her lap to lay their small heads on, she felt incredibly helpless.

Her poor babies.

She was certain that they'd be scarred for life by the shoot-out. And then there was the fire. The sight of her dream home going up in flames as they drove off made her feel nauseated again. Wiping tears, she tried not to recall each memory made in her home. Every laugh. Every smile. Every birth. Every celebration. They were all gone. Nicola had urged her not to look back as he carried her and the children to the truck, to forget it all. But how could anyone forget what she had just been through? Then another thought hit her, one adding a little more clarity to the situation. At least, everyone was still alive. *That Carmen girl was dead now simply because she was at the wrong place at the wrong time.*

Unsure of where she was going or who she was even with, she trusted her husband only to protect them. It was clear that she could not after huddling in a corner in the dark frightened out of her mind for what felt like hours.

Nicola had warned her.

No matter how she tried to oppress the thought, she couldn't help but wonder if this was all her fault, if breaking her silence had caused the attack. However, asking outright for an answer, she knew would give her no closure. Nicola would never tell her even if her suspicions were correct. He wasn't that cruel.

Riding behind him now, she kept her eyes on her husband. Nicola said nothing the entire drive. He sat in the passenger seat, looking out of the window in deep thought and occasionally looking back to check on them. She was only sane right now because he was. He didn't seem to be afraid at all by everything that happened.

Maybe you are in your element, she thought. *Maybe there is another side of you that I just don't know.* After all, he had called her naive, but naive to what?

The drive to their disclosed destination was short to her surprise. They pulled up to a huge mansion fortified by a bricked gate. Only the high peaks of the roof could be seen from the street and that was only because of the powerful lights strategically placed all over the lawn.

Guards were at the doors of the gate, carrying weapons like soldiers in front of an embassy. They looked inside and under the truck, flashing their lights, brandishing their intimidating weapons. She grabbed her children tighter to protect them. *Where were they? Who had sent for them?*

Boris spoke in Russian to the guard nearest the window then was allowed to pass through the entry. As the iron gate creaked opened, she saw the massive three-story house in full view. It looked out of place, like it didn't belong in Memphis.

The Land Rover pulled up the wide circular drive past the mansion and parked in the multi-care side garage. Turning off the SUV, Boris sent a text and waited for an answer. When he received a reply, he stepped out of the truck and motioned for Nicola to follow.

"Where are we?" she asked Nicola before he could get out.

"Safe," Nicola promised, getting out of the truck also. He opened the back door for her and picked up two of his sons out of her lap. They barely stirred, but even in their sleep, they whimpered. Clinging to their father, they nestled into his large muscular arms and fell back asleep.

Boris opened the other back door and picked up the other two children. Instinctively, Ivy reached out to stop him, but Nicola grabbed her. "Hey, it will be alright," he assured, rubbing her arm. "Come on, let's get you inside." He would have picked her up too, if he could have managed to carry all three of them. He had never seen his wife so afraid in her entire life, and the thought that he had not adequately protected them bothered him more than she could have known.

Ivy wanted to ask a million questions, but she knew that now was not the time. Pulling herself out of the truck, she followed her husband and Boris to a side door of the mansion.

Another blond guard opened the door and stepped to the side. This one was not wearing black fatigues. Instead, he wore a pair of slacks and a golf shirt.

However, he did have guns holstered and visible and like the other men, he was big, tattooed and brooding. Eyeing Ivy and Nicola as they passed, the man pressed his earpiece with his finger and spoke in Russian to someone else, someone watching them.

Ivy stayed close to her husband, wondering what he had gotten them involved in now. She could only think of one person who had this much money and was Russian in Memphis, and he was no law enforcement officer.

Her husband had spent nearly the whole of his career chasing Dmitry Medlov, and if she was now at his home, then she was also now lost in what her husband really did for a living.

Without a word and quite swiftly to be carrying two small children, Boris led the Agosto family through the palatial mansion, past rooms of people socializing, past artwork and sculptures that Ivy couldn't help but admire, past rooms that were decorated with such detail until she could barely take it all in in one glance, past crystal chandeliers and Persian rugs and elaborate bouquets and decadent luxury furniture to the east wing of the house.

When they came to a back row of marble stairs that led up to another long hallway, Boris stopped abruptly. "Is she alright to make it?" he asked Nicola while looking at Ivy. He could see the loss of color in her face, like at any minute she would be sick.

Nicola turned to Ivy. "Are you alright?" He wouldn't answer for her. She had been through so much, until she might have very well been sick now.

Ivy held on to the wooden banister. "I'll be fine," she said, ready to get wherever he was taking them.

The walked seemed longer to get up the staircase to the long hallway with limestone flooring and 20-foot, arched ceilings, then it did to get across the length of the mansion. Ivy realized when she got to the top why Boris had asked. Out of breath and shaking, she kept her composure but prayed to God for a place to sit soon. Even Nicola and Boris seemed a little out of breath with the children in their arms. They had moved quickly but carefully not to wake them, a thing that Ivy knew would have been impossible for her to do.

Midway of the elaborate hallway, Boris opened a door that led into a very large, very well-decorated bedroom with plush egg-shell white walls and matching carpet, a fireplace rumbling low, a towering king-sized sleigh bed, a 60-inch television mounted to the wall, a large wooden desk in the far corner and fine rugs and linen. In the corner was a gigantic flower arrangement of vibrant pink and white roses and above the bed was a painting so beautiful of the Mississippi River that she had to stop and gawk at it. The room smelled of fresh linen and jasmine and felt like a mid-summer's night dream. It took her out of her current hysteria and instantly soothed her.

Boris walked what Ivy thought was the closet and opened the door, which led into a smaller bedroom. It was far less elaborate but still extremely nice. Two twin-sized beds fit inside it with a small television and nightstands.

"Boss says for you to stay here tonight. The children can sleep in this smaller room," he said, laying both children in his arms on the bed carefully. They curled up together under the sheets already pulled out by the maid staff. He admired them for a minute without intending to and then turned back as he caught himself. "There is no outside door to this room. The only way in is through your bedroom, so they are safe." He pointed around the room so that they could see for themselves. He yawned in exhaustion and watched as Nicola laid Madison and Adamo in the other bed.

"Thank you," Ivy said quietly, "for saving our lives." She could barely look at the man. He made her uncomfortable with his rough, gravelly voice and menacing stare. Yet, something told her that he meant well.

Boris didn't like the attention any more than Ivy liked giving it. He blinked hard involuntarily. "You're welcome...*I guess*." He glanced over at Agosto and quickly changed the subject. "Food will be sent up. The boss will call on you when he's ready. Right now, he has things to do. My suggestion would be to get some rest. There is a bathroom connected to the larger bedroom. You're basically in this wing by yourselves. But a word of caution. You are not allowed to use the phones, internet...nothing. As a guest of Boss Medlov's home, I'm sure you can follow these rules, not make trouble, da?"

Nicola answered by offering his hand. "Thanks. Tell Dmitry that I appreciate it. We'll adhere to his wishes."

Boris shook Nicola's hand, but pulled away quickly. That was the first time that he'd ever touched a cop without killing him. It felt strange. This all did. Their boss never sent them on jobs like this, where people actually lived.

"Well," he said in a huff, "I'll leave you to your privacy now." Walking to the door, he opened it and paused. "Don't forget. No phones."

"No phones," Ivy said, feeling as though Boris needed to hear her say it as well.

Nodding, he closed the door and left them alone.

As soon as Ivy was certain that no one would interrupt them, she went back to look at the children in the adjoining room. Leaning against the doorway, she shook her head. "Nicola, tell me what's going on?" her voice was as wispy as feather. She didn't have the strength to argue, but she hoped that it wouldn't take that to get the truth.

Nicola walked up behind her and wrapped his arms around her waist. He was so happy to still have his family, so blessed. Kissing her shoulder, he pulled her long wavy hair behind her ear and whispered. "I'm doing what I have to do."

She struggled to turn around in his arms. Looking up into his eyes, she asked seriously, "What does that mean, Nicola?"

"Just what I said." His expression was terse. He held her shoulders. "I know you. You want to ask questions, you want answers. And you deserve them. But this is just one of those times that you're going to have to trust me."

"I do trust you," she said sincerely. "I'm sorry that I didn't before. I feel like this is all my fault. If I had just…"

Nicola frowned as he interrupted. "This is not your fault. Is that what you thought?"

"Well, yeah. The interview must have alerted the people looking for you," Ivy said, wiping tears.

Nicola held her tight, despite the odor coming from both of them of smoke and soot. "Baby, what happened tonight would have happened whether you did or did not do that interview. Listen to me. None of this is your fault. But I promise you this; I'm going to fix it. You will never worry about your safety or the children's safety again. And the people responsible for this are going to pay."

"Nicky, I don't want you to put yourself in anymore danger. It was different when I thought that you were just going to be solving a case, but people are trying to kill you."

"You know, when those guys came barreling into the house, I wasn't worried about dying, but I was scared as hell of the thought of not protecting you and my kids. A man's job, *his most important purpose in this life*, is to protect his family from all hurt, harm and danger. He ceases to exist as a man if he can't or won't do that. Me going after these people is not just about revenge, it's about my duty. It's about my purpose."

How could Ivy argue with him? Tucking her head into his chest, she closed her eyes. "Just remember that not only do you have a family to protect but also to raise. So, you had better come back to me."

"I wouldn't miss it for the world," he said, rocking her slowly. "Hey, let me run you a bath. You stink."

She couldn't help but laugh. "Yeah, well you do too."

"We might as well take advantage of the Boss's amenities, right?" He walked to the bathroom and opened the door. "Wow, get a load of this place. The tub in here is big enough for three people." He walked inside and turned on the light to illuminate yet another decade, luxurious room.

Ivy stuck her head inside and watched him sit on the end of the bathtub and run her water. She could tell that he was putting on a façade for her, trying to make her feel better and not worry. But it was not working. "Nicky, you're entire career has been about doing the right thing, the hones thing, and upholding justice. Are you going to throw it all away now?"

Nicola looked down into the tub and wade his fingers through the stream of hot water. "You can spend your entire life doing the right thing and not making a damn bit of difference in the lives of people who need you. Or you can do the wrong thing and change people's lives for the better for the rest of their lives. The hardest part of that kind of decision is to make it."

"And you've made it?" Ivy asked quietly.

Nicola didn't answer. Standing up, he walked over to the cabinet and pulled out a large towel. "Let me ask you a question?" He closed the cabinet back and walked with the towel over to her. "Do you feel safe right now?"

"Do I feel safe?" she asked, confused.

"At this moment, are you afraid for your life?" he asked.

Ivy shrugged. "Yes, I feel safe. No, I'm not afraid for my life at this moment."

Nicola pulled her shirt up above her head and took it off. Her long hair spilled over on to her bare shoulders. Looking down at her small, swollen bump of a stomach in sheer wonderment, he cleared his throat and kneeled to kiss her slightly protruding belly button.

"All that matters is that you feel safe," he whispered, kissing her belly button. "Because if you feel safe, then she feels safe."

Ivy rubbed the top of his head adoringly. Even in the middle of thunderous storm in their life, they still found a minute to be together. As he looked up, brown eyes burning through her, she knew that everything would be okay.

***

The *something* that Dmitry Medlov was doing that prevented him from receiving the Agosto family when they arrived at his mansion was not entertaining guests or being boss of a multi-national crime organization. He was on foot duty.

On the long sofa in the entertainment gallery of the west wing with the door closed and some sappy love story on the huge television mounted up on the wall across the room, he massaged his wife's aching feet after being in stilettos all night while she rested back in the nest of pillows and sipped hot tea.

With not a care in the world, they sat quietly under the dim lights, in a near trance as the world moved around them. With his large thumb, he pushed into the middle of her foot and massaged the sides with his fingers. Every once in a while, he would glance down at her perfectly painted toes and make sure that he wasn't hurting her.

She lay opposite him on the custom-made leather sofa sectional. With her designer cocktail dress pushed up on her thighs and her panty hose on the floor beside them, she fanned her hair out of its bun and yawned.

"I am happy for Anatoly with the new baby, his engagement to Renee and all of his success, but I'll be so glad when this wedding is over," his wife, Royal said, moaning as he hit a tender spot in her manicured foot. "Lower, baby." Her eyes rolled.

Dmitry obeyed. Moving his hand, he cupped her foot at the heel. "Right there?" he asked, kissing the side of her arch. He didn't feel the need to comment on her comment, especially since she was such a gracious host to the entire wedding party, but in truth, the traditional wedding hoopla didn't bother him. He rather liked it, considering that it was so new to his normal way of life. "You just need to be relaxed," he finally said.

Be relaxed?

Royal raised her head slightly at Dmitry's suggestive tone. Her pouty mouth covered in the stain of expensive crimson-colored matte lipstick opened, pearly white teeth exposed and another gasp leaped forward. "Yes, right there," she whispered. Staring down at him, she watched his eyes become hooded, gleaming back at her like light blue crystals. Swallowing hard, she opened her legs a little wider so that he could see her red lace panties under the slip of her crimson-colored dress.

Dmitry wasn't bashful about his beautiful young wife. Running a hand from her foot down in between her thighs, he found himself aroused by the wetness waiting for him.

She wiggled her foot into the opening of his crisp white dress shirt, ran it over the elaborate star tattoo on his shoulder and placed the ball of her foot over his heart. Feeling it thud, she smiled deviously. The Harry Winston diamond necklace he had given her just a month ago gleamed in the darkness creating a spectrum of brilliant lights across the room.

"I'm sure that I can find a way to make you enjoy your stay here." Licking his heart-shaped lips, he yanked her body towards his.

"And how do you plan to do that?" Royal asked, sitting up in his lap. She pushed her legs around him and pushed down on his snake-like erection. Raking her hand through his blonde curls mixed with just a hint of grey, she sucked on his bottom lip.

Dmitry cracked a smile. "There is nothing better than a woman who knows when to carry herself like a lady." Kissing her neck, he slipped a hand under her dress and moved her panties. "And when to act like…" He eyed her mouth, watching the excitement in her boil over. She pulled at his belt until she unlatched it, then stuck her hand down in his pants. Warm, engorged flesh begged to be free.

"I'm going to ride you right here," she said without smiling.

"Alright then," he said, resting his long arms back on the sofa. "I'll leave you to it." Raising his hips, so that she could pull down his pants, he prepared for his own idea of a late night snack when the door suddenly opened.

Anatoly walked in quickly and looked over at his father and stepmother, realizing that he had just interrupted something serious.

Dmitry didn't even bother to look back at his son. "This better be important."

"The package is here," Anatoly said, avoiding eye contact with Royal who had slinked into the curve of her husband and hid her body.

Dmitry raised his hand to dismiss his son. "Let them wait. I'll be there shortly." Right now, he had more important things to handle, like the hard on nestled in between his wife's thighs. He heard Royal giggle.

"You too are like kids," Anatoly said, rolling his eyes as he walked out of the door. Locking it behind him, he heard Royal laugh aloud as he walked with his men down the hallway.

Now Royal was curious. As Dmitry slipped his long member inside of her, she lifted his chin. "What package?" she asked, pulling him out.

"Royal," Dmitry growled. "Not now."

"What package?" she insisted.

"The Agosto family." Immediately he saw the concern on her face.

"The cop who was after you and arrested me? The guy that beat that thug up?" She grew more and more intrigued with each nugget of information. "And his wife? He's married?"

Dmitry chuckled. "*Da*, is that disappointing? Are you interested in him?"

Royal smiled. "No, but I want to meet *her*. I want to see what kind of woman married Nicola Agosto." Though she could not deny that he was an exceedingly attractive man, over the years she had come to find law enforcement officers abhorrent. Maybe she had been brainwashed, but maybe she was just in love with a seven-foot, blond haired, blue eyed, billionaire, mafia Adonis. Either way, she was certain that her husband would indulge her, if she asked the right way.

"I don't want you to," Dmitry said, wishing that they could get back to their original plan. They had spent far too much time discussing this man. "They have too much baggage right now. They should be quarantined like a disease until I figure out what exactly to do with them. Besides, I don't think that they are presentable from what Boris said on the way back from their burned down home."

"I want to meet them, Dmitry." She insisted like a child begging for a toy. "Please." Her voice was softer. Slipping him back inside of her, she couldn't help but gasp. She remembered a time that she would have wondered why the house was burned down and why they were there, but she had learned over the years not to be surprised by anything that happened here.

Dmitry could not deny Royal much of anything, no matter how ridiculous her request. He knew that he spoiled her far too much but he enjoyed it. Unzipping her dress, he palmed her breast and kissed her neck. "Fine, but later. Right now..."

A smile crossed her lips now that she had yet again gotten what she wanted. "Right now, I'm going to fuck you," she said, finishing his sentence.

***

It was nearly an hour and a half before anyone came to collect Nicola. Led by two men, one in front of him and one behind him, he was escorted down to the main floor and into the solarium where Anatoly was playing cards with Gabriel. The room was filled with cigar smoke and covered in beautiful exotic flowers and plants.

Anatoly looked up from the table for only a second, making sure to cover his hand. "You play?" he asked Nicola.

"What game?" Nicola asked.

"What game?" Anatoly shook his head. "Poker. What else?"

Take a seat at the wooden table opposite Anatoly and Gabriel; he looked around for the fourth player.

Gabriel pushed the vodka bottle to him. "We're waiting on Dmitry," he said, looking at his watch.

"Do you have somewhere to be?" Anatoly taunted Gabriel.

"No," he said, shortly.

"Your girlfriend is upstairs, sleeping in your bed. Yet, you act like you want to get out and see someone else…and I don't think it's about money. You're acting like there is some other woman on your mind." He touched his temple with his index finger.

Gabriel ignored him. "If you don't drink vodka, there is plenty of dark liquor back there on the bar," he said to Nicola.

"I've never been in a solarium equipped with a bar before," Nicola said, standing up.

"We're getting ready for my wedding," Anatoly said, laying down a card.

Nicola grabbed the entire bottle of Honey Jack Daniels and brought it back with him. Opening the top, he took a large gulp straight from the bottle and set it beside him.

Gabriel snickered. "That kind of day, huh?"

"Yep," Nicola answered.

When Dmitry walked into the room, the guards who were just relaxed and talking among themselves suddenly went rigid. Standing up from their chairs, they posted up in their positions and became silent.

With a distinct swagger in his long stride, he made his way over to the table and sat down in his chair in blue polo and jeans. Unfortunately, Anatoly knew why his father had been tardy to their meeting and why he had suddenly had to change his wardrobe. Ending the game in the middle, he collected all the cards.

"Bring me a shot glass," Dmitry said without taking his eyes off Nicola.

Immediately two men walked over to the bar. Nicola watched in amazement. Did this man ever have to do anything for himself? He looked across the table at Dmitry and shook his head.

"I do hold my own penis to piss from time to time," Dmitry answered, reading Nicola's mind.

"Good to know," Nicola said, taking another swig from the bottle.

Anatoly shuffled the cards and then took a swig of his beer. "So, papa wants to talk business with you," he said. Putting the cards down so that Nicola could cut them.

"So I gathered," Nicola said gruffly.

"We just saw each other what…four hours ago," Dmitry said with a curious look on his face. "I didn't expect you until tomorrow."

"Well, someone wanted me dead tonight," Nicola said, releasing a sigh. He cut the cards and Anatoly dealt them.

Dmitry rubbed the bridge of his nose. "What kind I say? Some people are just impatient."

"I would have been dead if you hadn't had your men there." Nicola didn't waste time being cool. He appreciated what they had done.

"That was not my doing." Dmitry pointed at Anatoly. "You should be thanking him for saving your family."

"I didn't send them there for that," Anatoly answered quickly.

"But he did make the call," Gabriel added. He winked at his cousin. "No one would believe it, but the guy actually has a soft side."

"I'm not soft," Anatoly snapped. "I don't trust you," he explained.

Nicola shrugged. "The feeling is mutual."

Dmitry picked up his cards. "So have you had time to think about my offer?"

Nicola put down a card. "You mean in between the gun play?"

"I have found that this is the time that men receive clarity," Dmitry said, face expressionless.

"Yes, I've had time to think about it, and yes, it looks like I have no choice. I'm indebted to you." The words felt like poison slipping from his lips. He pushed down the bile in his stomach and took another swig of Jack.

"You are indebted to us, but I want you to work for me in a way that you aren't always reminded of that." Dmitry watched his nephew put down the wrong card. Still expressionless, he played his own card.

"I'll remember that fact every time I look at my children," Nicola answered sincerely. His face twisted up. "I'm not rolling on any cops."

"That's not what I want you to do," Dmitry assured. "I've found it's hard to get complete cooperation when you ask a man to go completely against the grain."

"So what do you want me to do?" Nicola asked. He put down his cards and stared at Dmitry. "I've been a cop my entire life and after tomorrow, I'll just be fucking unemployed."

"You'd be surprised what can happen in a day," Dmitry said with a grin. "Tonight, you go up and see your wife and your kids. Tomorrow you put them on a plane and send them away. Get yourself ready to become a new man and tomorrow evening, you meet your new friends."

Nicola frowned. "Send my family where?"

Dmitry didn't look up from his cards. "To your family in Miami, I suppose. That had to be your plan at some point. You can use our jet. They'll be there in a couple of hours or less and then you can focus."

"I don't understand. You save my family. Send them off to keep them protected; offer me a job and all because I'm an honest man? Would an honest man even consider working for you after being a cop for such a long time?" Nicola rubbed a hand through his hair. "I don't know. I think you've got the wrong guy for whatever you've got planned."

"I don't make those kinds of mistakes. Of course you are the right man. You just don't know it yet. Besides good men make hard decisions all the time. They are not always what appears to be the right choice but they are what is best considering their options. And you, Nicola Agosto, are out of options."

Anatoly chuckled.

"It's not so bad," Gabriel said to Nicola. "I left the DEA, and I never looked back."

"But he left a rich man. You're leaving homeless and unemployed," Anatoly said, unable to miss an opportunity to stick it to Nicola. "I don't know why my father likes you so much, but just take the offer."

Nicola cut his eyes at Anatoly but chose to ignore his attitude for the moment.

"He's never in a good mood," Gabriel apologized.

Anatoly rolled his eyes and played his cards. "I don't like cops. And for the record, I think that this is a mistake."

Dmitry looked at Gabriel. "Make sure that goes down in the minutes."

Nicola picked up the bottle. "Look, I appreciate the room and board, the whiskey, the cards…but the fact of the matter is that I've got a hit list that I need to start on. Let's raise the stakes a bit. I'll come and work for you for good, not because I want to but because if that means that I can use your resources to kill the mother-fuckers responsible for trying to kill my kids and my wife, then it's worth it."

Dmitry raised a brow. "No locking anyone up?"

"Let me make this clear. I'm going to kill them or die trying," Nicola said bluntly. "Fuck honor, fuck my career, fuck it all. I want the motherfucker that gave the order, since the rest of the bastards who did the hit are dead."

Anatoly looked at his father, but did not speak. Dmitry nodded. "For good, you say?"

"Yes," Nicola answered quickly. "For good."

Dmitry stuck his hand out across the table. "Shake on it."

Nicola shook his hand hesitantly, knowing that this gentleman's agreement was the most expensive that he'd ever made in his entire life. "So, can I use your men? I'm ready to go tonight to start busting heads until I get a name and an address. I lost my only lead…the Roxie girl. So, I have to do what I do best and turn this city upside down until something falls out that I can use."

Dmitry liked Nicola's tenacity but knew that the man was emotional at the moment. "Revenge is a dish best served cold, my friend." He laid down his cards and smiled. "I win." Standing up, he tapped the table with his knuckles. "Go to your hearing tomorrow. Then you meet my men, and then you can get even. For now, have a drink, relax and then go and see your wife. Try to embrace and remember your last night as a free man. In the morning, we go to work."

"Why are you doing this?" Nicola asked.

Dmitry smiled. "Consider it an investment."

"In what?" Nicola probed.

"I'm a business man. There is only one answer. I want to secure my own personal interests." Winking at Nicola, he patted his son on the back and left.

28

Alone in the massive bedroom wrapped in a towel after her bath, Ivy sat at the end of the large bed staring into the golden embers as they rose from the fireplace. In contrast, cool air blasted from the vents in the ceiling above her, creating a relaxing, tranquil mood. Under any other circumstance, the opulence of the mansion would not have been lost on her, but at the moment, she could barely acknowledge all the work involved in making the beautiful mansion a palace for its guests.

A startling flashback paralyzed her. Guns shots. Fire. Screaming. Fear of death. The chaos still rattled around in her brain like a ricocheting bullet. Every time that she closed her eyes, she could hear her husband's voice. She could see him shooting back at the men who had come to their home to take their lives.

Fingers trembling, she clasped them together and said another prayer.

Thank you, Lord, for your deliverance, she mumbled. At just the thought of what could have been tears formed again at the corners of her tired eyes.

She knew that Nicola had been summoned by the great and powerful Dmitry but her heart worried for him. What had Nicola done? What had he traded for their safety? Every award and accommodation that he had received over the course of their marriage came to mind. And what about all the sacrifices, all the near death experiences? What about their life and all that they had stood for?

Was he about to throw it all away? Did he have to? Could she do anything about it? Her questions were still limitless, still unanswered. It caused a panic deep inside of her, down to the very core of her soul.

A gentle knock on the door pulled her from her thoughts. Getting up, she held the towel tightly to her body and walked to it. "Yes," she said, unsure of who it could be. She looked down at the bottom of the door and saw a shadow.

"I came to check on you," a woman's voice answered. "My name is…"

Ivy opened the door and looked out at the woman, stopping in mid-sentence.

Royal smiled warmly. "I'm Dmitry's wife," she said, raising her arms with a tall basket full of gifts. "May I come in?"

Ivy nodded. Stepping to the side, she let Royal in the room.

Royal walked in, and Ivy quickly closed and locked the door behind her.

Setting the basket on the bed, Royal began to pull out each item. "I bought you some things for the night. Underwear, sports bra, night clothes, a sundress for tomorrow, some lotion and hygiene products. It isn't much, but I figured it would help. I spoke with Boris, and he said that you all were extremely put out." Turning around, she stared back at Ivy, who appeared to be in shock.

Royal was a busty, curvaceous woman. She was mocha-colored with a long, bone-straight, inky black mane that stopped midway of her back. Its fullness bounced with her every move and spoke to careful care and attention as every part of her was. Heavy bangs lined her angelic face. Her features were distinctively beautiful and striking as was her appearance. Even in black yoga pants, a black tank top and Nike's, she appeared regal with four-carat diamonds in her ears, a Presidential Rolex on her arm and the smell of mind-blowing wealth on her skin. There was however a startling sight that contrasted with her stunning beauty. A scar across her neck, old but pronounced, drew worry and curiosity. Ivy tried not to stare.

"Aren't you Royal Stone?" Ivy asked in confusion.

Royal raised a perfectly arched brow. "I used to be in another life," she said, turning back around. "There are some other things in here that might be useful."

Ivy watched the woman from behind. She could see the tension in her shoulders. "My husband mourned your death a few years ago," she continued. "He told me something awful had happened to you. Your death was in the news for a week. He had worried that he hadn't done enough to protect you."

Royal huffed. "Well, what can I say? The dead has arisen." She didn't like sharing the details of her complicated past, but she could understand Ivy's sheer wonderment with standing face-to-face with a ghost. It was partly why she didn't bother to venture out into the city. Instead, she stayed behind the walls of her compound and treated it like a fortress of protection instead of a prison, like some people might have.

Ivy remembered herself. Walking up to the bed beside Royal, she looked at the gifts on the bed. This was kind of Royal, something that she didn't have to do. "Forgive me. I can't thank you enough," Ivy said sincerely.   She picked up the black cotton underwear, still with the tags on it. "The fire took everything that I owned." She huffed. "Even the smallest of things."

"Someone came after you?" Royal asked.   She looked over Ivy with pity and understanding that could only be shown if a person had some personal insight.

Ivy nodded.   "They would have killed my entire family, my children, my unborn child...everyone....if your men hadn't shown up.   We'd all be dead right now."

There was so much communicated between them at that moment that went unsaid but understood.

Without asking, Royal wrapped her arms around Ivy and hugged her tight.   Many years ago, nearly the exact same thing had happened to her.   She was brutally attacked by Dmitry's younger brother while she was pregnant.   To hear that someone else had been so offended made her blood boil with anger.   "You're safe now," Royal promised.   "No one can get in here to bother you."

Ivy felt herself tearing up again.   Her mouth watered and suddenly she could not hold in her pain. Sobbing softly, she held Royal tightly.   "Thank you so much."

"No need to thank anyone," Royal said, sitting her down on the bed.   "I think that to keep them from going straight to hell, Dmitry and the boys have to do one good deed a year.   It's written in blood somewhere."

They both laughed, breaking the tension.

"Are your children alright?" Royal asked, looking towards the door that led to their room.   "Where they injured in anyway? If so, I can call a doctor and have him look them over.   It won't be any trouble."

"Physically, they are alright, but emotionally, there is going to be a lot of work to be done to help them heal after this," Ivy said, wiping her face. "The most traumatic thing that ever happened to them before this was seeing their old dog, Henry, have a heat stroke." She was grateful for that fact at the moment.

"Just be there for them as much as possible. I have three children. One little girl and two twin baby boys. My oldest recently went through a very traumatic event that we are still helping her cope with. There are nightmares - terrible ones. Then the mood swings can be a bit much. I can tell you from experience that no one is ever the same after you dangle their lives in front of them. I don't care if it's a child or an adult. But reassurance goes a long way." Royal stopped herself, feeling that she had said too much. It was always hard to deal with outsiders. She was never sure of what to say or how to say it.

"Can I ask you a question?" Ivy knitted her fingers together.

Royal thought that she had been answering her questions. "Yes," she answered hesitantly.

"Has my husband been working for your husband?" Ivy's voice trembled.

Royal shrugged. "Who's to say? A lot of men work for my husband."

"A lot of men aren't cops," Ivy replied. Her disappointment showed. "He's a good man." She tried to wrap her mind around what she suspected. "Everything that I've ever known of him has been good. But if we're here..."

Royal stopped her with a raised hand. Her diamond ring sparkled across the room. "I want to help you. I really do, but my husband's business is just that. His. I can't nor do I try to control it. If you feel in your heart that your husband is a good man, then no one should be able to tell you any different. And he must care, otherwise, he wouldn't be here doing whatever he's doing to keep you safe."

Ivy needed more of an explanation than that, but she could tell that she wouldn't get it from Royal. "I appreciate that." Giving up on the subject, she clutched the clothes in her hand. "I better go and get dressed."

"Get some rest," Royal said, standing up as well. "I'm sure they will send Agosto up before long. And in the morning, please consider having breakfast with me and my family. I'm sure that being around them will put to rest any worries that you might have. We're not monsters. Just people, just like you."

Ivy truly doubted that but did not lead on. "I'd be honored to," she said, standing at the doorway of the restroom. "For what's it's worth, I'm glad that you're alive."

"Thank you," Royal said with a smile. "I'm glad that we're both here instead of the alternative."

Walking out of the room, Royal closed the door behind her. Quietly, she made her way down the hall, a guard waiting on her as she got to the stairway. On the way down, she saw Nicola coming up.

Exhausted and still in the same soiled clothes that he arrived in, he still was courteous enough to step to the side and bow his head slightly. "Mrs. Medlov," he said, face unreadable. The smell of alcohol permeated from his skin. Bags swelled under his tired brown eyes and his stubbly, five o'clock shadow raised above his square jaw. But even his dishevelment, he still was a picture of raw beauty.

Royal stopped a step above him. "How are you?" she asked, voice low.

Twisting up his wide mouth, he bit his lip. "I could be better." Then he shrugged at a thought. "I could be worse."

"Your wife is very sweet," she said with a smile. "Make sure to tend to her carefully."

"You don't have to worry about that." He saw her eyes run down to his hand, clasping the bottle he had taken from the solarium.

"I'm glad that you all are alright. Do have a good night," she said, turning to her bodyguard. "Get him some fresh clothes and bring them up."

"That won't be necessary," Nicola interrupted.

"Do it," Royal said abruptly. Her demeanor changed quickly. Remembering herself, she relaxed her shoulders and smiled. "Now, please." Her voice was softer with the last bit but not any less of an order.

The bodyguard nodded but did not speak. The unease in his face was evident. Standing behind her, he pushed on the earpiece in his ear and spoke in Russian.

Nicola smirked. "I see that you've managed to acclimate to your husband's way of doing things."

Royal didn't smile now. "It's the only way to do things, Mr. Agosto. A bit of advice. You might want to as well. These waters are a lot harder to negotiate than you're used to."

Nicola didn't speak. Rolling his neck, he took a swig straight from the bottle. "Thanks for the advice," he said, acutely aware of her meaning.

"We'll see you tomorrow. Do try and get some rest. I'm sure that you need it," Royal said, suddenly stoic and rigid. Stepping down past him, she slipped her hands into her pockets and headed quietly to the other side of her large house, bodyguard in tow. One would have thought that the man wasn't there behind her looming like a dark shadow. It took years of practice for such a thing not to bother a person. It took years of being watched and followed so often that one just learned to ignore it, to appreciate it, to count on it. And what time of enemies lurked outside to call for such a thing. The answer was sobering.

Nicola watched her as she went on her way and thought back to when she was just a young, clueless shop girl completely inept and over her pretty, little head. Now, she was regal, in-control and confident in her more-than-distinguished position. Other women in the underworld wanted to be her. They probably mimicked themselves after her. Bosses sought out women who looked like her just so they could be more like her husband.

And she did not flinch in the limelight. It was as if she barely noticed it.

He imagined that it was due to years of seeing more than her share of a world that just as dark as it was powerful. Every luxury afforded her was paid with the life of someone else, and she had learned to accept that fact.

In truth, he didn't want to see his wife lose her innocence that way. Royal, while extremely beautiful, was jaded now - a shell of the woman that she could have been had she not been introduced to a life where crime was a constant. Yet, even in the depths of her underworld existence, she still was safer than his wife. Her children were safer than his. The man following behind Royal and the many others strategically placed around her palatial home with fully-automatic weapons and till-death loyalty ensured that because of her name, she would always be protected, always be made to walk above the blood, bones and bodies of her husband's victims, so that she'd never have to feel the reality of who he really was.

It was that protection that he sought. It was that assurance that he needed. It was security that he was about to trade his entire life for…and it was worth it.

Headed up the stairs, he slowly came to grips with his new life. Whatever he was before this, he was no longer. All justifications for honor had gone. There was only one reality and that was that he had to keep his family safe.

Knocking on the door, he waited.

Ivy answered quickly. Changed into clean clothes and bathed, she looked more relaxed. The frantic worry in her eyes had gone. Lighting up when she saw his face, she wrapped her arms around him and held him tight, as if she had not seen him just thirty minutes before.

"Are you okay? I was worried," she said, pulling him into the room.

She was worried about him. After she was ostracized in the community she had worked her ass off to help, after she was fired from the job that she had worked in since college to become a partner, after she was shot at, house burned and children nearly murdered, *she was still worried about him.*

He closed the door and cupped her face in his large, dirty hands. "Baby," was the only word that he could muster before he found her lips and kissed her gently. The taste of her warm mouth was always its own sweet medicine for him. He relished in it, one slow evolution at a time. Picking her up off the floor, he carried her to the bed and laid her down on the softness of the pillows Rubbing his hands through her hair, he nuzzled his nose in the smell of it, let his fingers run through its silkiness.

Her eyes closed tight as she melted into him. Pushing his shirt up, she snatched it off his body and raked her nails over the stubble on his chest. Exasperated, she opened her legs as he pushed down in between them. A thick, engorged erection waited on her, pushing through his shorts, begging to be satisfied.

Nicola pulled her shirt up and bent to kiss her slightly bulging stomach. The roundness of it was so perfect and brown. Thank God that there were no bruises, no harm to his growing child. *I'll keep you safe*, he thought to himself. Placing his mouth over her belly button, he slowly caressed her before he helped her out of the clothes that she had just put on. Her perfect brown tips of her aching, rigid nipples pressed against his hot skin. The smell of smoke and sweat still lingered on his skin. Paying no mind, she kissed his neck and sucked on the lobe of his ear.

He growled, slipping a digit in between her thighs, happy to find her moist. The sudden penetration made her back arch.

"Nicky," she whispered.

"I love you," he said, kissing her breasts. Holding one in his hand, he carefully and softly massaged her.

"I love you so much, baby. I'll do anything to protect you."

Ivy rubbed a hand through his hair and felt tears on his breasts. He buried his head there in the fullness of her bosom as he fondled her.

"I know," she said, pulling his head to see his face. She nodded at him. "And I'm so grateful for it."

"Grateful," he frowned. "Oh, baby, you deserve so much more." Tears flowed down his cheeks. The pain swelled up in his chest, making it hard to speak. "I've never in my entire life known anyone more deserving of a good life. You just don't know how special you are...how wonderful you are. You and my children are my world. I don't exist without you." He kissed her again, this time deeper. "I don't exist..." he whispered in a raspy voice.

Ivy pulled down his shorts quickly. The feel of him lying on top of her so close that she could feel his heartbeat soothed her. "Let me make you feel better," she said, crying as well. "It's the only thing I know to do right now. It's all that I have to offer, but let me. Please let me."

Her hands glided over his muscular back, down the valley of ripples and his dark, tan olive skin. Cupping his buttocks, she felt him push inside of her. He was trembling as he entered. Raising up on his knees, he rested his upper body on his elbows to look at her. Grabbing her thigh, he pushed deeper and let out a moan. Eyes closing, he rested his head in the curve of her neck.

His wife. His beautiful, loving wife. She was still here, still his even after all that they had gone through. He was blessed, not lucky.

"Can you feel me?" she asked, holding him tight.

"Yes," he answered quickly, flexing his powerful hips. "All of you." He moved slowly in and out of her, forgetting the world around him for just a moment. The heady mix of love and sorrow fills the room, and they are now one just as they had been many times before. His breath is ragged and voice harsh as he feels himself grown harder inside of her. The silky feel of her body closing around him is intoxicating, paralyzing. Unable to escape the ecstasy of her touch, he realizes that he is as much hers as she is his, and that fact is the only thing that heals the gaping wound in his bleeding heart. All he had ever wanted was this woman, this temple, this joy. And as long as he had her, he could survive anything.

"This will always be your home. Not some building or some geographic location on a map," she said into his ear. Sinking her nails into his skin, she stole his attention. "Right here, in me. For as long as I have breath, this is your home, Nicola. Nowhere else and with no one else on this earth."

His large, naked body covered hers completely, but it was her body that hid him from all that mattered. "For better or worse until death does us part, so help me God," he said, raising his head to look at her. His hazel-brown eyes burned through her with a passion that she hadn't seen in years.

"Till death do us part. So help us God," Ivy said, raising her plump lips to his wet mouth.

While still connected in the darkness with only the fireplace to illuminate their illicit actions, they kissed slowly like the first time that they had met many years ago on the couch of his good friend's house, when she was just a college girl and he was just a young, lost man. He kissed her until the room began to spin around him and the sound of her moans took over like a hypnotizing melody. His kissed her until her tongue was woven around his own, and he could taste the sweetness of her words and the truth of her promises.

***

What was left of the burned down structure of the Agosto's formerly historic home was being hosed down with gallons upon gallons of water by the Memphis Fire Department. A sea of blue lights lit up the area. Police swarmed the neighborhood, interviewing scared neighbors who told terrifying stories of a shoot-out only meant for large-scale Hollywood productions. Cops walked the area with dogs and flashlights. News reporters stood on the perimeter in clear view of the crime scene reporting on the missing or dead family that lived inside. They connected without verification of the police department the slew of murders, bombings, and drive-by shootings that had taken place all over the city that night back to the Baby Boys case.

Suddenly, the question was raised about Sgt. Agosto's innocence. Had he truly been wrong in his attack on the dead DeMario Washington or was Ivy's profession of his innocence and her assertion that bad people plotting on them true? In the late hours of the night, as ambulances picked up dead bodies, the public opinion began to sway.

Ivy's interview promo was aired every break with people logging on to their computers to discuss the case on their social media outlets, while others called into the radio stations.

Ivy's parent stood outside the house crying and demanding answers with their friends who had rushed to
the scene as soon as they had heard the news. The
Security Squad that had snatched away Agosto's badge
and gun combed the area, while other detectives from
several special investigative units took as much evidence as they could find. Stepping over hundreds of
shells out on the lawn, crime scene investigators
quartered off large areas to start to find clues.

Getting out of his unmarked squad car in the middle
of the fiasco, Director Amway headed toward the house
dressed in his uniform. Immediately, reporters ran his
way, but officers blocked them from passing as cameras
flashed and followed him, screaming out for a statement.

"Director! Director!" They all shouted. "What
does the Memphis Police Department have to say about
the string of murders and bombings? What happened to
Nicola Agosto? Was his family murdered? What is the
Memphis Police Department going to do?"

He covered his face from the flashing lights and
stayed behind the crime scene line. Uninterested in
speaking with the media, he let his public information
officer take the lead, blocking the media from getting a
direct quote from her boss.

A large huddle of officers in uniform and SWAT
gear waited on him. Director Magnelli was in the
middle of the huddle, giving orders and sending out
squad cars to look for any possible signs of the Agosto
family.

"Where are we?" Amway said, as the officers
moved out of his way. He looked over at Magnelli in

surprise. "What are you doing here? You should be with your wife?"

"A lot of good that will do," Magnelli said, eyes red from crying over his dead daughter. He looked like death warmed over in a pair of jeans and MPD t-shirt with worn leather loafers. "We need to find whoever is responsible for this, and I can't help at the fucking morgue."

"I'm with you," Amway said, not pushing the issue. "I'm sorry for your loss. I really am. We've got several cars on your house. No one will get to your wife or any other member of your family. We're looking for your son right now."

"I saw that. I appreciate it," Magnelli said, shining the light on the map of the area. "We have officers saturating the area. We've called in those who are off duty. Investigators are out knocking on doors. Everyone is on full-alert. Johnson is in the hospital being treated for his burns and cuts. Steele is dressed and on the streets with a few guys. Ferris is under protective custody."

"Good." Amway clapped his hands together. "Alright men. I want confirmation of who is in that house. Agosto had four kids and a wife. If they are dead, I want to know. If they are gone, I want to know where they are. Put a cop on every corner if you have to. Activate all cameras. Find out how useful the Blue Crush system is. Since its open season on us, we're going to return the favor. Pick up any motherfucker that remotely looks at you wrong. I want every lead followed-up on and every stone turned over. I don't care if we have to fill the jail to capacity, we'll borrow space at the penitentiary. This shit ends now. We need answers, and we need them tonight. Let's send a message that this town still belongs to us."

29

Early morning crept through the heavily curtained windows of the bedroom where Nicola and Ivy lay asleep. The fireplace was still on and the silence of the room was peaceful and serene. Their boys were crowded around them, hugging them tightly, safely curled under their parents unharmed and out of danger.

Rolling over, Nicola's eyes popped open to the sound of gunshot ringing in his ears. Jumping up in a cold sweat, he reached for a weapon, but there was none. Suddenly, he realized the gunshot was actually a knock at the door. He looked over at his family, resting and let out a deep breath. *Just a nightmare.* Calming his beating heart, he pulled himself to the end of the bed and pushed his feet down into the carpet and walked to the door.

Boris was standing with a change of clothes for Nicola and the children. "Boss said for your family to meet him downstairs in thirty minutes." He passed him the clothes. "Don't be late," he said, walking off.

Nicola closed the door and leaned his head against the wall. Ivy slipped her hand from under the pillow and looked at him. "Good morning," she said, voice groggy. Before he could respond, she jumped up from the bed and headed to the bathroom.

Morning sickness. He couldn't be happier to see it coming. It meant that she was still pregnant, still healthy and carrying his child.

Putting down the clothes, Nicola followed her to the bathroom dutifully and bent over her to hold her hair as she threw up in the fine porcelain receptacle.

"Let it out," he said, rubbing her back.

Ivy wiped her mouth and flushed the toilet. "I should probably get something on my stomach. I'm sure the baby is hungry."

"So are you. I'll get the kids dressed. You just lay down until we're ready," he said, helping her stand. "You okay?"

"I'm fine," she said, holding her stomach. "Nothing I'm not used to." Going to the double sink, she grabbed her toothbrush and ran the water. "I'll help you get them up."

"Baby, you should rest," he insisted. He knew that she had to be weak after losing all of her nutrients. He didn't want her sick the entire day, especially before the flight.

"No, I want to help," she said, looking at him in the mirror. "I'll be fine. I promise. We don't have much time." She willed herself to pull herself together.

Twenty-five minutes later, Boris was back at the door waiting for them. Escorting them quietly through the hallway, he heard one of the twin boys ask about the guns under his arms. Ivy quickly hushed him and grabbed his hand. Taking them downstairs, he led them to the informal dining area where Dmitry sat reading a newspaper. Royal sat beside him, talking to a beautiful little girl who had a peachy hue and startling blue eyes like her father. Gabriel sat at the other end of the table, also reading a paper and flipping through his iPad.

The long dinner table was covered with flowers, fruit, biscuits, sausage, eggs, pancakes, and several other pastries. The aroma of freshly brewed coffee filled the room. It was a perfect way to start the day. As soon as the family entered the room, Dmitry put down his newspaper and stood. Walking over to Ivy, he took her hand in his own and smiled.

"Mrs. Agosto, how are you this morning?" he asked, escorting her to a chair near him. He pulled out a seat and waited for her to sit.

"Fine, thank you," she muttered, looking back at her husband.

Nearly speechless, she took in his monstrous size. He was easily seven feet tall and amazingly beautiful - too handsome to be a criminal and far too nice. He wore a tailored, crisp black shirt and black slacks. Evidently, he was an early riser. Nodding at Royal, who was also dressed in a black simple dress that only brought more attention to her tall, statuesque frame and fine jewelry, she felt completely underdressed.

"Did you sleep well?" Royal asked as a maid poured her more coffee.

"I did," Ivy answered quickly. Dmitry pushed up her seat to the table and patted her back. "Agosto, please have a seat with your wife," he said, going back to his chair at the head of the table.

"And kids come over here. Aren't you gorgeous," Royal said, standing to receive the children. She admired each of them, running her hand through their delicious black curly locks.

The children introduced themselves to the girl who watched the boys carefully. Royal couldn't help but notice the child's serious demeanor. Ivy drank in her beauty and her poise. The girl couldn't be any more than six, yet she behaved like an adult. Offering the boys a hand, she introduced herself as Anya Medlov then quickly went back to her breakfast.

Ivy wondered what could have happened to the girl to make her so ice cold, but she wouldn't dare ask. Then there was the other man at the end of the table, who nodded at her but did not address her directly. Quietly, he ate his food with a blond woman at his side. He barely spoke to her either. Instead, he immersed himself in work and occasionally gave a courteous smile. But he too was incredibly tall. His dark hair contrasted with Dmitry's but he looked so much like him until, she had to ask.

"Who is he?" Ivy whispered to Dmitry, feeling unusually comfortable with the man.

"He is my nephew, Gabriel. He's a bit put off today, but he'll be fine. And that is Briggy, his girlfriend. We're all one big family here." Dmitry watched Royal make his plate and then took it from her. "Thank you, sweetheart."

"You're welcome," Royal replied.

"Well, we appreciate your hospitality," Ivy said, looking over at Royal. "I slept like a rock in that cozy bed. And the kids slept well too. You're really too kind."

"It's the least that we could do considering how much you've been…put out," Dmitry said, looking over the children. He tried to use his words carefully. "Please, enjoy breakfast. There is plenty."

Settling down for breakfast, the initial shock finally wore off. Nicola and Dmitry spoke briefly about the news and the coverage regarding the attack, while Royal and Ivy spoke about the babies. There were no awkward silences or moments, instead the morning flowed like clockwork. Royal continued to play the gracious hostess, while Dmitry played the gentleman. Ivy nearly forgot that she was having breakfast with a notorious crime boss and his family. Instead, they were just Nicola's friends.

When breakfast was over, Gabriel stood and walked over to Nicola. Wiping his eyes, he adjusted the guns holstered under his bulging biceps. "We have to get your family to the plane," he said, looking at his watch.

Nicola looked over at Ivy and rubbed her back. "We don't have anything to take with us. We're ready when you are." He hated that his wife had to go away, but what else could he do.

Royal walked over to Ivy and hugged her. "Take care. Good luck with baby number five."

"You too," Ivy said, feeling as though she had made a friend. "Thank you again."

"Again, there is no need to thank us," Royal said, motioning for her daughter. "I have to get upstairs and check on the children, so this is good bye for me, but I'm sure that we'll be seeing each other again." Glancing over at Nicola as her daughter took her hand, Royal nodded. "Mr. Agosto."

"Mrs. Medlov," Nicola said as professionally as possible. He didn't even pretend that the relationship that Ivy was building with Royal carried over to him and Dmitry. From here on, it would be strictly business.

Dmitry cracked a smile at Ivy. He found her to be a breath of fresh air - so innocent and so caring. She was everything that he'd heard she was. Royal had gone on for quite some time the night before about the woman and her desire to see the family care for. "Don't worry, Mrs. Agosto. When you return, your home will be restored." He could feel his wife looking at him in approval.

Ivy smiled at the thought. Somehow hearing him say the words, made it true.

Four other heavily armed guards met the family and Gabriel in the foyer and escorted them out in the bright morning sun to a convoy of black Range Rovers with tinted windows parked right outside the house. Loading them up, they headed out to take Ivy and the kids to a plane on the outskirts of town in Millington to be flown to Miami where Nicola's family would be waiting.

When they were gone, Dmitry found Royal upstairs feeding the children with Briggy and a nanny. She looked up from doting on her son to watch her husband as he played with her daughter. "What plans do you have for Agosto?" she asked.

Dmitry raised a brow. "Why do I have to have plans?" he asked, cutting his eyes at her.

"Because you always do," Royal said, putting down the baby's snack. She rocked her son gently. "Do this without any intention of receiving anything in return, Dmitry."

He turned and looked at her. "Why should I?" he asked, putting his daughter on his lap.

"Because you can," she said seriously. "Because there is no need to turn everyone from their paths to suit you and your personal interests."

"Isn't not turning him in your personal interest?" he asked with a hint of sarcasm in his deep baritone Russian voice.

"I have nothing to gain from just helping them. There is not a personal interest involved," she said, rolling her eyes. "It's just after what nearly happened to Anya, maybe this is God's way of giving us an opportunity to pay it forward."

"Of course there is a personal interest for you. You like her. You want to save her," Dmitry said, rubbing through his daughter's hair while she played with her doll. She listened quietly, holding on to her father's every word.

"Just think about it," Royal said, refusing to argue the point. "It's worth a thought. This is an entire family that you're playing with," she stabbed.

Dmitry didn't like her choice of words. "I don't play."

"No, darling, you don't lose," she said, putting the bottle back in her son's mouth. "Now enough of this. We need to talk about Anatoly's wedding. Where is he anyway?"

"Busy," Dmitry answered without further explanation.

***

Ferris was shocked when he was told that despite him being in protective custody, he still had to be escorted to the police headquarters to answer questions about DeMario Washington. One would have thought that considering his home had been bombed and shot up that the investigation would have leaned toward other people - anyone but him. But Johnson had insisted.

With his legs wrapped in gauze, Johnson sat in the interrogation room in shorts and black t-shirt, shield wrapped in a single black band out of respect for Carmen's death, patiently waiting on Ferris to arrive. Steele sat on the other side of the booth, watching with Magnelli.

"This isn't a good idea," Steele said, pacing the room. "Johnson is holding on by a very thin string."

"Aren't we all?" Magnelli said, rubbing his temples. "But Johnson says that it's worth it. So, we need to speak with Ferris."

"Let me do it," Steele begged.

"No." Magnelli said shortly.

Steele knew that Magnelli was not thinking clearly. How could he considering his own tragedy. "I'm not worried about Ferris. I'm worried about Johnson screwing this up by doing something monumentally stupid," she said, leaning against the glass and looking at him. There was no way that she was going to leak that they had found those files, but she knew that they were close - too close to risk it.

"If he can get any information out of him, then it's worth it," Magnelli said, sipping his coffee. His voice was flat and void of all life as was his eyes.

She turned to look at him. He hadn't slept a wink and it showed. Walking over she touched his shoulder. No words could express her sorrow for his loss. His only daughter was dead and his son was missing. But here he was pushing forward with the investigation. "If there is anything that I can do…" she whispered.

Magnelli touched her hand. "Just do your job," he said, coldly.

She removed her hand quickly and went back to the glass just in time to see Ferris enter the room.

Johnson looked up from the table and stood. "Councilman Ferris," he said, offering his hand. "Thanks for coming in."

"I can't say that I'm happy to be here," Ferris said, looking around the small box of a room. "What is this about?"

"It won't take long. I'm sorry to drag you out but we were hoping that maybe you could shed some light on the situation with DeMario yesterday, since you were the last one to see him alive." He pulled out Ferris's chair. "Would you like some coffee?"

"There is no need for pleasantries, Johnson. I've had quite enough of them already this morning. Ask your questions so that I can go." He sat down and rolled his eyes.

Johnson looked at the glass and ran his sweaty hands down his shorts. "Okay," he said, grabbing his notepad and pushing the button to start the recording of the tape. "Did you know DeMario Washington before the attack on his life by Sgt. Agosto?"

"No," Ferris answered curtly.

"Are you in anyway linked to the Baby Boys murders?" Johnson asked, looking Ferris in the eye.

"What the hell kind of questions are these? Yes, of course I'm connected. I'm leading the public's interest in demanding the Memphis Police Department find the murderer responsible for four deaths," Ferris snarled.

Johnson sucked his teeth and looked over at the mirror. "What about your relationship to all four children?"

Ferris froze. "What relationship?"

"The fact that all four children were formerly at your child care facilities is one relationship." Johnson watched Ferris's face as it told on him.

"I wasn't aware of that? If it's so, then I'd be happy to help you in your investigation."

Johnson's voice lowered and sweat started to form on his forehead. "Don't you find it odd that you didn't know that before? That you of all people would lead this charge when they were all children you had come into contact with?"

"This interview is over," Ferris snapped. "I want my lawyer."

"Why do you want a lawyer? Didn't you just say that you'd be willing to help with this investigation? Don't you find it odd that a hit was put on myself and Steele only after we talked with you? And Mooky, DeMario's cousin was found dead, after we spoke with him. That's all too coincidental for me."

Ferris attempted to stand but Johnson pushed him back into his chair. "Sit your punk ass down," Johnson snarled. "And don't get up again, or I promise you, you'll regret it."

Steele panicked. "We need to pull him."

"Wait," Magnelli said, standing up. He walked over to the glass. "Wait for it."

"Did you put a hit on us with your partner? He was going to take care of us while you wrap the city around your pampered finger and run for mayor on the back of the same children that you were fucking. Is that about right?" Johnson asked, getting in his face. "But you didn't account for hiring fucking amateurs to do the job. So, you had to stage your own attempted murder."

Ferris had heard enough. "Now you listen to me. I won't take these ridiculous accusations. What? You're so inept at your job that you're grasping for straws by accusing anyone in sight? I have worked in this city for years. I'm an upstanding citizen and public official. I will not be harassed by some low-level detective who couldn't find a turd in a shit storm." He went to stand again.

Johnson reached into his cargo shorts and pulled out a field knife. Before Ferris could react, he grabbed the man's wrist, pushed it to the table and stabbed the knife through his hand straight into the table. The sound of metal tearing through bone and flesh echoed throughout the room.

Ferris screamed out at the same time that Steele went to the door to stop the investigation, but Magnelli held her down.

Blood began to paint the table in large oozing patterns. Pushing the handle harder, Johnson pushed Ferris back down into the chair. "I thought I told you to sit your fucking ass down. The next time you move, this goes through your short cock, you piece of shit." His nostrils flared, eyes blazed.

Ferris screamed out for help, but the door did not open. No help came.

"Give me a name!" Johnson spat. "Give me a fucking name!" He pulled his duty weapon and shot Ferris in the knee cap. "I will fill your ass full of holes if you don't start talking and there is not a damn thing anyone here can do about it." The door flung open but Johnson pointed it at the cop who came to Ferris' aid. "Back the fuck up!" Johnson growled. "A name, Ferris, dammit!" he screamed. Twisting the knife in the man's hand, he waited.

"Sammy!" Ferris yelled. "I don't have anything to do with it. I've just been paying people around the city to tell me anything that could solve the case and the only thing that I've turned up is a drug dealer named Sammy and a cop, but I don't know his name, and I don't know the drug dealer's last name…just Sammy."

Steele was at the door with the other cop now. "Detective Johnson," she said, gun pointed at him. "Please put down your weapon." She cocked her gun. "Dammit, don't make me fucking do this, Luke! Put the gun down!" she begged.

Johnson turned to Ferris and spit in his face. "I'm going to get you mother fucker. I promise you that. This isn't over." Dropping the gun, he raised his hands. "I need a shrink," he said as the police came in and handcuffed him. "I don't feel well."

"We'll get you some help, son," Magnelli said, walking through the door calmly. He looked at Ferris and spit on the ground. "Get this bastard some help in here," he said, turning away.

"I'm going to bury all of you!" Ferris yelled, holding his bloody hand as one of the cops pulled the knife out of his hand. "All of you!" As soon as his hand was free, he collapsed to the ground, knee throbbing and bleeding.

Carting Johnson off, Steele cursed. "Fuck, Johnson. Why?"

"Because it's time that we start playing by the same rules as them until we get some answers. Carmen's dead, Steele. She's dead and she's not coming back and someone has to pay for that."

Steele stopped walking and ran a hand through her hair. "But why does it have to be you?"

Johnson smirked. "I could give less than a fuck about myself," he said holding back tears.

"I'll take him," Magnelli said, walking up to them. "Steele, go back and make sure that we get that recording to the right people." He patted Johnson on the back and escorted him down the hall as officers looked on confused and in shock. "We're getting close," he said under his breath to Johnson. "I can feel it."

***

After Nicola and his entire family went missing, a meeting had to be convened by the police heads to decide what to do about his hearing. The mayor's office had already called and strongly suggested that his case be strongly reconsidered and investigated to make sure that no foul play had taken place. And the media was swarming around anyone at the police department who could possibly have answers. On the twelfth floor of the police headquarters downtown, a group of officials met quietly, hoping to come to some resolution on the matter, so that they could get back to the many other fires that they had to put out quickly.

"What the fuck happened today with Ferris," Amway asked, slamming his hands on the table. "It's not bad enough that we have a dead officer, slain in another cop's house during a clear assassination attempt, but we now have the lead guy pushing for our heads rallying the community for a news conference where he plans to publicly display his wounds from the hospital. More police brutality? This is your answer!"

Magnelli sat quietly at the table, eyes half closed. "The boy lost his cool. People lose their cool under these circumstances."

"Who let him in the room with the guy?" Amway asked, looking around at the men.

No one answered.

"Who?" Amway asked again.

"I did," Magnelli answered flatly.

Amway took a deep breath and swallowed hard. "Magnelli, I want you home. Do you understand? I don't want you on this case in anyway. Just go home and take care of your family."

"I plan to," Magnelli answered, "after this is done."

"Not fucking later, now!" Amway yelled. "I'm sorry about your daughter. I am, but I have everyone else and their families to consider too. You're off."

"My daughter's killer deserves to be caught!"

"Yes, her killer deserves to be caught. Those dead kids should have the same justice and so should De-Mario Washington and shit load of others. That's what we're here for. That's what we're paid for, to protect and to serve. And we weren't doing either when we put Johnson in the room with Ferris. I hate to say this, Magnelli, but your daughter isn't the first cop to die on this force. We've all had friends and family who have fallen to the same fate. My baby brother and Keegan's son. There are hundred just like us. But we took an oath. This has to be done through a process. This isn't the Wild West and we are held accountable."

"You think I don't know that?" Magnelli asked. "But let's face the facts. Something isn't adding up."

"Obviously," Amway gasped. "Right now, we are here to fix this. It starts with Nicola Agosto since half of the city is outside either demanding his head or demanding that he keep his job. The other half is out there to find out what we're doing about the dead kids and a few more are protesting about police brutality. This problem isn't going away until we fix it."

"Agosto is a good cop. It's obvious that he was framed now."

"Is it? Because no one in this room has brought me anything to say otherwise. The justice system doesn't deal in hunches. Bring me something, damn you! He's my friend too. He's a damn good cop, and no I didn't want this to happen to him and his fucking family. And you, Magnelli, you've been gunning for him since day one. What changed all of a sudden?"

"Everything changed. Hey, when I took the oath, I didn't suddenly become omnipotent and omniscient. I just put my fucking life on the line for over twenty-four years to keep people safe, some of which didn't deserve it. So, you'll excuse me if I don't feel sorry for some arrogant nigger with a hole through his fucking hand and knee, while my baby girl rots in a fucking box. The mother fucker had it coming!"

The men jumped up and caught Amway before he could charge across the table and snatch Magnelli up. "Nigger? Nigger? I got your nigger, you racist bastard. Get the fuck out of my office, Magnelli!" Amway screamed, trying to get out of the grip the men had on him.

Magnelli's eye twitched. "This city is going to burn, Amway. Do something about it before it does." Grabbing his jacket off the back of his chair, he turned and left, slamming the door behind him.

The men released him, and Amway snatched away, straightened his clothes and walked over to the window and looked out at the masses as they gathered in the streets with their signs and cameras, demanding answers. The crowd had grown from tens to hundreds in less than an hour. He had to focus, hand to regain control. The city couldn't burn on his watch. Turning around, he went back to the table and picked up his pen. "Get our riot unit activated and down here. Find out what time Ferris is going live on the air. We need to beat him. Keep our guys looking for Agosto and pull all the Intel together that we've found and get a target. I keep hearing the name Cane. Find out who and where the fuck he is and bring him here to me." He clenched his teeth. "Does anyone have a problem by law with pushing off the Agosto hearing?"

No one responded.

"Fine, we'll review this case at a later date pending further investigation into his actions," Amway said as his assistant walked to the door.

"Sir, the mayor is back on the phone for you," she said, hating to bother him again.

He nodded at her. "Put him through," he said, standing up. "Let's get this done, men...now."

***

As promised, the plane was waiting on the Agosto family on the private airstrip, gassed up and ready to leave upon their arrival. Getting out of the SUVs, the bodyguards secured the area while Ivy and Nicola said their last goodbyes.

"Do you think he's helping us because his wife is black?" Ivy asked, still lingering on her first interaction with Dmitry.

Nicola kissed her forehead. "No, baby. He doesn't care about that."

"Then what does he care about?" Ivy asked afraid. What could a man like that possibly want with her husband?

Nicola hated to see her worry so much. He touched her face and smiled. "He's a business man. He cares about his business. That's all."

Ivy didn't like the answer. Holding back tears, she closed her eyes and tried to calm her breathing. "When can we come home?"

"When it's all over, but you'll be safe in Miami for now. My folks won't let anything happen to you and there is plenty of security there. You'll be fine. Plus, I spoke with Dmitry. He has men there. You'll be under constant watch." He rubbed through her hair. "And I'll come for you soon. I promise."

Ivy grabbed his hand and held it to her face. "This is one promise that you better keep, Nicky."

"It's the only one that matters."

The door opened and Boris appeared stoic as ever. "Time to go," he said, reaching for Ivy's hand. He held it gently despite his outward rudeness.

Nicola quickly kissed all four of his sons. Time had run out for them. "I love you," he said, tears running down his face.

"Daddy, we don't want to go," Madison complained. "We want to stay with you."

"I know," Nicola said, wiping his face. "But it's okay. You're going to see Grandpa and Grandma Agosto. It'll be fun." He hugged them tight. His voice cracked. "Be good for them, okay? Be big men for me."

"We will," Adamo promised.

"And take care of your little brothers. They'll need you," Nicola added.

"We will," Adamo promised again.

"You must go now," Boris urged.

Helping the kids out of the truck, Nicola watched the men as they escorted his family onto the jet and then moved from the runway. Standing by the truck, he watched as they began to taxi down the strip.

He swallowed down his worry and said a prayer. *This is for the best*, is what he kept telling himself.

30

In all the years that Nicola had been a police officer, he had never been able to fully infiltrate the Medlov Crime family and its many layers. True, he had sent more than his fair share of undercover cops into the organization, but they had all returned with little evidence that would stand up in court against the city's most powerful criminal. Some had even been fired in the process of the investigations.

He had spent painstaking hours going over video and audio, trying to put together the pieces of a puzzle so elaborate until even knowing what he was looking at, he was often confused about its intricacies. Joint-task forces with the FBI had failed. Charges piling up in court had been dismissed. The city itself had been sued, and always Dmitry Medlov and his men stood above the ashes untouched.

Dmitry's reach was limitless as far as Nicola knew, but what he couldn't understand was why the man had chosen Memphis as one of his U.S. bases.

At the moment, Nicola sat in Dmitry's study back at the compound waiting for him to come and meet with him before they went to some undisclosed location to introduce him to the men who would help him finally put the men responsible for ruining his life in a box. It was quiet in the study, a peaceful place that was mixed with old world charm and modern art. The breathtaking view from outside the large bay windows made the room tranquil, but the many monitors displaying the many vantage points of the house, let him know that no matter how Dmitry tried to pretend that he felt untouchable, invincible, he was actually as paranoid and untrusting as any other man would be in his position.

Nicola's family was wealthy, but not like Dmitry. Nicola wondered if many men in the world were as wealthy as the man. No one knew just how much the Medlov family was worth considering that they were probably legitimately as wealthy through their legal businesses as they were wealthy through their illegal businesses. Dmitry's portfolio was extremely extensive crossing over ten industries including manufacturing, bottling, logistics, software, commercial real estate and pharmaceuticals.

In comparison, Nicola's father had amassed a fortune in Miami, but had done so the legal way. No one had died for his father's luxuries and no one ever would. He worried now about what his father would think of him if he knew what he was about to do. His entire life, the old man had preached honesty and loyalty. Now, here he was the former glory of his father's morals, about to become a turncoat.

Large footsteps echoed down the hall as Dmitry approached the study. Nicola stopped his daydreaming and focused. He needed to be exact in his expectations of this new partnership, even though he wasn't sure on Dmitry's end what was expected of him.

The door opened, and Dmitry entered alone. Without an entourage, however, he was no less intimidating. His presence was still overwhelming, both physically and psychologically.

But Nicola did not fear him. Instead, he wanted badly to understand him.

Who walked around in a suit all day anyway, Nicola thought to himself. A man who had conditioned himself after many years to be a reflection of what he wanted others to see him as *at all times*? Someone who had come from little to nothing? Someone who enjoyed but never took for granted all that he had come to obtain? Each summation was both a question and a statement, because so much was known about Dmitry Medlov, where he came from and where he was going. He was a constant enigma, a never-ending evolving portrait of success in America.

Nodding Nicola's way as he sat on the sofa, Dmitry closed the door behind him casually and walked over to his desk. Hiking up his pants, he sat down and grunted. "Did you see your family off?"

"Yes," Nicola said, putting down his cup of coffee. "Thank you again for flying them out."

"Of course," Dmitry answered. "And I see they gave you some better clothes." Sweeping a gaze of Nicola, he approved. When Nicola had come in the night before, he was covered in soot and blood. Now, he was dressed in new jeans and a shirt provided by Boris at Gabriel's request.

"Yeah, thanks for that too," Nicola said, looking down at his clothes. *Not his brand but nice.*

Dmitry turned on his large screen Mac computer and flipped through his financials quickly. Leaning back in the chair, he quietly scribbled something on a notepad and then turned his attention back to Nicola. "We don't have much time to do this. I have other pressing business. So, I have asked my men to expedite this process for you quickly."

"We've been on this investigation for some time, Dmitry. I hate to sound negative, but I don't know how you can just fix it just like that," Nicola said, unconvinced that such a situation could be *expedited*.

Dmitry was nothing if not efficient. He couldn't help but feel a bit offended by Nicola's lack of appreciation for his resourcefulness. He raised his hands and counted off his fingers as he spoke. "You need guns. You need men. You wanted that woman, Roxie, located and you want revenge. Does that about sum it up?" His hand held up four fingers. Dmitry didn't blink. His face was like stone carved into a beautiful statue of elegance.

"That sums it up," Nicola answered flatly.

"Four things. You need four things from me, and in return you will work for me." Dmitry tilted his head as though the exchange was too elementary for him to take seriously.

Nicola shifted in his seat. "Correct. I will come and work for you." His voice lowered as he said the words, showing his hesitation.

Dmitry picked up on it instantly. "Your concern is?"

"It's pretty obvious, right? All this time," Nicola spread his fingers as he spoke. "We've been on opposite sides. I don't know how you can trust me."

Dmitry scratched the side of his mouth and stared at Nicola. "We are gentlemen. We have a gentleman's agreement. Your wife and children have dined at my table. You have slept under my roof and received my kindnesses. As a gentleman, I can trust your word." He reached over and took a mint out of the crystal bowl by this computer and slipped it into his mouth. "Can't I?"

Nicola did not hesitate this time. "Yes. I don't go back on my word."

Dmitry turned up his lip. Voice low, he cracked a devious smile. "Neither do I."

"How do you want me to work for you? I'm not a cop anymore. I just don't understand how you plan to use me?"

"Let me figure that out. I have a few ideas, but I need to flesh that out more." Dmitry went back to his fingers. "Four things I've promised you...done quickly because of my other pressing business."

"Four things," Nicola repeated.

Dmitry narrowed his eyes. "I know it's killing you. You're sitting here in front of me, *needing me* and despising me at the same time. But you will learn that I'm not such a bad man."

"It's not you that I despise," Nicola said, swallowing down his pride. "I despise the bastards who tried to kill my family, who set me up, who killed those children." His eyes burned with hatred as the truth came out. "I despise myself for allowing this to happened, but I don't despise you. Is it killing me?" Nicola rolled his eyes. "You bet your fucking ass, it's killing me. But what am I going to do? Sit around and sulk? I don't think so."

"Men like us don't sulk," Dmitry said with a raised brow. "To make you feel better, I will answer one question for you...any question. Years of investigating me must be like torture now. And you know what, it will make you feel better. Knowledge always does.

Ask me anything you want to know, and I will answer it."

Nicola was taken aback. *Was he serious?* Just like that, he would divulge information about himself. He found it odd, almost insulting. Dmitry must have felt him to be less than nothing now if he would share *anything* with him, a complete non-threat.

Still curiosity peaked inside of him.

"Why Memphis?" Nicola finally asked. He could have asked a million questions about his operations, his family, his council, but that was what he really wanted to know. Memphis was Nicola's home, but it was a small, country place with the potential to be a mecca but the stunted growth of a sick child with its crime, poor education system, racial segregated mindsets, lack of creative influences and unskilled labor force. There was so much to do to make the city competitive, yet he chose this of all the places in the U.S. to call home.

Dmitry pursed his lips together, and Nicola couldn't tell if he was disappointed in his question or perplexed by it. Running his large, tattooed hand over the oak desk, he wryly replied, "I've always been talented in seeing a diamond in the rough. My wife and my chosen occupation are only two of the opportunities that I have acted upon. It's a gift of mine to see things for what they could potentially be if only given a chance. And in my entire life, every time that I've bet on the proverbial diamond, I have won, except once with my only relative. He was not…manageable."

"Ivan Medlov," Nicola said, watching Dmitry's back straightened at hearing his brother's name.

"Anyway, I came to Memphis to handle some other business, not pertaining to your question, and I saw a very critical thing for a man in my line of work.

Nicola was dying to know. Sitting on the edge of his seat, he listened with both his ears and his eyes, noting every inflection in Dmitry's voice, every facial expression.

"Did you know that the Port of Memphis is the fourth largest inland port in the entire country, served by all five of Memphis' Class 1 railroads with direct access to your interstates? I mean, you're literally on the Mississippi River. If you put that together with your corridors into other metros, your amazing logistical air transport options, your trucking lines, your alternative federal trade zone authorization for exporting and importing goods and the cheap commercial property that I buy up like candy, then your question is answered." Dmitry smiled. "Simple. Plain. Prosperous."

"And that's the only reason?" Nicola asked.

Dmitry shook his head. With his eyes locked on Nicola, he raised his finger. "One question."

Answering that one question for Nicola only made him want more, but he willed himself to stop. Right now was not the time to bite the hand that fed him. "So how do you plan to expedite this?"

"We had discussed previously, if you recall, having a meeting with my contacts in your department and other branches. Well, we are going to do that..." Dmitry looked at his watch. "Right now."

"How comfortable are these men with helping me?" Nicola could just imagine his accidental death by someone who felt that he was too much a risk.

"They are comfortable because I tell them to be," Dmitry answered as he stood. He could see that Nicola would have serious trust issues throughout their relationship, but he could hardly blame the man considering all that had happened to him. "Shall we?" Dmitry said, motioning towards the door.

"Sure," Nicola said, getting up.

***

Dmitry had no intention of having his key men inside of the police department and other agencies meet him at his compound. It was far too much of a risk for far too less of a return. However, he did feel that they all needed to meet on his territory to ensure full cooperation.

With a smaller contingent of men than usual, Dmitry loaded with Nicola, Gabriel and Boris into a black Escalade with pitch-black tinted windows and headed to the designated location. Bodyguards on fast black Mitsubishi bikes flanked them as they drove, though the common onlooker could not tell that it was a small convoy.

Gabriel sat up front while Boris drove, listening to talk radio and texting on his IPhone. He seemed completely removed from the situation, only there to protect his uncle, if needed. Neither he nor Boris spoke to each other or Dmitry the entire drive.

Dmitry sat back in the comfort of his plush leather seat with a television going and his ear plugs in while Nicola watched as the city's landscape changed from multi-million dollar homes to spotty commercial property to finally the old community of South Memphis. Jumping off of I-55 to Norris Road, they passed a large new church and an old golf course, before turning down the residential street Prospect and following it to a large industrial park that had been closed for over a year.

Dmitry's words echoed in Nicola's head. *Cheap commercial property that I buy up like candy.* There was just no telling what all Dmitry truly owned in this city.

Two guards in grey uniforms ran out from a small hut, unlocked the chained fence and moved the gate out of the way so that the men could rush in. They drove through the empty lot past vacant unloading docks for trucks until they came to a large warehouse. Pulling into the back of the building, they parked quickly beside several other cars and trucks that were already there.

Nicola's heart constricted. The men who would help him were waiting for him, and while they were ready for what they saw. He was not. What if he knew one of them? What if he knew all of them? How would he handle the idea of being in the dark for so long?

The bodyguards on the bikes checked the perimeter quickly and then signaled Gabriel and Boris.

"Uncle, they are ready for you," Gabriel said, opening his door. He looked back at Nicola for a moment and read his face. "Let's go," he said, closing his door behind him and opening Dmitry's for him to step out.

Boris didn't bother to open Nicola's door. *That was going too far for him.* In fact, this entire meeting made him uneasy. He could stomach Gabriel, a former cop, because of his father, his uncle and his position on the council, but such a courtesy could not be bestowed on anyone else. The code had already been bent enough.

Nicola opened the door and followed Boris, who donned an automatic weapon in the middle of the day like a sentry at a checkpoint. All four of them walked through the backdoors of the warehouse into the dimly lit space where he could hear distinct voices laughing and talking.

Without power in the facility, the building boiled in summer heat and smelled of chemicals and dust. Broken out windows above were the only places ventilation could get through. However, it was perfect for ensuring that no one could see the men meeting.

Taking off his suit jacket, Dmitry wiped his face with his handkerchief and muttered something in Russian. As they rounded the corner of the open space, past large separators that made the space appear to be divided into cubicle space, they came to a large group of men sitting around in metal chairs.

Nicola pulled off his aviator shades and looked around in complete shock. His mouth flew open as he surveyed the room. Sorrello, an FBI agent whom he'd worked the Medlov case with, was sitting down on an old desk, drinking out of a Gatorade bottle and sweating his ass off. Cory Hamilton, a man from his old unit and someone he genuinely regarded as friend sat across from Sorrello. Two men he only knew in passing from the bomb squad was there along with an old friend from homicide, Reynolds.

Dmitry passed his suit jacket to Gabriel, who stood behind him, and raised his hand. "Anyone *not* know this man?" he asked, pointing at Nicola frozen in his spot.

No one said a word. They all looked around at each other, unsure of how the new recruit would behave.

Dmitry turned to Nicola. "Anyone here that *you* don't know?" he asked.

It took a minute for Nicola to speak. Pushing himself to say something, he fumbled over his words. "No…" he shook his head. "No," he said louder. "I know everyone here." He looked around, cursing each man in his mind.

"Everyone isn't here," Cory said, sucking his teeth.

Dmitry looked around. "Where is he?" He rolled his eyes in frustration. There was no time for tardiness. He had other more pressing things to handle more important than this *charity* work.

"He said that he was a couple of minutes out max," Cory answered, standing up. He walked over to Agosto and offered him a hand. "We heard about what happened. Just here to help you out, bro."

Nicola looked down at Cory's hand. *What was a handshake anymore?* "Thanks," he said, stepping back. He looked at Dmitry. "So, this is why I couldn't make a case stick as long as I was after you? You had my own men in your pocket?"

Dmitry smacked his lips. *Oh the drama.* "There are many more, Agosto," he said in a matter-of-fact tone. "I just pulled the ones you needed for t*his* job." He clapped his hands together. "It's hot as fuck in here, and I want to leave. So let's get on with the part that requires my attention. I will let you gentleman handle the details."

Cory took the floor. "I guess until he gets here, I'll start," the young man said, looking around the room. "Based upon what our friend, we have two primary targets." He passed around files to each man and opened up a laptop on the table. "Cane, a man that we all know, otherwise should not be in on this meeting and Councilman Ferris are the targets."

Nicola's head snapped.   "What?" he croaked. *Councilman Ferris?*

Cory passed him the folder. "The night that you were extracted from your house, Dmitry's men also captured one of the hit men. A guy named Sammy. You know him?"

"Yeah," Nicola snarled. "I know him."

"As you can imagine, it took some convincing for him to come clean. He wasn't really budging or saying a word until Anatoly came over this morning," Cory said, shaking his head. "He worked the guy over. Got some good Intel, but if you want to know much more, you had better get in there quick. The guy isn't going to last much longer."

"What else is there to get?" Dmitry asked, walking up to look at the computer.

"Well, he told us some shit that you're going to want to know," Cory said in a lowered voice as the last member of their party arrived. His eyes locked on the tardy man and put his hands on his hips. "It's bad," he said, looking back up at Dmitry.

"How bad?" Dmitry asked.

Cory swallowed hard. "Let's just say that it's not all about Agosto anymore. Sammy had a little more to say than what we bargained for."

Nicola followed Cory's eyes to the man at the door. To his surprise, it was Deputy Director Magnelli. Standing like a ghost of the man he once was, he barely recognized his old subordinate, peering back at him through disbelieving eyes. "Agosto," Magnelli said, like nothing was wrong.

Nicola needed a seat. Was there anyone that Dmitry Medlov didn't have his claws sunk into? Leaning on the back of the metal chair in front of him, he looked down at the filthy ground below. "Son of a bitch," he cursed. "Not you too."

Magnelli was unmoved by Nicola's undoing. "Yeah, me too." He came in and took a seat. All of the officers got up and began to pat him on the back, giving their condolences for his loss. The onslaught of attention only made things worse. Fighting back tears, Magnelli raised up a hand to stop the men. Pulling out his flask, he took a swig. "I'm sorry, but I just don't want to hear it anymore. Every time someone mentions it, it reminds me all over again that she's dead." He rolled his tongue around his mouth and huffed. "The only reason that I'm helping you, Agosto, is because it will lead me to Carmen's killer."

Agosto understood. He was in the same position. They were all here out of necessity - he hoped.

"Bring him out," Dmitry said, wiping the sweat from his brow again.

Boris and his men stepped away from Dmitry quickly and disappeared into the factory.

"Bring who here?" Nicola asked.

"You'll see," Dmitry said. Not wanting to waste any time, Dmitry got to the business that he had come for. "Each man here has a purpose. I've only used police officers as using my men could present a bigger problem for me later. Cory will access any records that you need. Magnelli will help keep the MPD off your ass for as long as possible. Sorrello will help with an Intel regarding a federal investigation that could come about as a result of this job. The bomb specialists...*well, that's pretty self-explanatory*. Gabriel will assist you will the hardware needs, and you all can divvy up the wet-work. When a plan has been properly put together, then you report it back to me. Until this is over, Agosto you will stay at the loft above the clothing store." He knew that Agosto was familiar with the place, considering he had put it under surveillance many times before.

"Do we still have eyes on it?" Nicola asked Cory with a hint of sarcasm in his voice.

Cory crossed his arms over his chest. "Just me." His eyes quickly averted from Agosto's, knowing that this would forever be a sensitive subject for the two of them, no matter what capacity they worked in.

The sound of a body being pulled across the hot ground make them all look up. Boris and one of his men pulled Sammy, broken and bloody, by his arms back into middle of the men and dropped him. He wheezed and gurgled, trying to breathe out of his broken nose and through his broken ribs. Unable to see through his blackened eyes, he stumbled as he tried to sit up on his own. Boris quickly booted him in the chest and made him crumple back into the fetal position.

Nicola could barely look at the man, and the stench of his urine and bowels colored the room with death to the point where he had to cover his nose.

"My son takes his work seriously," Dmitry said, unbothered by the scene. "Cory, you said he had more to share. What is it?" He walked up to the man and kneeled to pull the man's head up by his sweaty face. "Can you speak?"

Sammy choked. "Yes," he whispered. Blood spilled from his mouth.

"Ask him about the person responsible for Carmen's death," Cory said, looking over at Magnelli.

Dmitry looked up at Cory.

Cory shrugged. "I wanted you to hear for yourself."

"Tell me," Dmitry said, grip tighter now.

"It was botched job done by Collin Magnelli and one of Cane's men. No one knew that she was inside," Sammy sputtered. He inhaled a shallow breath. "Please, just kill me or let me go."

"We'll get to that soon enough," Dmitry said, looking over at Deputy Magnelli who quickly stood and walked over to the man.

"What did you say?" Magnelli asked, eyes wild.

Dmitry stood up and stepped away from the man, giving Magnelli plenty of room to get to the man. He wasn't exactly moved by the murder of some local cop during a drive by, but he was very moved by the murder of a man's only daughter by his only son. He had a daughter, and Anya was his pride and joy. There was no separation in emotion evoked at the news. Everyone in the room was stunned, and he was no different.

Tears formed in the corners of Magnelli's eyes. Screaming out in anger, he snatched Sammy up, jerking his head as he choked him. "Don't you fucking lie to me, you bastard!"

Sammy tried desperately to breathe. With the little strength that he had left, he pried at Magnelli's fat fingers from around his Adam's apple. He began to turn blue, drifting into a full black out.

Nicola stepped in and grabbed Magnelli's arm. "Let him breathe, man," he said in a low, calm voice. "At least until you find out for sure."

Magnelli shook in anger. Face red, he trembled as he held Sammy, wanting right then to choke the life out of him. However, Agosto was right. Loosening his hands just enough for the man to breathe slightly, he bent lower. "How do you know this? How do you know my son killed my daughter?"

"Collin works for Cane," Sammy whispered. "He is part of the three wise men."

"The three wise men being Cane, Ferris and Magnelli," Cory added for clarification.

"Is there anyone else?" Nicola asked Sammy. "Was Twist involved?"

"No, just the three of them," Sammy answered, wincing in pain. He spit blood. "It was always the plan to get Twist out of the way. Your investigation just made us have to push up the timeline. Twist already had his suspicions and he got confirmation from his main Molly dealer…some bitch named Roxie, tailed Cane to a meet with Ferris after Agosto spooked him at the house."

Cory chimed in. "Why does Cane still need Ferris? Since he was cleaning house, why didn't he get rid of him too?"

Sammy struggled to put together a cohesive thought. "Cane can't get of Ferris because he knows that he has evidence against him. They needed Magnelli to be the mole on the inside. He was cyphering infor-mation out of you," Sammy said, trying to peer out of his swollen eyes at Magnelli.

"But why kill all those kids?" Nicola asked confused.

"The kids were not a part of the original plan. Ferris provided Cane with startup capital for his drug operation in turn once the operations were up and running, Cane would fund Ferris's run for mayor and upon his election would push to have Magnelli replaced with Magnelli. There were never supposed to be any kid deaths, but Ferris' problem got out of control."

"What problem?" Nicola pushed.

"He's a pedophile," Sammy sobbed. "No one knew until after. He was using the sample Molly that Cane was giving him on the children, and they kept overdosing, so we had to keep getting rid of the bodies. Cane was worried about the heat that would come down but Ferris said that he could..." Sammy began to lose consciousness.

Magnelli slapped him in the face. "Hey! Hey, Ferris what?" He shook him.

Sammy's eyes opened lazily. "Ferris set everyone up to make himself look like the savior. Cane knew once they put Agosto on the case, there was a high probability of it being solved so, he set him up after he had surveillance put in his house and figured out his triggers. Then Cane had Ferris kill DeMario in the hospital with a bad fix. But then Johnson and Steele showed up, so Cane sent Magnelli and some of his men to get rid of them before they could connect the dots. He wanted to get rid of any loose ends. He sent us to kill everyone except Ferris. We were only supposed to make it look like a hit was put on him. The only one we couldn't find was Twist's girl, Roxie."

Dmitry pulled his gun from out of the holster under his arm and set the gleaming weapon on the table beside Agosto and Magnelli. Voice soothing and calming, he shoved his fists down his pants pockets. "You've been very forthcoming, considering your condition. Why?" He tilted his head and looked at the tortured man in mock concern.

"If you're going to kill me, please just kill me. I've cooperated," Sammy said, collapsing as Magnelli stood up and let him go.

"I told you, Anatoly really fucked him up," Cory said, shaking his head. "He beat him with a link chain for half the morning."

"Should we put him on an IV until this is over? He might have more information that we'll need," Dmitry asked the men in the room. It would be their choice, but he knew the answer even before he asked the question. They were out for blood and justice, not prisoners.

Nicola was listening the entire time, fuming over the fact that this man, despite his sudden willingness to cooperate, had come into his home the night before with the sole intention of killing his family. His wife. His children. His unborn child. He had helped get rid of the bodies of innocent, murdered children. He had plotted and schemed like a snake in the grass. And now, Dmitry wanted to offer him life. Just a minute more was too much for him.

Picking up the gun on the table, he pointed at Sammy and pulled back the hammer.

Dmitry looked over at Nicola and released a sigh. "Are you ready to cross that final line, Agosto?" he asked in a sinister voice.

Before Dmitry could get a response, Nicola pulled the trigger. The first shot took everyone by surprise. No one could believe that the man they once dubbed a *boy scout* would actually shoot an unarmed, beaten, bloody suspect. But they were all wrong. As the bullet entered Sammy's chest and knocked him backwards, Nicola put both hands tightly around the trigger. Standing over him as he moaned and writhed, Nicola emptied the clip into Sammy's body at point blank range one slow bullet at a time. Watching the murder was surreal for most men.

Many of them had bet secretly that Agosto wouldn't turn - that even despite the loss of his job, his house, his name and nearly his family, his moral code would kick into high gear.

But they were all wrong.

When the clip was empty, Nicola turned and offered the gun back to Dmitry. Wiping the sweat from his brow and blood spatter from his face, he swallowed down his own self-disgust. "You can go now," he said to Dmitry. "We've got it from here."

31

Collin Magnelli had never received so much attention in all of his life. Every time that he put down his cell phone for a second, someone else called. If it wasn't family checking on him, then it was a reporter, begging for a statement from anyone in the Magnelli family since the Deputy Director and his wife were not talking to the media.

Female officers whom he had previously jumped through hoops to start a conversation with were initiating a call to him just to see if he was *alright*. Two uniform officers, in a show of support parked outside of his Mid-town bungalow, while other officers circled the area. For the first time in years, there was a feeling of solidarity between officers no matter what rank, color or gender. For that second in time, they were all blue, all brothers. And all that it took was killing his own sister.

Guilt grew heavy in his heart with each passing hour about what he had done, but the will to live was far too great to expose himself. As he had driven off the night before from the scene of the crime, he had actually thought about turning himself in to the authorities and letting them have their way with him.

But then reality kicked in. He was a cop killer and a cop. His father was one of the heads of the MPD with a damned-near unblemished record and he was on his way to replacing him once Ferris was mayor.

What was done, was done. There was no going back and changing it and he had to accept that. However, he did need to focus on getting his story straight about where he was the night before, remembering not to look guilty and to behave as though he was grieving for Carmen, not because he had killed her but because she had been killed.

When this was all over and the drug operations were fully kicked into gear, he would do something special for Carmen's daughter, Laila to make amends. But for now, it was game time. And he had to perform. Cane had told him to lay low, abruptly end all communication until further instructed and to keep an ear out for Roxie, just in case she popped up. Other than that, after he and his family buried Carmen, all he had to do was sit and wait.

Looking critically at himself in his bathroom mirror under the bright halogen light, he picked up his razor but decided against shaving off his stubble. The more worn and exhausted he looked, the better. It would ward off some people from bothering him.

Plus, his boss - a man that was a consistent asshole his entire time on the task force - was actually nice to him. He had told him to take as many days as he needed off and to *let him know if he needed anything*. As far as he was concerned, he wouldn't have been more shocked if the man had offered him a blowjob. Lt. Shuls was a smug, overly analytical douche bag who had never once given him an opportunity to prove himself on the team. But maybe now, he would be a favorite, sort of like Anderson on vice who had suddenly gone from a shit bag to a mensch after his father, who was a second-generation tough cop had died. The guy was promoted and lauded like he had found the cure to cancer, and it was all because people liked his old man and wanted his legacy to continue.

Another thought slipped into Collin's mind. This one was far more personal. He wondered with Carmen out of the way, if he could actually develop a closer relationship to his father. She had always been in the way. True, he had cared about his sister, but the truth of the matter was that she had been his father's primary concern all of his life.

He got the scraps that fell off the table compared to her lifestyle. Everyone considered her mother a saint and his mother a cheap, strung out whore from the trailer park. No one had even mourned his mother when she died. It was just another inconvenience to add to her long list of inconveniences.

His father would actually need him now, and he planned on being there for him.

With the towel around his waist, he walked into his dingy bedroom and plopped down on the end of the bed across from the television. Rolling his neck, he tried to pop out the kinks earned while sleeping nearly standing up all night because of his paranoia and the fear that either the cops would come or Cane would send his guys to kill him too.

Neither had happened, proving that he worried too much.

There was no one to connect the dots but Cane and Ferris, and they were in just as deep if not deeper than he was.

If Roxie was still alive then she wasn't coming back to Memphis just to get killed and Johnson had not seen his face, so there were no witnesses.

Resting back on the queen-sized bed, Collin closed his eyes and drifted off into a light sleep while the TV played and the ceiling fan above him rotated on high.

Suddenly, his cell phone rang again but this time, his father's special ringtone sounded with a picture of the two of them the day that he graduated from the academy.

His heart skipped a beat. Popping up in the bed, he rolled over and grabbed the phone off the nightstand before it could hang up.

"Hello," Collin said, trying to sound as groggy as possible.

"Collin, where the hell have you been? I called you twenty times last night?" Magnelli asked, fuming.

"Sorry, dad. When I found out about Carmen, I think I did what every other cop did. I headed to my unit to see what could be done." That was not a lie. As soon as he ditched the vehicle from the night before, he grabbed his gear and headed to his headquarters to ensure an alibi. He tried to sound less defensive. "How are you? Does Mom need anything?"

"No," Magnelli bit out. The fact that Collin had even referred to his wife as his mother made him sick to his stomach, but for the moment, he hid his disgust. "Are you going to the vigil for Carmen? You should be there."

Collin looked at his watch. That was in less than an hour. "Yeah, of course I planned on going," he lied.

"Text me when you get there. I'll be alone. Your...mother can't make it. She's a mess right now."

At least one part of that statement was true. He had texted his wife all day to make sure that she was alright, but she only replied with two word answers. Still grieving her daughter's death, she had barely gotten out of bed once, so his sister was at his house helping to take care of her.

"Sure, anything for you," Collin said, sounding a little more pitiful. Covering his mouth, he covered up a yawn. "I just got out of the shower. I'm on my way."

"Good. Then I'll see you there," Deputy Magnelli said, hanging up before he gave himself away. "It's done," he said, taking another swig. "The little shit will be there."

"I know that this must be hard for you," Nicola said, putting his hand on his shoulder. "But you did say that you wanted the person responsible for this. I promise you that he'll pay."

"What's hard is that my baby girl is gone," Magnelli answered. He stood up and went over to the map of city hall. Running his hand over the markings, he picked up the Glock 17 assigned to him and slipped it in the back of his jeans. "This plan had better work. We only have one chance to do this right."

Agosto racked his shotgun. "It'll work," he said, passing another shotgun to Cory.

***

It was ironic to Councilman Ferris that he was back at The Med so quickly after killing DeMario, but the only hospital that treated gunshot wounds in Memphis was this place. Looking at the gauze covering the throbbing stab wounded hand, he cursed. "What the fuck are you going to do about this?" he screamed at Director Amway, who stood with Mayor Thompson and his support staff. "That man should have never even been allowed to interrogate me. He should have been on some sort of leave, locked in padded cell or getting treatment for his obvious PTSD."

Mayor Thompson was the first to speak. Pushing his tie down in his suit, he tried to act as though he was concerned about more than just being sued. In truth, he hated Councilman Ferris and everything he stood for. It was no mystery or secret that he was going to run against him in the next election, nor was it a secret that Ferris was using the Baby Boys case and all of the chaos surrounding it to build a platform.

"We have taken Johnson to Lakeside," the mayor said, repressing his grin. "Right now, he's under psych evaluation. After that, we will hold a hearing."

"Fuck a hearing. I want him fired!" Ferris spat.

"By the time that you finish firing police officers, there will be no one to protect you," Director Amway said under his breath.

Mayor Thompson looked back and tried harder not to laugh. "The point is that maybe you should go home and get some rest. We'll sort through this and take care of anything that you need."

"Why was he allowed to interview me?" Ferris asked again, almost hitting his wounded hand on the bed in his fit.

"He was authorized to do so by Deputy Director Magnelli, who is also on leave at the moment. I'm sure you can understand why," Amway answered.

"Then why was he allowed to authorize Johnson to interview me?" Ferris continued. "All you people ever do is pass the buck around here. Who is going to take some fucking responsibility?"

Amway stepped closer. "I'm here. I'm responsible," he said, voice stern.

Mayor Thompson interjected. "We're going to have a car to take you back to your hotel. You'll have around the clock protection."

Ferris interrupted again. "You know what? I don't want it. I've seen what your protection can get me. I was under your protection when I was stabbed and shot by a lunatic claiming that I was responsible for the Baby Boys murders. Me? I'm the one who has pushed for this investigation. It would hardly make sense if I were the killer." He threw his head back as a pain shot through his body. Taking a deep breath, he rolled his eyes. "When is the vigil?"

Thompson looked at Amway. "I don't think that your presence would go over very well at the candle light vigil for Sgt. Magnelli," he said, looking back over at Ferris. Politics began to play out. "You should rest after your emergency surgery."

"You mean I should not give a statement to the press who want to know exactly what happened to me," Ferris snarled. "Forget it. I'm going. I don't care how many pain pills I have to take or what I have to do to get there. The people want me there. Every family that I've comforted, every community group and church group that I have begged to help raise awareness about this case…"

"Every television station," Amway said before he knew it.

Ferris pointed at Amway. "You just don't want to look incompetent as you obviously are."

Amway had had enough. He walked up to the bed where Ferris was sitting and bent over him. "Now, you listen to me you sniveling little bastard, we have put in more man hours, arrested more people, took more reports and followed more leads in this case than any before it. We have Intel from drug dealers and users all over the city who are alleging that something big is going down and I'm going to get down to the bottom of it, I don't care if I have to go out and solve this investigation myself."

Mayor Thompson tried to pull Amway back, but he quickly jerked away. He was going to say what he came to say to Ferris once and for all. "Johnson may have been wrong for attacking you, but I doubt very seriously the man was wrong for interrogating you. I saw the tape. In all my years on the force, I know a guilty man when I see one. And you're up to something. When I find out what, I'm going to slap the cuffs on you myself."

"You may want to start looking for another job, Director," Ferris said with venom lacing his words.

"What makes you think that I give a fuck, Councilman," Amway said, moving in closer.

Ferris moved back, obviously intimidated by the man.

Amway stood up straight and turned back to look at the mayor. "We're going to solve this case," he said walking to the door. His administrative assistant and public relations officer followed behind him. "But for now, we're going to pay our respects at the vigil. I'm sure that we'll see both of you men there."

As Amway left the room, Mayor Thompson turned back to Ferris. "We're close to a riot here, Ferris. The citizens of Memphis are literally chomping at the bit for justice. Don't give them a reason to distrust us further by attacking the police department publicly any more than you already have."

Ferris ignored Thompson's advice. "I paid for a poll a couple of weeks ago, and you know what? I'm beating your ass by 23 points. That's an awfully big swing." He sucked his teeth and smiled. "Scared that tonight when I'm in front of those cameras that I'll gain more voters?" He rose up in the bed. "You should be, because I'll be there. And I'll be ready to answer any questions they have about you, that piece of shit director and this case."

"This isn't about votes," the mayor said in disgust. "Our city needs us. How is jumping in front of a camera going to help solve this case or put the people at ease?"

Ferris smiled. "I guess we'll have to see." Resting back in his bed, he looked at the television mounted on the wall and hit the monitor beside him. "Nurse, I need more medicine."

Mayor Thompson knew that was his cue. Nodding at his Chief of Staff and his press secretary, he walked to the door. As they opened it for him, he turned back and looked at Ferris one more time. "Do you know why I'm not worried about your 23 percent, Ferris? It's because there is a big difference between numbers and people. And you only care about one of those and it's not the important one. I care about what happens to my citizens and so does Amway. So regardless of how this turns out, I can assure you that you'll never win."

Ferris didn't bother to look at the mayor. "Numbers don't lie, Thompson. Numbers don't lie."

When he was finally alone, he dwelled over the rest of the events in front of him measuring out the outcomes in his head. Cancelling tonight's appearance was not an option. He and Cane had already hatched a plan. He was to use tonight's vigil as his personal stage. He would publicly condemn Amway and Thompson, while pulling votes and giving spectators something very special, a show that they would not forget.

***

The people of Memphis were in complete outrage about the untimely death of the beautiful Sgt. Carmen Magnelli. A decorated officer, mother and friend on the force, the media hailed her as a fallen hero who had been struck down in her prime by a mysterious but deadly criminal faction, possibly retaliating against the detectives on the Baby Boys case.

In remembrance of Carmen, the mayor asked the city to fly the American and Tennessee flags at half-mast. Officers covered their badges with black bands and homes across the county put candles in their windows. Every talk radio station across the city only wanted to discuss one issue - the Baby Boys case.

Ivy's interview aired to the most viewers in the station's history at five o'clock on the dot. National media outlets remotely broadcasted from outside of the police station among the nearly one thousand people who protested, demanding justice for the children who had been killed. People held up signs asserting that in light of all of the chaos, the city had forgotten its responsibility to find the killer or killers.

Plus, no one knew where Agosto was. Even after searching the city for an entire day, there was no sign of him or his family. And while the autopsy reports from the bodies recovered from the fire confirmed that he and his family weren't among them, the question many people had was had they been abducted.

Ready for payback, police officers patrolled the streets in full force, on guard and anxious to get revenge. They were locking up anyone who gave them a hard time, filling the jails to capacity. Criminals, used to guarding their territory, opted to abandon their posts on the corners to seek safer shelter inside of homes and store fronts. Word had gotten out. Amway had let his hell hounds out and he wanted answers. Those who didn't know anything were afraid of being mistaken for those who might. So the normally packed places like basketball courts, car washes, parking lots, bars and clubs were empty. Every pedophile with a record was being or had been hauled in for questioning and every possible hitter in the city was being monitored.

Memphis had finally reached fever pitch and was on the country's center stage for everyone to witness a complete meltdown.

In preparation for the candlelight vigil at city hall and the large group protesting from one end of the police precinct to the other, the riot and TACT unit had been activated. The goal was to move everyone from off the streets in front of the police station and get them to disburse quietly. Since there had not been an application submitted for a peaceful protest to take place. Knowing what could happen, he had to act swiftly.

However, he also had the difficult task of not disturbing the vigil only blocks away, where the city's top leadership, mourning friends, family, and concerned citizens were gathering for the hour-long memorial.

The last thing he wanted was for the wrong people to be harassed, while one troublemaker got away with inciting a riot.

With heavy protection on the mayor, he and about 100 police officers as well as the entire city council, county commission and part of the Magnelli family gathered in front of hundreds of people holding candles and signs. The mall was completely covered with people as they prayed and watched on waiting for a word from their leadership.

About ten blocks down, the only place that parking was available due to the large crowd, Collin parked his unmarked and got out to walk with the masses head to the vigil. He had put a call into Cane and told him that he was coming, and asked about any news that he might need to know. Cane had told him very specifically to go dark with communication until later. While he didn't know exactly what had happened, he knew that all of his men from the hit were dead and that Agosto was missing. The news was enough to shake Cane up and make him tighten up his operations until he could figure out how to finish what he had started.

Cane had, however, looped Collin into the last of his favors/stunts for Ferris. Evidently, the two of them were orchestrating a riot at both the peaceful vigil taking place at city hall and at the police station using the same calling card from the night before. Ferris felt that it would throw the scent all the way off of him and onto a more mysterious figure. He also felt it would make the powers that be look even more incompetent, just what he needed for his big announcement tonight.

In return for Cane's favor, Ferris had promised to deliver him Amway's head on a plate via heavy litigation and a part of the settlement from the city. In the past, Amway had busted up and locked down countless of their stash houses around the city and locked up his men, which is why Collin had been recruited in the first place - to give him sensitive Intel to stay ahead of the prick. Also when the time was right, Ferris would also go after any of the police officers in special units who had been a problem for Cane, once he was in office.

Collin would never understand politics, but what he did understand was that based upon the climate of the city right then, if a riot broke out, it just might burn down.

Unwilling to take any chances, he brought his department-issued weapon with him, looking out for any familiar faces that might be imbedded in the crowd to start the ruckus.

When he got to the packed courtyard, he saw his father standing near the front of the large crowd of dignitaries facing the crowd in full uniform. Headed up to him, he also saw a man pushing Ferris in a wheelchair towards the podium. Avoiding even looking Ferris' way, he made his way to his father and shook Amway's hand.

"Director," Collin said nodding.

"How are you holding up, Collin?" Amway asked concerned.

Collin shrugged. "We've all seen better days."

Deputy Magnelli locked eyes with his son as soon as he said the words. Forcing himself to seem civil, he moved to the side. "Come and stand by me, Collin." When he saw Ferris, he leaned into Amway. "I know you and I had our words today, but you can't let that son of a bitch speak at my daughter's memorial."

Without flinching, Amway agreed. "I had no intention of it," he said, cutting his eyes at Ferris while he shook hands with the oblivious participants soaking in his bullshit. There was no question in Amway's mind that he didn't like Magnelli. He was a closet bigot and hypocrite who had been exposed over the years as being biased and preferential. But the man had never pretended to be any more than what he was. However, Ferris was a different type of monster. He cloaked himself with flowery words and promises that he never intended to keep all while advancing his own personal agenda.

The golden, yellow sun was starting to set on the nearly seven hundred people who had come downtown to show their respects. It was a mix of races, ages and sexes all peacefully gathering near the trolley line all the way up to the front door of city hall. Musicians played their saxophones and guitars, singing songs of loss. Others held up homemade signs.

In the backdrop of the Mississippi River, surrounded by riot police and lowered flags, the program began.

Bishop Hall, head of the local Catholic Dioceses, walked up to the podium, placed right beside a large photo of the fallen officer and began his prayer, a heartfelt dedication to the passing of Carmen Magnelli. People bowed their head in silence, wiping their eyes and holding hands. Officers hugged each other and wiped the sweat from their brow. And even despite the sweltering heat, people didn't complain like normal. Their sorrow was overwhelming.

Collin looked around and finally felt the full brevity of what he had done. All of these people could not have been wrong. He plucked down a future leader of this city and pillar in his family, the only child of his stepmother and the only daughter of his father all because he wanted something that he could not earn on his own. His own greed and jealousy had caused this and there was nothing he could do to fix it.

As he listened to the speakers, Collin began to wipe tears from his own eyes welding up in the corners of his eyes. Remembering her face, her smile, their many years together growing up in the house together, serving on the department together, laughing and debating at his father's house all washed over him like a river of guilt. Suddenly, he began to buckle.

He glanced over at his father, who had not shed a tear and knew that something was wrong. The man stood with a scowl on his face, so angry until the lines in his cheek seemed etched. His gaze was locked on Ferris and he was willing to bet that he hadn't heard anything that the speakers were saying.

Was it possible that his father knew? How could he?

Just a few blocks over at the police headquarters on Poplar Avenue, riot police were moving against a now hostile crowd. They gave orders over their loud speakers and pushed the masses away from the front of the police station as they held up signs demanding justice for the four murdered children and demanding Agosto and Johnson's arrest for DeMario Washington's death and Councilman Ferris' attack.

News cameras snuck behind the lines to get a better view of the crowd. The shouting and screaming was deafening in what seemed like minutes what was a peaceful group had turned into a mob. People pushed and shoved against the police, trying to get to the doors of the station. Others stood across the street holding up signs and cursing at the police, refusing to move.

"Disperse immediately or you will be arrested," the officer said over the loud speaker.

"Fuck you!" one of the white men towards the front of the crowd screamed. "You pigs can't keep us from a peaceful protest!"

Standing behind their riot gear, the police pushed the crowd, prepared with their less than lethal weapons to begin arrests.

The lieutenant running the operation gave the word and officers slipped their gas masks over their heads. Tear gas bombs were released into the crowd and the officers lined up and advanced against the front line of protests.

Other officers grabbed those who had begun to throw bottles and arrest them.

However, in the middle of the crowd, a group of young men were not there to protest but to wreak havoc. Sent by Cane, they embedded themselves in the center of the crowd of people with their backpacks and hoodies. They had been waiting for the tear gas, waiting to be masked by the coughing and wheezing masses to pull out their Molotov cocktails. Pulling down their ski masks, they pulled out the bottles, lit them and began to throw them toward the front of the police line and towards the buildings on the opposite side of the street. As soon as the fire bombs hit the ground and the shield of the police, they exploded. The bombs that were thrown through the windows of the bail bonds businesses and law offices on the other side of the street exploded as well creating a large plume of smoke that could be seen over city hall.

Mass hysteria broke out immediately not only at the riot occurring at the police station but also at city hall. Seeing the smoke and hearing the hundreds of people only a short walk away caused panic in the crowd.

Amway put his hand on the mayor's shoulder as he spoke and interrupted. "You have to go inside," he whispered into his ear.

The mayor at first resisted. There was no way that he was going to let common thugs and rabble-rousers make him flee his own podium. Looking out at the crowd, who was torn between listening to the mayor for direction and looking at the burning streets behind them, he pulled the microphone closer. "We can't let them win," he said, forgetting his speech. "Right now, you need to leave and get to your cars and then to your homes safely but make no doubt about it, we cannot and will not let them win. This is our city. Memphis is our home, and we can't give it up to those who would simply use it as their criminal playground." He looked over at Ferris and snarled. "Or to push their own agenda."

Amway stepped in. "You have to go now," he said forcefully as officers flanked the mayor and pulled him back into the safety of the building. While the city dignitaries were escorted inside the glass doors, Amway spoke with his men to get situational report.

Sirens erupted as officers dealt with chaotic crowd control. Firefighters rushed to the scene to put out the building directly across from the police station while ambulances rushed to help officers and protesters who were burned by the small handheld bombs.

Carmen's memorial had been thoroughly ruined.

Amidst the crowds moving and the police locking down downtown, Ferris took the opportunity to get his five minutes of fame. Having supposed to have been placed on the program and then abruptly taken off, but still a member of the city council, he too was taken into city hall along with several cameras and reporters who slipped in to get response about the riots from public officials.

"Councilman Ferris," a female reporter asked, walking towards him. The cameraman followed her. "Do you have any comment regarding the attack on you earlier today by Detective Luke Johnson?" She shoved her microphone into his face.

Ferris could barely repress his smile. He looked out of the glass at the people running and screaming, police shoving the masses away from the doors and shook his head. The entire city was falling apart and the hottest story was still him. He couldn't have planned it better.

"I was attacked today by an officer who obviously is out of his league when it comes to the Baby Boys investigation. I have been encouraging the community to come together and share any possible leads in an effort to help the police department, who has obviously dropped the ball not only on this case but also on keeping the people of this city safe. He was enraged about not only that but my own desire to get to the bottom of the Agosto's case. Seeking revenge, he stabbed me in my hand and shot me in the knee."

"Shouldn't you be recovering right now instead of out here at the memorial?" she asked, loving every minute of the prime time interview.

"I have always put this city first. I have pushed for better schools, better pay of our government workers, better upkeep of our community centers and better care for our elderly. The Baby Boys case has been a major priority in my life because some of the children were once students at my afterschool and preschool programs. When I found this out, it just broke my heart to know what had happened to them. The parents deserve answers and justice." He moved closer to the mic. "And you know this all is a reflection of our city leadership. The mayor has not done a good job of leading our departments or our efforts to keep our citizens safe."

"So what do you suggest that we do?" she asked, seeing other reporters come up to join in the discussion.

Ferris relished in the attention. He waited for the two other reporters to get in position first. With all the lights on him, he looked into the cameras and spoke to the people. "I'm going to run for mayor in the upcoming election, because I know I have what it takes to lead our city out this despair that we've been knee deep in for many years."

Amway watched from across the room in disgust. He knew it. This entire show was about Ferris getting what he wanted. Mayor Thompson watched on as well. Stepping closer to Amway, he leaned into his ear. "Get him out of here," he said, nostrils flaring.

Deputy Director Magnelli having watched from afar as the entire situation unfolded saw the golden opportunity that he was waiting for. "Stay here," he told Collin, who stood beside him. He made his way over to the mayor and Amway. "We've got TACT guys who can move these people out of the general area. The unmarked are parked down in the garage. I say that we start to get them in cars and get them to their homes out of this mess."

The mayor couldn't agree more. "He's right. We should get them out of the area."

Amway didn't agree. "The safest place for them is in here," he said, looking on outside at the grounds covered in tear gas and smoke. The police were pushing hard against the crowds and slowly they began to disperse.

Mayor Thompson looked over at Ferris, still talking to the cameras. "We have enough officers in here to drive the council and commissioners to safety. We need to do that," he urged, voice straining.

"I'll have to agree with him," Magnelli said, turning his back to Ferris. "We have to do something. They shouldn't just be here like sitting ducks."

Amway paused. Everything in him told him that this was wrong, however, he had the mayor at his back urging otherwise.

"Fine, but I don't want you anywhere near Ferris, especially after that stunt earlier today that Johnson pulled. You just take a car and get you and Collin to safety. Take the rest of the day to just get some rest and be with your family. You're on leave; you shouldn't be working." Amway looked at Magnelli's tired eyes and felt sorrow for him. "Get some rest."

Magnelli nodded. "I appreciate it. I will," he said, signaling for Collin. "But first, I'll make sure the men know what to do."

"We are truly sorry for your loss," Mayor Thompson said, offering his hand. "We'll do everything in our power not only solve this crime, but also to comfort your family."

"I appreciate it mayor," Magnelli said humbly. He looked over at Ferris and rolled his eyes. "It's nice to know that some people here actually give a damn."

When the officers got word, they quickly began to take the public officials down to the garage in shifts. Loading them up, they quickly exited the gate and headed out into the streets with escorts to get them to safety.

When it was time to escort Ferris, an officer in tactical gear walked up to him and offered his hand. "Hello sir. I'm Cory Hamilton. I'll be escorting you to your hotel."

Ferris shook his hand. "Nice to meet you."

"Nice to meet you too," Cory said, straitening up. "I voted for you in the last election. You're over my district. I was a campaign volunteer."

"You don't say," Ferris said as Cory pushed his wheelchair through the packed lobby to the elevators. "Well, I hope to have your support in my run for mayor next year." The elevator buzzed and opened.

"Count on it," Cory said, nodding towards Magnelli as he pushed him inside. When they got inside the elevator, Cory carefully pulled Ferris' brown leather coach bag off the side of his chair and gave it to the officer standing beside him.

"I just don't see why we didn't wait longer to be escorted out. The streets have to be packed." Ferris huffed. "Just another poorly laid out plan by Amway and Thompson."

"Hey, I just do what I'm told," Cory said as the door opened. "But hey, I promise to get you to your destination safely. With the firepower that we're carrying, it would take an army to pry you out of our possession."

Ferris laughed. "Well, that's comforting."

Cory and two other officers led him to a Black SUV parked near the back of the garage. Loading him in the back of the truck carefully, they put his wheelchair in the trunk area and then prepared to head out into the traffic. In the long processional of cars and bike police, they entered onto Main Street and headed south in the bumper to bumper traffic.

Ferris frowned. "I'm at the Marriott," he said, looking out of the window. "Why are we going this way?"

"Someone would like to see you first," Cory explained.

"Who? What is this?" Ferris said, looking for his bag.

The officer sitting beside him raised the bag up and snatched it away. Opening the bag, he fished out Ferris's phone and passed it to the officer in the front passenger seat.

"Who are you?" Ferris asked, trying to sit up.

Nicola turned around in the seat and smiled. "No introduction is really needed, is it?" he asked with a devious grin.

"Agosto?" Ferris said in shock. "What…" He went for the door, but the man beside him pulled a weapon.

"I wouldn't do that if I were you," Agosto said, turning back around. "You might as well just sit back and enjoy the ride."

"I'll have you all arrested!" Ferris protested.

Pulling out a syringe, the officer beside him grabbed the struggling man by his arm and stuck him in his neck. Feeling dizzy instantly, Ferris flung his head back on the seat and passed out.

"Check mate," Agosto said, smiling at Cory.

32

It took nearly an hour for Cory and Nicola to get out of the heavy bumper-to-bumper traffic of downtown Memphis after the riots began. Blue lights lit up the district; officers chased on foot after troublemakers; riot police locked down entire blocks and pushed traffic away from the streets; families grabbed their children and strollers and bolted back to their cars; pepper spray fogged the littered streets and complete and utter chaos took over what unbelievably, the business district of the city had been set ablaze and firefighters were working to put out many historic buildings that were attacked.

The men drove with their blue lights on and siren blaring for most of the way to their destination, moving through traffic easily and unnoticed with their dark tinted windows. Every radio station in the city was advising listeners not to go out in the streets. Every television station recapped the event and did live shots of the on-going struggle to get the city back under control. Many local analysts on site at the studios said that the riots could have been worse; the injuries could have been more if only Director Amway had not been ready.

Nicola listened carefully to the reports, waiting for reports that Councilman Ferris had been lost or abducted during the chaos, but no one had noticed yet...or didn't care.

He looked back at the man still unconscious and felt the sudden overwhelming desire to shoot him.

"Not yet," he said aloud.

"Not yet, what?" Cory asked. He looked back at Ferris also. "Oh, him."

Nicola rested back in his seat and looked at his watch. "We're behind schedule."

"Yeah, well no one was counting on a fucking riot." Cory turned off the expressway onto Highway 64 and headed towards Eads, not far from Cane's horse range.

"Where are we going?" Agosto asked.

"One of the Medlov safe houses," Cory said, turning off his lights and siren. "We're meeting Gabriel there."

Nicola had to ask, although he promised himself that he would not. "Tell me something."

Cory's stomach tightened. "Sure. What?"

"Why did you do it? I mean, you were a good cop. Why did you turn?" Nicola needed an answer for his own resolve, although he didn't feel as though Cory was obligated to answer.

"My mom," Cory answered with little guilt in his voice. "She was dying and I couldn't afford the care. Plus, my cover got blown. So, I made a choice to keep my life, save my mother's and make some money to take care of us both."

Nicola couldn't think of a more noble answer, but he still felt betrayed. He had trained Cory, brought him up, watched over him and vouched for him for years. To know that he was reporting back to Dmitry Medlov and his men the entire time felt like the ultimate slap in his face.

"I guess that I can understand," Nicola finally said. He instantly saw Cory relax more. "But how did you deal with it…I mean…knowing that you were a mole?"

Cory turned up his lips. "It's still hard," he said with a frown. "This is never who you intend on being."

Crossing over into the unincorporated county, the worry of getting Councilman Ferris out of the reach of the MPD became a null factor. The department had no jurisdiction in the county, and the sheriff's department wouldn't likely pull over a government vehicle that wasn't breaking any laws. They were nearly home free.

"So what's in this stash house?" Nicola asked, unsure of what to expect.

"Weapons…" Cory corrected himself. "Big ass weapons. The kind that you don't sell to street thugs or small time gangsters."

Nicola was intrigued. "So all this time, he really has been operating within the city?"

Cory smiled. "Dude, get off the job."

Nicola raised his hands. "Hey, I just want to know. This is my life's work just thrown away. It would be nice to at least have the puzzles put together for me."

The officer in the back wasn't so sure that that was a good idea. He cleared his throat and kicked Cory's chair.

Nicola looked back at him. "You don't agree?"

"I don't want to piss the Medlov's off," the cop said, shrugging his shoulders. "Why don't you just ask them?"

Cory chuckled. "Do us a favor and ask Gabriel. He'll be there when we arrive if nothing has change. If he's comfortable telling you, then you'll find out, but

Maurice is right. There is too much to lose by saying too much too soon."

Agosto nodded. He could appreciate that. After all, someone had to be loyal to something. And after only a day, he wasn't exactly one of the boys yet.

Pulling into an upper middle class community of contemporary two-story homes and luxury cars, Cory turned down the quiet dark, dizzying lanes until he arrived at their location. It was a cozy southern-style, two-story home with red brick and white shutters in the middle of a cul-de-sac with a well-cared-for lawn, expensive exterior lighting, sprinklers running, and nice tall fencing to prohibit anyone from seeing the back-yard. In no way did the house stick out; instead it set the tone for the street, appearing inviting and non-threatening.

Nicola had to give it to the man. Dmitry was smart. He put everything in plain view and let them all run over themselves looking for his product. There was no telling how many homes just like this one were in the county under different names, and the selling of just one shipment of guns paid for the house several times over. It was a *win-win* for him and a big *fuck you* to law enforcement.

Cory pulled into the double garage and closed it after him. Quickly Maurice jumped out to help get the councilman inside.

"Is this place safe?" Nicola asked, looking around the garage at the organized yard tools and holiday decorations. He stepped out of the truck and closed the door. The sound echoed in the small space as well as their voices.

"It's got a big basement, one of the only ones in the subdivision. No one will hear a thing," Cory said, walking around to Nicola's side to help with Ferris' limp body. He put on his leather gloves and tied them down at the wrist. There was no way that he wanted to touch the pedophile with is bare hands unless he was choking him to death. "Hey Maury, give him another shot will you? I don't want him waking up in the middle of this."

***

In the master bedroom of the stash house, the sound of a woman's erotic, sexual moans spilled out beyond the confines of the room into the hallway and down the quiet corridor, echoing through the hollow rooms like a throbbing pulse. As the men entered the kitchen with Ferris' body, Cory and Maurice snickered to each other, while Nicola locked the door behind him.

"The alarm code is 4545," Cory said, dropping Ferris on the tile floor. He rose up and stretched his arms. "The fucker is heavy."

"No shit," Maurice said, going to the stainless steel refrigerator to get a beer. "I need a cold one before we tote his ass down to the basement."

The woman screamed again.

Nicola walked to the doorway and looked through the house. There were at least six bodyguards who stared back at him, all carrying weapons and wearing suits. He turned back without saying a word to them. "Who is that?" he asked Cory as the strange woman made a low throaty noise and said something vulgar and inviting.

"Heidi and Gabriel," Cory answered before Maurice could. He looked at his watch. "He should be done in a minute."

"It takes longer and longer each time. Are they falling for each other?" Maurice asked. He looked through the refrigerator for something to eat. "It would be beneficial for her, at least, if they did."

"He's not stupid. It's easy ass man. That's all," Cory said, rolling his arms.

Nicola walked back to Ferris' body, bent down, picked him up and threw him over his broad shoulder. "Where do you want him?" he asked, annoyed by the sound of the woman. He had to get away from it. It made him miss Ivy even more. He should have been home right then making love to his wife and playing with his kids not lugging around kidnapped politicians and working for international organized crime rings.

Cory could see Nicola's aggravation and felt for him. "I'll walk you down," he said, twisting the top off of his beer. "Do you want one?"

"Sure," Nicola said with a huff. "It's fucking boiling outside, even with the sun down."

Maurice walked to the window and looked out as more cars pulled up. "The guys are here. Looks like everyone except Magnelli."

Nicola nodded. "Good. Then we can get started soon."

Cory led Nicola to the basement adjacent to the kitchen. Flipping on the light, they descended down a long stairwell to a full basement. One side of it was stacked with crates full of ammunition; the other side was an authentic electric chair with worn leather straps under an unforgiving halogen light. Nicola placed

Ferris in the chair and Cory helped strap him in. When they were done, they looked at the man, sweating, leg wrapped, hand covered in dirty gauze and felt no remorse.

"How long will he be out?" Nicola asked.

"No more than an hour," Cory said, pulling the tripod and camera out of the corner. "You said you wanted a full confession on tape, right?"

"Yeah," Nicola said, hearing footsteps behind him. He looked over at the stairs to see Gabriel, standing shirtless with only his jeans on. He walked over to them, still glistening from sex and stared at Ferris.

"So this is what all the trouble is over, huh? Doesn't look like much." He popped open his beer. "Then again, pedophiles never do."

"He'll be up in an hour," Cory said again.

"Do you have something to bring him to quicker," Gabriel asked.

"Yeah, if you want," Cory said, ready to go back upstairs. He had seen what was done down in this basement and it gave him the creeps, but if anyone had it coming, this guy did.

"What parts of the puzzle are we missing before we start?" Gabriel asked Nicola. He wanted to get it over with as much as they did.

"Magnelli and his son. They are supposed to be on the way." Nicola looked down at his watch. "Hey did you get me that phone?"

Gabriel pulled an iPhone from his back pocket. "Yep," he said, extending his hand to Nicola. "It's not traceable. You can talk as long as you want to the wife."

"I've got something that I need her to do." Plus, he missed her voice. He wouldn't wait to talk to her, to know that she was fine and to let her know the same about him. She had to be worried out of her mind. He had told her to call her folks as soon as she got to Miami to let them know that she and the kids were safe, but he had given her strict instructions not to mention how they got there, who brought them or anything at all about the Medlov family. He was certain that she understood and that he could trust her to keep their secret.

"Do you guys need me right now? If not, I'm going back upstairs and grab something to eat," Cory said, walking towards the staircase. He could hear the men talking upstairs among themselves.

"No, you're good," Gabriel said, looking at Nicola. "But you, I do need to speak to."

Nicola raised a brow. "I'm all ears."

Cory excused himself on that note, and the men were left alone.

Gabriel having been an agent way before he was a crime boss wanted to see where the man's head was. In fact, it was imperative considering everything that he had seen. It would be Agosto's death for sure, and he felt responsible for telling him so.

Gabriel grabbed a seat across from Ferris and sipped his beer. "Do you know what you're doing?" he asked, green eyes narrowed. The bright light shun down on his large muscular form and black as night hair.

"Yes," Nicola answered flatly.

"It's just that you've been a cop for as long as you've been a grown man. How are you going to deal with this once it's all over and you've gotten your man?"

Nicola answered truthfully. "I haven't planned that far ahead yet."

"When I came here to this…world…I knew that I didn't belong. And I expected a hard transition, but the incentive was that I was gaining a family more important than the one that I was losing. And by family I mean the men that I served with."

"I know what you mean," Nicola said, sitting down opposite Gabriel and Ferris. "You've never had children have you?"

"No," Gabriel answered proudly. "Lately, I've been thinking that I don't really need them considering my line of work. It only holds me down, makes me more vulnerable." He thought about the botched kidnapping of Dmitry's daughter Anya only months before and felt the goose bumps form on his arms again. He could never tell anyone but that experience had changed his life permanently. For that matter, it had changed Anatoly's as well. "But I do know what it means to nearly lose someone you love. So, I get why you are here, I just want you to understand that why you are here today may not be enough of a reason for you to stay committed tomorrow. The only thing about the Medlov family is that you don't have a choice. Once you are in, you are in."

"Yeah, I've gathered that," Nicola said, looking back at the crates. "I'm a man of my word. I'll do everything that I said that I would do, because you all have done everything that you said you would do."

Gabriel clenched his jaw. "Well, let's go upstairs. There's a completely different thing to handle up there."

"Magnelli and his son..." Nicola huffed. "I wouldn't want to be Collin."

"Shit, me either." Gabriel stood up off the chair, hovering over Nicola. "Let's get to it."

***

Collin had no idea where he was. His father pulled up to a house packed with cars and parked. Thumping out his cigarette, Magnelli pulled himself from the car and motioned for his son to follow him. He had had time to think on the drive and was finally at peace with what he was about to do.

"Pop, where are we going?" Collin asked, glancing around the quiet, dark neighborhood.

"A friend's house. I told some men on the department that I'd meet them here," Magnelli said, walking to the front door. He rang the doorbell and waited.

"Do I know him?" Collin asked. He swatted a mosquito off his neck.

"You know a few of them," Magnelli answered as the door opened. It was Cory.

"Hey man," Cory said, nodding at Collin. "Glad you could make it."

"It's a fucking mad house out there tonight," Magnelli said, stepping inside. "You know my son, Collin."

"Yeah," Cory offered his hand, though his flesh crawled. "How are you?"

"I'm making it," Collin said, a little more relaxed. He knew Cory Hamilton from around the department. He worked for Agosto. The thought bothered him mildly, but he knew that most people on the force did know Agosto and had worked for him or with him at some point.

The two of them walked in the house past Cory and into the chilled air. Collin could hear men laughing and talking as he stood in the foyer, which also made him drop his guard a bit. That was until he rounded the corner and saw the Medlov guards.

"Who the fuck are they?" Collin asked his father.

"Friends," Magnelli said, turning to his son. The other police officers emerged out of the kitchen still in uniform and greeted Magnelli, circling around Collin without him realizing it.

"How are you Collin?" Reynolds asked, hitting Collin on the back. He offered his hand.

Collin knew that Reynolds had been on the force nearly as long as his father had. He offered his hand and shook it. "Good to see you," he said, on guard.

Reynolds shook Collins hand tight at first, and then suddenly snatched him forward, throwing Collin off balance while from behind Cory grabbed him, and then Sorrello took his weapon.

Collin tried to fight but in seconds the men had him on the ground. Without a weapon, he was defenseless. Struggling, he looked up at his father. "What's going on here? Let me go! Dad!" he called out for his father, but it was in vain.

Magnelli bent over his son and looked at him. "Why'd you do it, Collin?" he asked, shaking his head. "Of all the people on the force, why'd you have to kill your sister?"

"I didn't kill anyone!" Collin exclaimed. "You have to believe me. Pop, please. Listen to me," he said, struggling. His voice trembled. "I didn't kill anyone."

Magnelli wanted to believe him but couldn't. "We'll see," he said standing back up. "Take him downstairs with his friend and duct tape his mouth. Tonight, we're going to get to the bottom of this."
***

When Ferris woke up, the first thing that he felt was sheer, agonizing pain. Pushing his head into the back of the chair, he let out a scream and tried to reach for his pulsating knee. It was then that he realized that he was strapped to the chair by his arms, waist and legs. The hot light above him had him sweating and irritated. The top of his head, especially around his balding center, was burning hot from the relentless beam off the 100-watt bulb above him.

The thud of his heart pounding inside of his chest was nearly audible. Licking his cracked lips, he scanned the room. To his surprise, Collin Magnelli was sitting tied and bound to the right side of him in a metal chair. He looked over at him and frowned.

"Where are we?" Ferris asked as burning sweat dropped into his eyes.

Collin tried to speak but the gray duct tape around his mouth and head prevented him from talking. All he could get out was muffled moans. He shook his head, trying to prevent Ferris from saying too much.

In Ferris' haze, he could barely think. Closing his eyes, he swallowed, hurting his dry throat. His croaked words. "Agosto is alive."

Collin shook his head again, begging Ferris to be quiet.

Ferris opened his eyes again, the light above nearly blinding him. "Is Cane here?"

Agosto walked across the room. "Afraid not," he said, coming out of the shadows. "But don't worry. He'll get what's coming to him."

Ferris locked his tired eyes on Nicola as he drug a seat across the concrete flooring and sat down on the back of it. The guns in the holsters under his arms gleamed in the light. "We're going to talk, and you're going to tell me everything that I want to know."

Ferris snarled, despite his situation. "And if I don't," he said, still trying to free himself from his bonds.

Nicola sucked his perfect teeth. "Then I'm going to kill you...slowly," he said with a smile. "And nothing would bring me greater pleasure. I promise you that."

"Well, I promise you that you're bringing a shit storm down on yourself and your family," Ferris promised.

Nicola shook his head. "Do you really believe that?" He looked around and then rested his bulky arms on the back of the chair. "Look around you, Ferris. This isn't a hearing...this is a last stand. You're either going to tell me what I want to know or you're going to die...just like Sammy."

Ferris paused. Just what did Agosto know? His tone instantly changed. "I have money. Get me out of here and you can write your own ticket."

"I can write my own ticket now." Nicola reached in his pocket and pulled out a notepad. "Just to stay on task, I've written a few questions down. If you answer them, then your time here will be less pleasant, if you know what I mean."

Ferris looked at the notebook. The pain radiated through his entire body as he tried to shift his aching bottom in the chair.

"We're short on time. So shall we begin," Nicola asked. He eyed Ferris, waiting for an answer.

"I'm not telling you shit," Ferris spat. The saliva hung to his mouth, showing another indication that he was dehydrated.

Cory walked over with a bottle of water out of the darkness and set it beside Nicola. Looking over at Collin, he tilted his head. "Well, at least we know that they know each other. The question is now is what else can they tell us."

Nicola ran a hand over his head, scratching through his dark mane. "What is Cane planning? Where is he? Where is your playground? What is your part in this? Four questions," he said, raising four fingers. "Four questions answered and you keep your life."

"The police will come looking for me," Ferris promised. "And when they do, they will bury you under a prison cell. You'll never see the light of day again, never see your family."

Nicola stood up. He walked over to Ferris and stood over him. "Four questions. That's all you have to do is answer them. And yet, you sit here like the pompous asshole that you've always been trying to play the tough guy." He smacked his lips. "Okay, we'll make it five instead of four. Who ordered the hit on my family, on Johnson, on Carmen, on Steele?" He pulled the man's head back and stared in his blood shot eyes.

"Fuck you," Ferris said, trying to pull away.

"Fuck me?" Agosto said, teeth showing. "Fuck me?" he screamed. "No, Ferris, fuck you." He reached back and landed a dizzying blow to Ferris' head.

Coughing up blood, Ferris tried to speak, but Nicola hit him again, this time harder. The sound of the blows echoed around the room, making Collin flinch in worry. Landing one blow after another to his battered face, Nicola finally stopped and stepped back. "I can do this all night," he said without raising his voice.

Ferris' head fell. Dark red blood oozed from his mouth in a long string down to his soaking wet trousers. He sobbed quietly, unable to even touch his wounds.

"I don't' know anything," Ferris said pitifully. "You have the wrong man."

"Oh, I've got the right man," Nicola said without guilt. "You're just giving me the wrong answers." He opened the bottle water and took a sip then walked over to the corner and pulled out a blow torch. "I'm new to this torture thing. You see, up until you decided to try to play God with my life, I was a good cop. I didn't believe in this type of thing." He lit the torch and walked towards Ferris. "But it's amazing what a man will do once he sees his family nearly killed." He put the fire only inches away from Ferris' face. "They tried to shoot us, and when that wasn't successful, they tried to burn us. Do you know what fire feels like?"

Ferris' eyes bulged in fear. He tried as hard as he could to pull away from the hot blue flame of the sun-like fire. "I don't know anything," he lied. "You have the wrong man!" he screamed.

Nicola's eyes blazed. Putting the fire to his cheek, the sound of flesh burning filled the room. It was enough to make him sick but he held back his own nausea and prayed for answers. Hiding his own disdain for his actions, he pressed with the interrogation. "Five questions, Ferris. It will turn into six and you're torture will turn in to an all-night affair. It's all up to you." He put the fire near Ferris' crotch. "I can' find other things to burn."

"No!" Ferris screamed and cried. "Alright..." He threw his head back. "Alright. What do you want to know?" He cried aloud as the pain of the burn caused him to rock in the chair.

"I told you want I wanted to know," Agosto said, looking Ferris in his wounded face. "What is Cane planning? Where is he? Where is your playground? What is your part in this? Who ordered the hits?"

The sound of men coming down the staircase from the main floor of the house to the basement caused Collin to look away from the horrifying sight to the processional of officers, including his officer.

Cory walked up to the camera and turned it on. Zooming in on Ferris, he waited.

"How do I know that you won't just kill me once I tell you what you want to know?" Ferris asked, spitting more blood.

"You'll just have to trust me," Nicola said, chuckling. "It's a hard choice. Trust me. I know, but you've made your own bed. Now, you have to lie in it."

Collin kept his eyes on his father. Tears formed at the corners of his eye lids and fell down on this tape around his mouth and cheeks. Unable to look at him any longer, he released a frustrated sigh and looked down his taped feet.

"Cane is planning to take over the illicit drug business with a powerful new type of Molly that is completely undetectable once in the human system. He's been testing it for months and now it's in production. He has orders from all over the country and he has a partner out of New York, a woman, but I don't know her name. I just know that she exists."

"Is this new Molly what killed the four children in the Baby Boys case?" Nicola asked, unable to let go of the case that had haunted him since he had agreed to take it.

"Yes," Ferris answered reluctantly.

Nicola chose his next question carefully. "Let's go back to Cane for a minute. Where is he producing this new drug? We've searched the city and he's not around. Where is he?"

"In Millington," Ferris answered, looking at the blow torch. "His father has a farm out there. It's still in his mother's name. He's using it to produce the product and prepare it for production."

Collin threw his head back in disgust.

Nicola looked over at him and twisted up his lips. "Is Collin a part of this?"

"Of course he is. Why else would he be here?" Ferris answered, feeling absolutely no loyalty. "Collin kept the scent off of Cane while he prepared for the deal. Those possible dealers who knew had amnesty as far as Colin was concerned, plus he reported to us on the Baby Boys case and what Magnelli was planning."

Collin shook his head.

Deputy Magnelli emerged from the shadows and walked over to Ferris. He leaned into the man with his gun pointed. "Who killed Carmen?" he asked, cutting through the chase.

Ferris swallowed hard as he looked down the barrel of a gun for the first time. "Collin killed her accidentally. He was supposed to kill Johnson, but she was there." He looked up at Magnelli and pleaded. "I had nothing to do with that."

Collin tried to speak. Screaming muffled words at Ferris, he tried to break free.

"Seems like he would beg to differ," Nicola said to Ferris. "Take the tape off," he said to Magnelli.

As soon as Collin could speak, he screamed. "Ferris ordered the hits because Johnson and Steele linked him to DeMario's death. We had no intention of using him, but we had no choice. Dad, you have to believe me. Killing Carmen was a God's honest mistake."

Magnelli started to shake. "God doesn't make mistakes, you evil, twisted bastard! I should have never allowed your crack whore mother to give birth to you. I should have never taken you in to my home. I should have never allowed you to come home from college, and I should have never trusted you in my house when you joined the police department."

"Dad," Collin cried. "Please forgive me. I had no idea. I promise you, I had no idea that Carmen was there."

Magnelli ignored his cries. "Bobbi told me the day that I brought you home after your mother overdosed that you were trouble. And I promised her that you weren't, even though I knew that you were born out of sin. Even though I knew that I didn't love you, no matter how I tried!" He pointed the gun at his son.

Nicola stepped back and listened on like the rest of the men in the room, shocked at the reality of their relationship. But no one would stop him. His revenge was just as needed as everyone else's.

"You have to believe me, Dad," Collin cried.

"I promised Bobbi that I'd find the man responsible for her only child's death and I'd put a bullet in him. Do I look like a liar to you?" Magnelli screamed. "Do I?"

Collin stopped crying and looked up at his father in pain. "I'm sorry," he said, voice cracking.

"So am I," Magnelli said, pulling the trigger. He shot his son three times. Once in the head and twice in the chest. Lowering his weapon, he looked over at Ferris who wept for himself. "You make him pay, Agosto, or I will," he said, walking to the staircase. He had to leave, get away from what he had done and what his son had done. Jetting up the stairs, he left the men to do what they needed to do.

"Next question," Nicola said, ignoring Ferris' sobs. "What is Cane's next step?"

Ferris didn't hesitate this time. "He plans to distribute day after tomorrow to all the clubs that Twist owned, to his pharmacies where his men will sell to the locals and through the trucking line that he recently bought. It's being produced in mass quantities at the farm. If you just go there?"

"Where?" Nicola screamed.

"I don't know the fucking address. I just know that it's in Millington," Ferris said afraid.

Nicola stepped closer. "Where is your playground? I know that you have one. You wouldn't have killed those children at your house, so where do you play?"

Ferris shook his head. "I didn't kill those kids."

Nicola pulled out his gun and shot Ferris in the knee that had not already been injured. "Now is not the time to fuck with me!"

Ferris screamed out in pain. "I don't…"

Before he could lie again, Nicola shot him in the arm. Unable to take the pain any longer, he confessed. "I bought a dry cleaners on Stage Road. It's been closed for years. In the back. The playground is in the back," he cried.

"What's the address?" Nicola said, determined to keep his promise to Mrs. Naples.

"555 State Road!" Ferris screamed.

"How do you get in touch with Cane?" Nicola asked, turning his back on Cane to look at Cory.

"I use the track phone in my bag," Ferris cried. "Just please don't kill me. Please." He begged.

"Oh, I'm not going to kill you," Nicola said, putting his gun back in his holster. "But I'm going to make damn sure that you never hurt another child in your life."

33

After six long hours of torture and interrogation by Nicola, Magnelli, Maurice, and Cory, the dark basement of the stash house stunk of blood, shit and piss. At first when the esteemed councilman felt untouchable, he had tried to play stupid, but after some rigorous encouragement with a cattle prod and blowtorch, Ferris had given them everything that they needed to go after Cane.

They knew the warehouse vicinity, location of the drop points for the Molly, the players involved minus the supplier *who was still a mystery to everyone except Cane*, the reason that Twist was killed, who had put the hits on Johnson and Steele and who had put the hit on Nicola's family. They even knew how and why Nicola had been set up.

Hearing the elaborate plan come directly from the serpent's mouth had been a sobering experience for everyone in the room. They listened on speechless as Ferris revealed everything one sordid fact at a time.

When it was all done, everyone was exhausted.

There wasn't a calm heart in the room, especially since they all had families of some sort. It could have been any of them in Agosto's place, any of their families put on a hit list, any of their jobs in jeopardy.

Nicola had to give it to the self-proclaimed *Three Wise Men;* they had planned out their strategy very well. But they had not accounted for one thing. Leaving him alive. And now that he had survived their botched attempts, he planned to make good use of his existence by ending theirs.

Glowering down at Ferris with his large, muscular arms across his wide chest under the hot halogen light, Nicola decided he was done for now with his interrogation. It was dawn and there were other things to handle.

Ferris drooped over in the wooden chair, exhausted, weak, and nearly unconscious. Mumbling something to himself first, he let out a pain-filled gurgle and then threw up green bile that spilled out of his swollen mouth onto his torn shirt.

The sight of what Ferris had been reduced to didn't make Nicola as sick as he had first thought it would. *Maybe because the bastard deserved it.* He was a man who didn't exactly believe in the methods he had used to get Ferris to talk, but he was coming to see that sometimes rules needed to be broken to get things done.

"I'm starving," Cory said, standing beside Nicola. His stomach growled loudly. He spit on the concrete floor beside Ferris. "Worthless piece of shit. Should we cap him now so that we can get going?"

Nicola had never had a hard on to kill someone more. But he had made promises, promises he was sworn to keep. "No," he finally answered regrettably. "Leave him for the time being." He walked away from the man, needing to get some distance before he changed his mind.

"You have the proof that you need," Cory said, pulling out his weapon and stepping closer to Ferris. He covered his nose and looked back at Nicola. "Why are you letting him live? Magnelli killed his son for killing a grown woman. You're really going to let this baby killer live? He raped and murdered at least four children." He pushed the muzzle of his gun to Ferris' head. "He doesn't deserve to take one more breath. Am I right, Maurice? Tell him."

Maurice was in the corner on the couch nodding. Hearing his name, he sat up and looked over at Cory. "What?"

"Shouldn't we kill him already?" Cory lobbied.

Maurice set his head back on the couch again. "I thought that was what we were doing."

"Look, I know that he deserves it. You don't think I want to kill the motherfucker right now for what he's done to me, my family and three other families?" Nicola's voice rose in frustration as he turned back around, veins popping out of his neck. "But that would just be doing him a favor. He needs to suffer beyond any measure of the word that he could have ever fathomed. He needs to be publicly fucking humiliated and stripped of every single recognition and every ounce of respect and then thrown in with the rest of the animals to spend the rest of his life being fucked up the ass and treated like the dog shit that he is. Tell me if you think hard enough about it that you don't agree?"

Cory put the gun down. "You know how broken the system is. Hell, if it weren't, we wouldn't be here. So, what are you going to do when he walks away with no charges and starts giving names and ranks on everyone in this room? Then who will be getting fucked in the ass?"

Maurice looked over at Nicola and waited for an answer. Cory had a point.

"We don't hand him over until the case is concrete," Nicola said, looking at Ferris, and if Nicola didn't counter offer something better, then they'd make an executive decision to kill Ferris themselves.

"He's beaten to shit," Cory said, pointing at him. "And he witnessed the murder of another cop." He pointed to Collin's lifeless corpse still tied to the chair in the corner. "Tell me how that shit will stand up in court. He'll pay one of his high-price lawyer friends to get him off on temporary insanity and he'll be back at home fucking ten-year old boys before you know it." Cory knew that would piss Nicola off.

It worked.

"I made a promise to deliver this son-of-a-bitch with a bow to the families who are now forever ruined because of him. What about their justice? What about their peace of mind?"

"Him being dead is justice and peace of fucking mind enough," Cory pleaded. He pointed the gun one more time at Ferris and whined. "Just…" He stuttered in anxiety. "Just let me cap his ass, Agosto. Live for once."

Nicola almost gave in, knowing that he had to keep the men in this room on his side in order to get the job completed, but the interruption saved him from having to make a decision right then.

"There *is* a way to keep your captive silent for good but keep him alive for your public humiliation plan," Anatoly mocked, walking down the staircase. He had been quite intrigued by the exchange between Nicola and Cory. Evidently, the young cop had grown some balls over the years working for him, because when they first met, he was a sniveling little pussy, scared of his own shadow and eager to keep his hands clean.

"How?" Nicola asked, leaning his hands on the end of the wooden worktable in the corner. He heaved a heavy sigh, growing more and more tired of dealing with Ferris.

With Gabriel and Boris behind him, Anatoly stepped off the bottom step and down in what had become a makeshift dungeon in a black leather suit completely unfitting for the hour. Evidently, the man had been out all night and decided to stop in and check on everything before retiring back to the compound.

Gabriel's face instantly turned up at the foul odor radiating from Ferris, but Anatoly was used to this form of retribution, was unaffected by the smell of men losing their bodily functions. He cracked a smile at Ferris, a stab right to the politician's heart, as he crossed the room. "It's one of my father's old techniques. You cut a man's tongue out, his hands off, and you cripple him. You leave him as ugly on the outside as he is on the inside. We call it the *mirror method*."

"It will definitely make it hard for him to testify," Cory said, slowly changing his mind. He could live with Anatoly's plan. "By the time that they are able to get someone to even remotely try to understand him, the proof will have him incarcerated."

"Who can do that *mirror method* thing effectively?" Nicola asked, unwilling to volunteer. He still had some sanity and didn't want to lose it cutting off hands and tongues.

"Vasily is pretty good at it, but he's away right now. I'll have him take care of it once he's back in town." Anatoly walked over to the table and looked at the map as if giving such an order was an everyday thing. "So what's on the agenda for today, gentlemen?"

Nicola pointed at the red circle on the map. "This is where Cane's warehouse is. It's out in Millington, not far from where the private airstrip is. About fifteen miles away from the military base. That's going to be the last spot we hit tonight. We have to move quickly before word gets out that Ferris and Collin are missing, and that I'm not one of the bodies from inside the house. Once Cane finds all of this out, he'll immediately pack it up and move. Right now, he can't put all the pieces together. We need to use that to our advantage and attack now."

"That's all fine, but what is the first spot you're going to hit?" Anatoly asked.

Gabriel shook his head. "He's got pre-wedding jitters," he explained to Nicola. "I tried to talk him out of it, but he thinks one last hurrah before the wedding will be good for him."

"These men are going to be heavily armed," Nicola said to Anatoly frowning. He wasn't expecting the boss' son to really get in this. After all, it wasn't his fight. Plus, if something did happen to him, Dmitry would be on his ass.

"Before I was a boss, I was a boy, doing exactly what you're doing right now every day before breakfast, after lunch and sometimes for dinner," Anatoly said flatly. His face was emotionless.

"But you're not a boy now." Nicola rolled his neck. "You're a boss. And you and I both know that you don't have to get involved. Sammy was enough. I mean. I'm grateful for it, but this is asking too much."

Anatoly was a man of few words, and even more than that, he didn't feel as though he owed anyone except his father and sometimes his fiancée an explanation. But just this once, he would explain himself just so that Nicola didn't get the wrong idea. "This isn't about you," he said, sucking his bottom lip. He looked into Nicola's face, hazel brown eyes blazing. "Someone, *who will remain anonymous and is no longer with us*, kidnapped my baby sister not long ago for a very handsome payoff. The plan was to sell her back to my father, *but* if he didn't cooperate or if he got too close, the secondary plan was to sell her to someone else. They were going to rape her, make her a slave." He pushed the words out like poison as his gaze became distant. "Since that day, I promised myself that I'd never let anyone get close to my family, especially the children. And I'd send a message to anyone who even thought about harming myself, my daughter or any of the women in my family. Now, obviously these rednecks are not threatening us, but your recent situation speaks to something in the core of my father, my cousin, and myself. You should feel lucky. If nothing had ever happened to Anya, you might be dead yourself right now."

Nicola was speechless. He wasn't aware that Anatoly even had a daughter. And no one that he knew on any law enforcement agency was aware that Anya had been stolen or even that she existed. However, it did put things into perspective for Nicola. It proved that the Medlov men were actually human.

"Well, we could always use another hand then," Nicola said, changing his tune. "By all means, if you want to get your hands dirty killing drug dealers and mangling pedophiles, who am I to stop you?"

Anatoly looked at his watch. It was already six thirty. "Back to the agenda."

Nicola looked over at his bomb guy who was in the corner of the room carefully connecting wires to his latest masterpiece. "I need a bomb for breakfast. And I need a hit team for dinner. During lunch, I plan to call in some other friends on the force who will help me lock down Cane's second drop point. It's a strip club that Twist used to own called Lollipop."

Anatoly nodded. "Gabriel knows the place well." He looked over at his cousin and smirked.

Gabriel rolled his eyes. "I'm in too. Just tell me where you want me. Hell, I haven't done any real cop work in a while."

Anatoly took off his jacket and laid it on the table. Finally, he could have a real bachelor's party before the nuptials. "Well now you have two additional men. Just make it interesting. Boris, get us some gear."

***

Vasily felt as though he had stepped out of reality and landed in some western film from another century. Looking around what was considered to be Guymon, Oklahoma from the top of the metal stairs attached to his boss' leer jet; he slipped on his black designer shades and checked his Rolex.

9:30 a.m. on the dot.

Two hours was all that he was giving himself to get what he came for and get the hell out of this state. Alone for his trip, he hiked down the staircase and jumped into the black SUV waiting for him on the tarmac while the stewardess watched from the opening of the door hatch.

The drive to Keyes, Oklahoma was about fifty miles away through flat undeveloped land as far as the eye could see. There was little commerce in the area with a population that was 90 percent white, most of whom had never seen or spoken with a real Russian. The average income was below $50,000 a year, less than the price of his watch. And the town folk were sure to be nosy as hell.

He was headed to see a Roxanna Little aka Roxie Lite. His boss had told him that this woman was his priority for the moment. "A necessary means to a desired end," was how Dmitry had referred to her. So as far as Vasily was concerned, nothing else in this world mattered except finding and extracting this woman. *In two hours.*

***

After Cane had killed his father and burned down the pharmacy many years ago, he had it rebuilt and took it over with the goal of making it a regular drop stop. Hiring only handpicked, cooperative pharmacists who also moonlighted on his team as chemists who prepared his Molly, he had learned the value of having legitimate businesses to cover for his illegal ones. Before he had killed Twist, he had begged his old partner to go half with him on building new pharmacies all over town and expanding their static locations, but Twist had said no, claiming that it would bring too much attention to them and eventually land them in jail. It was decisions just like that one that had prompted him to kill him in the first place.

Now that Cane was completely in charge, he planned to revisit his initial idea and buy up buildings in different areas around the city where he already had a lot of users and bring his vision in to fruition.

It all started with today.

While he sat outside of his makeshift warehouse in the woods drinking coffee and listening to the chirping birds, a group of men loaded up the freshly prepped Molly for his first full production delivery into the back of a white delivery van. Packed in small plastic baggies and then stuffed in stolen pharmaceutical boxes, the drugs were finally ready to make their debut on the streets of Memphis.

"Ready boss," the driver said, closing the back of the truck.

Cane walked over, holding his coffee cup in one hand and a can of snuff in the other. "You boys better make sure that shit gets delivered with no problems. I don't want no excuses, you hear?"

"Sure thing," the driver said, nodding obediently. "I'll be to the pharmacy by seven thirty and to the club by nine. I'm dropping off to Dr. Wayne at the pharmacy and to Hannity at the club," he said, going over the instructions that had been pounded into his head. "Tonight be back here at five thirty to pick up the shipments for the dealers."

"No, damn you. Be here at three o'clock. Don't you think it's going to look pretty odd you driving through the fucking hood delivering shit to drug dealers after dark? You want to appear like you're on the up and up, not that you're carrying $200,000 worth of fucking Molly, you idiot!"

"Three o'clock. Yes, sir."

"Get out of here," Cane said, wishing Sammy was there to handle the day-to-day. It had been a mistake to send him to Agosto's house. Now, he was down a man during the most critical time of the operations, but at least Agosto was dead. It had been worth the cost in the long run.

If he had been able to, he would have put everything on hold until he figured out just what the hell was going on, but he was on a tight deadline with his New York supplier and had to get the product out on the street immediately to start to see a return.

***

The sun was already bright and glaring down on everything under its path by the time that Nicola, Gabriel, and Maurice arrived at their first checkpoint. With a growling stomach, a five-o'clock shadow that was turning into an Armani beard and bad breath that made it hard to breathe, Nicola waited impatiently in the passenger seat of a newly stolen black Tahoe.

"I forgot how much I hated stakeouts," Gabriel said to Nicola before he pulled out his newspaper. He figured that he might as well get some reading in if they were going to be sitting for a while.

"Yeah, that was never my favorite thing either," Nicola said pitching the untraceable phone Gabriel had given him on the dashboard of the truck. He wanted to call Ivy badly but could not risk it just yet. Without a word, he slipped on his shades and sunk down in the passenger seat.

Gabriel checked in the rearview mirror for any possible witnesses. "Maurice, what's your status," he said into the air piece.

Maurice answered quickly. "I'm on my way back. Package is hot and ready to be opened." He appeared from the corner of the pharmacy and ran across the street to the SUV parked and waiting.

"Check," Gabriel answered, back in his old law enforcement mode.

"He is so used to deactivating bombs, until I guess setting off a few is the only thing that keeps him tamed," Nicola said, watching Maurice drive away. He'd known the guy for years and even before finding out that he was a mole, he knew that he was mildly off.

"Never used him before." Gabriel sipped out of his Starbuck coffee cup. "I'm sure I will though." He looked out of the dark tinted window as the delivery truck pulled up to the back of the pharmacy, and then backed into the dock. "Okay. Here we go. Right on time, just like Ferris said. I guess the bastard is good for something."

"Is that them for sure?" Nicola asked, looking through the binoculars. "I'd hate to kill the wrong men." He watched the driver jump out and open the back door. As he bent to put down the boxes, his gun holster popped out of his uniform jacket. "Yep, that's him."

"Sure?" Gabriel asked.

"How many drivers do you know who wear guns on their deliveries if they aren't armed car security?" Nicola raised a brow at Gabriel.

Gabriel chuckled. "Everyone who works in Queens." He opened the middle console and pulled out the black detonator. "You want to do the honors?" Gabriel asked, passing it to Nicola.

Nicola flipped the top of the detonator open and watched as the driver and his partner walked into the back pharmacy. Normally, he would have been concerned about the men, trying to find a way to lock them up instead of kill them.

But that was before…

Thinking of his screaming children, he looked over at Gabriel. "Fuck'em all."

Between Nicola pushing the button across the street from the pharmacy and the time that it took to explode there were only milliseconds of time. Before he could blink, destruction unlike the community had ever seen was unleashed. Nicola and Gabriel reverted back to children at a fireworks show. In utter, quiet excitement they watched the pharmacy explode and large black plumes of red-hot smoke and fire rise up into the morning sky. Along the back of the small pharmacy, the truck connected to the dock also caught on fire and exploded. Glass from the front of the building exploded out on the streets causing passing cars to swerve; bricks flew out onto the parking lot and every single solitary Molly pill was gone.

Quietly Nicola watched one of the men who had not been instantly killed by the bomb run several feet on fire before collapsing to the ground. This gave an entirely different meaning to the old saying *if you were on fire, I wouldn't even piss on you.*

He couldn't help it. Nicola smiled a long easy smile that eventually rose up to a teeth-showing laughter.

Gabriel couldn't help but laugh to, glad that Nicola was getting some justice. "Well alright. Let's go get some breakfast," Gabriel said, pulling off.

34

Cane had not been home in a day and a half, but some of his men had been charged with staying there and maintaining and watching over the large horse farm in his absence. As long as the tyrant was gone, things were relaxed. The guards at the gate played their music and drank Bud Light in the shack; the bodyguards watched television and played video games and some of the other stragglers enjoyed the pool and Jacuzzi.

Ricky, one of Cane's buddies who had been with him for years, hiked up from the house to the shack with more beer for the men in the mid-afternoon heat, while drinking a beer of his own and smoking a cigarette. It was like a paid-vacation for him. He had taken a bath in Cane's two-person garden tub, laid in Cane's extra-large bed and watched Sports Center all morning and did blow right off the dining room table while the maid served up barbeque for breakfast.

When he got to the shack, he knocked on the door and raised the six-pack.

"One of you fuckers order a beverage?" he joked.

The men opened the door and welcomed him. "Now that's what I'm talking about," one of the men said, grabbing the six-pack. "Bout time, man. Took you thirty minutes to bring'em. We done been ran out."

Ricky laughed. "I was busy ordering up some cooch for later. Betty says she's going to bring some girls by."

The men perked up. "You gotta let us in on the action, man. We're burning up out here," one of the guards said, opening the bottle of beer.

"Just don't shit faced before they get here," Ricky warned. "Girls don't like drunk dick. I don't care what your momma told ya."

All three broke out in laughter and started to pull out the beers for immediate consumption. However, they were so thoroughly enthralled in their conversation and getting a buzz until they fail to notice the three SUVs approaching at an accelerated speed.

With Cory driving, Nicola was coming fast, approaching the shack at nearly 80 miles an hour down the private street. On cue, he cocked his automatic weapon and cleared his cloudy mind. Letting down the back window, stuck his gun out and prepared.

Right behind him, Gabriel pushed down on the gas and opened the sunroof for Anatoly to squeeze up top. With a hand-held rocket launcher, he aimed at the fortified gate.

"Say ahhh, mother fuckers" Anatoly said, squeezing the trigger.

The *thud* of the rocket zipping out of the container was followed by a dead-on impact into the gate. The explosion blew open the complete right half of the shack and the fortified entrance. Before the men inside of the shack could get their bearing, Nicola was unloading his first clip. Bullets rang out like notes of a song. Hitting two of the men while they were still crawling out of the burning shack; Cory stopped so that Nicola could jump out of the truck. He landed on the ground, gun pointed. When Ricky raised his head up out of the rubble, Nicola pulled the trigger and shot a hole through his head. Before the man's body could fall back down in the pile of debris, Nicola was back inside of the truck.

Maurice and Boris followed as the tail of the convoy, barreling through the burning gate. As soon as they cleared the fire, Boris popped out of the sunroof and when he was in distance of the house, he too unleashed the fury of a rocket, which made impact at the front door. Anatoly and Gabriel headed towards the right side of the mansion; Boris and Maurice headed toward the left side of the house and Nicola and Cory headed straight through the burning door.

The men inside the mansion were completely taken by surprise by the sudden attack. As soon as they heard the commotion at the gate, they grabbed their guns and headed toward Ricky's aid, but their weapons were inferior to Dmitry's military grade fire power. Where they had shot guns and pistols, Nicola and his men had machine guns, rockets, high-powered rifles and grenades.

The fact that there were more of Cane's men than Nicola had didn't matter. It was a clear demonstration of the fact that Cane's local wanna be thugs were outclassed by police and organized crime experience in the field.

Nicola burst through the front doors in full tactical gear, running so fast until the men could not get one good shot out. As soon as his foot hit the threshold, he started to lay bodies down. Diving behind the large sofa in the living room, he popped back up from behind the barrier spraying the room while Cory gave him cover on the other side of the foyer. Every person they saw, they shot without prejudice or hesitation. Large caliber bullets ripped through the palatial home, tearing through drywall, destroying fine furniture and paintings.

When the Cane's men though that they had cornered Nicola in, he did a quick tactical reload, dropping one magazine on the floor while popping another one in his M4. With one hand, he pulled the trigger; with the other he threw a grenade across the room towards the men, blowing a hole in the wall.

Bodies flew everywhere. Blood splattered and men began screaming in pain ill prepared for the encounter. Cory quickly picked up the slack by throwing two more grenades into the other rooms, blowing out more walls and returning gunfire.

The sudden commotion disoriented the men toward the front of the house and scared the men toward the back of the house. As they tried to escape through the game room door leading out to the pool, they were met by Gabriel and Anatoly who unleashed the fury of automatic weapons and concussion grenades.

Maurice and Boris cleared the other side of the house with little trouble leaving no one alive before Maurice threw down a black satchel by the stove in the kitchen.

"Head out; head out!" he screamed into his earpiece as he and Boris bolted out the side door and ran around the side of the mansion toward the truck.

"Let's go!" Nicola screamed to Cory.

"Heard it!" Cory said, returning fire again.

All six of the men quickly exited the perimeter of the house, running as fast as they could while still shooting at the clueless men who thought Nicola and his team were retreating. As soon as they arrived back at their trucks, Maurice hit the detonator and a loud explosion brought the once beautiful house to its knees. The bomb rocked the ground beneath Nicola, feeling more like an earthquake than C4.

In seconds, they were back in the truck and headed back out of the burning gate onto the road.

There was no need to stand around and watch the mansion burn, because without a doubt, there was no one left alive.

***

Dmitry stood in front of the pile of perfectly cut, blue diamonds splayed out on the dining room table with his arms crossed and his hand under his chin. In deep thought, he contemplated which ones he actually wanted to keep and which ones he wanted to sell. Bending down, he picked up the cool precious stones in his large hand and studied them.

"They are worth about $100,000 a piece," the Israeli dealer said, watching his boss for a decision. "Compliments of your former competitor in Yemen. We took the notable spoils of war and brought them to you. Most of it is being housed at your home in Miami, but these were important enough to make a special trip." He hoped that Dmitry was impressed with his work and willing to contract him again.

Dmitry turned his lip up and scanned the pile. Who knew that Al-Shaqqaf was into the precious jewels trade? Maybe if that was all that he was involved in, he might still be alive.

"How many are here? Dmitry asked.

"There were at two hundred and ten," the man said, standing taller.

Dmitry smacked his lips. "I can't make up my mind," he finally said, putting the diamonds back down. "Anya!" he called out.

As soon as his voice rose, the door opened and the maid was there to answer him. "Can I help you, sir?" the short, frumpy Hispanic woman said with a warm smile. She looked up at the tall man with extreme admiration in her eyes.

Dmitry smiled back. He absolutely adored Mary. "Bring me my Anya. I have a job for her," he said, walking over to the buffet. Fishing through the crystal bowl, he picked out a shiny green apple and took a bite. "I know how to settle this once and for all. Then you can be on your way back to Miami to see how much I can get for the rest of our friend's belongings."

The Israeli man frowned. Wasn't Anya his daughter? What could a child offer to the multi-million dollar decision? However, he didn't dare voice his concern. Everyone knew how Dmitry Medlov felt about his only daughter. Quietly, he waited for the girl to answer her father's summons.

Within minutes, Anya walked into the room with a doll in one hand and book in the other. Dressed in a simple pair of jeans and a Tinker Bell t-shirt, she walked over to her father. "Mary said that you wanted me," she said, eyes traveling over to the other man in the room. She gave him a distrusting look that sent chills up his spine. Evidently, the girl didn't care for strangers.

Dmitry bent down and picked his daughter up. Kissing her rosy cheeks, he walked with her in his arms over to the table. "Pick your favorite ten and then we'll send the rest with this nice man," he said, sitting her on the table beside the pile.

"Just ten?" she asked, looking at all the sparkly stones.

"Just ten," Dmitry repeated. He ran an adoring hand over her angelic face. "Be quick about it, please. Daddy has other things he has to do."

Anya turned and looked at the stones, putting down her doll for only a second. Picking up the biggest ten that she could find in the pile, she handed them to her father and then picked her doll back up. "Can I have ice cream, papa?" she asked as he set her down on the marble floor.

Dmitry looked at her shirt. "It looks like you've already had some," he said, pointing out the smudge of chocolate on her shirt.

"Mommy said that I can't have anymore, but I wasn't full yet. Can I have some now?" she asked again. "I did a favor for you, picking out your diamonds. All I want is something to eat." She did not blink or smile. However, her argument for deserving more dessert was compelling.

The Israeli man watched on learning something new about his boss even as he handled his child. This family believed that nothing came free. A favor for a favor, no matter how small.

Dmitry smiled and nodded. He always loved negotiating with his princess. She would be a formidable force once it was time. "Fine, you can have one more serving of ice cream. Tell Mary to fix it for you."

As she headed back to the door, he stopped her. "Anya, did you forget to say something?" He put his hands on his hips and waited.

"Did you?" she asked, opening the door with her small hand. Leaving Dmitry alone with his guest, she closed the door behind her quietly.

Dmitry seemed nothing if not pleased with the girl. Turning back to the man, he pointed at the ten that she had selected. "Leave those ten and take the rest to be sold at the store in South Beach."

"As you wish," the man said, picking up everything but the ten diamonds that Anya had picked out and placed them carefully in the titanium case.

Another knock on the door drew Dmitry's attention. "Mary, I told her that she could have some more ice cream. It's fine."

"It's me, boss," Vasily said.

Dmitry looked over at the Israeli man motioning toward the door. "The men will see to your arrangements for the night at the Peabody," he said as Vasily walked in past him.

As soon as the man was gone, Dmitry sat down on one of the upholstered fine satin chairs by the table. "Did you find her?"

"Yes," Vasily said, wiping his tired eyes. It had been a long trip, although no one cared. He yawned and leaned against the table nearest the door.

"*Well*, where is she?" Dmitry asked, frustrated that he had to probe.

"In the trunk," Vasily answered. He shrugged at his boss cutting his crystal blue eyes at him. He quickly explained. "She's a handful. I had to improvise. You told me to bring her here whether she wanted to come or not. Well, she didn't want to come. I found her working in a tire shop in Keyes. Evidently, her parents didn't want her at the farm. So, she hitchhiked to the farthest place that she could get before she ran out of cash. The place was a real hell hole. She should have been glad to come back."

Dmitry ignored the rest of the Intel. "She's in the fucking trunk right now?" He stood up and walked towards the door. "Take me to her."

Out in the garage, Vasily popped open the trunk of Dmitry's white Bentley to find Roxie duct taped and tied down with rope. Dmitry bent down to the woman, whose eyes grew wide with fear at the size of him, and snatched the tape off her mouth. He was about to apologize for his man's treatment of her when she interrupted.

"Ouch!" she screamed. "What the fuck! Where am I? Am I back in Memphis? Did Cane send you?" Her eyes were wild with fear and anger. "What do you want from me?"

Dmitry looked at Vasily. "What's that smell?" he asked, trying to ignore Roxie and wishing that he hadn't taken off the tape.

"I pissed in your fucking trunk! You mother fuckers can't just kidnap someone." Taking a deep breath first, she screamed out. "Help! Someone help me!"

"Please be quiet," Dmitry said, voice low. He massaged his temples.

"Help!" she screamed again. Her shrieking voice carried through the garage and wounded Dmitry's ears. "Someone help me!"

"Please..." Dmitry took a deep breath. "Stop yelling."

"Help!" she screamed again. "Someone, please!"

"Shut! Up!" Dmitry growled. His voice boomed and scared her. Oddly enough, it wasn't even a scream, but his baritone was so forceful and so deep until the base sent chills through her spine.

Immediately, Roxie quieted down.

Gathering his composure, Dmitry put his hand on the side of the car and tried to speak in a low, calm voice. "Cane couldn't have found you if you had hid under his ball sack. I sent for you."

"Who are you?" Roxie asked, looking between him and Vasily. "And what do you want with me?"

"That depends," Dmitry answered.

"On what?" she asked, trying to raise her head to talk to him.

"Are you going to stop screaming? If not, I'm going to leave you out here until you start to stew in your own urine. However, *if you behave and keep in mind that there is no reason not to*, then Vasily will take you someplace where you can have a hot bath, fresh clothes, and something to eat." He raised his long index finger. "In exchange for that kindness, I want to know what you saw the night before you fled the city."

Roxie's face changed and Dmitry knew right then that she knew a hell of a lot more than she should have.

"I'm waiting," he said irritated.

"How do I know that you won't just kill me as soon as I tell you?" She rolled her eyes. "Uh uh. I gotta get something out of it."

"How about a chance to get out of the trunk, you rude little bitch," Vasily snapped.

"That's enough, Vasily," Dmitry ordered. "Roxie, that's your name right."

"What difference is it to you? Last time I checked you didn't need to know a person's name to pop a cap in their ass," she screamed.

Vasily shook his head. *Like he had told his boss, she was a handful.*

"Roxie," Dmitry said, heaving a deep sigh. He pointed his long finger at her. "I don't have time for this shit. Okay, so don't take my kindness for a weakness. Tell me exactly what you know *right now*. If you're worried about Cane, I can assure you that he's the last of your worries." His eyes narrowed. "But you do need to worry about me. You have some information that I want, and I get what I want. Do I make myself clear? You're in the back of a Bentley in my garage. If I wanted you dead, you'd be in a hole out in the desert that I just spent time and money extracting you from. Now, if you want to push me, then I'll just hand you back over to Vasily and he'll harvest your organs and sell them so that I can recoup my money." That last part was a joke but Roxie didn't find it to be funny.

Just then the garage opened and Nicola, Anatoly, and Gabriel came pulling in from the trip out to Cane's house.

Dmitry looked up and waved them over as they got out of the SUV.

"What's this?" Anatoly asked, looking at the girl with a stone face.

"This is Roxie," Dmitry said, cracking a smile. "Evidently, she has bigger balls then the men that we pick up. Won't say a word...yet."

Nicola walked up to the truck with a bottle of water and his flak jacket thrown over the side of his shoulder.

He instantly recognized her. "You found her!" He said, amazed at Dmitry's abundant resourcefulness.

"Who are you?" she asked, still fidgeting in the back of the trunk.

Nicola caught a whiff of her urine and bucked his eyes. "I'm...I'm Nicola Agosto," he said, stepping back a few feet.

"So you brought me back here?" Her eyes blazed with fury. "All you had to do was answer the fucking phone when I called the first time."

"Better late than never, right?" Nicola said, reaching to pull her out of the truck.

Dmitry stopped him. "No, not until she tells us what we want to know. Now it's about principle."

Nicola let go of her bound hands. "Well..." He waited just like the rest of them.

"It's here, okay. I still got it but..." She paused and huffed.

"What's here?" Nicola asked.

"I have the real jump drive with the recording of the cop, the politician, and Cane meeting earlier that day, and I recorded Twist getting shot by Cane that night on my phone. It's all on the fucking jump drive." Wiggling again, she growled in frustration. "I have to piss again."

"Well, I'll be damned," Nicola said astonished. She really was the key to the case. "Where is the drive?"

Roxie cleared her throat. "In me?"

"Excuse me?" Nicola said with a frown.

"In me. I use a plastic receptacle like the drug mules do to keep it up in my pussy. I knew it would be my only chance at staying alive, so I keep it close."

"On that note, I'll leave you gentlemen to it," Dmitry said, turning and walking back to the entrance of the house. "You men come and see me when you're done." He threw up his hands.

Gabriel couldn't help but laugh. With his balled up fist to his mouth, he hit Nicola on the shoulder. "You can fish it out if you want to, but I'd use gloves though."

"Let her up," Nicola said to Vasily. "She told us what we wanted to know."

Vasily cut his eyes at Roxie. "You help her out. I went and got her."

Shaking his head, Nicola pulled the little woman out of the back of the Bentley and stood her up on her own two feet. However, two much time in the car had her nearly too weak to stand on her own. Grabbing her before she collapsed, Nicola picked her up in his arms.

"Don't bring her in the house," Anatoly said, walking away.

"Well, what am I supposed to do with her?" Nicola screamed out.

Gabriel passed him the keys to the SUV.

"Take her to the stash house. Let her get a bath, some clothes, and food and then Gazelle, the girl who runs the house, will put her back on a commercial plane to Oklahoma. Don't forget to get your precious jump drive from her," Vasily said, headed back towards the house. He was absolutely exhausted. All he wanted was something to eat and a bed for himself. But Anatoly quickly stopped him.

"Turn around. You're going with him," Anatoly said, stepping in front of Vasily. "You did a good job, and I appreciate it, but I need one more thing. Well, two things actually. At the stash house, there is one dead body of a cop that I need you to get rid of and there is one man still alive that I need you to mirror."

Vasily dropped his shoulders. "Boss, that's going to take all night. I'm exhausted."

"Get something to eat and grab a nap there then." He hit Vasily on the shoulders. "Just get it done tonight. Tomorrow will be too late. And Nicola and I have some things to handle. He's going to drop her off, we're going to regroup and go back out to finish this shit. I've got a fucking wedding the day after tomorrow."

"*Da da*, boss. I'll do it," Vasily said obediently. "But I'm not getting in the car with her." He looked over at Roxie as Agosto loaded her in the back of the SUV. "I'll drive another car."

"What you don't like the smell of piss?" Winking at Vasily, he turned and walked into the house with Gabriel who was waiting at the door.

35

Late in the afternoon, a young black man in his early thirties with dreads pulled back, wearing a navy polo shirt and pair of crisp dark jeans rang the doorbell of the stash house and waited with a techy backpack thrown over his arm. Without a word, Nicola opened it quickly, stepped out to make sure that no one was following him, escorted him inside, and then closed the door behind them.

"I'm Rah," the man said, taking off his shades and replacing them with black thick-rimmed glasses. He offered his hand.

"Agosto," Nicola said, shaking it.

"Yeah, I've seen your work online," Rah said flatly.

"Don't believe everything you see on TV. Come with me," Nicola said, leading the man down the long corridor passed the bodyguards who sat in the living room watching television to the office at the end of the hallway. Opening the door to the study, he pointed at the computer on the large oak desk. "The jump drive is already in the computer. From what I've been told, the laptop is not traceable. So, you can do your magic without it being traced. How long will it take?"

Rah sat down behind the desk, opened the MacBook Air and typed in his password. "I've worked on this computer before. From time to time, Dmitry or Anatoly has me leak something to media when they want someone to know something." He didn't elaborate any more than that. "With regard to the information on the drive..." He tapped his fingers on the desk as he contemplated something. "How far do you want it to go?" He turned his lip up.

Nicola shrugged. "Well the ass beating that I gave DeMario went at least nationwide." He huffed in frustration of the thought. "Can you match it? I need every major network, all social media...the works."

"Can I?" Rah smiled arrogantly. "I can make you popular in Egypt by midnight. They'll be begging you for interviews in New York in an hour."

"Just give me thirty minutes to give a friend here the heads up and you can make me famous in Calcutta for all I care," Nicola said, turning to walk out. He stopped abruptly. "Can I get you anything before I go? Water? Red Bull?"

Rah didn't look up from the computer. He was already typing. "Nope, thanks. I'm good."

Leaving Rah to his *Internet magic*, Nicola headed to the dining room where the weapons were being brought up from the basement, unboxed and loaded on the elaborate rectangular table.

"Don't scratch the wood," Gabriel ordered, passing off a long, black zipped bag to Boris. "Take this and get in position. Don't let anyone out the front." He passed the other bag in the corner to Maurice. "Are you good with sniper rifles?" he asked, pausing before he placed it in his hand.

"Are you trying to insult me?" Maurice asked, snatching the bag. "I'm a fucking Marine, dude, not a DEA agent."

Gabriel smirked. "Don't let anyone out the back. There are no windows so they only have a couple of options. Whoever built this place was a real idiot, but it works in our advantage today since Nicola plans to go all *Sparta* on their asses."

Nicola walked over to the table and looked at the sniper rifle it the open hard case. "How did you get your hands on a Stealth Recon Scout?" he asked impressed.

Nicola didn't know it, but Gabriel's second love in life was hard-to-get, high-powered sniper rifles; *the first love was a secret to everyone except him*. He gave a big bright, toothy smile and walked over the weapon. With his hands on his hips, he sighed. "Well, the short answer to your question is, we stole a few thousand off the back of a secured train coming through Chicago. But the real question is why? You see, the SRS is the most versatile sniper system in the world. It is nearly a foot shorter than conventional sniper weapons, maintains ½ MOA or better accuracy and can easily be adapted to individual missions, like yours, where you need to change the weapon's caliber and length. This bitch can shoot 50 yards or one mile. So the question is who wouldn't have one?"

Maurice rolled his eyes. He had heard the speech literally a hundred times before.

"The Medlov family specializes in getting the shit in built that your local gun man can't even pronounce yet and all of it is completely un-fucking-traceable. We've got these and Hard Target interdiction rifles and anything that you can possibly dream up in our arsenal for just this little mission alone." Gabriel picked up the weapon and passed it to Nicola. "Now, I wouldn't recommend this one for you for this evening's *party* but in the future, I suggest that you take it out for a dance. You might like it."

Nicola held the sleek rifle in his hands and looked it over. It was portable and lighter than most sniper rifles, but he was nowhere as giddy about it as Gabriel was. "You really get a hard on with these things, huh?" Nicola asked Gabriel, passing it back.

"Dude, I'm toting a boner right now," Gabriel said with a wink.

Nicola stepped back a few inches. "Nice to know. So, what would you suggest that I take with me to-night?"

Gabriel walked over to the far corner where stacks of weapons were piled on a dark gold satin upholstered chair. "This is the SRS Covert, purposefully designed for police and military snipers needing ultimate conceal ability. It's the shortest sniper rifle in the world with a quick caliber conversion feature. So you have the option of either suppressed subsonic ammunition or full-power standard ammunition with ½ MOA accuracy. Now each hard case has the six magazines, attached bipod, scope, suppressor, and secondary kit." He picked up a case of smaller, machine guns. "When you get a chance to get up close and personal, we have two options. This one is your standard Israeli Mini UZI SMG."

"These are self-explanatory," Nicola said, knowing he would need both.

"Easy enough for a ten year old to operate, though that's not our demographic," Gabriel said, pulling out an even smaller case. "And these are your best friends. Glock 19s. We've got more of them than the MPD has bullets. So help yourself." Pointing over to the stash on the buffet, he raised a brow. "Concussion grenades, the regular grenades, night vision goggles, radios, flak jackets, K-bars… it's all over there."

Nicola turned up his lip. "Damn. I'd say that we're ready."

"When you are." Gabriel looked at his phone. "What time is this shit kicking off?"

"I need Boris and Maurice to head on over and set up. Once they are in place, they need to radio in," Nicola said, going back to the map. "We need to cut off the two road ways that head into the small warehouse and we need eyes 360 around the perimeter."

"I can handle all of that with Boris and a few guys that are already here," Maurice said ready to get this over with. He did have a life outside of Nicola Agosto and Dmitry Medlov, regardless of what they thought. His oldest of four girls had a ballet recital in the morning and his wife was nagging the shit out of him about being gone so much over the last week.

"Alright. Well, the brave team should head out of here at the most in an hour," Nicola said, looking at his tactical watch. That should give us enough time to…" He stopped, hearing blood-curdling screams come from the basement.

Gabriel motioned to Boris. "Close the door to the basement, *please*. I don't want to hear that bastard scream all night. Damn."

Boris got up from his chair and stalked down the corridor toward the kitchen and basement.

"Is that Vasily working?" Nicola asked, hearing Ferris scream again.

Gabriel hated that part of his job. "Yep," he said, disgusted. "I don't know why he doesn't just cut the tongue out first. It's so annoying. I think the sick fucker likes to hear them scream all the way up to the end." He shook his head. "Vasily needs a girlfriend."

Nicola continued, trying not to think of what parts Vasily was cutting off of Councilman Ferris at that moment. "We should be able to get suited up and out there in an hour."

"Anatoly will be here in about ten minutes. I'll get him up to speed. After that, I'll see you when I see you," Gabriel said, offering his hand.

"Thanks." Nicola shook his hand sincerely. "I appreciate it all."

"Oh, my uncle never does anything for free. You'll see." Gabriel winked at him.

This wasn't Nicola's first time hearing that. Still, he couldn't let that bother him for now. When it was time to pay the piper, he would. "Give me a minute. I need to make this call," he said, pulling out his non-traceable phone.

***

"Hello," Steele said, hesitant of answering a blocked number on her cell phone.

"Steele, it's Agosto," Nicola said, walking out of the living room. He knew that he could trust her to handle what needed to be done in the eleventh hour of this push. But he hoped more than that that she could keep her mouth shut about how she did it.

Steele froze. "One second," she said, putting her hand over her phone and popping up from the table.

Director Amway looked up at her and frowned. "Who is it?"

"My…" Steele didn't know how to answer and lying to the Director wasn't an option. "Give me just a sec, okay. I'll be right back."

She was in a meeting with Amway and ten other men about the connection between the bombing of Cane's house in Eads and his pharmacy in Memphis. They were promptly putting the pieces together with the Bomb Squad and knew that whoever was responsible for the bombing of Agosto, Johnson, Ferris and her house using Molotov cocktails was not the person or persons responsible for the professional bombing the buildings that day that had used C4.

Their bomb guys had referred to the two bombings as Amateur Night at the Apollo versus Beirut. Obviously the MO led them all to believe that the latest one was in retribution of the previous. The question now became who did it?

There were no fingerprints and no witnesses at either location. Ferris was missing and up until this very moment the entire Agosto family was gone. People were still demanding answers, only now they were louder, speaking to the media every half hour. They wanted to know who was responsible for the Baby Boys murders, the bombings, the riots and they now believed that Agosto could be innocent.

And reporters were creating a complete frenzy over the downtown riot the night before, which could have potentially been a lot more destructive if Amway had not had his men prepared.

Plus, everyone was still talking about Ferris announcing his decision to run for the city mayor's job after Johnson stabbed him in the hand and shot him in the knee.

What the media did not know was that Collin Magnelli had vanished into thin air. The Deputy Director had come in just this morning and put out a missing persons report on him after he got drunk at Mother Russia the night before and bolted out of the restaurant, demanding to be simply left alone.

Going into the adjoining bathroom of Amway's office, she closed the door and whispered into her phone. "Are you and your family alright? We've searched everywhere. The fucking FBI is involved. Where are you?"

"I'm fine," Agosto said, pulling out a small piece of paper. "Something is about to hit the air. You need to know that, *but when it does*, I suggest that you already be at 555 State Street claiming that your unit cracked the Baby Boys case."

"What?" she said in raised voice. "How?"

The men in the room next door curiously turned their direction to the bathroom.

"It was Ferris all along, Steele. And there isn't going to be an easy fix for this. You have to trust me. Go to 555 State Street, with or without a warrant and raid the place before the news hits, which will be in 30 minutes or less. In the back room of the building there is a latch to an opening in the floor. Open it and go downstairs. It's a pedophile playroom with drugs, DNA, video...God only knows what else. The building is registered to Ferris."

"How did you find out?" she asked, pulling out her small notebook to write down the address.

"You don't want to know. Also, considering I just gave you a career case, you have to hold me as a confidential snitch. No one can know that we spoke."

"If this Intel is correct, you don't have to worry about that. You don't say anything and I won't." She looked at her watch. "I gotta go if I'm going to make your timeline."

"Good. Make sure you take care of Johnson. He's a good honest cop."

"I will," Steele said, opening the door. "Take care of yourself."

***

The panic in Cane's eyes could not have been more pronounced if he had been at his house when it was bombed. Hanging up the phone on one of his men who had been able to get through the traffic to see the destruction for himself, he turned to his men standing around in his office looking at the news and screamed.

"What the fuck are you going to do just standing there looking at that damned television?" He hit the table with the fat fingers balled up into a frustrating fist.

The men turned and looked over at him with a look of fear and disgust. He wasn't such a bad ass now that he wasn't the one behind the trigger. Wiping the hair out of this face, he twisted his John Deere hat around on his head and stormed out of the office into the warehouse where fifteen people in scrubs worked quietly to produce and package his new synthetic drugs.

"I'm only on day fucking one and shit is already going straight to hell," he said, pacing around.

"What you want us to do, boss?" one of the bigger men asked.

Cane cursed under his breath and then bit his lip. "We gotta...we gotta move. I want everything stopped. Break down the equipment and get ready to move. I'm going outside to see how many trucks we got parked at the back of the dock. We need to get this shit out of the state."

"Where?" The man asked.

"Someplace safe, you fucking moron! Do you think that they are going to just stop once they blow up my fucking pharmacy and my house? They're next move is going to be here as soon as they find out about it, and considering that I can't get Ferris or fucking Magnelli on the phone, the assholes responsible probably already know."

He walked to the back door and flung it open. The evening sunlight shined in his face. Throwing a hand up over his eyes, he knocked his hat off his head. "Fuck," he bent down quickly to pick it up and a bullet whizzed right above his head into the building and hit one of the workers on the end of the assembly line placing the pills into small baggies.

"Oh shit!" Cane said, crawling back inside. As he slammed the metal door behind him, shots rang out again from across the lot in the bushes penetrated through the door leaving large holes.

People scattered immediately. They all ran, including Cane toward the front of the building. "Get the guns!" Cane screamed. "Get the fucking guns."

Perched on the grassy hill under camouflage, Boris touched his earpiece informing. "They know we're here."

"Copy that," Nicola answered, riding in the SUV convoy headed straight toward Cane's warehouse.

Grabbing his AK-47 from behind his desk, Cane went towards the front door on the other side of the warehouse with his men. "Open it," he told one of his guys, standing beside him.

Sweating in fear, the man hesitated as he reached for the knob. "Open it now!" Cane said, pointing his weapon at the man. He spit snuff on the floor beside them. "Open it now or I'll kill you myself. I swear to God!"

Feeling that he had no choice, the man inhaled a deep breath and opened the door to peer out quickly. As soon as the golden sunlight hit the man's face, Maurice, 50 yards away in the bushes, shot the man dead in the head. Brain matter splattered into Cane's face, making him jump back from the body. "Front secured," Maurice said into his earpiece, before the man could hit the concrete floor. He popped his bubble gum and settled back down in the bushes, completely undetectable.

"Copy that," Nicola said with almost a grin in his voice. He was only fifteen minutes out from Cane's place now and didn't want the man touched until he got there. But for now, at least, they had him cornered like the animal he was.

Cane shot the gun up in the air to quiet all the ruckus inside. The men and women who were working on the assembly line turned off the machine and boxed up the Molly as fast as they could, while Cane and his twelve men went to get as many guns as they could.

"Fuck!" he screamed, kicking a box of Molly beside him. Pills scattered on the floor beneath him. "Who in the hell is that?"

"We need to be figuring out what the hell we're going to do," one of the men said. "I could give a fuck about who they are?"

"Jim Bob, who do you think you're talking to?" Cane screamed.

Jim looked at his friends behind him first, then turned to Cane with a sympathetic nod. "You ain't in charge no more, *boss*. We all gotta figure out how the hell to get out of this place alive. They have both exits blocked. They done blew up your house and your business from what the news say. You ain't got much in the way of means right now. So you can point that gun at one of us again, and we gone do you ourselves." Jim pumped his double action barrel.

"I wonder if we shouldn't just see if we give him up will they let us go," one of the other men behind him said, pointing his gun at Cane.

Cane weighed the situation carefully and changed his tune. "Do you really think that they killed two men without a fucking word and expect to bargain with you?" Cane screamed. "Your best bet is with me. You hear! I still got a bank of money, and if I get out of this, anyone who helps me is gonna get rewarded. I mean a hundred thousand for each of you. Now that's more money than you boys ever seen. Then we can just restart somewhere else."

"Somewhere like where?" Jim asked. "We'll find some place. But if we don't figure out how to get out of here and they keep shooting at all these chemicals, then we're going to be incinerated by the shit in all these barrels."

He knew that they were in a tight fix. The warehouse was filled with combustible chemicals that could take out the entire area if blown up. Even if he got out alive, *which was his first priority*, then it would be impossible to get his entire product out. But maybe, he could use some of the chemicals in here to keep whoever was outside off his ass.

"What you think boys?" Jim asked as the self-appointed leader of their mutinous group. He was honestly tired of Cane and ready to kill him for all the trouble he had caused. The entire time that Cane had been developing this scheme against their former boss Twist and with his so-called business partners, he'd promised one thing after the other and never came through. Jim was still living in a trailer park, driving a shit pick-up and living paycheck to paycheck while Cane was relaxing in a 6,000 square foot farm house. In truth, he was sort of glad to see the bastard's place blown to hell. It was justice for him if no one else.

"Hundred thousand sounds real nice," one of the shorter men behind Jim said. "And what if it's only two men out there with guns. Hell, it's ten of us left plus the workers. We could swing it."

That was not what Jim wanted to hear but he knew that he couldn't do it all alone.

"Well, alright then," Cane said, putting down his hands. Sweat poured down off his neck onto his shirt. "Let's go find a way out of here then." He turned the workers and screamed, "Get those barrels and bring the half-full one over here to the front door. Get some to the back door and move quickly!"

"Boss, you gotta see this quick!" one of the men screamed from Cane's office.

"What is it now?" Cane asked, running into the room with the rest of the men.

On the monitors they watched as a long convoy of black Tahoe trucks approaching at a fast speed headed toward the entry gate of the long private gravel road. Barreling through the old gate, they knocked the temporary barricade out of the way. Metal shrapnel flew up in the air as they zoomed in, headed right toward them.

"There are five trucks," Joe said, "There goes the whole more of us than them theory." Suddenly, he wanted to revert back to giving up Cane. It seemed like a better idea than going up against the men coming.

Cane rolled his eyes. "Get your guns and get to the doors," he said in a low defeated growl.

Nicola and his men were doing at least eighty miles an hour down the gravel road. Cocking their guns, they did one last radio check before they headed into position.

"What's the status around the perimeter of the building?" Nicola asked into the radio.

"No movement in the back," Boris said, looking out of his scope.

"No movement in the front," Maurice said, checking his cell phone. Sending his wife a text, he focused back on his weapon.

"ETA two minutes," Nicola said, looking over at Cory. "You ready to end this?"

"Oh yeah," Cory grinned, pushing down on the gas. "Let's light these motherfuckers up."

The trucks entered through the thick trees, turning their lights on bright as they approached their destination. Pulling up to the white old warehouse, each SUV stopped at one of the four corners of the building and blared their blinding lights on the building lighting it up in the dark. Jumping out, the men pulled out their weapons. Standing behind the open doors of the truck, they pointed their guns and put their fingers on the triggers.

"They've got us surrounded. I count fifteen of them, all carrying automatic weapons and wearing tactical gear," Jim said, even more nervous now. "What are we going to do, boss? We gotta do something! Can't just sit here like a bunch of damned deer to be picked off!"

"Just let me think, damn you!" Cane screamed, getting behind a wall in the middle of the building where he could take cover as well as return fire. He crouched down behind the concrete wall and wiped the sweat from his furry brow. "I gotta do everything around here myself," he mumbled under his breath.

Outside of the building, Nicola and his men took their positions among the high trees and brush. With the owls hooting, the cricket chirping and lightning bugs flying around, they quietly waited. "Settle in and wait for the signal," he said into the ear piece. Getting on the phone, he dialed on his cell phone.

"Yeah," Deputy Magnelli answered.

"We're in position," Nicola said, spitting on the ground.

"Alright." Magnelli put his hand over the phone. "Hit it now, Billy," he said, speaking into the radio.

"Yes, sir," the man answered.

At that moment, the factory went completely dark. Walking a few feet away from the entry, Anatoly shot a cannon round into the front door, blowing off the knob and leaving a huge hole in the door. Immediately, Cane's men started to fire at the door blindly. Anatoly's man quickly ran up to the side of the door and waited a second to make sure that it was clear. As fast as he could, he opened the door, threw in the bag, closed it shut, then darted back to the safety behind the truck.

A minute later the generator kicked on and the lights came back on. The frantic men inside were still shooting toward the door. Looking around the corner of the wall, Cane stood up. Putting his hand out, he screamed. "Cease fire!"

"I told you that they wanted something," Jim said going for the bag. "There is something inside."

"Be sure it ain't no damn bomb!" Cane screamed.

They waited a second before Jim picked the black bag up and felt how light it was. "Feels like a football," he said reaching in. His hand quickly snatched back. Turning back towards the door, he dropped the contents on the floor. "Son of a bitch!" he screamed as he looked down at Sammy's severed head. Attached to it was a note. You're next.

Cane came from round the wall and walked up to it. Wiping his face, he growled. "Fuck you!" he screamed.

Anatoly could hear him screaming from the hole in the door. Laughing, he rolled his tired neck. "I told you that would fuck him up," he said into his earpiece.

Seeing the note, Jim eyes went wild. "That note says that you're next. Not us." He walked toward the door.

"What are you doing, Jim?" Cane asked, pointing his gun at him.

"They don't want nothing to do with us," he said, pointing his gun back at Cane. "This ain't my fight."

Grabbing the door, he screamed out. "If you want Cane, you can have him. We just want to get out of here alive."

"You traitorous son of a bitch!" Cane screamed to Jim. Pulling the trigger on his shotgun, he blew a hole through Jim's black Jack Daniel's shirt, sending him to the ground.

The other men froze, shocked that their boss had killed their friend in cold blood.

"The mutiny begins," Anatoly said, pulling out his grenade.

"Let 'em fly," Nicola said over his earpiece.

The men all released their grenades at once, throwing them toward the building. Running back a few feet to take cover, the loud explosion crumbled the outer walls of the warehouse, rattling everything and everyone inside.

For what seemed like minutes, they rolled around the concrete floor among the debris deaf and dazed. When their hearing finally returned, the ringing in their bleeding ears paralyzed them.

That was enough for the workers. Running toward both the front and back doors away from Cane, they came out shooting, determined to get out of the warehouse alive.

As soon as the workers darted out, Nicola's men began to mow them down, one at a time. In what seemed like slow motion, their bodies flew back into the walls and onto the ground as the high-caliber bullets ripped through them.

Cane watched in utter fear. For the first time since all of this began, he realized that he was facing death.

"What do you want from me?" he screamed, crouching behind the wall. "Who are you?"

"I asked the same thing when you sent your fucking punks to kill my family, you piece of shit," Nicola screamed back to him. Anger blazed in his eyes.

Cane froze. "Agosto is that you?" Shit, he thought he was dead. Fucking Sammy couldn't do anything right. Slapping his forehead, he stomped the ground quietly. None of this would be happening if it weren't for Ferris. Killing everyone else had given that wop-bastard time to prepare for his men to arrive.

"Who else would it be?" Nicola had had enough. He didn't want to kill anyone else. He just wanted Cane. The final piece to this puzzle.

Cane knew that he was dead. There was no way out of this situation. He grabbed a handful of Molly tablets and swallowed them down. "You know what they say. Never send a boy to do a man's job." He stood up and shot towards the opening in the door. "I should have offed you myself. Killed those little dusty ass nigglets of your and fucked your pregnant nigger wife up the ass."

Anatoly went for Nicola, but it was too late. En-raged, he ran full speed toward the warehouse, blowing the rest of the battered front door off the hinges. As soon as he was inside, he ducked behind a pile of debris and unleashed the fury of his SRS. The bullets tore through the building and interior walls, hitting the men hiding behind the wall in the office and killing them instantly.

"I'm going in!" Gabriel was second in the building, giving Nicola cover. He caught two men hiding behind the assembly line and returning fire. Putting his gun on burst, he blew the men and the assembly line up. Fire exploded, knocking him back.

Anatoly was the third to enter. He came in with his infrared pointed and cleared the side of the building with his Uzi. The bullets moved so fast through the wall until those crouching behind it had no time to take cover. They fell fast and hard.

Cane hid behind a large table shooting directly toward Nicola, but the continual burst of Gabriel's gun sent him to the floor for cover. As he did, Nicola dove over the table, kicking the gun out of his hand and sending it across the floor.

"You wanted me; you got me," Nicola said, grabbing Cane up by the shirt. He drew his arm back and punched Cane directly in the face, knocking out his two front teeth. Cane fell back on the floor and Nicola kicked him in the stomach with his steel toe boots.

Cane screamed out. Grabbing Nicola's foot, he tried to throw him to the floor.

"What's wrong?" Nicola asked, guns firing around him. He kept his eyes on Cane. "You don't seem so bad now that I'm here to kick your fucking ass!" He pulled his foot free from Cane and kicked him again, this time in between his balls.

"Fuck you!" Cane screamed again in pain. With his hands on the floor, he tried to pull himself back against the wall, as he did, he reached behind him and grabbed the gun tucked in his belt.

As Cane came around his waist with the gun, Nicola dropped down on top of the man and grabbed his hands. Punching him again, he fought to get the gun out of his hold.

Cane rolled over on Nicola putting his full weight on him trying to get a better grip on the gun.

Nicola threw his head back and butted Cane in the eye. Rolling back over out of Cane's grasp, he grabbed the K-bar attached to his pants leg. Stabbing Cane in the kidney twice fast and deep, he twisted the knife in his bulging side and grabbed the gun out of his hand.

Cane grabbed the knife, trying to pull it out of his side and screamed again, spitting blood on the floor.

Nicola stood up over the man and noticed the gunfire had stopped. "Look me in the eyes, you piece of shit. I want you to know that this time you fucked with the wrong man's family."

As Cane looked up and began to speak, Nicola pulled the trigger shooting him in the same manner he intended for him to die. Then he shot him twice in the chest for good measure. Throwing the gun back down on his bloody body, he spat on him and walked away.

Gabriel pulled at his flak jacket and huffed from across the room, standing over another dead body. "Can we please go home now?" he asked with a grin.

"With pleasure," Nicola said as Maurice walked in the building. "Yo, you ready to blow up some shit?"

"Been waiting all damned day," Maurice said as he threw in three black bags of C4 under a box of chemicals in the center of the building. "We've got five minutes gentleman before the fireworks begin!"

All the men loaded back up into their trucks, leaving the piles of dead bodies behind and low-rising fire behind. Quietly, they made their way through the long succession of trees and thicket out into the clear night sky and drove nearly a mile down the gravel drive. When they got to the gate, Maurice happily pushed down on the detonator. "Enjoy the fireworks, gentlemen," he said into his earpiece.

Behind them a large plume of smoke erupted, echoing for miles around. It would be only a matter of minutes before the authorities not only saw but heard the bomb and came to the scene. As they entered out onto the highway, they separated and headed into different directions.

Nicola drove quietly under the full moon with the window down and music on low, watching the fire off in the distance with a true sense of calm. For the first time since this all began, he felt like himself, and he knew that his children and wife were safe. What would happen in the days ahead would be up to everyone else, but he had done his part. He had solved the case, brought the men responsible to justice, and kept his promise to the woman who had come to his doorstep. All it took was him breaking every law that he had ever upheld and turning to men whom he'd formerly despised.

He looked over at Gabriel now, resting quietly in the passenger seat beside him and wondered just who he had been really chasing all those years. The man beside him had put his life on the line, not because of him or his mission, but because of the love for his family. The Medlov men, no matter how corrupt, had been his only ally.

Gabriel must have felt Nicola look over at him, even with his eyes closed. "Funny how shit works, huh?" he said with a chuckle.

36

Director Amway looked over his notes in the silence of his office, prepping for a joint news conference with the mayor that would take place in less than an hour. He had a lot of information to cover in a short period of time, most of which, he could barely believe himself.

Ferris had been one of the three masterminds behind a horrendous case that had upset the nation all for lust and power. And he had done it right under his nose. The idea was mind-blowing and yet another reminder why he couldn't trust anyone…nearly anyone.

There were still people that he trusted; people whom he knew upheld the badge and oath behind it, like Nicola Agosto. No one could give him credit for his work in bringing Cane, Ferris and even Magnelli's son, Collin, down, because he was technically dismissed during the investigation, but those who were in the position to make real decisions knew that he was responsible for solving the case and finally giving the city what it needed to begin the healing process.

Sure, Steele might have found out what was going on eventually, but it would have been too late, and even if she had dug up the truth, Ferris would have found a way to kill her and Johnson, who was now resting at home on leave *with pay*.

It wasn't like Ferris was going to file charges. He had been delivered to the front of the police department in a crate with a video of him confessing to everything that they already knew he was involved in. Plus, the police officers who witnessed the stabbing and shooting by Johnson had suddenly recanted their initial statements saying that Ferris had gone for a weapon. Sure it was a sloppy cover-up, but no one cared, not the media, not the public and damned sure not the police department.

Agosto had saved the city, but in his quest he had left one piece of evidence that put him at the drug factory on the outskirts of town. A gun, charred with bloody handprints found in the debris told the story that everyone wanted to know. They had pulled the prints off the pistol and discovered that it was one of their own that had cracked the case. A huge favor to the local municipal law enforcement had paid for the weapon to be handed over to the MPD and ultimately lost in transport.

Now, he was responsible for fixing things and preparing tomorrow for Carmen Magnelli's funeral.
Scratching through his notes as he thought of how to put in words his plan to work with the mayor to renew the city's trust; he was interrupted by a knock on the door. He looked up to see his secretary standing at the entrance.

"It's Deputy Director Magnelli," she said in a soft wispy voice. "Should I see him in?"

"Yes, please," he said, putting down his pen.

Magnelli walked in and closed the door behind him. He looked haggard with bags under his eyes and a full beard. Setting down his coffee mug on Amway's table, he took a seat.

"What brings you to my office? Aren't you supposed to be preparing for your daughter's funeral?" Amway asked, narrowing his eyes at the man.

"I came to ask you one final favor," Magnelli said, threading his long fingers together.

"One final favor?" Amway asked, ears perked up.

Magnelli laid the paper in his hand on the table. "That's my resignation. I know that you want it. You want to move this department into a new era, he said with irritation in his voice. "And I want to move into my condo in Boca with the wife and spend some time on the green, enjoying what's left of my life."

Amway looked at the paper like it was a million-dollar check. "So what's the favor," he asked, reaching for the paper.

Magnelli put his hand on the edge of the paper and looked Amway in the eyes. "I don't just want Agosto re-instated."

Amway took off his glasses. "Okay…" he waited.

"I want him to take my job," Magnelli said without blinking.

Amway pushed back in his chair and took a deep breath.

"Look, I know that you and I have had our problems. Like the fact that I called you what I called you and I was dead wrong for it. I apologize, but…"

"But you had to get out of here that day and you knew that calling me a nigger would do the job," Amway said, smacking his lips. "And you were the last one with your son the night before. I'm guessing that Agosto told you that he was in on it. So you did him yourself. Then you got rid of the body. I'm sure that we'll never find it. And don't worry, I don't plan on looking. I wouldn't dare waste the tax payers' money. But why do you feel like you owe Nicola this? The Deputy Director's position is for someone a little more seasoned in diplomacy."

"He'll *learn* to be diplomatic. I'm not worried about that," Magnelli said, not even bothering to deny Amway's accusations.

"What are you worried about then, Magnelli?" Amway interrogated.

"As of today, nothing at all as long as you agree that the job is his. I'll walk out that door and never come back or I can stay here until you can't stand the sight of me."

"I already can't stand the sight of you," Amway said with a stone face.

"Is it really that bad of a trade off?" He tilted his head and let go of the paper.

Amway huffed and pulled the letter towards him. "No, it's not." He read the first paragraph and smiled. "Fine. I'll talk to the mayor but I don't believe that there will be any resistance."

Magnelli stood up and offered his hand. "It's been a pleasure."

Amway shook his hand. "Take care of yourself, old timer. I'll see you tomorrow at the funeral and after that we'll mail your gold watch to Boca."

***

It was a perfect day for a summer wedding. The sun was shining bright with not a cloud in the blue sky. The entire house was buzzing with joy. People had been running about all morning to set up for the gathering, setting up tents, putting out chairs, delivering food and flowers. And now it was actually time.

Anatoly stood with Gabriel and the other groomsmen in the backyard of his father's mansion as the music began and the small gathering rose from their seats.

"You ready for this? I mean killing is one thing but dying a slow death is another," Gabriel said, hand crossed in front of him. He pulled at his black tuxedo and twisted up his lip. Weddings always made him nervous, but lately, the idea made him want to crawl out of his own skin.

"Don't fucking start, Gabriel," Anatoly snapped under his breath. "Just because you finally figured out what to do with your dick after all this time doesn't mean that the rest of us should wait for you to catch up."

The priest cleared his throat and narrowed his eyes at both of them.

"Sorry father," Anatoly said with a smirk. He looked over at Royal, who was standing with the children and cradling his daughter in her arms, and took a deep, calming breath. She nodded back his way, giving him an equally warm smile. They had talked earlier that morning and she had given him a new perspective on things.

Still, he was nervous. Deathly nervous. Not of getting married, just of getting it wrong. Renee had become his everything and given him a reason to be a better man. In truth, he knew that he didn't deserve her, but his father hadn't deserved Royal, yet he had her, despite her Vietnam-Vet father who was boycotting the entire event because he hadn't asked him for her hand in marriage.

He quickly shook that thought off. He'd deal with that on another day.

Dmitry escorted Anatoly's fiancée Renee down the aisle. Dressed in a long flowing white gown covered in Swarovski crystals that contrasted with her dark chocolate skin, she embodied what he'd always imagined a bride would look like. Heaven in a word.

Even Gabriel paused when he saw her. Straightening up, he darted a glance over at his girlfriend standing on the other side with the bridesmaids and shook his head. "She's going to get ideas," he whispered to Anatoly.

"This isn't about you," Anatoly said through his teeth. "Now shut up."

***

Nicola stood over Ivy in the darkness of his old bedroom in his parent's house watching her sleep, curled up in one of his old football jerseys from high school, looking like a schoolgirl. Tears stained the side of her nose and the pillow below her, evidently from another night of crying herself to sleep. She had been through so much yet had managed to stay so incredibly strong.

Kneeling beside the bed to get a better look at her angelic face, he ran a careful hand through her soft tendrils and sucked in her breath as she exhaled. The scent of her always made him insane, ever since the first day that he met her. He wanted to kiss her pouty mouth now, suck on her bottom lip and taste her essence.

After nearly losing her, the only thing that mattered to Nicola was never letting her out of his sight again.

The desperation of that mission was even more pronounced watching her now. Over the years, he had committed to memory the straight lines of her nose, the sweep of her high cheeks and the thick arches of her eyebrows. He had memorized her favorite words, her most vivid dreams and her biggest fears. He knew it all, but what he hadn't known before all of this was just how far he would go for her. Now he did. Till the ends of the earth.

"I love you," he whispered.

Feeling someone present, Ivy stirred awake, brown eyes slowly opening to stare at him. She blinked hard, body as still as a statue. "Nicola," she said in a whisper. Her finger clinched the side of the pillow as she raised her head slightly, black hair spilling down on the white pillow below her. *Was he actually there or was this yet another one of her haunting dreams?*

It was only when she reached out and touched his face that she knew that the heart shaped mouth smiling back at her was actually her husband's. His brown eyes sparkled in the darkness and the adorable dimple in his chin became more prominent as her sight became clearer.

"Hey, baby girl," he said in a low, deep baritone. "How are you?"

"Nicky!" was the only word that she could muster before she pulled him into the bed and held him as tight as she could in her embrace. "Oh my God. I thought I was dreaming," she said, exasperated. "But you're here. You're really here." Tears ran down her face on to her burning cheeks.

He caressed her long narrow back, crooning to her in a soothing tone. "Yes, baby. I'm here."

Pulling away for just a brief moment, she searched his body, feeling his chest, then his back and arms. "Are you alright? Are you all here?"

"I'm fine," he said, taking her hand in his own and pulling it to his face to kiss each digit. "It's done. We're safe."

Ivy swallowed hard. She knew had seen the news and had an idea that everything that was brought to light about the men was because of something that he had done. She nodded at him sympathetically, pursing her lips together. "Whatever you had to do...I love you for it," she said cupping a hand behind his thick neck.

Nicola closed his eyes and pushed his forehead up against her, melting into her as he held her close. "God, I love you too." Picking her up by her waist, he turned her around and straddled her on his lap. His deep breaths made his rock hard chest swell. "I want you so badly."

Ivy's pressure began to rise when his thumbs grazed against her body. She could feel him growing underneath her inch by thick engorged inch with every second that passed.

"Take me, she hissed.

The intensity of his fever pitch gaze made chills run down her spine.

He looked down at her rigid nipples poking through his jersey and clenched his jaw tight. Pulling off her shirt, he wrapped his bulging arms around her tender flesh and kissed her neck with his open mouth.

A gasp escaped her mouth. Opening her legs wider, she felt him moving below her, grinding into her needy body.

With one swift move, he rolled her over on the bed and pulled off his shirt. She raked her nails over his carved abs and then grabbed his belt buckle.

Nearly snatching his pants off, he bent over her body and lifted her thick thigh. Pushing himself inside, he let out a moan that he buried in her breasts. "Damn," he moaned.

Ivy arched her back and widened her legs to let him all the way in. Quivering, she pulled his face up to her own and kissed his open mouth.

"Oh Nicky," she said as he pumped slowly into her body.

Just then the door opened.

"Shit," Nicola said, grabbing the covers and pulling them over them. He hid them just in time. Wearing Transformer pajamas and a wild curly mop of curls on the top of his head, Adamo switched on the bright light while rubbing his tired eyes, completely unaware of what was going on. "Mommy can we sleep with you?" he said in a pouty, groggy voice.

Suddenly, his flushed face lit up. "Daddy!" Running across the room at top speed, he dove over in the bed and crawled to his dad, pummeling his father's balls in the process.

"Argh!" Nicola yelped, laughing at the same time that he nearly doubled over. "What's up, little man?"

The other three were quickly behind him, screaming and giggling to the top of their lungs, hugging their father and kissing his face, happy to see him. They asked a hundred questions, one right after the other, snuggled on top of the covers in between their parents.

Nicola looked over at his wife in the bed, children curled under her while she clung to the sheet and laughed. This was his perfect life.

Epilogue

Nicola had never been one for shiny uniforms and big elaborate offices with his name on the door and pictures of him and the mayor on his desk. He was more of a jeans and t-shirt, and shitty closet space office kind of cop. But he was slowly getting used to being in Magnelli's former position and one of the new top brass on the department. The perk of a secretary helped too, especially when he wanted to lie and tell someone that he wasn't available, only sometimes even she didn't do exactly as she was told.

With one knock on the door, Johnson peeked his head inside of the office boasting a sly grin and a Yankees baseball cap. "Is this the missing's person bureau, because I'm looking for a stubborn old bastard who used to work with me," he said, coming in and closing the door behind him. He wore his normal dark straight legged jeans, a black button down rolled up to his elbows and his badge swinging from his neck.

"Look what the cat drug in." Nicola smiled. "And what did I tell you about calling me old?"

"Looking good," Johnson said, checking out Nicola's new digs. *Impressive.* Walking to the chair in front of Nicola's desk, he took a seat and slouched down. "Damn, I guess they hooked you up, huh?"

Nicola honestly couldn't tell if that was meant to be a compliment or if he was condemning him. "How are you?" Nicola asked, concerned for his friend. He'd heard rumors that Johnson had been distant from everyone and everything since Carmen's death.

"I'm good," Johnson said, expression serene. "Really, I am."

"Good," Nicola said, putting away a confidential file on another case. "Let me know if there is anything that I can do for you."

"You mean that?" Johnson cocked his head.

Nicola knew the tone. "Of course, I *mean* it." He frowned. "Or is that why you're here?"

Johnson smiled again. Pulling a newspaper out of his back pocket, he threw it on the table. "Normally, Dmitry Medlov comes and goes, but this time, he's staying."

Nicola picked up the newspaper. "What am I looking at?"

"B3. Top of the page." Johnson scooted eagerly towards the end of the chair.

"Magna Carta Munitions coming to Memphis," Nicola read out loud. "Okay," he said, throwing the paper back down.

"Magna Carta Munitions specializes in weaponry, Agosto. It is owned by the parent company Hutton Industries, a London-based front that's been around for a couple of decades. Both are owned by the one and only Dmitry *fucking* Medlov. He's moving his new factory right over on Presidents Island right off the Mississippi River. The bastard even applied for a 15-year PILOT with promises of bringing in jobs to the city and using the prisoner re-entry program. It's a big *fuck you* to all of us."

Nicola chose his next words carefully. In no way did he want to give Johnson any kind of idea that he had a dog in this fight. "Is Dmitry the one out front with this project?" he asked, his face inscrutable.

Johnson huffed. "Hell no. When is he ever? But Gabriel Medlov is. The nephew."

"I know of him," Nicola said, pushing back in his chair. This was all too much to process in front of Johnson. He needed time to think. "So what do you want from me?"

Johnson didn't understand why he had to spell it out for the man. "Now that I've been promoted and have my own team, I wanna get one of my guys in there. See what's what. I know he's up to something, and I would do it my damn self, but after the Baby Boys case everyone knows my face. I'm a fucking celebrity around here." Johnson was nearly giddy. "This is a career bust. If I can prove that Magna Carta is a front from the Medlov family's organized crime activi-ties...." He shrugged his broad shoulders. "The possi-bilities are endless."

Nicola cut him off by raising a hand. "You gotta have some proof first, Johnson, to get authority to start an undercover investigation. Get me that. It's not illegal for the man to own a munitions company. He's never been charged with anything that stuck in the states, and he's not on any Interpol list."

"That's because there is never a witness to testify. *But okay*. Hypothetically, let's say that I have proof...then what?" Johnson asked, frustrated that Nicola couldn't see the brilliance in his plan.

Nicola tapped his finger on the table, contemplating what he could say to his subordinate that wouldn't be scrutinized later. Everything about Johnson said that he already knew more than he was saying, but to push the issue might set off an alarm. He kept his tone even. "Then we'll see."

"And I have your word on that?" Johnson asked.

"If I tell you something, Johnson, that is my word."

Johnson backed off. *The old man was getting touchy again.*

Looking at his watch, Nicola stood up. It was time to go. "Look, we can talk about this later, *okay.* You're not going to bust Magna Carta before they move here. Take some time and think about what I've told you. *Plan accordingly.* Today is my anniversary, and I want to get home to my wife. I've got something special planned and if I mess this up, then she'll have me by my short and curlies."

Johnson stood up and huffed. "Yeah, sure thing. I'll get in touch with your secretary and see if I can get on your schedule soon."

Nicola reached a hand across the desk. "Take care of yourself."

"You too," Johnson said, shaking his hand and then grabbing the newspaper. "Don't want to forget this."

***

Ivy was getting big as a house. She was a little less than a month away from the big due date, and they still hadn't decided if they wanted to know the sex of the baby. Nicola thought that Ivy might have known because a few months ago, she stopped letting him go to the monthly doctor's visits. He was hoping for a girl to top off his perfect little family, but Ivy said that she felt like it might be another boy because of the way that she was carrying it…whatever that meant.

When he pulled up to his house, he put his code into the new gate and waited for it to open for him. Driving up, he saw that the painters had gone for the day and Ivy was finally home. During the day, she spent most of her time shopping for new furniture as the rooms were finished by the contractors or picking out neutral clothing for the baby.

As soon as he hit the door, she wobbled from the entertainment room and hugged him tight.

"Happy anniversary!" she said, kissing his lips.

"Happy anniversary, sweetie," he said, pulling a small black box out of his pocket. "For you."

She took the box in her hand and smiled, raising up on her tiptoes. "Can I open it?" she asked.

"Well, I was hoping that you could wait until after dinner, but I was so proud of myself for not getting something late or screwing up by being late until I wanted you to at least see it." He said all of that, but he knew that she wouldn't wait. It wasn't in her nature.

Ivy ignored him. "Now's as good a time as any." Opening the box, she screamed. "Diamond earrings?" her eyes widened and her mouth dropped. "These are huge!" They flickered hues of blue in the dimming sunlight coming through the window.

"Two carats," he said, pulling back her hair so that she could look in the mirror in the foyer at them up against her delicate ears.

"Now, that's what I'm talking about." Grinning she turned and hugged him tight again. "I couldn't have asked for a better gift. Thank you."

"Okay, so let's get ready for round two. I was thinking that we could go and have dinner at Fleming's Steakhouse; I've already reserved your favorite table and after that…who knows."

"Well…I figured that considering that we just got our back in our house that we could spend the night here," she countered.

"After all that complaining for the last year about not me taking you out for your anniversary, now you want to stay at home?"

"Shh," Ivy said, grabbing him by his arm. "Follow me."

Nicola followed her to the dining room that was decorated with candles in silver candelabras and a huge dinner already prepared. He took off his jacket and threw it on the chair in the corner. "Wow."

"All your favorites," she said, walking up to the table and motioning over the food like Vanna White.

"Home it is then." He kissed her forehead. "Plus, you're saving me money."

Ivy clasped her hands together, ignoring his quip. "There's more. Two more things actually," she said, wiggling her nose. Leading him to the head of the table, she sat him down and passed him her own box.

"What's this?"

"Open it," Ivy said, eyes bright.

Nicola opened the box slowly and pulled out a pair of pink infant booties. A huge smile tugged at his lips. "Is this what I think it is?" He pushed back from the table to stand up and hug her.

But Ivy stopped him abruptly. She motioned for him to stay seated. "Yes, but there is something else in the box. Pull the little cover from the bottom."

Nicola reached back down in the box and removed the foil paper to find a second pair of booties. He had had this experience before...twice.

Suddenly, he felt light headed and he hadn't had a thing to drink. "We're having twin girls?" His vision blurred.

"Twin girls," she repeated. The look on her face was pure accomplishment. "Aren't you excited?"

"Oh yeah," Nicola said, mouth agape. "I'm going to need a second job."

Ivy's smile became brighter. "That's your second gift. Today, while I was out, I got a call from a recruiter. Evidently, there is a big munitions company coming here from London, and they need a V.P. of Marketing. And guess who owns it?"

Nicola didn't ask, instead he just shot up his brow.

Ivy continued. "Royal Medlov. She recommended me first to head hunters and said that I was the type of woman that she felt like could lead the company. Did you hear what I just said?" Her eyes were hungry with ambition. "My first order of business will be to pick a PR team here in Memphis to help me manage local messaging." She brimmed with joy. "And my old boss is interested in pitching us." Taking a breather in between her long-winded explanation, she snorted in devious laughter. "I can't wait to see that bastard's face when he finds out that he's got to pitch to me. You know I'm going to turn him down. I don't care if it is the best pitch I've ever seen, the answer will be *hell no*."

Nicola sat with his arms on the table cupping his mouth and had gone completely pale. "So you want to take the job?" he asked.

She put up a finger. "I know what you're thinking, Nicky. There are certain *relationships* there that are a bit questionable, but Magna Carta has never been under any investigations that have gone public. It is owned by Royal...well Chloe and this is an opportunity for a major munitions company to be run by women."

"It's owned by Dmitry Medlov. It will be run by Dmitry Medlov," he said, shaking his head.

"Don't say no, Nicky," Ivy begged. "I need this."

"Is Royal going to be the face of the company?" He hardly doubted it. There would be no way that he would put his wife in front of any public scrutiny.

"No. Gabriel Medlov is going to be the face. He's been named CEO as of today according to the recruiter," Ivy said, pulling a seat up beside him. "This is a golden opportunity. The pay is $300,000 the first year, plus stock options and benefits."

"And you'll be only in charge of public relations and marketing?" he asked, still completely unmoved.

"Yes. There is no way for me to get caught up in anything crazy. And I promise you that if things get out of control, I will quit." She promised as she put her right hand over her heart.

She said it like that would push Nicola's doubts away. He had major reservations, but at the same time, he could barely argue with her considering his own situation.

"I'm going to be honest. I don't like this at all. I think taking this job is a big mistake and I think that we both are playing with fire and not expecting to get burned."

Ivy felt herself bristle with his statement. "Do I at least hear a *but* coming or is this just your way of saying no?"

Nicola huffed. "But I'll agree to it only if we set some hard boundaries between what you will and will not do for Magna Carta or anyone associated. I don't care if you and Royal become best friends and start having sleepovers where you braid each other's hair and talk about boys; you will not cross the boundaries that we set." Nicola wiped his face with both hands and put down the booties.

She nodded and stuck out her hand. "Deal."

Nicola smirked but seeing her sudden seriousness, he shook her little hand firmly. "Deal."

His approval was all that she needed to perk her right up again. "Thank you," she said, getting out of her chair and sitting in his lap. Holding his face close, she kissed him. "This is all wonderful stuff. You'll see. We're going to have *six* kids, more than anyone else in this entire neighborhood. I have a new job lined up after the babies are born, and now you're Deputy Director. The house is nearly complete and we've got a second chance."

Looking into her eyes, Nicola knew there was no way that he could not be happy for her. She deserved to be rewarded. Rubbing her bulging stomach, he kissed her hand and sighed. "You're right, baby. I am happy." He corrected himself. "I'm grateful more than anything. You've always wanted to run your own shop. Magna Carta is a big company. You'll do well."

"Good," Ivy said, happy with herself also. "Now, I'm going to go and grab the bread pudding out of the oven, and I'll be right back." Standing up, she left him alone with his thoughts.

"Unbelievable," Nicola said aloud, resting his head back on the chair. Suddenly his private cell buzzed. It was a blocked number. Automatic alarms went off in his head and he started to let it go to voicemail but the situation with Roxie still hand him leery about that. "Hello," he said, pulling at his uniform shirt.

"Agosto, happy anniversary," Dmitry extended gleefully.

Nicola sat up straight. "Dmitry."

"The one and only," he said unapologetically, sitting across from Royal at a five-star restaurant in Belgium. When the waiter was finished serving him his meal, he nodded and continued. "Do you remember when I told you that I'd come calling soon enough?"

"How could I forget," Nicola said, looking around the corner to make sure that Ivy wasn't coming. He got up quickly and walked toward the corridor leading toward the bathroom.

"Well, it's soon enough," Dmitry said, putting forth his smooth palm on the linen table cloth and looking at his nails. "I need a favor."

Nicola knew the day would come, but did it have to be his anniversary? He lowered his voice and closed the door as he went into the hallway bathroom. "I thought that we agreed that I'd do that favor, *not my wife.*"

Dmitry picked up the wine glass in front of him and swirled the contents around. "Oh, I didn't call your wife. Royal did. She seems to have an affinity for her. Plus, I don't think that her offer was unreasonable, from what she told me."

"Depends on what you consider to be reasonable," Nicola said under his breath. "I want to make it clear to you that she won't be involved in anything illegal. She's worked too hard to be the subject of a federal investigation just because there was no one else to be the fall guy."

"I'm hurt that you'd think I'd do such a thing," Dmitry said, taking a sip of his wine. "If I wanted to frame someone, it wouldn't be a V.P in Marketing. You can't go to jail for bad PR, but I do appreciate your candor."

"I just want to make sure that we're clear." He checked his face in the bathroom mirror. "So…what *favor* do you want from me."

Dmitry smiled. *A man of his word to the death.* That was why he liked Nicola Agosto. "Two words. Luke. Johnson."

THE END

About the Author

National bestselling author Latrivia S. Nelson is the author of fifteen interracial romance novels. When she's not writing great books, she's the President and CEO of RiverHouse Publishing, LLC, located in Memphis, TN.

Nelson is the proud mother of two children, Tierra and Jordan, and a devout lover of life.

www.latrivianelson.info
Latrivia@LatriviaNelson.com